"Evoking ... n a
culture br ... *elist*

"Unger dc ... *el's*
travails—s ... *dity*
against his g. ... *eekly*

"David Unger's tale utterly seduces with its mix of the exotic and the familiar."
—*Toronto Star*

"Unger's rendering of human contradiction is masterful, for in the space of Samuel's four days of awe, Unger reveals life's slippery terms of engagement in all their complexity with a clarity that still contains compassion ... We can be grateful for the message of this wondrous book: despite our fears, even the least heroic among us can find the will to go forward." —*Review: Literature and Arts of the Americas*

"David Unger spins a fascinating tale of weird redemption in *The Price of Escape*, leading us on a tense journey from 1938 Nazi Germany all the way to Guatemala. The sinister United Fruit Company casts a giant shadow over this vividly rendered landscape, devouring everyone and everything in its path. Unger has created a compelling protagonist in the flawed and anguished Samuel Berkow, a man on the run from his own demons and the terrible forces of history."
—Jessica Hagedorn, author of *Dream Jungle*

"*The Price of Escape* is a supremely well-crafted emotional and historical tale of a lonely Jewish man's flight from Nazi Germany to Guatemala, a supposed tropical paradise that is also cursed, and where he must carve out a new life."
—Francisco Goldman, author of *The Art of Political Murder*

"*The Price of Escape* is a fresh, provocative, and deeply moving historical novel that explores the fate of a young Jewish man who narrowly escapes Nazi Germany, only to find himself ensnared in the squalid underbelly of a Guatemalan port town. In the unusually compelling character of Samuel Berkow, author David Unger has authentically captured the profound sense of displacement—physical, emotional, and spiritual—that all of the dispossessed must face."
—T Cooper, author of *Real Man Adventures*

# THE MASTERMIND

### BY DAVID UNGER

This is a work of fiction. Certain liberties have been taken regarding historical events and characters for the sake of the narrative. All other names, characters, places, and incidents are the product of the author's imagination.

Published by Akashic Books
©2016 David Unger

**APR – 1 2016**

ISBN: 978-1-61775-442-5
Library of Congress Control Number: 2015954058

First printing

Cover design: Jorge Garnica/La Geometría Secreta, used by permission from Editorial Planeta Mexicana
Cover photo: Stock.Xchng

Akashic Books
Twitter: @AkashicBooks
Facebook: AkashicBooks
E-mail: info@akashicbooks.com
Website: www.akashicbooks.com

*To Salar Abdoh: friend and fellow writer who, like me, straddles two worlds and knows the risks. And the infinite pleasures.*

*To Anne: my partner and best reader.*
*Gratefully.*

# LIFE IN THE FOG

*2009*

When Guillermo Rosensweig wakes up his left cheek is pressed against the kitchen floor. A sliver of saliva curls out of his mouth, forming a sticky pool. He is butt-naked and his arms hug his shoes as if they are a lifesaver.

Blinking several times, he tries to recall why he's on the floor. His mind registers nothing. With great effort, he raises his head—which weighs exactly thirteen pounds—and looks around for clues.

He draws a blank and drops his head back down to the floor. The sunlight drills into his eyes through a hole in the window. Judging by the ache in his body, he has probably passed out again. At least this time he managed to take off his shoes.

The phone rings.

"Jefe," the voice says, with undisguised certainty.

"Say what?"

"Do you need some intervention?"

Oh, code-talking time. It's his driver and bodyguard Braulio Perdomo: his shadow, his do-anything-you-want-me-to-do; actually, more like his common law wife at this point. *Intervention* is the code word if he's been kidnapped, his car sequestered, someone is holding a gun to his head, or if his tires need air, or his stomach antacid.

"No, no, I'm fine. A little tired is all."

"Swallow two raw eggs, with lemon and chile. It will lift the cruda."

There's a long silence, long enough to walk to the garita, chew the rag with the guard at the entrance to his gated community, and stroll back home. Before Guillermo can round up a reply, the chauffeur adds, laughing, "On Sunday morning such things are permitted. The raw eggs might even give you an erection."

Guillermo obediently looks down at his mostly hidden pecker, sound asleep in its bed of hair, and then curses Braulio's arrogance. Why had he accepted Miguel Paredes's offer of Braulio's protection? In a mere three week's time, Braulio has managed to gain control of his employer.

But better to focus on the first clue: it's Sunday morning. "Did I ask you to call me today?"

"It's about tomorrow. You wanted me at nine, but I can't get there before ten. My wife, she has a doctor's appointment, and the children, you know, one of us has to take them to school, what with the violence—"

"There's no school bus?"

"I guess you've forgotten that two were commandeered last week, held for ransom. Can't chance it, jefe."

"Please don't call me jefe."

"Whatever you say, Guillermo, but that doesn't change things."

What the fuck. "Ten is fine. But on the dot. With the car washed."

"I washed it before leaving on Friday. Remember, *jefe*?"

Guillermo can actually *see* Braulio smirk. "So we're set."

"We are all set. Enjoy your Sunday," Braulio chimes.

Yes, enjoy Sunday. Too scared to drive your own car to the supermarket, even though the BMW has bulletproof glass and sensors on the chassis; too suspicious of the gardener, the guards, the maid, your own up-till-now trustworthy chauffeur. *Enjoy your Sunday.* Things have degenerated fast.

In Guatemala, your own shit betrays you.

Guillermo pushes himself up and walks over to the sink. He opens the tap and slurps water like a guppy. Unpurified, it might sicken him, he knows, but something's bound to kill him anyway. It's only after the third mouthful that he realizes the water smells of dog puke and spits it out. No need to help the executioner.

He manages to stagger across the living room to his bedroom and fall facedown on the bed. If he could get one brain cylinder to fire up, he might force the cloud to lift in his mind and bring a brief moment of clarity. At least there's hope for that.

He could call Maryam. She would know what to do. Then he remembers that she is dead, and is the reason he has lost the will to live.

His head pounds. He needs jugs of purified water and a handful of ibuprofen, but he's nailed to his bed. Where are his clothes?

In the shower he could whistle "Oh What a Beautiful Mornin'" and do what? Beat his shrunken meat, as Braulio often suggests? Go bicycling? Maybe jog to work?

What work? What day?

The cloud's lifting and his dim brain begins to strategize.

He should stop these alcoholic binges. But for whom? For himself? Not for his wife and kids who left him for Mexico. Actually, his *ex*-wife and kids because Rosa Esther became his ex eighteen months ago, when he wouldn't break off his relationship with that mierdita arabe—that "little Arab shit," as Rosa Esther referred to Maryam. This was ancient history, back in the days when dinosaurs walked the earth and he was bewitchingly in love—with Maryam, that is, the one true love of his life.

Is this the way to refer to what happened? To his loss? Someone should pay. Someone will. Maybe he is ready to do what Miguel Paredes has asked him to do, and set the whole world aflame. *What's the point of living?*

Guillermo closes his eyes, relaxes his body. Inhale three deep breaths, exhale through the mouth because your nose is clogged. Pranayama yoga. Dispel all thoughts and concentrate on the soft point of light issuing from the blue cloud of emptiness. If he does this for ten minutes every day he will unlock the door to the sanctum of tranquility where he can begin to reorganize his life.

Breathe in, breathe out, in and out. The road to nirvana. It's that simple.

After only fifteen seconds, he opens his eyes, his mind wandering, his breath distorted. He turns on his back. The fan circulates above him, the lines on the ceiling becoming constellations he recognizes but cannot name.

He maneuvers across the mattress, swings his legs down, and sits at the edge of the bed. The German shepherd next door begins yodeling from the terrace. Bandits must be scaling the building walls or a zompopo circling and confusing the Aryan dog's head. *Arrrrrroooo. Arrrrroooo.* If Guillermo had a gun, he'd blow tracers into the crevice between its lidded eyes. *So long, Rin Tin Tin. Hasta la vista, baby.*

Without the strength to sit, he falls back down on the bed. The breathing has helped. His mind's perfectly clear now. He clasps his hands behind his head and lets a bemused smile form on his lips. His eyes close and he begins to recall the sweetness of life, when he fell in love with Rosa Esther because of the softness of her skin, and her devotion to the grandmother who raised her. Then there were Sunday lunches at Casa Santo Domingo in Antigua, weekend trips to Lake Atitlán. This was during the golden era of their matrimony, when Rosa Esther still believed she had married a good man—one foregoing dalliances, committed to her, to the Union Church, and of course to their children, Ilán and Andrea.

His eyes well up as he acknowledges his deceptions. He had become an expert in betrayal. All he'd needed to do was call home and say he was working late with an important client on a case so hush-hush he couldn't whisper a word about it over the phone. Rosa Esther, who embodied trust, would believe him, releasing him to meet with Rebecca, Sofia, then Araceli, and finally Maryam, at the Best Western Stofella for a few hours of boozing and pounding the mattress and floor.

Johnnie Walker made him invincible. Two, sometimes three fucks an hour, the hotel manager often banging on the door because the neighboring guests complained of the commotion . . . fucking against the walls, down on the floor, on the bathroom sink, or in the tub when most guests were getting dressed for dinner in the Zona Viva.

With Maryam it had started the same way. She was the daughter of his client Ibrahim Khalil. Unlike Rosa Esther, she had a fierce and magnetic practical intelligence. And her beauty: her dark hair sparkling like ebony filigree, green eyes, and a mouth that turned down whenever she doubted what Guillermo was proclaiming—which was often. Maryam became the love of his life, and he willingly foreswore seeing other women to be exclusively with her. But how can you be with "the love of your life," when you're married, when she's the married daughter of your best client, and when your social standing depends on being a good husband, father, and community model?

Here's where his lawyerly thinking comes in handy. He has argued in civil case after civil case that while the law cannot be circumvented, circumstances, more than strict adherence to legal strictures, determines culpability or fiduciary responsibility. Similarly, the marriage contract is valid by decree, yet he can have girlfriends as long as he fulfills his marital, filial, and community responsibilities to the letter of the law. And why not? His affairs never hurt anyone. Moreover, Rosa Esther had begun denying him his conjugal rights.

And he swore fidelity to Maryam.

Guillermo opens his eyes and smiles at his cleverness. Guatemala is a country where allegiance to law, family, and religion matter equally, so church and state often agree. Every political leader speaks about maintaining the "social fabric." Forty-four years of armed conflict can be neutralized by a document that insists on constitutional statutes which have never been even remotely upheld. The Peace Accords marked a return to social stability. *Stability for whom?* Soldiers ceding power to return to the barracks? Fractured Indian families with thousands of dead relatives reclaiming arable land near villages that no longer exist? Guerrillas laying down arms to attend trade schools where they can learn to fix cars or splice electrical wires? Drugged orphans foregoing their knives and guns to volunteer to feed paraplegics in medical centers throughout the country?

He turns his head to his night stand. The clock says eleven something. He should begin the day. He thinks: *My life is wretched: I have nothing to live for. Even Braulio mocks me. Before Maryam was murdered with her father, she was going to leave her husband Samir to live with me. We were going to do a thousand things together—walk on beaches, climb volcanoes, stay in bed all day drinking and making love. All destroyed by a ball of fire. Since then I have lost clients like pearls unstrung from a necklace. My mother, and especially my father, would be ashamed of me. Rosa Esther is happy in Mexico City, far away from me, and my children no longer care if I live or die. Why should they?*

Sweat like condensation on the walls of a cave breaks out on Guillermo's face. As soon as he stands up, he feels dizzy and decides to crawl to the bathroom. His heart thumps wildly in his chest. When he reaches the toilet, his mouth opens and a stream of alcohol and all the bits of his cruel, undigested life pour into the white ceramic bowl.

It's approaching noon on no particular Sunday. When is he going to stop abusing himself until he passes out?

From somewhere outside the building he hears a group of kids singing "Humpty Dumpty" in English. It makes him want to cry.

He vomits again, trembling, assured that this is the time for all the king's horses and all the king's men to put his life together again.

It might be too late. The knot in his stomach is unrelenting. His whole body is trembling as he feels a wrench tightening in his gut. He vomits one more time and then howls.

He won't fight it any more. He will do exactly what Miguel Paredes wants him to do, even if that means he won't be around to watch the world explode.

Let the fun begin.

# CHAPTER ONE

## LAMPS FOR SALE

*1977*

**E**very afternoon when classes end at the Colegio Americano in Vista Hermosa, Guillermo hitches a ride downtown with his chauffeur-driven friends. The driver drops them off at the Portal del Comercio amid the crush of polluting public buses, and they make their way between the stands of cheap clothes and toys lining the arcade to the Klee Pharmacy and El Cairo, where the promenade starts. They stroll the length of Sixth Avenue to the San Francisco Church looking into shop windows and cafés, hoping to catch sight of one of their female classmates drinking a Coke or having ice cream at one of the sidewalk cafés. If, after a block or two, no one has been sighted, they settle down at a window table of some dive to drink beer and talk, gossip. To see and be seen.

The truly rich girls park themselves at Café Paris, Restaurante Peñalba, or L'Bonbonniere near the Pan American Hotel, and drink large Cokes through straws. They are the shapely and more stylish versions of their mothers, many of whom now wear Reeboks and sweatpants when they go downtown. The boys—dressed in their Farah pants, Gant shirts, and wingtip shoes—are younger versions of their businessmen fathers, without the mustaches.

The boys in Guillermo's group like going to the Fu Lu Sho because it's dark and the food is cheap. The restaurant is angular, with little round tables and booths with red upholstery. The boys act like big shots for about an hour, but the girls never come in because they aren't interested in boys pretending their parents don't have money. Then around five they scramble off to meet a mother or father or aunt or uncle, who gives them a ride home to Los Arcos or Vista Hermosa or Simeón Cañas. This is the daily pattern now, awaiting graduation.

Guillermo lingers behind because he will hitch a ride with his father, who leaves his lamp store, La Candelaria, at precisely six. For that one hour from five to six, he sits alone and watches the secretaries and stenographers who work in one of the Edificio Engel businesses come down for a Fanta when they're cut loose at five. He fantasizes about hooking up with one of them, one who might want to join him for a beer and egg rolls. He ogles the ridge of their breasts popping out of their patterned Dacron dresses. Acrylic sweaters are tied around their shoulders to fend off the night air—he loves their dark, shapely legs, their cheap high heel shoes, the red lips with too much gloss. If they would only look at him! But these older girls don't even know high school boys exist.

Fridays are different. Guillermo and his friends hurry downtown to see the four o'clock feature at the Lux—the latest Paul Newman or Robert Redford film—or they go over to the Capitol Mall to play video games under the haze of cigarette smoke.

In March he meets Perla Cortés at La Juguetería, a toy store. He's there buying a new soccer ball. She's getting a plastic dump truck for her baby brother. She's a "neighborhood girl" (the term used for someone whose parents aren't rich) in the tenth grade at the Inglés Americano, a second-tier high school. They talk, go have a mixta and a Coke at Frankfurts, and immediately she becomes his first steady girlfriend. They begin meeting on Fridays and going to the movies, since her mother works as a nurse until six at the Cedar of Lebanon Hospital on Eighth Avenue and 2nd Street. He takes her to the movies at the Cine Caitol and buys luneta seats, always near the back, where he can put his arm around her.

As the credits are rolling on their first date he accidentally brushes her firm breasts while standing up. She actually purrs, pulls him down, and snuggles closer. He feels an erection forming and puts a hand on her left leg. She happily takes his hand and brings it to her panties so he can feel how wet she is. She opens her legs, slips his hand under the band toward her pubis. She directs his forefinger inside of her and begins squirming and grinding, letting out little whimpers. At some point she pulls his penis out of his pants and strokes him till he comes mostly on the cinema floor.

Three of their dates end like this.

But on the occasion that Guillermo's pants become the target of his sperm, he decides he can't continue seeing Perla. Their sex feels mechanical, and he has difficulty accepting the fact that she's the one initiating the foreplay. He thinks the man should be in control.

He arrives at his father's store late, with his shirttail out.

This is the last time they are together.

"I want you to start working with me, Guillermito." Nothing would make Günter Rosensweig happier than to have his son become the financial controller of La Candelaria. His daughter fell in love with a woman and is living in San Francisco. "My only son, working alongside his father."

"Dad, I don't want to talk about it now." They are at home. It is a Sunday, a week after Easter. If a resurrection took place the week before, thousands of years ago, Guillermo is unaware of it. Lunch has just ended. His mother is in the kitchen barking instructions at the new maid. He has to escape upstairs, get away, do anything but discuss his future employment with his father. "I have to study for my finals."

Günter smiles proudly. He imagines his mathematical son overseeing sales, handling the ledgers, while he continues to attend personally to the customers. "You would be a big help to me. You know I like Carlos, but I don't want him inheriting my business."

"Pop!" the boy yells desperately. His father has a round, freckled face. His stringy red hair is combed back. His brow is always knitted and his eyes are constantly looking at the world with genuine expectation: the prospect of being liked, of concluding a sale; wanting the world to conform to his desires. There is expectant hunger in his eyes.

"I won't live forever." He had a heart attack two years earlier which almost did him in. Guillermo knows that it would kill his father outright if he had to leave his business to Carlos, his most loyal employee. He knows he is being baited, and usually concedes that he will eventually take over the store. For once, however, Guillermo says nothing.

"You never want to talk about it," Günter presses.

"Not now," Guillermo says, standing up. He is grateful that he has inherited his mother's dark Romanian features. If he looked like his father he would end up playing chess every day with a group of bespectacled friends and eating salty pickles. They have nothing in common.

"You don't want to talk about it now, so when? Give me a date. What about next week after your classes end—"

"That's way too soon," the boy says, not turning around. "We can talk about it in the fall. I've already made graduation plans with my friends for the summer."

"What? You want to go to parties and sleep late?" The father shifts in his chair, stands up. "I want you working with me," he bellows, rooster-like.

This is his father's fantasy—to have his son at his side, if only for a few months. It's a scenario enhanced by Guillermo's failure to apply to college in the fall. In truth, Günter has no illusions that his son will take over the business permanently. Though he has scrimped and saved for years, Günter knows that when he retires, he will sell the store rather than leave it to Carlos. He realizes that it's impossible to get his son to do anything other than hang out with his friends.

"Go study," he says crossly, knowing that he and his wife have made a mistake raising their son as they have, pampering him. But Guillermo is already halfway up the steps to the aerie where he lives, where he eats potato chips and daydreams, away from everyone else, hearing nothing.

When Guillermo finishes high school, graduating in the middle of his class, his father starts in on him again. He expects all the after-school and weekend activities to come to an end and work in the store to begin.

"Pop! Have you forgotten about my graduation trips?"

"What?"

"The trips, the parties! Next week I'm going waterskiing in Likín. Then Rosario has invited us to a weekend barbecue at her family home in San Lucas. And Guillermo—"

"You're Guillermo!"

"My *friend* Guillermo Contreras," the boy says, exasperated with his father who never hears a word he says and doesn't know the name of a single friend, "has invited the class to go on his yacht and swim and dive in the Río Dulce. And Mario and Nora have planned a spelunking excursion—"

"Spelunking? Speak Spanish!"

"Cave exploration. The caverns outside of Quetzaltenango."

Guillermo is convinced that his father knows nothing that doesn't involve either hanging or repairing a lamp. He has never been to Tikal or Quiriguá. He thinks that Cobán and Copán are the same place. When Guillermo mentions working as a volunteer digger with the University of Pennsylvania in September at one of the Mayan archeological sites near Uaxactun, Tikal, or Piedras Negras, his father draws a blank.

"This is what I want to do. All my friends are going to college in August, and I plan to live in a tent in Petén and work with a team."

"In the jungle? With a shovel in your hands?"

"Yes, we might discover a new pyramid."

"And what about La Candelaria?"

"This fall, Pop, this fall."

His father shakes his head. He knows that as soon as September arrives, his son will come up with another excuse. He can't understand why Guillermo will do anything to avoid working in his lamp store.

By mid-August the trips are over and Guillermo's high school friends are preparing to set off to college. He won't miss all of them, just his best friend Juancho.

And contrary to Günter's prediction, Guillermo has finally run out of excuses for not working at La Candelaria. Since he studied accounting and business math in high school, it makes sense for him to work alongside Carlos, the bookkeeper, in the glass-partitioned office perched above the sales floor.

Carlos has big droopy ears, mole-like eyes, and breath soured by too many Chesterfield regulars. To escape the smoke clouds, Guillermo constantly skips down the spiral staircase to have cup after cup of coffee at El Cafetal.

"I am so proud that you are here—with me. I could not expect this of your sister."

There's nothing Guillermo likes about his father's store. It's a long tunnel with hundreds of lamps, some lit and some not, hanging on hooks from the ceiling rafters. There's no order to the store, and certainly no style. It's just a tapestry of hanging lights, with a tiny bamboo forest of pole lamps squeezed together at the back near the bathroom. A counter for storing smaller table lamps runs along one length of the store. Anibal, the security guard, walks around like King Neptune with his trident. Actually, it's a pole with a hook to bring down whatever lamp the customer might want to see up close.

"Selling lamps is an art," his father says. "It is an art defined by practical-ity since a lamp has both an aesthetic and a utilitarian function. You will learn about how the shades determine the amount of light filtering into the room. Clients need to know how the switches work and whether they accept bulbs of varying intensities and colors, or just one type of bulb."

"I know all this, Pop. You've been telling me the same thing since I was five."

His father ignores him; he needs to continue making his speech. "Do they want cheap rubber or cords wrapped in silk? Lamps dangle, sit flat, snake out of corners, hug walls like sconces or torches. They flood, they focus. They suffuse from the top, the bottom, or the sides."

Guillermo nods his head, but it only encourages his father.

"The shades can be conical, round like pumpkins, bouncy like lanterns. They can be translucent or almost transparent. The customer has to decide."

To his father, the purchase of a chandelier for a living room or a lamp for a bedroom, a dining room, or a den is a major decision, like the buying of a sofa, end tables, a desk, a refrigerator, or even a car. Customer need has to be met so there will never be a question of returning the lamp *within seven days for a full refund*, which of course spells disaster, since the lamp cannot be sold as new.

His father refuses to initiate a no-return policy. He is the epitome of the ethical small businessman and he works for the purpose of servicing his customers honestly and efficiently and making them feel satisfied.

Though this is an admirable quality, Guillermo doesn't want to spend his own life as a lamp salesman. It is too demeaning.

Günter Rosensweig arrived in Guatemala penniless in the early fifties from Germany. He had a drop or two of Jewish blood—not much—though its lack of traceability despite his last name had allowed his own father to maintain a bookkeeping business in Frankfurt during the war, while many of his Jewish associates were hauled off to concentration camps. It helped that there was a renowned Count Rosensweig living in a sprawling castle in Ardsberg who famously declared to the press that "the best Jew is the dead Jew." This Count Rosensweig adage was quoted broadly among other Germans.

It saved his father and mother.

Günter had avoided army service because he was asthmatic and had a heart murmur. The postwar years in Germany were difficult and unruly, and he had no reason to stay and help his countrymen rebuild. His parents were both dead, he had no siblings, and he was driven by the desire to emigrate to a new continent, away from the chaos of Europe.

Pictures reveal that Günter had been taller once, and passably hand-some. This is the man Guillermo's mother Lillian, a dark-haired beauty from Cobán, must have met. Her own Romanian father had been a cardamom grower and her mother a Rabinal Maya. Lillian was a few inches taller than her husband, and had an attractive face with chestnut eyes that, while not clever, were certainly seductive. How they ever got together was always a mystery to Guillermo, who felt that someone had erroneously mixed together pieces of two different puzzles, say a weasel with a jaguarondi. Guillermo resembled his mother. People said that he had been spontaneously generated from Lillian, without any of his father's genetic traits. His sister Michelle had the round face and stringy reddish hair of their father. She would never be at-tractive, everyone said so, but with his dark brooding eyes, Guillermo would break hearts.

Günter was twenty-three when he began working in Abraham Sachs's lamp store on Seventh Avenue and soon became his associate. Two years later, after Günter had married Lillian, Abraham died of a cerebral hemorrhage when a fifty-pound lamp landed on his head. With no heirs, Günter inherited the lamp store. A true godsend.

But godsends don't necessarily extend to the second generation. When Guillermo's application to take part in a dig is rejected, he has no choice but to stay on with his father, even if he considers the lamp store a penitentiary.

As soon as he starts working there, Guillermo begins making up all kinds of excuses not to drive in with his father at eight thirty in the morning. *I couldn't fall asleep last night, my head aches.* He takes the bus on his own downtown and arrives around ten, just in time to go out to El Cafetal for coffee and donuts.

Günter does not scold his son. Moreover, he is oblivious to his suffering. After six weeks of working, or rather not working, Guillermo confesses his misery.

"The store is killing me, Pop. Working with Carlos is giving me lung cancer."

Günter Rosensweig is not completely humorless. "At least you don't have to buy cigarettes to smoke them."

"Very funny."

"What would you like to do instead, son? What about coming downstairs and helping me with sales?"

Guillermo frowns. If working with Carlos is life imprisonment without parole, then working with his father and his overweight, poorly dressed, forty-five-year-old employees in black scuffed shoes is a death sentence. They all wear paisley aprons and rely on Anibal to lower lamps for the customers with his trident from the garish helter-skelter night sky. And he would have to hear his father's sales pitches, which have always embarrassed him. He would also have to wear a blue apron every day. What if one of his friends' parents—or worse, one of his former schoolmates—were to see him dressed like this?

La Candelaria is the only lighting store left in downtown Guatemala City. Zone 1 is becoming increasingly dangerous, less trafficked, and more derelict as the months go by. Maybe the 1976 earthquake, when hundreds of the old colonial buildings simply collapsed, had been the first nail in its coffin. By 1979, when Guillermo is eighteen, La Candelaria's business has already begun to suffer from stores in the malls outside of the city center that not only offer lamps and small electronics, but also feature nearby cafés, restaurants, and boutiques in a more attractive setting with plenty of parking. Guillermo tells his father that he should open another store in Zone 9 or 14, but he swats away the idea: "People will always come downtown to shop."

The noise, the smoke, the heat, the traffic is increasingly horrific. The once elegant downtown streets have become a dumping ground for dozens of improvised stands that front the shuttered businesses and crowd out pedestrians.

Günter declares: "I think you'll be happier working downstairs with me."

Guillermo's eyes well up with tears. What is he doing in Guatemala? All his friends are gone, and he is given a choice between sucking in stale cigarette smoke upstairs hidden from view, or working the floor in plain sight, where the parent of any of his friends might see him. "I can't do this. It'll kill me."

His father doesn't know how to react. While he is upset that Guillermo doesn't want to work alongside him, his son's misery breaks him. "What about doing deliveries?"

Guillermo wipes a tear away from his eyes, smiles weakly.

So throughout the early fall, Guillermo drives a battered Volkswagen van and delivers lamps and chandeliers to private homes. Sometimes he stops in the Zona Viva to grab a coffee or a Gallo beer at a café. He misses Juancho terribly. Driving around, he at least sees the sunlight and pine trees, people and clouds.

But he also sees how Guatemala City is increasingly populated by poor Indians, clogging the streets and making driving dangerous. He blames the government for not rounding them up and placing them in work camps, and for having allowed the guerrillas to control the highlands in the first place.

He is falling into a selfish depression with no sympathy for anyone but himself. The worst part of driving the van is making deliveries to the homes of friends who are off at college. He prays that he can hand the boxes to a maid or a houseman, but every once in a while he bumps into a parent and has to experience his humiliation completely . . .

By December his parents are distraught. Guillermo can't be a van driver for the rest of his life. Or can he?

They decide to give him a generous gift: enough money to tour the major capitals of Europe for the next four months. It won't be in style, but he'll be in a new environment. And he will be on his own.

## CHAPTER TWO

# FROM THE LOUVRE TO GROWING ARTICHOKES

**Guillermo hopes that the experience** of walking the broad avenues of Paris and Madrid, visiting the great museums of Rome and London, and standing atop the dikes in Holland will somehow illuminate the course his life should take. He believes that, after seeing Velasquez's *Las Meninas* or Michelangelo's *Moses*— or even visiting the Heineken brewery in Amsterdam—he will wake up one sunny morning and see his future life flash before him.

But Europe does little for him. He awakens each day in a sour mood, and with an erection he sometimes attends to and other times does not. There are too many other boys lying awake in nearby bunks at the hostels where he is staying. He longs for the aerie in his parents' home.

He feels terribly forlorn. He sees how the other trekkers manage to hook up for a while and travel together, but for some reason he is unable to become part of a group. He is a lone wolf. He realizes that his body language indicates to others that he is unapproachable and not sociable. He thinks back to his month with Perla Cortés and wishes he could find someone like her here in Europe. Someone to wrap his arms around, even if it means allowing her to dictate the terms of sex.

Whenever he feels the need, which is every three or four days, he visits the red-light district of whatever city he's in. He enjoys the power of money. Sex is cheap and safe in Europe, though in Barcelona he finds dozens of moving black dots in his underwear and feels a horrifying itch. He imagines that he has contracted syphilis and goes to a clinic in the Barrio Gótico suggested by the youth hostel manager. A nurse examines him with gloves and tells him he has crabs. For six nights in a row he has to sleep with a frothy lotion on his crotch, and must desist from having sex. His style is cramped, but now he is a survivor, a kind of war veteran, having come down with crabs.

He develops a unique strategy for each city he visits. While he takes in all the required tourist attractions, he also seeks out one under-the-radar museum or park in order to feel different and unique. In Rome, it's the Villa Borghese, with its immense grounds and lovely Canova sculptures. In Paris, it's the Marmottan, which has the huge water lily paintings Monet completed in Giverny near the end of his life. In Florence, the Brancacci Chapel of the Santa Maria del Carmine Church is his choice. Masaccio's dazzling *Expulsion* makes Guillermo feel right at home with its depiction of banishment. In Madrid, it's Goya's black drawings in the Prado. He sends postcards to Guatemala that he writes while sitting on park benches in front of these museums, to his parents in Vista Hermosa, to his friend Juancho in Tempe, Arizona, and to his sister Michelle, who has decided to pursue a master's degree in education at San Francisco State.

Guillermo goes to the American Express office religiously in each new city to receive news from home. He hears from his mother that his parents are toying with the idea of moving from Vista Hermosa into a gated community in Los Próceres because of the increasing violence in the country. His sister nervously confesses that she likes women (duh), and has begun to explore her new identity with her Mexican girlfriend Marcela. From his father he hears that the guerrillas are making inroads among the Maya population in the highlands. His good friend Juancho writes that he is so homesick he's planning to drop out of Arizona State and return to study business at Universidad Marroquín—a new institution opened by Guatemala's business elite to counter the increasingly radical San Carlos University.

Guillermo feels that Guatemala is changing without him but continues his aimless journey to new cities and museums. He is lonely, and would like nothing more than to go home, but he feels obliged to complete his four-month sojourn.

To conclude his travels he hitchhikes through Southern France and sleeps in seven-dollar-a-night hotels. He has the money, and prefers to avoid the socially inept stays in youth hostels. He visits Avignon, Arles, Saint-Rémy, Les Baux, and Aix-en-Provence, talking to no one but getting a feel for why the Old World is what it is: old. He is charmed by the Roman ruins, sarcophagi, and aqueducts in the south of France. He doesn't know exactly why, but maybe it's because they stand in marked contrast to the beauty of the landscape. It's an unseasonably warm spring, and his nose becomes attuned to the smell of fresh lavender and thyme pushing up through the earth. He sees trees with tulip flowers growing above the crown of leaves.

In these smaller towns and villages of Provence, he has stopped seeking out brothels, because he doesn't want to contract another case of crabs, or something much worse. He is happy masturbating in his bed, with toilet paper at his side, imagining pulling down Perla's panties and letting her receive the deposit of his sperm—which traditionally fell on the movie house floor—inside her body.

In April, as summer warmth spreads into the streets of Paris, Guillermo returns to the home he has known since he was a child. After telling his parents all about his many adventures—but leaving out the sexual ones—he once more becomes a slug in their house, occupying the studio apartment built for him when he was in junior high. It is his castle, his aviary, his lair, where he can listen to Nat King Cole and Andy Williams cassettes, leaf through photography books, sneak up *Playboys* he bought in an El Portal newsstand, and fondle himself in peace. And this he does with more fury than pleasure.

Finally, after weeks of his son's slothing, Günter once more climbs the stairs to his room. The man has aged rapidly, making Guillermo wonder if he is sick. He asks the question he is so fond of asking: "What are you going to do with your life, Guillermo?"

"I don't know, Dad," the boy replies without any hesitation.

His father glances around at the rumpled clothes in the corners of the room, the stacks of magazines. It takes a big effort, but he says in a high-pitched voice: "I want you to take over La Candelaria. I want to retire."

Guillermo's heart sinks. He recognizes that as much as he does not understand what motivates his father, his father does not understand him in the least.

"I want to do something on my own, Dad. Make my own mark. Maybe take up farming."

This is a new one for Günter. He is almost speechless. "Farming? And do what? Grow cabbage?"

"I was thinking of artichokes," Guillermo says, remembering how delicious they had tasted in France, the meaty leaves dipped in a warm sauce of butter, basil, and garlic. He has never even seen an artichoke in Guatemala, but he is certain they can grow here. Maybe not in abundance, and certainly never to find a way to his father's table, but the soil and the climate would be appropriate for developing a large harvest.

"Is this what you got out of three months in Europe?" His father is frowning. The reddish hair on his head is turning gray. "That you want to grow artichokes?"

"I was away for four months."

His father glares at him, exhausted. "Okay, four. What difference does it make? You go to Paris, London, and Amsterdam and a light goes off in your head that you want to be a farmer and soil your hands?"

"I don't want to be stuck in an office," Guillermo says, recalling Carlos and resisting the instinct to joke about a light going off in the head of the son of a lamp store owner. "And I'm not good at selling."

"What about studying something of value? Instead of you planting artichokes, what about the *business* of farming? Let somebody else do the heavy work." He remembers his son's cockeyed dream to work in an archeological site in the middle of the Guatemalan jungle.

"Agronomy?"

"I don't know what it's called, but it puts food on the table: farming, distribution, sales. Anything to avoid seeing you on your hands and knees in the dirt."

Once in a while the old man has a good idea, Guillermo has to admit. "I wouldn't mind becoming a rich farmer, Father."

"This is what you have learned in Europe?" Günter goads. "That you abhor working for a living? You would prefer being a gentleman farmer to taking over a proper business that has been developed by your father?"

Guillermo doesn't want to argue. "I don't abhor poverty, I just don't want to live in poverty. Poor people sicken me."

"So now I understand why we have Indians and guerrillas fighting together in the mountains of Guatemala—because they have chosen to be poor? And you feel that Europe is a tired continent with lots of museums. Is that what you think?"

"Europe is worse than Guatemala," he tells his dad. "At least here there is hope of change. There are only fossils over there."

Günter Rosensweig is exasperated. He turns on his heels and starts walking out stoop-shouldered. Guillermo recognizes this posture as the same his father uses on customers, which he believes will result in sales. But this time there is no sale in sight. The customer will never call him back.

"I don't want to wear an apron every day," says Guillermo, his voice cracking.

Günter turns around. Guillermo is holding his breath. Again he has tears in his eyes. The father understands how his son sees him. In an apron. Like a maid.

"Come here, son."

Guillermo runs into Günter's open arms. For months he has been holding in his frustration, his sense of utter failure. He hates his emotions and promises himself that he will never be so weak as to lean on anyone again. He doesn't want to wound his father—he isn't sadistic—but he doesn't want to be trapped in a life he finds repellent.

Günter strokes his son's head as his own tears come flowing out. Yet they are crying for different reasons. Guillermo wishes he could stop, but he can't. Maybe this is what happens when you tell your father that the work he does is demeaning, or maybe it's because it has been months since another human being has touched him with something resembling love.

It is 1980 and a very dangerous time in Guatemala. Most of Guillermo's high school friends decide to stay abroad, taking courses, working, or traveling over the summer. They are advised not to come home. Their parents must tend to their stores and offices, risking being kidnapped, but why should their children put themselves in danger? The mother of a Colegio Americano friend is kidnapped, and when the family fails to pay the million-dollar ransom quickly enough, she is shot five times and left on the side of the road by Chimaltenango, with her jewelry still on her.

The message is quite clear: *Pay up, and pay up well, or die.*

Guillermo is nineteen and President Lucas García claims the country has never been safer. This is the real stupidity, to speak of order and the rule of law as if history has ever been civilized. Guillermo remembers that the Mayan golden age offered the seventh century a vicious hierarchy, superstition, and the yanking out of still-beating hearts, not to mention slavery and constant warfare. And the Romans and the Gauls let thousands of their soldiers die in futile combat.

It was a butcher shop then, and so it is now. In Guatemala City, businessmen are hiring twenty-year-olds with automatic rifles, buzz cuts, and bench-pressed muscles to determine who lives and who dies with the flick of a wrist.

His father sells lamps. In high school Guillermo was just another boy who dreamed of kissing the girl who barely knew he existed, but smiled through him just the same. The girl knew that his father sold lamps, while her own father owned factories, had three white convertible Impalas in the garage, membership at the Mayan Golf Club in Amatitlán, and a house in Likín with a motorboat and skis. Without saying a word to their daughters, they knew they would never date anyone with a background like his.

So Guillermo finally tells his father he wants to be rich, filthy rich, so he won't ever have to hesitate at a restaurant before ordering steak or lobster. And he will never touch a lamp again, unless it is to turn the switch.

Since he only spent two thousand of the four thousand quetzales that his father had given him for his trip, he has enough money to pay for a semester's worth of courses at Universidad Marroquín, where Juancho is now studying. His friend insists that he start taking summer courses immediately, not to wait for the fall term.

The Chicago school of economics is the rage at Marroquín. Everyone prays to the god of capitalism and that god is named Milton Friedman. The theory is simple—reduce or eliminate taxes and let money do what it has always done: create more money. Somewhere down the line the quetzales will trickle down to the bootblack or the street sweeper.

There's no place for guilt about inequities or the gap between the rich and the poor, because economic policy rewards those who take initiative. Allow the merchant class to make money freely and they will use their profits to further fertilize the fields of bounty. The Promised Land will have glass buildings, streets paved with gold, papaya and avocado trees growing in the backyard of every house. It will be paradise on earth.

Guillermo has no trouble with this philosophy. In fact, he embraces it. Soon enough he is reciting Friedman quotes—sculpted into the wooden signs at the entrance to the library and the other buildings on campus—by heart. *A society that puts equality before freedom will get neither. A society that puts freedom before equality will get a high degree of both.* But his favorite quote is, *He moves fastest who moves alone.*

"John Maynard Keynes" and "federal government" are bad words. The university is filled with serious young men planning to be millionaires by the time they turn thirty. Guillermo has become one of them—but since he is a loner, he does not join any clubs.

He believes that free enterprise is king.

He plunges into his studies. He hates his literature and philosophy courses, where the idea of economic success is, if not belittled, then considered an obstacle to social equity. The novels he is forced to read and the philosophy he is obliged to study all stress the negative, but Guillermo is now interested in emulating systems that allow unfettered wealth and happiness.

In high school, everyone read existentialist literature voraciously. His classmates thought that Camus's *The Stranger* was the greatest novel ever written: a man who feels nothing when his mother dies, who kills another person for no apparent reason, who refuses to repent for his sins, who not only doesn't believe in God but spits in His face, and who happily awaits his execution hoping that a big noisy crowd will be there to see him hanged. They loved the novel because it had nothing to do with their actual lives.

His courses in macro- and microeconomics, organizational management, propensity theory, business economics, and motivational factors in economic growth, however, are too theoretical and dry. He realizes that what he likes most now is not studying and memorizing economic concepts but arguing with his fellow students. He has become an acolyte to capitalism, his new religion, but even more so, he's become a skilled debater. He is convinced that he can actually win a debate defending the position of either Marx or Engels.

Marroquín counts among its students the sons of the wealthy: the Paizes, the Sotos, the Halfons, the Habers. No matter what political or economic positions his fellow students stake out, Guillermo always goes one step further to the right. While his classmates fear a Communist takeover, many of them consider Ríos Montt's military coup against Romeo Lucas García regrettable because it involves a distortion of the rule of law. Guillermo, however, alone among his classmates, happily applauds it.

"Are you going to sit on your hands while the guerrillas take over your father's factories, kidnap your family, and ransom them for millions of dollars? When will it stop? When your parents are impoverished and your sisters sold into prostitution?"

He argues not only because he has mastered the facts, but because he has worked hard to develop the skill to distort them. He is gifted in foreseeing his fellow students' counterarguments, like a champion chess player. He can see two steps ahead of them and he revels in the anticipation of his successes, even before achieving them.

By the second year, Guillermo abandons his business studies to pursue law, an occupation better suited to his developing skills as a manipulator. He takes courses in commerce and procedural law at Marroquín, but also graduate seminars in constitutional and tax law at the Landívar. The more knowledge he acquires, the more power and money he is sure to have.

For the first time in his life, Guillermo knows what he wants to do.

When he was in Paris, Guillermo heard a French diplomat say about his own country, *C'est un pays de merde.* If France is a shitty country, Guillermo wonders, what would this same man think of Guatemala? At best, *C'est un pays trop bizarre.*

## CHAPTER THREE

# FEEDING ELEPHANTS

One Sunday in May, Guillermo and Juancho decide to go to the Aurora Zoo, the scene of so many happy childhood outings. There's a palpable tension between the boys, as if something remarkable has happened to change their relationship. In reality, nothing has, but Juancho feels scared of his friend now that Guillermo has become so combustible. He doesn't want to end up feuding. Juancho is pleased to be driving, so that he need not look his friend directly in the eye.

They park close to the zoo's entrance. The walkway is sprinkled with visitors—grandparents, parents, and children on bicycles or scooters, Indian families, worker families, all kinds of families, except those of the very rich. The jacarandas are in bloom, with their inverted cones of scarlet flowers, and the shrubs are pockmarked with white and red berries. The clouds in the sky are thick and tuberlike: it might rain later that afternoon, but now the sun is shining, not too harshly.

The aroma of cotton candy, sugared nuts, tamales, and mixtas—hot dogs with avocado wrapped in warm tortillas—hangs listlessly in the air.

"I'm hungry," Guillermo says suddenly, putting out a cigarette. He picked up smoking in Europe as a way to calm his nerves and to feel more self-assured, but never smokes in front of his parents. He doesn't want them to remind him of how he complained about Carlos's smoking.

"I could eat something," Juancho replies hesitantly. He's thin as bamboo.

They go over to a food cart and wait their turn in line. Guillermo shakes his head when he sees the menu on the side of the cart saying that the mixtas cost thirty-five cents each, and a small Coke twenty. This is all chump change, yet he feels obliged to complain. "We used to pay a nickel for them at Frankfurts near the Cine Capitol. Do you remember?"

Juancho nods. "And the Cokes used to cost six cents."

"Life—and inflation—in the damn tropics," Guillermo says.

He orders two mixtas for himself, one for Juancho. He would prefer to drink an atol de elote, but he knows he'd have to leave the zoo. The cart man prepares the mixtas deftly, as if he were a machine, putting the hot dog on a griddle-warmed tortilla and then slathering it with guacamol. He pulls two cans of Coke from his Styrofoam ice chest behind the cart.

Guillermo gives the man two quetzales, and refuses the change. "Keep it—you should invest in a new cart."

The man nods and is already taking a new order. He has a look on his face as if to say the world is filled with sergeants and few soldiers.

"What do you think?" Guillermo asks his friend. They are sitting on wobbly stools on an elevated table piled high with napkins and soiled wax paper.

"They taste the same to me."

Guillermo shakes his head, watching half of his second hot dog fall to the sidewalk as the tortilla breaks in half. "The ones at Frankfurts were grilled, not boiled, and the avocado was dolloped on a thick corn tortilla from a big plastic container that sat cold in the icebox. These tortillas are made of wheat flour."

"Nothing's what it was," says Juancho resignedly.

"You are so right," agrees Guillermo, with more than a hint of disgust in his tone. "Let's pay a visit to our old friend La Mocosita."

The elephants are around the corner from the mixta cart. La Mocosita, the erstwhile baby now fully grown, seems unusually agitated. She keeps walking back and forth in her pen, dousing her back with water and trumpeting. Guillermo looks at her and swears there are tears in her eyes. When the two friends try to feed her bananas, she turns her back on them. That's when they see the broken arrow sticking out of her haunches. Someone has shot her, and a thread of blood issues from a small hole near her tail, trickling down her left leg.

Thousands of gnats can kill an elephant, Günter Rosensweig used to say, so his son would understand that the smallest creatures can accomplish a lot if they decide to work together.

"Can you believe this?" says Juancho, horrified.

"My stupid father . . ." Guillermo whispers. He pulls a Pall Mall from his shirt pocket and lights up.

"I don't understand what your father has to do with anything. We need to find a zookeeper."

". . . always talking about the importance of people working together when he should have been telling me it only takes one asshole to wreck a beautiful thing. What kind of person would shoot an arrow into an elephant's backside, in a zoo no less?"

They look frantically for a guard around the neighboring lion and tiger cages. They go to the exhibit where three Galapagos turtles sleep like prehistoric rocks on a grassless stretch near a standing pond with storks and ibises. They finally find a zookeeper sitting on a bench with the *Prensa Libre* covering his face. He is snoring loudly.

Guillermo pulls the paper off his face.

"What's going on?" says the keeper, shielding his eyes from the sun, his legs kicking in the air.

"Someone shot an arrow into La Mocosita."

"Huh." The zookeeper raises his shoulders. "I'm in charge of the reptiles. You need to find Armando, the keeper of the large mammals."

He makes no effort to get up. They see why: there's an empty pint of rum next to him. Furthermore, he packs more pounds than a grown sea cow. He would fall on his face if he tried to stand.

"You drunken piece of shit."

The keeper flays both his arms in the air as if trying to punch them, but he can't get himself up. He looks like a fat cartoon character with elephantiasis.

Guillermo and Juancho run over to the monkey house. A zookeeper, wearing green rubber pants and boots, is hosing down the cement floor of the cage while some gibbons hang from rings and growl from above. They tell him what they've witnessed.

"Hijos d'puta, huevones. Maricones. Sinvergüenzas. Last week someone cut off the ear of the pygmy rhino. A month ago a red panda was stolen. What's going on in this country? Do the guerrillas think that torturing animals will overthrow the government?"

Juancho laughs nervously. He understands that Guatemala is going down the tubes, but not for these reasons. Armed conflicts don't necessarily spark mischief.

"What's so funny?" the zookeeper asks, closing the faucet. "Don't you believe me, you skinny piece of shit?"

"Everything is the guerrillas' fault. The postal worker strike, the pollution from the buses, the eruption of the Pacaya volcano," Juancho says facetiously.

Guillermo has never seen a guerrilla, but he has bought the line that those trying to overthrow the government are Marxists on the Cuban payroll. He has seen college students with beards and mustaches drinking beer and cursing the military government at Gambrino's Lunch or at Café Europa behind the Lux. They are skinny boys with ink stains on their shirt pockets and black pants with cuffs rising up to the ends of their white tube socks. They wear Che Guevara glasses, with thick tortoiseshell frames, even if they have twenty-twenty vision. Their shoes are black and badly scuffed. They are not exemplary members of the human race, but they certainly don't arouse fear. Most of the time they occupy tables near the Paraninfo where they sell copies of *Alero*—a literary magazine—or try to get their fellow students to sign petitions protesting the latest government assault in Quiché. Guillermo knows that they are not wholly innocent but it's hard to imagine these scholarly types living in the mountains and jungles, surviving on plant roots and handouts from sympathizers, and planning raids against fully armed military garrisons. The radical core do their recruiting away from the public eye.

They follow the zookeeper to La Mocosita's cage. His wet boots squeak as he walks.

A dozen people are trying to attract the elephant's attention, to get her to come nearer. Not in the mood, she lounges in the back of her enclosure, resting on her right leg. The long tears coming out of her eyes flow like strings down her gravelly face.

The zookeeper picks up a towel from the guardhouse and goes into the elephant cage through a back gate. La Mocosita doesn't even stir. He moves over to her and gently washes the crust off her face with the towel as if she were a child. She lifts her head in pleasure and lets him rub her jowls. He then looks at the arrow, shaking his head. In one gesture, he breaks it against the surface of her left haunch. She groans forcefully four or five times, shaking her head back and forth. He shoves a clean towel flush against the wound and holds it there, stanching the bleeding until the elephant calms down.

"Let's get out of here," Guillermo says.

They decide to go to Pecos Bill, a hamburger joint on Sixth Avenue in Zone 4 about two blocks from the Hotel Conquistador. As kids they used to go there with their parents on Sundays, spending the whole afternoon swimming in the Motor America Hotel pool nearby and then eating the best hamburgers in the city. The restaurant has a little courtyard in back where the families often sat while the kids played on the seesaws and jungle gyms.

The restaurant is mostly empty. Juancho and Guillermo need a beer—they are driven by thirst, not hunger. They take a table near the entrance, where they can gaze out at the Esso gas station across the street and, a bit beyond it, the 235-foot Torre del Reformador, which is a mini Eiffel Tower given to Guatemala by the French in 1935.

To the right is a table occupied by two girls in their early twenties and an older woman—perhaps their grandmother—dressed in a long black Mennonite-style dress and wearing too much rouge and mascara. Her hair is dyed dirty blond. Guillermo glances under the table and sees that the older woman is wearing high pumps. The three look like they have just come from church, maybe Mass at the nearby Union Church.

One of the girls attracts Guillermo's attention, a strawberry-blonde with lots of freckles. Later he learns that Rosa Esther Castañeda's mother was born in Ireland, but had come to Guatemala to study Spanish in the early sixties. She eventually married a local businessman who owned the Chrysler franchise in Guatemala. Rosa Esther took after her mother, while her sister resembled the father—a short, plump man with dark, vivid eyes.

The waitress comes over as soon as they sit down. Guillermo orders his Gallo and Juancho another Coke. When their bottles come, Guillermo thanks her as he squirms in his seat to make eye contact with Rosa Esther. Their eyes meet for a split second before hers shift away.

Guillermo is handsome, with dark wavy hair. Rosa Esther notices his full lips and dark, probing gaze. Guillermo is beginning to realize that his good looks can make some girls tremble. Juancho, on the other hand, is a string bean of a person. He seems brittle next to Guillermo, like a porcelain statue about to shatter, the kind of man a girl on a mission of mercy might find attractive.

Juancho orders a cheeseburger from the waitress when she brings them the beer and Coke. As she saunters away, the grandmother has a coughing fit and looks as if she might upend the table.

Guillermo gets up at once, and brings Juancho's untouched soda over to her. "Please, drink this."

The woman blanches, and waves him off with two bony white hands. She is gasping for air, and is clearly embarrassed.

"Please, I haven't touched it. Have a drink," he says.

Rosa Esther's sister stands up and takes the bottle, jams the straw in the old lady's mouth, and urges her to drink. The woman takes a few sips, then pushes the bottle away.

"Something got caught in my throat, I couldn't breathe. I'm so sorry. We were just leaving. Let me buy you another Coke—"

"Don't worry about it. "

"That was so sweet of you," Rosa Esther says, standing up and rubbing soft circles into her grandmother's bony back.

"Are you okay now?"

"Yes, thank you, young man. May the Lord bless you . . . I don't even know your name."

"Guillermo Rosensweig. And my friend over there is Juancho Sánchez. If we can be of any further help—"

"You've done more than enough," the old woman says. "Girls, don't just sit there. Introduce yourselves and thank the young man."

"Ay, abuelita, give us a chance."

The two girls introduce themselves as Rosa Esther and Beatriz Marisol Castañeda. Juancho stands up and waves shyly, and then everyone sits back down. There's a sense in the empty restaurant that there's been a bit too much commotion for a Sunday afternoon.

Guillermo is smitten with Rosa Esther's milky-white skin, the ethereal air around her, her blue eyes like shallow pools. She seems to almost float lightly above her seat as she sits between her grandmother and sister. Her hands are thin and delicate, blue-veined like her grandmother, barely visible under her long-sleeve white blouse.

About five minutes later, the three women get up to leave. Guillermo, who has been stealing glances as he talks to Juancho, feels a sharp pang in his chest as Rosa Esther turns around, waves to him, and mouths a *thank you*. She is the last one to walk through the screen door to the parking lot, and Guillermo notices how white and shapely her calves are. He quickly jumps up and goes bounding after her.

"Rosa Esther, wait."

She turns around and manages to hold the door open for him. Her blue eyes sparkle like bits of cobalt.

"I don't know how to say this—"

"You would like to see me again," she slips in.

"How did you know?" He is surprised by her gumption.

She nods, raising her eyebrows. "It's all over your face."

"Can I have your phone number?"

She shakes her head. "I am not that easy."

"So how can I see you again?"

"You can't."

He looks at her confused, in desperation, thumping one foot. "I want to see you again," he says insistently, a bit uncomfortable that she is forcing him to be so declarative.

She nods a knowing smile. "I go to the Union Church every Sunday. Maybe one day you'll stop by and share the Mass with me."

It's a strange request, totally unexpected, and his "Okay!" is equally odd, as if he doesn't quite know how to respond.

He has never gone to church to pray or to seek any sort of solace. He really doesn't believe in God or His son. It is all a bunch of idiocy. But it would be a greater folly not to go now that she has invited him so openly.

Sure, he can give religion a second chance.

## CHAPTER FOUR

# LOVE & MARRIAGE: A HORSE & CARRIAGE

**G**uillermo seems to fall in love with the idea of Rosa Esther. The following Sunday, he puts on a suit and white shirt, borrows his father's car, and drives over to the Union Church near the Plazuela España. He luckily finds a parking space around the wide circle. It is just before noon.

He takes a deep breath before entering the church. When he reaches the back pews, he happily realizes that the services are about to end. The pastor has finished his homily on a piece of scripture and is preaching that only through God's grace, not through good works, can salvation be achieved. The only way to receive this grace is to accept Christ into your heart as the only true God; only in this way will the sinner be forgiven his sins and be born again. He concludes by saying that one day the Lord Jesus will return to this godless land and the final and complete resurrection of the dead will occur. This will lead to the establishment of a new heaven and a new earth and the elimination of suffering, evil, and even death in this new glory and the holiest of holies—as things were before the fall. The saved will share in the everlasting glory while those who fail to accept Jesus will suffer eternal punishment. The righteous will be part of an endless banquet while the damned will fight for morsels of food.

Guillermo has heard these things before, but this pastor—obviously not Guatemalan—says it with a kind of fatalism that seems almost admirable. He is pleased not to have heard another wishy-washy speech about how Guatemalans need to reach out to the poor. The sermon is in English, and clearly the majority of the seventy-five or so parishioners are comfortable with English and Anglican culture. This could be a service anywhere in Europe or North America. Looking over the crowd, Guillermo sees just a few people—including Rosa Esther's sister—who are authentically Guatemalan. Everyone is applauding enthusiastically.

To Guillermo, this sermon only underscores how simply Jesus Christ brings salvation to believers. It is all a bit too easy. He smiles as he stands in the back of the church, watching the parishioners hug one another as they make their way out. He too could believe in Christ if it meant he could kiss Rosa Esther over and over again on the mouth. He is not beyond duplicity.

Guillermo cranes his neck but doesn't see her. Beatriz Marisol is there with her grandmother; Rosa Esther is nowhere to be seen.

More than disappointed, Guillermo feels betrayed. Why would she suggest he come if she weren't planning to be there? When, with much embarrassment, he asks after her, Beatriz Marisol tells him she was there for the nine o'clock service but volunteered to accompany the children's church to the Aurora Zoo.

"And your parents?"

Marisol drops her eyes. "They're dead. We have an uncle, Lázaro, who lives in Mexico City. Otherwise we are alone, " she says somewhat melodramatically.

Guillermo can only say, "I'm so sorry."

"Don't be. It happened long ago."

Guillermo returns to the Union Church the following week, arriving a half hour earlier. Once more he wears his only suit, from his high school graduation. He wants to look the part, though he is only there for one reason.

This time he sees Rosa Esther from the church doors, where he waits out the service. She looks lovely in a long white dress with little violet and yellow flowers and a buttoned sweater.

When she comes out of church with her grandmother and sister, he approaches them to say hello. He's a bit giddy. She doesn't seem surprised to see him.

"Ah, the gallant boy from Pecos Bill," the grandmother says.

"Yes, it's me. I've come to ask your granddaughter if she would join me for coffee and dessert at Jensen's across the street."

Rosa Esther begins making excuses, but her grandmother interjects: "Do you have your own car?"

"Yes," Guillermo answers, pointing behind himself with his thumb.

"Please take her from us. She's been too much of a recluse lately. Try to cheer her up."

It is over croissants and tea at Jensen's that Guillermo learns her parents died in an Aviateca flight that crashed in the jungles of the Petén when she was six and her sister four. Her grandmother volunteered to raise the young girls. Guillermo pretends to listen attentively but his one desire is to unbutton her white dress and lick her equally white flesh.

So this is how the courtship of Rosa Esther begins. Guillermo realizes that she is no Perla Cortés and he won't be able to put his hand under her dress so easily. He has to embark on dating—traditional Guatemalan-style dating. Formal, polite, and virginal.

Guillermo is attracted to her inaccessibility and emboldened by her grandmother's approval of him.

What does Rosa Esther see in Guillermo? She is attracted to his boldness and has always had an innate desire to tame wild stallions. She is up for the challenge. She has also grown bored of her life with her sister and grandmother and wants to escape.

At the moment there is a surge of violence in Guatemala. The country is gripped by its worst years of armed conflict—the massacres, the forced conscription of Indian villagers, the wholesale emptying of towns, the militarization of the countryside, the killing of student and union leaders in the capital, and the president's daily rants.

But Guillermo and Rosa Esther are soon locked in a state of courtly love, immune to the chaos, engaged in what could be described as "spiritual dating." They kiss, sometimes for two or three seconds, never deeply, and certainly never touching tongues. But under it all there is a passion stirring, like water on the verge of boiling.

More than fearing the qué dirán, Rosa Esther's religious upbringing doesn't permit her to venture beyond certain forms of mild petting. So Guillermo thinks. But Rosa Esther knows what she is doing—she is an expert fisherman who knows that patience, above all, helps reel in the big fish.

This foreplay goes on for five months. But when Guillermo is granted a full scholarship to attend the master's program in corporate law at Columbia University in New York City, he realizes that something has to change. He wants to take Rosa Esther with him, and the only way that that can happen is if they are married.

When he asks Rosa Esther's grandmother for her hand in marriage, she grants it instantly, knowing full well that she is condemning Beatriz Marisol to a life of unconditional devotion to and caring for the grandmother.

Rosa Esther apparently has no say in the matter. Or does she?

Juancho is the one most surprised by the liaison. "Why Rosa Esther?"

"I love her."

"You do?"

"I love looking at her and seeing how she despises filth."

"Is that enough to sustain a marriage?"

Guillermo looks at his friend with a condescending sympathy. They are so different. "She is the perfect wife for a young lawyer. She will give birth to my children and she will see to their education and pleasures, without requiring much from me. And she will fuck me any time I ask her to."

"Is that enough?" Juancho repeats.

"If it isn't enough, I know the places to go to get it." Juancho shakes his head as Guillermo gives him a hug, whispering, "Don't forget, I'll be a lawyer. If it doesn't work out, we can always get divorced."

And marry they do, in a small, quiet Lutheran ceremony in August of 1983 at the Union Church. Günter Rosensweig does not understand a word of English so he hardly follows the service, and neither does his wife Lillian. Guillermo's sister comes all the way from San Francisco with her lover and raises more than a few eyebrows by holding her partner's hand throughout the service.

Guillermo's parents behave as though they are not gaining a daughter but losing a son—a son who will never be the proprietor of La Candelaria, a son who is leaving Guatemala to study abroad. The lamp store has become a failing enterprise now that the middle and upper classes have abandoned the downtown. Soon there will be no store.

Guillermo is happy to be going to New York. He feels he finally holds the reins to his own future. He has direction and knows where he will be in a few years' time. And Rosa Esther is also happy because she has married a man in the eyes of God, as her dead parents would have wanted. She can also see that, while she is not exactly looking forward to living in New York City, Guillermo's degree will bring them a life of leisure and luxury when they do return to Guatemala.

Guillermo is fascinated by the whiteness of his wife's skin, by her hard, perfectly shaped pink breasts, by her flat stomach. The first night they make love at the Camino Real Hotel in Guatemala City, they do it missionary style. She complains when he tries to enter her, but after some kissing and rubbing, she welcomes him gently. They make love twice that night, in the same position, each feeling a sense of conquest over the other.

In the morning there's no blood on the sheets. He is certain Rosa Esther is a virgin, and the lack of blood surprises him, but not enough to question her. He has heard of situations in which riding a horse or using a dildo breaks the hymen, so he feels no need to embarrass her or make an issue of it.

He has a strange dream around daybreak on the first night of their honeymoon at Casa Santo Domingo in Antigua. He sees himself lying in an enormous nuptial bed with Rosa Esther. The mattress and box spring are on the street in front of the Plazuela España, and cars are whizzing by. He assumes they are about to make love but he isn't able to get an erection—he feels no sexual desire. He knows she is naked under the sheets; he can see her legs spread apart. People are streaming by. He asks her to help him bring the mattress and box spring upstairs where they can have some privacy. She shakes her head and gets up, telling him that this is his duty, not hers. He is a bit taken aback, but decides to comply, and carries the bed alone upstairs.

After dinner on the second night of their honeymoon, Guillermo is overcome with such desire for her that as soon as they return to their room, he rips off her clothes. He is so hungry for her. He throws her down on the queen-size mattress under the large cross overlooking the bed, and tries to go down on her, to taste her sweetness. But as soon as his mouth touches her, she pushes his head away like a joy stick and brings his mouth up against the crook of her neck.

Guillermo relents. He has slept with mostly loose women whom he never had the desire to go down on, where hundreds of men had released their sperm. With Rosa Esther it is different, and he knows in time he will be back there and she will permit him to taste her.

To an outsider, sex between them might appear perfunctory. Yet Guillermo is seduced by her desire to always be below him, to allow him to thrust into her—to violate her purity—to push into her as hard as he can. She always lets out quiet yelps or sobs seconds before he ejaculates. It is hard, carnal sex that lasts no more than a few minutes.

Guillermo is sometimes puzzled because he cannot tell if she is achieving an orgasm or simply tightening her vaginal muscles, urging him to finish quickly. The act is done and consecrated. He attributes her lack of adventurousness to her sense of duty, as if it has all gone according to plan, her plan. He doesn't attempt to improvise, assuming there is nothing she expects from making love but procreation.

And yet he later discovers that she uses a diaphragm. She does not want to get pregnant, not now anyway, or perhaps not until they return from the States. But this causes him to question her actions: is his wife a kind of dominatrix who doesn't want to cede control to him? To anyone?

## CHAPTER FIVE

# SEVEN SEASONS IN NEW YORK

**I**t's hot, humid, and disgusting on the August day they arrive at Kennedy Airport. Guillermo and Rosa Esther are committed to making the two years in New York City happy ones. Through Columbia University's housing office, they rent a one-bedroom apartment on the sixth floor of 566 West 113th Street, between Broadway and Amsterdam Avenue, next door to the Symposium, a little Greek restaurant painted a light lapis lazuli. When there is some kind of special occasion to celebrate, like the completion of an exam or paper, they go downstairs and eat moussaka, okra, taramosalata, lamb flank, and octopus on lacquered wooden tables that seem to have been removed from an old sailing ship. The food is good if unspectacular, and the retsina, though a bit earthy and tasting of fern, becomes their passion.

Their neighbors are mostly graduate students, many of them from Latin America or Asia who, like Guillermo and Rosa Esther, are happy not to be in their homelands. In time they learn that the problems in Guatemala pale against those in Indonesia, Lebanon, Argentina, and Uganda, and that none of their fellow students want to leave New York, no matter how crime- and poverty-infested it is. New York is a very dangerous city, but Columbia manages to make the Morningside Heights neighborhood a kind of oasis of calm. The biggest nuisance is the woman who wears a plastic flower pot on her head and aggressively sings, "*I'm gonna live forever,*" from *Fame*, at passersby on Broadway.

It doesn't matter that most of the windows of their apartment face walls, and ivies and philodendrons are the only plants that thrive in the dim light. They live with unpainted furniture from the Gothic Store, bookcases that are wobbly hand-me-downs, and a kitchen table with chairs that were probably rescued from a nursing home.

Their closest neighbors are the Wasservogels, an old Jewish couple living in a tiny but immaculate studio adjoining their apartment who invite them for tea and cookies on the day after they arrive. They are childless Holocaust survivors, with numbered tattoos on their forearms, and their apartment smells the way the elderly often smell: a combination of talcum powder and artificial air fresheners. A week after their arrival, Herbert, a former philosophy professor, is hospitalized with a severe stroke. His wife Irma, who resembles an egret with her elongated neck and white skin, dutifully visits him every morning at St. Luke's Hospital and stays until seven at night, though there is little she can do. The stroke has paralyzed him, and he is fed through a plastic tube. He dies a week later.

Irma is devastated. If she were a pessimist before Herbert's death, she now epitomizes gloom and doom. His passing is only the latest episode in a life that began happily in Vienna but was almost lost in the Sobibór concentration camp, where she and Herbert were among the few survivors, and has ended in a solitary studio prison in New York.

While Guillermo goes through orientation at Columbia, Rosa Esther helps Irma by doing the shopping for her. Irma lasts another month before she dies of grief and is replaced by a fat nurse who works twelve-hour shifts at St. Luke's, and then sleeps.

The loneliness of some New Yorkers barely registers with Guillermo who has never been happier. He is relieved to be away from his father and his decrepit store, his complaining mother, and the small-mindedness of life in an ugly Central American capital. He feels he can breathe without looking over his shoulders, without guilt, without questioning why he is doing what he is doing. He has escaped the armed conflict and all the competing claims by the government and the resistance.

He takes his classes at Columbia Law School on 118th Street, atop a plaza spanning Amsterdam Avenue and overlooking the main campus to the west and Harlem to the east. He is impressed by the huge bronze Lipschitz sculpture of a Greek hero wrestling Pegasus that lords over the plaza with its flying hooves, flapping wings, and gnashing teeth. It is the fitting symbol for the anarchy that rules the world. Guillermo understands that as a law graduate he will be among the forces of order who will attempt to tame this chaos. He will be ready when the time comes.

Though Rosa Esther doesn't want to, Guillermo insists she take classes to improve her English at Columbia's School of General Studies. The courses are expensive, but her grandmother covers the tuition fees with the idea that one day her granddaughter will run the Sunday school at the Union Church. Rosa Esther is hesitant at first, but soon proves astute at and happy with learning an English that has little to do with the Bible and scripture.

Rosa Esther makes friends with the other female students in her class, and soon gossips about them with Guillermo. She learns a few words of Twi, Ga, and Urdu, enough to greet her classmates from Ghana and Pakistan. She is fascinated by the strange habits and customs from other cultures: the prevalence of polygamy, arranged marriages, even clitoral circumcision. After three weeks, she knows more about life in Nigeria, Korea, and Japan than she does about the many Maya groups in Guatemala.

Guillermo and Rosa Esther seem to be a happy couple: he impressed by the beauty of his ice queen and she admiring him for his animalistic looks, if from a distance. They are both proud to be seen with someone so different in appearance, character, and appetite. Is it magic? Perhaps. But they also share a distaste for the ordinary.

Theirs is a love sealed by a contempt for the commonplace.

There are lots of cheap coffee shops nearby—Tom's Restaurant, the Mill Luncheonette, and the College Inn—that make cooking almost unnecessary. Guillermo and Rosa Esther eat out almost every night since she—having grown up with maids, cooks, and a very solicitous grandmother in Guatemala City—has never had to learn to cook. For $3.45 they can have a baked chicken dinner, boiled potatoes, and, yes, soggy broccoli, a green salad that edges closer to brown, and colorless pink tomatoes with no taste. Their favorite waitress minds the manor at Tom's: Betty is severely wrinkled, a taller and more vibrant version of Irma Wasservogel, defying her age with dyed blond hair and tons of rouge and makeup.

"What'll it be today, baby?" is her mantra as she comes up to their table with a wet cloth in one hand and an order pad in the other. She always passes the cloth over the table, whether it's clean or dirty, dancing figure eights around the dishes, napkins, and utensils. When you give her the order, she looks at you and smiles, never writing anything down. Her pen never strays from its saddle behind her right ear. She never gets an order wrong and is known to give you an extra chicken leg if she sees you have cleaned your plate. She is greatly admired by all the former students who now live in the neighborhood because it seems that when they protested Columbia's ownership of Dow Chemical and Halliburton stock back in the sixties, Betty had provided them sanctuary at Tom's. She also authorized the donation of food to those who had taken over faculty buildings on the Columbia campus. "You're not going to billy club my babies," she'd apparently told the riot police, defiantly holding a mop across her body to bar their entrance into the restaurant.

On Thursday nights when Guillermo's corporate law course ends late, he often goes with his classmates to the Gold Rail near 110th Street, where he orders a well Scotch for $1.25, a beer for seventy-five cents—not Gallo or Cabro, but good enough to do the trick—and the blue-plate special for $3.75. The students debate Reagan's criticism of big government and his belief that social Darwinism will resolve society's ills. Reagan is Guillermo's hero, though in this he is in the minority. He passionately defends Milton Friedman's theories favoring a free-market economy with minimal government intervention. His classmates argue that government is needed to balance the capitalist urge, but they all agree with Guillermo that the social responsibility of business is to increase profits, and to engage in an open and free competition without deception or fraud. These are the ideas he hopes to bring back to Guatemala.

In the meantime, Old New York still exists. You can get a homemade bagel or a bialy stuffed with white fish for three dollars or a huge corned beef sandwich with a sour kosher pickle for two, and drown it all down with a fifty-cent lime rickey, or an egg cream from the Mill Luncheonette. There are three vegetable stands between 110th and 111th streets where the competition is ferocious. Everyone agrees that the tomatoes are soft and tasteless, the cucumbers pulpy, and the avocadoes usually brown and bruised at all three stands, but at least they are not in cans. The local bodega on 109th Street sells Ducal refried beans from Guatemala, frozen yucca from Costa Rica, and every once in a while huge five-pound bags of papayas from Mexico, for thirty cents a pound.

When Guillermo has some free time, he and Rosa Esther go together to Papyrus and Bookforum, bookstores on Broadway that even have Spanish-language sections. He surveys the law textbooks. She looks for novels written by Latin Americans. Her favorite author is Manuel Puig and she devours his *Kiss of the Spider Woman* and *Betrayed by Rita Hayworth*. She has him sign copies of his books when he visits New York and reads from *Pubis Angelical* at Columbia University's Miller Theatre. Soon she is reading the latest novels by Cortázar, Vargas Llosa, García Márquez, and even Nelida Piñon, either in Spanish or English. But her favorite novel is Isabel Allende's *The House of the Spirits*, which becomes a best seller in the United States. She identifies strongly with the protagonist Alba, a lonely child who plays make-believe in the basement of her house and is raised by her grandmother. It might as well be her own story.

During their second year in New York, Rosa Esther volunteers as a teacher's assistant at the Cathedral School of St. John the Divine, even though it is not her church or religion. She likes reading books to the first graders, taking them out to the playground, and looking for the peacocks who strut around the gardens when the weather is nice.

Guillermo and Rosa Esther go see movies on weekends, either at the college student union in Ferris Booth Hall, or at the New Yorker, the Thalia, and the Olympia—dilapidated movie houses on the Upper West Side. They don't know much about film, and they take this opportunity to see the classic works of De Sica, Rossellini, Godard, Truffaut, Renoir, and Fellini—films that had never been shown in Guatemala. They also enjoy seeing classic American films like *Sunset Boulevard*, *Casablanca*, and *Citizen Kane*, which may have come and gone at the Lux, Fox, and Reforma generations before they were born, but reveal so much about the country in which they now live. Guillermo comes to prefer the new European cinema of Lina Wertmuller, Fassbinder, and Herzog, which he adores for their chaos and wild, irreverent sexuality. Rosa Esther hates them for their lack of moral value. In fact, these European films frighten her, like when Guillermo drinks too much and tries to go down on her, or asks to enter her from behind.

She insists on taking Guillermo to the eleven a.m. Sunday services at the Church of the Ascension on Morningside Drive, because it is small and the Mass more intimate. She begins to wonder if she would be happier becoming a Catholic and joining the Iglesia Yurrita back in Guatemala City because she finds the Union Church service bland and mediocre in comparison. She knows this would not make her grandmother happy. She'll cross that bridge when she has to, but for now, she consumes the Catholic ritual as if it were forbidden fruit.

Guillermo and Rosa Esther are never bored with one another because there is always something new to do in New York. Besides studying, reading, and teaching, Rosa Esther goes to free concerts at the Manhattan School of Music and the Bloomingdale School of Music. Twice a week she swims laps in the Columbia gym and often attends afternoon lectures at the Union Theological Church. When Guillermo is studying at night, she watches American television—*All in the Family*, *Dallas*, *The Jeffersons*, *Diff'rent Strokes*, *The Cosby Show*—to try to understand this strange new country a bit better. Soon she is surprised to admit she knows more about the United States than she does about her own native country.

Rosa Esther and Guillermo become fast friends with lots of Latin Americans who left their homelands to escape the military juntas establishing dictatorial rule throughout the Americas.

There's the Chilean poet Marcelo Fontaine (nicknamed El Pucho—the cigarette butt—because his mouth and clothes reek of nicotine and he always has a rash on his face), who is getting his doctorate in comparative literature, and his wife Chichi, who is as intellectual as a washerwoman. They live on the first floor of their building and Marcelo has a side job as a porter, help-ing the superintendent remove garbage from the elevator well twice a week. They tell heartrending stories about crossing by foot into Bolivia's desert to escape Pinochet's secret police, eventually making their way to the United States. Guillermo likes the way Chichi looks at him, with sexy eyes and a pouty mouth that seem to beg him to lend her his penis. He imagines she would know what to do with it.

Carlitos and Mercedes—a handsome, well-mannered couple—are from Buenos Aires and are rumored to be related to one of the junta chiefs. Car-litos is getting a degree in international relations while Mercedes, a blond, blue-eyed former TV newscaster, is studying sociology. They are interested in how the military manipulates the media at home, and they mourn the arrest of poets and painters for simply being the children of well-known opposi-tion leaders. They have a lovely daughter named Valentina, also with blond hair and blue eyes, and enough money to hire a full-time nanny so they can pursue their studies. They are waiting for civilian rule to be reestablished before returning to Buenos Aires. Guillermo also finds Mercedes—Meme—attractive.

Catalina is the daughter of a famous Chilean poet who wrote a memo-rable poem about a helicopter that, crashing into the Andes, symbolized the overthrow of President Allende.

Mario is a bad Uruguayan poet whose father died suddenly and whose family fortune was swindled by his caretaker uncle in Montevideo. Mario has sad eyes and digs into his bag of tricks to try and seduce every girl he can.

And then there's chubby Ignacio, a Peruvian Communist architect who lost a hand designing homemade bombs near El Cuzco, and who fled the military by sailing down the Amazon on a raft. He is helplessly in love with the even chubbier and religiously American socialist Hope Wine (everyone calls her Deseo Vino), who often hosts the most elaborate of dinner parties. Within six weeks of meeting one another, Ignacio and Hope get married, assuring he will never be deported.

From their friends, Guillermo and Rosa Esther learn new names for tradi-tional Guatemalan vegetables—choclo for elote or maize, palta for aguacate—

and eat canned erizos (sea urchin) with pisco or aguardiente. There's always plenty of cigarettes, lots of dancing, endless political arguments, and harmless kissing across couples, as can happen when people in their midtwenties are ruled by liquor and hormones.

Rosa Esther allies with Mercedes, who also shies away from too much physical intimacy. They are always the first to tell the others to quiet down.

New York becomes an endless fountain of pleasure and culture. Guillermo and Rosa Esther live happily for over a year distracted by both the richness of their studies and their adventures, far away from the pettiness and the boredom of life in Guatemala City.

But Günter suffers a stroke in early December, barely three months into his second year at Columbia. Between attending final classes and finishing semester-long research, Guillermo calls home two or three times a day to get reports from his mother. At first he feels a bit of relief. Despite some mild paralysis, the stroke doesn't seem serious—mostly a warning that his father must sell La Candelaria and retire. But two weeks later, as Guillermo is finishing his finals and making plans to fly home with Rosa Esther for the Christmas holidays, his father dies suddenly from a second stroke, a blood clot that loosened in the carotid artery and went directly to his brain.

His death is awful, but the timing couldn't be better. Guillermo's sister Michelle has already gone back to be with their mother and make the funeral arrangements. Guillermo and Rosa Esther arrive just in time for the wake at the Funeraria Morales in Zone 9 and the simple burial in the Cementerio General.

Guillermo stays in the aerie of his childhood home to help his mother, while Rosa Esther spends time with her grandmother and sister in their house near the Union Church. The prodigal son fulfills his filial duties during the month-long winter break. He must reward Carlos and the few remaining employees for their years of service and close down the store near El Portal. La Candelaria has, at this point, lost nearly all of its business to the fancier, more hip lighting stores in the malls, and the best Guillermo can do is get forty-three thousand quetzales for all the remaining merchandise. The downtown store has always been leased—a miracle, because at this point it would be impossible to sell the building for anything other than a huge loss.

After Michelle returns to San Francisco, Guillermo is able to sell his parents' house in Vista Hermosa and set up their mom in one of the high-rises off Avenida Las Americas in Zone 14, close to the Gran Centro Los Próceres. He feels that she will be safer and better taken care of there. With the money his father has saved over the years, he hires her a chauffeur and a live-in maid. She will be well provided for, because Guillermo finally understands that there is a payoff to all his father's money-pinching. He has left his wife with oodles of cash.

But three weeks later, on January 6, the day of the Epiphany, the maid discovers that Lillian has simply died in her sleep. She is sixty-eight years old. An autopsy is required by law, and indicates there has been no foul play in her death. No trace of drugs, no unusual illness. With nothing left to live for, she has simply up and died. Guillermo pleads with his sister not to come back. What for? For a second burial? He ends up burying her in Verbena Cemetery; thirty of her friends, most of whom Guillermo never knew, attend the funeral.

So within three weeks he has lost both his parents. He is more stunned than grieved. Rosa Esther doesn't know what to say or do to quell Guillermo's loss. She has lived her whole life without the support of parents; she does not understand why Guillermo suddenly starts crying at odd moments. She seems angry at his tears, walking away rather than embracing him. Guillermo begins to feel a greater distance from her. Maybe he doesn't really need anything from her. Not anymore.

Certainly not their usual sex habits.

Only Guillermo can understand Lillian's death. The night before she died he had a dream that the Angel of Death flew over his bed and sprinkled droplets of poison on his face. He survived by keeping his mouth shut. The dream is a premonition that he will be constantly stalked by death. He is not frightened. Forewarned, he will live his life vigilantly, but will have a long life.

Guillermo and Rosa Esther return to New York for the final semester at Columbia. These have been happy years for them, he with his studies and freedom, and she with the variety in her life. The subway costs thirty-five cents—there is music, art, theater, and literature everywhere in this city, and despite occasional muggings they are living in peace. When they get together with their friends, the others complain more vociferously of the violence in Argentina, Chile, Peru, and Uruguay. They express fear for the safety of their relatives, but also for themselves. They have been vocal in criticizing their homegrown dictatorships from abroad and are fearful of spies.

In truth, they live with the tense knowledge that their student visas are about to expire. By July 1 all of them must return to their homelands. None of them are ready—they've grown comfortable with the peace the United States offers them.

To stay beyond the two years of his academic visa, Guillermo applies for a postgraduate fellowship at New York University's business school. He wants to study banking and finance but is rejected. And with the death of his parents, Rosa Esther is more intent on returning to Guatemala to spend time with her own familiy. She wants to be around should her grandmother become sick.

"This is our reality," Rosa Esther says to him. "The fun's over."

"I don't want to go back."

"Well, I do. And if I return, you do too."

He glares at her, realizing that the love and respect he had for her has turned to something else. He recalls what he said to Juancho when the latter challenged his marriage.

It's not yet time for a divorce, but he's ready to push the envelope.

As if to deny the future and upset his wife, Guillermo buys himself a fifteen-gear Peugeot and Rosa Esther a three-gear Raleigh. If they are going to leave New York, they might as well spend their last months exploring the city.

"This is the most foolish thing you have ever done. I will *never* ride that bike," she tells him, more angry with his lack of consultation than the waste of money. She knows that his parents' deaths have left them without money worries for years.

He simply shrugs. Every weekend or holiday at daybreak he takes his bicycle down the elevator and rides through Riverside Park or Central Park. He makes a habit of biking over the Brooklyn Bridge to Fulton's Landing, where he eats ice cream and stares at the monumental beauty of the Twin Towers in the distance. He discovers Sahadi's on Atlantic Avenue and buys dates from Morocco and ma'amoul from Yemen for Chichi, Mercedes, Deseo Vino, and even his wife. On several occasions he rides to the Bronx Zoo, where for the first time he sees a red panda, and thinks back to his many visits to the Aurora Zoo with Juancho.

One day, he bicycles all the way to Brighton Beach, where he eats potato and mushroom knishes and watches the many Russian immigrants sunning themselves on the boardwalk. He does not want to leave New York, though he knows their visas are about to expire. And anyway, Rosa Esther would make good on her threat to leave him.

At least he will return armed with a master's degree in commercial and international law from Columbia University. And the years in New York have allowed him and Rosa Esther to establish independence from their families, or this is what they tell their New York Latin American friends. But there is no need to justify their actions. Everyone but Ignacio and Deseo Vino has decided to return to their birth countries to reintegrate. As foreign citizens without working papers or green cards, they have no choice but to leave since no one wants to stay illegally.

There are parties every Friday and Saturday night in May and June. Marcelo starts his drinking early and by nine o'clock is snoring in his chair. He's always the first to pass out, leaving Chichi tantalizingly alone. Rosa Esther finds this spectacle of drunkenness distasteful and she returns alone to their apartment as soon as dinner is over. She nods her head in disbelief when her husband says he will be home by midnight. She acts as if she doesn't know it, but she is convinced that Guillermo has been making love to Chichi since April.

But she is wrong—it began two months earlier . . .

At the beginning of February, Chichi and Marcelo had decided to host a Valentine's Day party in their ground-floor apartment. All the friends were there, drinking heavily and smoking grass, dancing with their partners. At one point Guillermo went to the bathroom to pee. He didn't see Chichi sitting on the toilet seat. Closing the door, he finally noticed her and glanced down at her crotch, her thick black bush, and then their eyes locked. Chichi immediately stood up and approached Guillermo, turning the bolt behind him. Her eyes were on fire; she had waited a long time for something like this. And so had he.

He could taste her cigarette breath as she kissed him and put her hands on his jeans. Then she knelt down on the bathroom rug, pulled down his zipper, and put his penis in her mouth. She rubbed his testicles while she consumed him.

Guillermo could hear Jim Morrison singing over and over again: "*When the music's over, turn out the lights . . .*" The bathroom door was vibrating. He pulled out of Chichi's mouth and lifted her up. He thrust himself inside of her and they started making love standing up, tightly clenched. He was trying to hold back his orgasm, but he couldn't. He was too excited to be inside a woman who truly wanted him. He came as he heard her begin to sing in her poor English: "*Before I sink into the big sleep I want to hear, I want to hear the scream of the butterfly . . .*"

She clung hard to him. He felt her nails digging into his back through his shirt. He had come, but remained hard, and she used his hardness for her own pleasure. In another couple of minutes she let out a series of soft cries that he tried to cover up with both his hands.

This was the first of many trysts. In fact, Guillermo visits Chichi every Tuesday and Thursday morning when Marcelo's Shelley and Wordsworth course meets. After class, Marcelo always goes straight to Butler Library to study. They make love without protection and by May she is pregnant. Chichi doesn't care who the father is—what she wants most from life right now is a child. And Marcelo, ignorant of everything, is pleased to have an heir.

What neither Chichi nor Rosa Esther realize is that Guillermo and Mercedes are also having a romance. Mario, the sympathetic bachelor, has given each a spare set of keys to his apartment so they can get together every Friday morning.

If making love to Chichi is animalistic, lovemaking with Mercedes is slow and romantic, an instrumental duet, though she insists he use a condom. Mercedes feels she could fall in love with Guillermo and his dark features, and this makes their liaison every bit more dangerous. She tells him not to worry, but he does. They could fall in love and wreck two marriages.

Each week Guillermo's balancing act becomes more complicated. He is certain that one of his three women will discover the truth. Still, he is cautious in his planning and movements and, surprisingly, feels no guilt pleasuring three women; well, two. He has discovered the true power of sex, and wants to explore it even more.

But the dalliances soon come to an end. The military is overthrown in Argentina after the Falkland Islands debacle and Mercedes and Carlitos are invited to return to Buenos Aires immediately and form part of the new Alfonsín government. Marcelo and Chichi are returning to Chile because Marcelo has been offered a professorship in English literature at Valparaíso University, a position he can't decline. Neither Mercedes nor Chichi speak with Guillermo about leaving Rosa Esther.

Rosa Esther announces proudly to her husband and to the group of friends in June that she will be giving birth in late November. She has known since March. Guillermo is taken aback by this public announcement, and he wonders if she held back telling him because she was suspicious about his affairs. He doesn't question her in private, but he is inwardly pleased to know that his wife will have something to distract her from his affairs when they return to Guatemala. This is all having a child means to him right now.

It looks as if the group will part as friends—until the moment the shit hits the fan. Chichi and Marcelo have passed herpes back and forth for years, and during a flare-up, she passes it on to Guillermo, who passes it on to both Mercedes and Rosa Esther. He has no option but to confess his infidelities.

All three couples are prescribed antiviral medication that will curb the symptoms, though it will never eradicate the disease. Chichi and Marcelo don't really care; Carlitos doesn't want to hear the details, but is willing to forgive his wife if she declares (which she does) that she will stay faithful to him from now on. Guillermo tries to fabricate excuses for his behavior: how the death of his parents unhinged him; how the women seduced him; how it all happened because no one wants to go home. But Rosa Esther fumes. She is unwilling to forgive Guillermo for putting their baby in jeopardy. She feels more betrayed than heartbroken, and will punish him for this sin of biblical proportions. She also fears the medication will damage their baby.

Guillermo admires himself for confessing to being the culprit, and actually convinces himself that he is a victim of circumstances, and of seduction by their female friends.

The last party toward the end of June is unusually quiet and tense. It is filled with maudlin speeches, pointed accusations, and empty promises to keep in touch. There's a sense that an era has ended.

The timing of their departures could not be more perfect.

CHAPTER SIX

# ALL UNHAPPY FAMILIES ARE UNHAPPY
# EACH IN THEIR OWN WAY

**B**ack in Guatemala following graduation and his parents' deaths, Guillermo uses his inheritance to buy a house with a spacious backyard in Vista Hermosa not far from the campus of the Universidad del Valle. Their house is at the top of a hill, on a corner, and it has views of the lights of Guatemala City off in the distance. It is palatial.

Without discussing it, Guillermo and Rosa Esther settle into the typical married life of well-to-do Guatemalans: they buy matching Oldsmobiles, begin amassing objects to fill their home and their lives. While there is pleasure in populating one's house with furniture, sophisticated electronic systems, landscape paintings, and Mayan artifacts, this is accompanied by the increasing emptiness in lives obsessed with accoutrements.

Soon they will be going on weekend trips to Antigua and Panajachel and of course doting on their child when it arrives. He will take up golf or tennis like the majority of the men of his generation. She could begin studying French now that she has mastered English, or go to exercise classes, but instead abandons her shift to Catholicism and becomes more deeply involved in the Union Church.

Rosa Esther bonds with the religiously conservative but socially liberal parishioners. They believe that their maids and groundskeepers should be treated with utmost enlightenment, having them work no more than fifty hours per week and providing them housing in which only two people occupy a room. The hired help is almost like family, and the parishioners often orga-nize fundraising events to secure money for special operations to repair cleft palates and other deformities in their workers' families.

They are preparing to be saved on Judgment Day.

Following the rush to marry and recalling the wonderful and inspiring chaos that was New York, it becomes clear to Guillermo that he and Rosa Esther have little in common. They are unsuited in temperament and philosophy. He wants to socialize with work associates and she prefers to spend time only with her sister and grandmother, and eventually with her newborn child. He loves to eat fresh papaya with fried eggs for breakfast, and she prefers yogurt and granola. They cannot even agree on the kind of coffee to have in the morning.

Guillermo was raised by a Catholic mother and a half-Jewish father, and though he had an extremely strong moral base as a child, he has no real in-terest in religion. Rosa Esther, on the other hand, thrives on the activities of the Union Church and insists that they build a truly Christian home. Their sexual drives were dissimilar from the start, but after his various infidelities, there is a more apparent religious undercurrent to hers. She now thinks of sex solely as a means for procreation and is dismissive of it as a release of tension or for recreation. At best it becomes a biweekly, sometimes monthly indulgence, performed more out of obligation than passion.

Guillermo becomes sentimental when he recalls his graduate studies in the States, what he refers to as "the period of intimacy, of shared experi-ences." He often wonders if they had been alone, without friends and without the distraction of a magical New York City that glittered in their hearts and in their imaginations, if their relationship would have begun to unwind earlier. He knows that his heart or at least his penis is bursting with passion, and he finds it difficult to discount his trysts with Chichi and Mercedes as isolated events.

No, they were clearly more than that, and formed the foundation of his new morality—something he cannot discuss with his wife. As he goes about building his reputation as a financial lawyer with some success—first working for the Banco de Guatemala and then for Credit Suisse—he discovers that he can atone for his betrayals by pledging allegiance to the God of Onanism: masturbation, in lieu of sex, brings him pleasure.

After Rosa Esther gives birth to their first child, Ilán, and two years later to their daughter Andrea, she withdraws from the physical realm, and he can see the window of their life as a unit closing down. He fondly remembers cavorting with Chichi on Tuesdays and Thursday mornings, and his Friday soirees with Mercedes. He sees these moments as the highlights of his married life. Spilling his seed two or three times a day on a toilet seat is hardly a sin.

But giving his wife herpes certainly was.

Rosa Esther falls deeper and deeper into family and church. It is clear to both Guillermo and Rosa Esther that they have lost the thread from her heart to his, and vice versa. Since he feels wounded by and sometimes furious at her judgment, he never wants to bring the subject up. And for her own reasons, neither does she.

One night they are lying in bed reading. Guillermo is unable to concentrate. The buzzing of his lamp and the occasional drip of water from the bathroom faucet is distracting him.

"Something has come between us," he says, putting down the newspaper.

"I don't know what you're talking about, Guillermo." Rosa Esther is wearing glasses and reading a book in English about Pilates.

"We used to want to make love," he says, surprised at his directness. He is aware of his erection.

"Never," she answers icily, not taking the eyes off the page. "Well, maybe before you started seducing your best friends' wives."

He rolls over to her side of the bed, pulls off her glasses, and attempts to straddle her.

"What are you doing?" she gasps, trying to push him off. "Have you gone mad?"

"Look at me!"

She does. Her eyes bulge, adding color to her creamy white face. He is much stronger, so she stops resisting him.

He relaxes his grip and in that moment she hits him hard on the forehead with the edge of her book. It is a sharp momentary pain and he is more hurt by the fact that she has struck him than by the bruise. While he is holding his head, she bounces him off her and stands up.

"If you ever touch me like that again, without my permission, I will leave you and take both of the children. Do you understand?"

He doesn't know what he has done wrong and is too frustrated to respond. He is starting to hate Rosa Esther and because he sees the children as extensions of her, he is beginning to resent them as well.

While Guillermo and Rosa Esther were living in New York, Juancho was getting his BS in international banking from Universidad Marroquín. Afterward he landed a job as a financial advisor for the Taiwan Cooperative Bank, which was looking to develop financial opportunities in Guatemala, one of the few countries in the world with which Taiwan had diplomatic ties. In short order he married Frida, a pharmacist with a thriving practice near the Campo de Marte. They bought a house in Vista Hermosa, not far from where his parents lived. He soon found his banking work boring and his employers inscrutable, so he decided to become a loan officer for the Banurbano of Guatemala—in this way, he could help small local businesses grow. But this job as well was not to his liking. His superiors forced him to deny loans to young entrepreneurs that he would have preferred to approve. He was also told to funnel tens of thousands of quetzales to businesses he suspected were shell companies, certainly not in need of capital. He had no one to complain to, and he felt that basic decisions were being made for him. He was simply being asked to execute them.

But Juancho is no liberal hero. He does not believe in social welfare, or that the government should be doing anything to correct the injustices in society. In this, his thoughts mirror Guillermo's, but his ideas are expressed with much less hostility. At best, government should be a referee to make sure the capitalist system functions properly, and that no single corporation can establish a monopoly. Taxes should be kept at a minimum, just high enough to fund the necessary departments of government: the military, the police, fire, sanitation, airport management, earthquake relief. The private sector should be in charge of everything else, even schools and parks. He will never vote for anyone who is overly progressive, criticizes the military, or attacks right-wing governments. Like most Guatemalans, he does not want to dirty his hands to ensure the enforcement of his ideas. He believes that honesty and transparency in government are important. No one should be asked to do things that are counter to the principals of God and country, and certainly not under-the-table work. He is a decent Guatemalan who believes that corruption is a worm that can pervade all walks of life and needs to be extracted. But he is not a fighter or whistle-blower.

So just as Guillermo and Rosa Esther are returning from New York, Juancho decides on a change of life. He purchases a hectare of land on a sloping plateau in San Lucas Sacatepéquez, about twenty-five kilometers from Guatemala City. Unlike Guillermo, he does not want to become a gentleman or corporate farmer. He wants nothing to do with corruption and illegal activities. He wants to work the earth with his own hands and have it produce bounty.

Juancho buys two hundred three-year-old avocado saplings and hires Marco Zamudio, an agronomist and botanist, to help him start an avocado farm. The soil in San Lucas is rich, the weather temperate. He and Marco embark on an ambitious grafting program, which allows them to reduce the period of juvenile growth and to spur the development of the fruit in half the normal time. So within two years, the saplings will begin to bear fruit. By the fifth year, if all goes as planned, the land will be producing ten tons of avocados—sweet and fresh and untainted—which Juancho hopes to sell to supermarkets and high-end restaurants in Guatemala City and Antigua, and possibly even export to the United States.

But one Wednesday Juancho is driving his truck from his house to the farm in San Lucas. Suddenly he loses control of the pickup, goes off the road, bounces over a gutter that is more like a trench, and slams right into a sprawling rubber tree on the side of the road. His head collides with the steering wheel. Juancho has apparently suffered a heart attack, and is dead on impact. The heart attack must have been strong, sudden, and severe. He is only twenty-six years old.

Guillermo is among the first to get a call from Frida. He is in anguish over his friend's death. It's not only the loss of friendship, which has been side-lined, but the awareness of how quickly things can change. Life is ephemeral, like cigarette ash or pollen carried off by a gust of wind, leaving nothing behind. He is troubled by the suddenness of Juancho's death. He doesn't want to appear paranoid, but he does wonder if his friend really had a heart attack or if he was killed as punishment for being unwilling to do something illegal at his job at the Banurbano.

A wake is held in the Funerales Reforma a few blocks north of Calle Montufar in Zone 9 on the following Saturday. The casket is left open for viewing, but something has gone wrong with the embalmment of the body. Noses start twitching and hands cover faces. An odd odor floats in the room, like a cloud. People cough and put handkerchiefs to their mouths. The stench is awful.

Since everyone is too polite to say anything, it is a ghastly wake. And while Juancho's two-year-old son is running around, as if his father's casket were a big wooden mansion atop a table, Frida is beside herself in grief. She knows something has gone wrong with the embalming but she is unwilling to address the problem, for fear of creating a disturbance. She is more concerned with when the priest will arrive to direct the services, since he is an old family friend traveling all the way from San Salvador. It is a long trip that can become longer with mountain mud slides.

Rosa Esther accompanies Guillermo to the wake, but she provides him little solace. She finds the viewing macabre, especially with the peculiar mixture of decomposing flesh and formaldehyde in the air. She is grateful that she never took the steps to convert to Catholicism. She is suddenly repelled by the pomp, by the eerie rituals, and yearns for the simplicity of the Union Church. At one point, her hand grazes Guillermo's shoulders. It is a tender touch. For an instant they look at one another the way they did when they first met. He reaches out to grab her hand, but she merely nods and walks back to her seat.

When the priest finally arrives a half hour later, there's a collective sigh of relief. Instead of wearing a full-length black cassock, he is dressed in dark pants and a black shirt with a white collar. A simple red cross dangles from his neck. He is young, even handsome, and looks something like a beatnik. He touches his nose nervously and confers with the director of the funeral home. The mourners observe how he keeps nodding his head.

He immediately approaches the coffin and closes it, draping the top with a small sacramental cloth he has brought with him, which depicts an embroidered, mostly naked red-and-blue Christ lying on a yellow mattress. He whispers a few prayers under his breath, then asks the attendees if anyone would like to say something.

It is midafternoon, and everyone is tired, hungry, and impatient after the long wait. A few family members say kind, innocuous words amid tears, but there is a sense of futility and hollowness in the air. Words cannot undo the deed. Juancho's death seems so unnecessary, so premature, so incongruent; no kidnapping, no mugging, no nothing to awaken political speculation or thoughts of bribery. A death without the violence that now characterizes daily life in Guatemala seems too simple to get worked up about.

When the speeches end Juancho's mother asks the priest if he can deliver her son his last rites. The priest grabs her hand and says that extreme unction is only for the gravely ill or the very recently departed, before the soul goes to heaven. He assumes that Juancho was a good Catholic and there is no need to question whether he was penitent for his sins or not. He is already in a state of grace.

Juancho's mother is distraught and a bit confused by the priest's trenchant comments. She leans more heavily on her daughter-in-law's shoulder, using it mostly as a crutch.

The priest finally realizes he must say something meaningful and kind to comfort the attendees. He calls the mourners around the coffin and initiates the Prayer for the Dead.

The weeping of the crowd is widespread and audible.

By the time the mourners head for the Cementerio General for the burial it is nearly three o'clock. The clouds are low, almost touching the tops of the trees. It is cold and raining.

If the mood was undeniably dreary at the Funerales Reforma, it is down-right grim at the cemetery. Fully three-quarters of the mourners have decided to opt for lunch and skip the burial, and there are barely a dozen people, all under umbrellas, to witness Juancho's descent into the ground.

On the drive home Guillermo is utterly depressed. His parents are gone, he feels lost without his wife's love and companionship, and now his best friend, who countered his increasingly strong diatribes against the liberal government, is dead.

He finds it increasingly difficult to believe that Juancho had a heart attack while driving. Something or someone else must have been behind his death.

After nearly five years of living in Vista Hermosa, Guillermo and Rosa Esther decide to give up their house and move to a four-bedroom apartment in the Colonia España, in Zone 14. Crime continues to rise and be more targeted, and he does not want his wife or children to stare down the barrel of a gun held by someone who simply had to scale a brick wall. Their new neighbor-hood is tranquil—more bubble-like than an Israeli settlement on Jerusalem's West Bank—and has armed guards at the entrance.

Rosa Esther finally accepts Guillermo's repeated suggestion to celebrate their eight-year anniversary with a long weekend alone in Panajachel, leav-ing the children with her sister and ailing grandmother. They stay in a corner suite at the Hotel del Lago with a gorgeous view of Lake Atitlán, and a handful of dormant volcanoes visible from their fifth-floor balcony.

On Saturday morning they walk through the gardens to the hotel's pri-vate beach. The sky is cobalt blue, and there are half a dozen turkey vultures floating high in the sky. The lake water is too cold and murky for Rosa Esther, so she watches from a chaise longue as Guillermo skims the surface of the water, flexing his well-toned arms as he swims in broad strokes.

When he comes out, Rosa Esther stands up and gives him a towel. "I had forgotten that you could swim so well."

Guillermo smiles, thinking that his wife remembers little about what he's told her. The swimming has been exhilarating, but he is exhausted, and he is very much aware of how out of shape he is. "When I was in high school, I took swimming classes at the Pomona. Do you remember where that is?" he asks nostalgically.

"Of course. It's on the same block as Union Church."

"You might have seen me swimming on days you went to church," Guillermo says, wrapping the towel around himself and lying down on his chaise longue next to her.

"I don't think I would have noticed," she says.

It is a funny comment, and Guillermo has to check his laughter. He wants to tell her that when he met her she was much more open to things than she is now. Open to him. But he already feels that too much water has gone under that bridge. Had she *ever* been in love with his virility, or was he simply a quick ticket out of becoming her grandmother's lifelong companion?

Still, he is willing to try to recover what they had in the weeks after they met at Pecos Bill, if only to feel less lonely and to foster a sentimental connection in her.

Later, in the afternoon, he asks Rosa Esther where she would like to dine. She tells him that she's tired and would prefer to eat at a table overlooking the lake in the hotel dining room. He says that it would probably be too cold and he meekly suggests they order dinner to their suite and have a table set at the edge of the balcony. They can have the fireplace lit. The swimming, the fresh air, has invigorated Guillermo. He wants to see if there's anything he might do to recapture the passion they once felt for one another.

Surprisingly, she says yes.

He calls the front desk and asks for someone to bring up some wood, light the fireplace in their room, and set up a small table for dinner. He orders a bottle of Châteauneuf-du-Pape, which will cost him more than eight hundred quetzales—a small price to pay to rekindle romance. Guillermo thinks that though he isn't as captivated by Rosa Esther as he once was, perhaps a couple glasses of wine will animate him to plunge back into her, just as he dove into the cold Lake Atitlán waters.

A hotel porter brings a little round table for them and sets it up near the chimney with a white tablecloth and pewter candlesticks. He even brings a slender vase, with a long-stemmed yellow rose.

At six p.m. a waiter comes up to set the table and open the wine, which they drink while eating crackers and imported Gruyère and chorizo. Guillermo keeps sniffing the wine, which is both bold and full, and he feels a bit drunk after two glasses. Rosa Esther is also drinking, but warily.

They have a lovely dinner, talking mostly about the children. Guillermo mentions the possibility of visiting New York as a family next year for Christmas, and watching the ball drop in Times Square. Rosa Esther says maybe, which is better than no.

When Guillermo has drunk most of the bottle, he calls downstairs for two Hennessys even though his wife says she has had more than enough to drink. He closes the balcony door and tipsily puts more kindling in the fire.

The waiter brings up the cognacs in snifters and removes the dirty dishes. Guillermo gulps his down as if it were water, and feels the heat of the alcohol warming his ears. Then he grabs the other snifter, takes Rosa Esther by the hand, and lifts her from her seat. When he tries to bring her down onto the brown shag rug, she initially shakes her head softly but finally acquiesces.

For several minutes they sit silently, holding their arms around their own legs, watching the flames ignite the new wood in the fireplace. The flames shoot up toward the flue; small branches crackle and spark. Guillermo feels his heart filling with something like love as he begins to sip Rosa Esther's cognac. She has moved a bit away from him and still has her arms wrapped around her legs, but now her eyes are closed. He leans into her gently and tries placing his lips on her mouth, but he loses his balance and his kiss lands sloppily on her chin.

Startled, she opens her eyes and pushes him away. "What are you doing, Guillermo!" she says rather harshly.

"I'm sorry. You looked so beautiful. I thought you were remembering us—"

"You're always thinking about yourself. You have no idea what I was thinking about."

"Why don't you tell me, then," he says softly, trying to reach out to his wife. His head is spinning.

"I don't think you would understand." She pushes herself up and moves toward the bathroom. "You know that you ruined it in New York with that Chilean whore. Ilán could have been born with herpes."

He looks down at the rug and says, "Rosa Esther, they were all our friends. We were younger. I was careless."

"Why?" she asks. "Because you didn't use a condom with Chichi?"

"I've apologized for that." He gets up to go after her, unsure of what he wants to do, but he upends the glass of cognac at the edge of the rug. He stops to watch the golden liquid dribble across the parquet floor.

"Yes, you did. And then there was Mercedes," she says, entering the bathroom and slamming the door behind her.

He collapses on the rug, defeated. It seems her religion won't allow forgiveness.

When the nightlight is turned off on her side of the bed, Guillermo is surprised to feel Rosa Esther snuggling into him and actually touching his briefs. He is taken aback. They haven't made love in nearly six months.

He is aware that he is drunk, but he's cautious because of their previous conversation about Chichi, Mercedes, and herpes. *What does she want from me?* he asks himself, waiting for her next move.

She touches his briefs again, as if lightly knocking on a door, and lays on the mattress.

His penis hardens in its web of cotton. He lifts her nightgown and moves down the bed. He wants to drink from her. As he puts his mouth on her stomach, she closes her legs and tries to pull him up. He clamps her hand down on her legs as she squirms to get free, but he will not let go of her. He puts his forefinger in his mouth and then pushes it tenderly inside of her. She buckles her legs, throttling them to the side as if he were trying to brand her with a pike, and then suddenly relaxes her body. As he keeps wedging his finger in and around her vulva he can hear her licking her lips, swallowing, and gasping a word that sounds like his name.

She grinds against his finger, helping him find a more pleasurable spot deep inside of her. When he feels her lips on the side of his face, he lifts his forearm to free her.

Her legs are open wide now, willing him to enter. She pulls down his underwear harshly, bruising his testicles, and with both hands pulls out his finger. He crushes his penis inside her and she arches back. She pulls his buttocks in steady strokes, leaving his hands free to caress her breasts. He pinches her nipples, hard.

Without warning, she lets out a long scream and gulps for air. She has not waited for him. He keeps pressing into her, and she digs her nails into his back as if insisting that he not stop.

When he is about to come, she wriggles an arm under him, grabs his penis, and jerks it out. His semen falls onto the sheets. He's still feeling it bubbling out of him when she turns over and clutches the pillow on the far side of the bed. Her body is shaking with the aftershocks of her orgasm. She might be crying.

"Rosa Esther, are you okay?"

"Don't even talk to me," she answers bitterly, evidently angry at having given in to her pleasure.

Guillermo is the first to wake up the next morning. He sees Rosa Esther sleeping peacefully with her head on the pillow, her hair spread out behind her.

Guillermo feels sick, like the character from *Nausea* who one day looks at a tree and only wants to vomit. Instead of feeling pleasure or satisfaction when he awakes, he feels abundant terror. He imagines he will live like this forever, having occasional, meaningless sex with her and finding pleasure with other women. There is a point of accommodation in marriage that is satisfying, almost expected; there is comfort in repetition: the Sunday excursion to a social club and the two o'clock meal; the shrimp cocktails, the baked potatoes, the guacamol, and the cuts of puyaso; the drive home to their bunker-like apartment after playing tennis or softball with the children, who are aligned with her.

He looks at her, this alien who doesn't stir. He hears a woodpecker pecking. He thinks he can survive this marriage. The two of them can live comfortably inside a tent of indifference.

* * *

The rest of the weekend passes by unremarkably. Guillermo and Rosa Esther are civil to one another, both in their own bubbles. He realizes he should never assume that his experiences can be shared with another person. Not with Rosa Esther anyway. They may share pleasures and delights, even physical ones, but they will do so occupying parallel planes in a three-dimensional universe.

She will continue to share his bed, but makes it clear without using words that she is not interested in making love to him. If this seems like punishment, she expects him to bear it dutifully, and to remain faithful according to the terms of their marriage contract even though he has broken it more than once.

This is all implied, not discussed.

As Guillermo is putting the suitcases in the car for the drive home and Rosa Esther waits in the lobby, he remembers the time he found Chichi in the bathroom of her apartment and they attacked one another, Jim Morrison and the Doors in the background. Her mouth smelled of too many cigarettes and bad wine, but he loved the feel of her stiff nipples against his cotton shirt. Had she been masturbating on the toilet seat awaiting him? As soon as he entered, she had come to him.

When he came he had looked into her face, and he could tell that she was happy, probably having experienced something she had not had in the years of being married to Marcelo. *The scream of the butterfly.* Like Rosa Esther, the night before.

But now he remembers what had happened next. Someone knocked on the door and Chichi quickly pulled herself away, took off her clothes, climbed into the shower, and closed the black curtain. Guillermo zipped up his pants and opened the door as she turned on the water. "Thank God it's you. I really have to pee," Rosa Esther had said to him, pushing her way in and sitting on the toilet seat. "Who's in the shower?" Guillermo had said nothing, and simply left the bathroom.

Had the two women spoken later? Rosa Esther never said anything to him about the incident. But she must have known that he had made love to Chichi, for something had shifted, undeniably changed.

Even before all six friends had herpes.

Guillermo and Rosa Esther live their lives like two lines that intersect at only one point—the children. She has her girlfriends, her family, and her church. He has his work—which is quite consuming—his club, and the dalliances he manages, or so he believes, to keep hidden from his spouse. He is becoming the typical Guatemalan man, having multiple adventures outside the house, but not even considering the idea of ending his loveless marriage. He is not interested in finding a permanent lover—he enjoys the excitement of speed-coupling.

Until he meets Maryam Khalil.

## CHAPTER SEVEN

# IT WASN'T THE HUMMUS THAT HE LIKED

**G**uillermo will never forget the moment he first saw her.

It was in February of 2006 that he first met Ibrahim Khalil, a new client. The president of the republic had asked Khalil to serve on the honorary board of the quasi-governmental Banurbano of Guatemala—the same bank where Juancho had worked—to oversee the legitimacy of loans to various private businesses and nongovernmental organizations.

It didn't take Khalil long to figure out that there were cash credits to companies that weren't even officially incorporated or registered in Guatemala. These were ghost firms receiving funds to build essential factories in the middle of the Río Dulce or plant sea grass in the mountains north of Zacapa! Half the firms had no street addresses, just PO boxes and articles of incorporation in El Salvador or Honduras. Khalil reached out to Guillermo because he had received threatening phone calls after he made an incendiary statement during a contentious board meeting, claiming that he suspected someone or a group of managers was misappropriating funds.

Pure and simple, Khalil had sniffed out money-laundering swindles. And unlike Juancho, he wasn't about to keep quiet.

Two days after he brought his discovery to the board meeting, he threatened to contact the supreme court—not the president whom he didn't trust—to initiate an investigation into the financial shenanigans. This was when the threatening phone calls began. The first call—a female voice telling him he did not understand how Banurbano works, and that he should stop his probing—he simply disregarded. But the second call was a manly voice ending with the threat, "Or you'll be sorry."

This was when he contacted Guillermo Rosensweig's firm.

After two short phone conversations, Ibrahim hires Guillermo not necessarily for protection (there are a dozen firms in Guatemala that offer armed bodyguards and all kinds of effective monitoring equipment), but to help him figure out how to proceed (should he contact the press?) and identify who is threatening him and who are the final recipients of these loans. As a board member Ibrahim has no real fiduciary responsibility, but he takes his work seriously and believes that he has been entrusted to oversee the administration of public funds. He sees his role as essential for maintaining public trust in the Guatemalan government.

During their third phone call, Guillermo tells Ibrahim that he doesn't think he needs added physical protection for now, but that it would be wise to keep his opinions to himself, especially since there will be another board meeting the following week. After Guillermo hangs up, he realizes he has made a mistake and calls him back to set up a time to meet. Because of his business background, he offers to go over the documents himself at Ibrahim's office above his textile factory in the industrial zone behind Roosevelt Hospital.

Ibrahim's textile business is doing well and needs oversight but not daily intervention. He feels he has a good management team, and the foremen and workers appear to be happy. He has blocked attempts at union organizing because he believes that business owners should have full say regarding the decisions that involve their primary investments—the workers and the products they make. He isn't interested in sharing power.

On the day he meets Guillermo, Ibrahim is wearing a blue jacket, checkered gray slacks, a blue shirt, and a striped black-and-red tie. Guillermo can't imagine who has dressed him. When he turns seventy-four, he thinks, maybe he won't care what he looks like either. Nothing the man wears seems to match.

They have a good first meeting. Ibrahim trusts first impressions, and he thinks Guillermo is intelligent and, more importantly, an upright man. He gives the lawyer two folders filled with ledger documents and bank transfers and says to him, "Guard these with your life."

Guillermo nods. The phone rings and Ibrahim answers. To give him privacy, Guillermo takes the opportunity to go to the bathroom. When he comes back, Ibrahim says, "Guillermo, my daughter Maryam is picking me up in ten minutes. I'm going to have lunch with her in her apartment in Oakland. I would be pleased if you would join us."

Guillermo knows that Rosa Esther is waiting for him at home. She decided that morning to have the maid cook chayotes stuffed with canned crab meat, even though the meat is usually salty and dry despite mayonnaise dressing. Why did Guillermo even think that someone who knows nothing about food could instruct their maid Lucia to cook?

"Shouldn't you ask your daughter?"

Ibrahim waves an arm in the air. "She's always thrilled to meet one of my new associates, especially one as trim as you. Maryam admires athletic people," he says politely.

Guillermo smiles. It is a strange comment, somewhat enticing. "Well, I used to be an avid cyclist." He is in good shape, but hardly athletic anymore. "Let me check with my wife—she's expecting me for lunch."

He excuses himself and goes into the hallway to call Rosa Esther. He tells her that a last-minute business engagement has trumped their lunch plans.

"Will you be home for dinner?" she asks. "I want to know because I've received an invitation from Canche Mirtala to have dinner and play bridge with her friends tonight."

"I'm not sure."

"Guillermo, I don't want to waste another evening waiting for you to decide if your evening plans include me or Araceli Betancourt."

His temples throb, but he ignores her comment. "Why don't you go to Canche's? If I finish early, I'll meet you there. If not I can always fix something for myself at home."

Rosa Esther hangs up without saying goodbye. Twice already she has warned him that she will take the kids and go live with her uncle in Mexico if he doesn't break off his chain of affairs. When she last made this threat, Guillermo complied, taking a break from his cavorting in order to keep his children close. He told himself that he would be faithful to Rosa Esther—but this only lasted until the next tight skirt rolled on by. Sex has become a drug, a good drug that makes him feel powerful, alive, and renewed. He is a devotee to erotic encounters.

When Guillermo comes back into the office, Khalil has already put a gray Stetson on his head and is standing by his desk.

"Ibrahim, I would love to join you." He is curious to know more about Khalil's daughter, whom he imagines will be around forty.

The old Lebanese man's eyes light up. "It will be a party," he says cheerily.

There's an armed guard at the entryway to the textile factory—security is a top concern in Guatemala. It is common knowledge that for a mere five thousand quetzales, three vetted guards can decide to take their coffee break at the same time so a kidnapping crew can carry off a heist.

When the two men step out onto the street, Guillermo sees a black Mercedes parked in front of the building. The driver's tinted window rolls down and before he can see a face he hears a female voice calling out tentatively, "Papá?" The appearance of a stranger has troubled her.

"Don't worry, Maryam. Guillermo is an associate of mine. Actually, a new lawyer. I've invited him to join us for lunch," he says, walking over to the front passenger seat.

"You should have said something when I called," his daughter reprimands softly. "I would have planned a larger lunch."

"Guillermo's a light eater. That's how he stays so trim," her father replies as he opens the car door. With his head, he signals for Guillermo to sit in the back behind him. "Let me move the seat up," he says, pushing a button on the side of his door.

"You don't need to," Guillermo says, opening his door. Ibrahim is a shrunken man who probably wasn't very big to begin with. From his seat, Guillermo can see the back of Maryam's head. And of course he can smell her Coco Mademoiselle perfume.

Maryam has thick black hair that falls over her neck and the headrest.

This, along with the profile of her right cheek, is all he sees of her, since she won't turn around to look at him. He can feel the icy mist of anger forming between the front and back seats like a glass partition. It is obvious that she is bothered by her father's last-minute invitation. Guillermo has half a mind to simply get out and call for a rain check, but something holds him back.

Maryam starts the engine and begins driving out of the lot. Finally Ibrahim breaks the silence and says, "Maryam, Guillermo Rosensweig is helping me figure out where all the money is going at Banurbano. I want you to be nice to him."

She actually humpfs as she zooms across the gravel of the parking lot, dousing Guillermo's parked car in dust. "I am nice to everyone." She pulls up to the fifteen-foot gate that encloses the factory, the offices, the loading dock, and the garbage dumpsters, and gives the attendant a ten-quetzal note.

"Maryam, he is my employee."

"Whatever, Papá. I don't want him to forget how nice I am to him, should a kidnapper want to make him a rich man one day."

"Please. Fulgencio has worked for me for twenty years."

"Precisely," she says, striking the steering wheel for emphasis. "He doesn't need much convincing to know he needs a change."

She rolls her window up and turns to Guillermo. "Sorry for making you feel less than invited. Papá knows that I want him to give me some advance warning when he invites someone to my apartment. It might be a mess or the cook may not have made enough food, but it's also a question of safety."

The guard opens the steel gate and Maryam proceeds rapidly over the speed bumps, turns left, and drives the six blocks to Roosevelt Avenue. Guillermo tries to get a better look at her through the rearview mirror. She seems anything but radiant. She is wearing a white T-shirt; her tanned face sports no makeup; her lips are colorless.

Guillermo imagines she is wearing a short white skirt and matching sneakers with puffy balls on the heels, and that she has been playing tennis all morning. Typical Guatemalan wifely style. And he is sure she hasn't showered this morning because he can smell her sweat winning the battle over her perfume. He wonders if she has shapely legs, and this causes his penis to stir.

Before he can say a word, Ibrahim asks his daughter: "Will Samir be joining us for lunch?"

"No," Maryam says. "Something's always cropping up at the hardware store. Or maybe he has a meeting with his Lebanese Committee friends." Samir must be her husband. Her lukewarm response implies there's trouble in the marriage. Maybe this Samir is just like him, prone to lying and engaged in multiple affairs.

"So," Ibrahim says triumphantly, "it will be just the three of us."

Guillermo wonders what's on the man's mind. It has happened all too quickly. There is no way he planned it this way.

Maryam pushes some buttons on the dash, and instrumental Arabic music starts playing. A female, possibly Fairuz, starts singing. She has a soft and plaintive voice, and Guillermo can hear a lightly strummed lute in the background.

He can't take his eyes off Maryam's thick and lustrous hair. At one point she leans into the mirror to see behind her and their eyes meet quite by accident. Almost immediately she sets hers back on the road.

"Guillermo is an avid cyclist! That's how he stays trim," Ibrahim says, after an inordinately long silence. "If I didn't have this pacemaker I would take up the sport myself."

Before Guillermo can say a word Maryam laughs. "Father, I don't think your old pacemaker is the reason you don't bicycle. You could always get a training bike for your apartment. But if Guillermo thinks riding a bicycle in Guatemala City is a way to stay healthy, he doesn't really value his life very much."

"I live in Colonia España in Zone 14. It's very safe there, with lots of gentle hills perfect for cycling. And the air is pure."

"I've only driven through once. It felt like being in a private city," Maryam says. "I'm told there's an area in Colonia España full of modern mansions."

"I wouldn't know. Our apartment is average sized, really."

"Isn't that where Boris Santiago lives?"

Guillermo is surprised by the question. "The drug lord?" he asks, somewhat hesitantly.

"There would only be one. I read an article in *El Periódico* on the Guatemala Cycling Federation that he is an avid cyclist, and one of its principle donors. I thought you might know him since you live in the same area."

"Maryam, please," Ibrahim says.

"No, it's okay," Guillermo says. "I don't have much in common with a drug lord."

"Do you live there alone?" she asks, driving with both hands on the steering wheel.

Guillermo realizes that Maryam hasn't noticed the huge wedding ring on his left hand. "No, with my wife Rosa Esther, my son Ilán, and my daughter Andrea. Now you know everything about me," he replies somewhat provocatively, as if Ibrahim were not within earshot.

Guillermo imagines Maryam smiling. "I wouldn't say that. Men are full of secrets," she says. "I hope you won't think I was prying. I only like to know who is coming to eat at my apartment."

"Maryam, *please*—" Ibrahim interjects for a second time, almost playing the role of a referee.

Guillermo taps his client's shoulder. "No offense taken."

After an awkward silence Ibrahim says, "You must have strong legs, Guillermo. I mean, to do all that cycling."

"Strong enough to get me up the hills. Riding is my passion and my joy. I love it. I like being alone. The exercise and the release of tension are added benefits."

Maryam snickers aloud. Guillermo thinks she might actually have a sense of humor—or is she simply laughing *at* him? His imagination is getting the better of him. He is already putting them naked together in bed. Maybe this is the ideal situation. He and Maryam are married, both unhappily, if he's reading her relationship with Samir correctly. Ideal for meeting up for an occasional fuck.

As soon as the car is parked in the basement of her building, Maryam races ahead to call the elevator. Guillermo can see that she is indeed wearing a tennis outfit; she does have nice legs, evenly tanned. And she has puffy pink balls on her heels, which somehow warms his heart.

Guillermo springs out of the car and opens the door for Ibrahim, who struggles out of the front bucket seat. They walk arm-in-arm to the elevator, where Maryam is pressing the button to hold the door open. Once inside, the elevator climbs slowly to the sixth floor. Maryam steps over to her father and holds his hand. She does not look at Guillermo, but he can see that she has dark eyebrows, a broad nose, and thick lips. Her eyes are green. When the elevator opens, they are facing a dark wooden door with an upside-down turquoise hand nailed to its middle.

"What's that?" Guillermo asks.

"Fatima's Hand. It keeps away the evil eye." Maryam unlocks the door and welcomes them in. "Have a seat," she says to Guillermo, indicating a brown leather chair, "while I change. My father will make you a drink."

"What will it be, Guillermo?"

"Chivas on ice. And a soda on the side."

"A man who drinks a man's drink . . . I'll join you, though I shouldn't," Ibrahim says. He disappears into the kitchen for a few minutes and returns with a small silver tray with three glasses—Guillermo's highball, with plenty of ice, and soda on the side, and for himself a Scotch, neat, in an ornate crystal goblet.

"To your health," Guillermo says, raising his glass.

"*Fee sahitkum*," Ibrahim answers.

"Guillermo, I hope you like Middle Eastern food," Maryam's voice rings out as she comes back into the living room. She has changed out of her tennis outfit and now wears a brown, fitted skirt and a floral yellow blouse, making her appear only slightly less suburban. There's makeup on her face: her lips are dabbed pomegranate red, and purple mascara outlines her eyes. She is ebullient, almost girlishly so. She looks at least eight to ten years younger than she did in the car.

They sit at one end of a large dining room table. The cook has prepared a lemon and ginger soup, which is followed by a plate of grape leaves, hummus, and baba ghanoush. The main meal consists of rolled chopped lamb with plenty of mint-like parsley and flakey rice with peas.

The conversation is light-hearted and full of pleasantries. Maryam asks

Guillermo to tell them about his family, which he is more than happy to do. When he mentions that he and Rosa Esther lived in New York City when he was studying at Columbia, Maryam says that she has cousins there. They operate a small store importing Middle Eastern delicacies for the large Arabic community in Brooklyn: apricot in flat sheets, tahini, all sorts of olives and dried fruit. Somewhere on Atlantic Avenue.

"Sahadi's?" Guillermo offers.

"No, it's called Aleppo Station. My brother Mansur married a Syrian woman. They threaten to visit us every year, but we are the ones who have visited them. Hiba," Ibrahim calls into the kitchen, "bring us the grebes and some Turkish coffee at the tea table."

They adjourn to a small table by a corner window, which has already been set with small cups and plates for dessert. Guillermo enjoys the cookies, which are made with bleached wheat flour, butter, and sugar. The Turkish coffee is strong and bitter.

Maryam's hair falls across her face every time she drops her head to eat, forcing her to constantly brush her face and tuck her hair behind her lovely small ears. Guillermo would like to bite them, especially her right ear, which is oddly flattened.

Guillermo doesn't recall feeling this happy in months.

## CHAPTER EIGHT

## *MERDE ALORS*

In the succeeding month, Guillermo accompanies his client Ibrahim to his daughter's apartment three more times for lunch. There is something kinetic building between them, but since they are both married and Ibrahim is always present, the attraction remains muted and almost hidden.

As the weeks pass, Guillermo learns that Ibrahim dislikes Samir immensely, though he approved of him at first. This aversion is partially the result of the guilt he feels for convincing Maryam to marry him. He just about calls Samir a liar for pretending he had lots of money saved up from his hardware store and would be a good provider for his daughter's future. Ibrahim now realizes that his son-in-law has very little money and absolutely no ambition.

Still, his dislike of Samir—who is almost his own age—does not justify pairing Guillermo with Maryam. But he enjoys having the younger man around, and there is no doubt that these lunches please him, if only to make Samir remotely jealous.

Guillermo wants to invite Maryam for drinks or dinner without her father as chaperone, but he suspects she would laugh in his face. She is not the kind of woman he can simply invite for a romp in bed at the Stofella, or so he thinks—she is much more elegant, and comes from a decent, if conservative, Maronite Christian family. In this, Ibrahim's family more closely resembles Rosa Esther's than Guillermo's.

What he especially likes about Maryam is that she has a desire to know what is going on in the world. While most Guatemalan women read *Vani-*

*dades* and *Cosmo*, she has a subscription to the *Economist* and *Poder*, and is comfortable reading novels in both English and Spanish.

They talk politics, especially about the Middle East. Maryam is convinced that Iraq will end up like Lebanon—dozens of competing factions held at bay by a cold peace once the Americans leave. Or it could be worse: civil war.

The embarrassing thing is that during these lunches, Guillermo sits at the table sporting a huge and painful erection. Going to the tea table for dessert, for example, has become an awkward maneuver for him, and there have been several occasions when he has noticed Maryam glancing at his bulky crotch.

There is another issue too. Since Guillermo has begun having affairs, he has divided the women he knows into two separate types: the proper, marrying kind, and the cavorting sort. He wants nothing to do with the former, whom he can spot immediately, so he gravitates to those women who are either single, divorced, unhappily married, or only interested in a physical encounter. Guillermo cannot imagine finding a woman who is independent and sensual simultaneously unless, of course, she is unhappily married. He can foresee bedding down with Maryam, if he can get her alone, but only after several expensive lunches at Tamarindos and lots of tiny gifts of chocolate and perfume. At the same time, he realizes she is his intellectual equal, having secured a degree in economic history at the Universidad del Valle.

From the first day he saw her in her perky tennis outfit, he knew she had a luscious body, one built to please him—short but shapely legs, full breasts, a kind of sassy spring to her movements. He suspects that her vulva tastes of mango, or something sweeter.

He is afraid to take things to the next level because of his budding friendship with Ibrahim and the complications with Maryam's husband and Rosa Esther. He imagines that the next step might be off a cliff.

And how could he even arrange the next step? He doesn't have her phone number, and sending her a letter at home is much too risky. What he would like to do is slip a note into her pocket asking her out for lunch at La Hacienda Real and let things go from there. He is now fantasizing about her all the time. She has become a kind of obsession, even though nothing has happened between them but a mild, almost sardonic tease. He is becoming so sexed up that he begins masturbating again, simply to keep his attention on his work. And he has begun seeing one of his lovers, Araceli, at least twice a week, even at the risk of Rosa Esther finding him out.

Maryam must know that he is constantly staring at her with something more than desire. He is in fact undressing her, and she seems to like it, this lust, though he knows she will not act on it. In Guatemala, a woman rarely hankers after a man, especially a married man, more so if she herself is married. The woman is never the aggressor.

One Wednesday, as soon as he steps into Ibrahim's office for their weekly meeting, the older man grabs him by the forearm.

"Guillermo, I have to confess something to you. I know that we respect one another, but what I have to say to you now cannot be shared with anyone, especially not with Maryam. I need you to swear it on your life."

Guillermo is unflinching. "More than my client, you are now my friend."

"And you are mine. But all the same, I need you to promise me. Do I have your word?"

"You don't even need to ask."

Ibrahim drops Guillermo's arm and goes over to the window, which looks down from his third-floor office above his textile factory to the parking lot and the surrounding fence. It is an ugly view of cars, concrete, and loading docks in an area that lacks plants and trees. He then walks back and signals for Guillermo to sit across from him at the table in his office. They were supposed to discuss the possibility of moving his company's accounting offices to El Salvador. Since banks there operate strictly in US dollars, it would be easier to transfer money to Ibrahim's accounts in Miami. Also, the president of Guatemala has begun talking about nationalizing the banks.

"Besides the occasional threats, someone is now tapping my house and my cell phone conversations."

"Are you sure?"

"I used to have clear connections on both but now there is static, and a kind of muffled echo. I called Guatel to complain. They claim there is nothing wrong with my phone lines or connections. I brought my cellular to be examined, but the serviceman says it is in perfect working order. And I continue to get strange calls with the heavy breathing. This isn't normal."

"Well, these winter rainstorms have been a nuisance," Guillermo says, unconvinced by his own words.

Ibrahim stands up and grabs his forearm again. "Guillermo, I am trying to tell you something and you are trying to calm me down by giving me silly explanations. I don't need a lawyer for that." He sits back down. "At our last board meeting, Ignacio Balicar—the president's representative and the chairman of the Banurbano advisory board—interrupted my presentation on the suspicious dispersal of public funds to say that it is dangerous to make wild accusations I cannot prove. He says that the president's enemies are acting more boldly, and he has asked his staff and associates to be careful with what they reveal to the press, especially in this climate."

"What climate is that?" Guillermo asks.

"Balicar said that everything is very combustible—in case I didn't know it. *Combustible,* I said back to him, *that's an awfully charged word.* Balicar smiled and just kept nodding. Then he said—almost as an afterthought—that the president and his wife are upset because they sense there are members of the opposition party who are trying to encourage the army to overthrow him. And he is not going to let that happen."

Guillermo whistles. "That's quite a conversation."

Ibrahim goes on: "He was looking straight at me when he said it. Actually, I don't think you know that Ignacio is also a vice president of Banurbano. He is both an employee and an advisor, something I consider objectionable."

"So his opinions aren't really objective."

"Exactly. Ignacio went on to say that independent accountants from Pricewaterhouse have already audited the bank's financial statements for the last three quarters. The board was convened simply as an informational courtesy to assure Congress that there is transparency at Banurbano. He reiterated that the accountants are quite content with the books and that our role is not to question them."

"My. I am surprised that they were audited. I'm certain he didn't produce any Pricewaterhouse documents to prove compliance. *Cooked* would have been the more appropriate term."

Ibrahim sticks his finger at Guillermo and wiggles it in his face. "Touché, my friend, touché. I wasted no time in saying, *I may be seventy-four years old and a bit forgetful, but I have never rubber-stamped anything in my life. I am an honest man, an honorable man.* When I was asked to serve on the board, I told Ignacio it was with the understanding that we would be independent of management and that we would be able to question or address anything that seemed controversial or unseemly. That is, we could challenge and even overturn any unusual loans the government was making to private businesses or nongovernmental agencies. Since I joined the board I have also challenged the president's wife's policy of giving monthly cash payments to the poor. First of all, she was not elected to office to oversee these expenditures, and secondly, I have never believed in a social welfare state. There is no way to know who is getting the bulk of this money, nor if it is being used to buy votes for her run for the presidency . . . But never mind, with this we were talking about expenditures of ten or eleven million quetzales a month, but when I saw monthly transfers on the level of forty to fifty million quetzales . . . that's why I hired you. Can the government be involved in a money-laundering scheme? Are they using strange maneuvers to deposit money in overseas accounts or are they simply placing money in national dollar accounts they secretly control? This is what you and I have been looking into."

Guillermo nodded. "And what happened next?"

"I was told not to worry. You and I saw the same kinds of ledger manipulations last time we met. But I can show you what they did last month, only with smaller quantities, and in a less apparent way. Balicar and the board secretary both laughed at me and said we needn't worry about such small transactions when the Guatemalan government has a budget of nearly a billion dollars. There you have it, Guillermo."

"But why are you telling me this? Is there something you want me to do?"

"First the threats, then the garbled phone calls, and now I think I'm also being followed."

"Oh shit."

"Yes, *merde alors*."

"This is dangerous."

"It is. In Lebanon we say, *Yellah!*"

"Which means?"

"*It's time to go.* We have to do something."

Guillermo scratches his chin. "You need around-the-clock protection. I will get it for you."

"I am sorry, but I prefer to die than to live like that," Ibrahim responds.

"This isn't some kind of joke. These people are serious."

"Sorry, Guillermo, but that is out of the question. I already have more protection in the office and factory than I need." He rubs his very wrinkled face with his hands. "Maybe I shouldn't have mentioned anything to you. We should get back to discussing the possibility of moving the accounting and budget personnel of the textile factory to another country with lower taxes—"

"Don't be silly. You have others who can advise you on that. On the contrary, Ibrahim, as your principal lawyer I must know everything that is going on in your life. You need someone on staff who sees the big picture."

"I have given you complete access to both my thoughts and my files."

"I want to have a security team check out the safety systems in your car, home, and factory to make sure there are no possible leaks. I want them to check your phones and your complete phone records." Guillermo sees an opportunity. "And I want them to inspect Maryam's car and apartment as well. In fact, I want you to give me Maryam's home and cell numbers right now so that I can be in touch with her."

"But what for?"

"To determine if her phones are tapped. My chief concern is for you and your daughter. I want to make sure I can contact either one of you whenever I need to. I'll also need Samir's cell phone."

"Why Samir's? He's not involved in any of this."

"Yes, but he's also a likely target whether you like him or not. I'm going to use my connections at Guatel and the Ministry of Defense to see if I can figure out what's going on."

Ibrahim writes the numbers down on a small card. After that, the two men get back to business.

"You won't believe what's happened at Banurbano since our last meeting." Guillermo raises his eyebrows.

"Take a look at this." Ibrahim gives him a folder with the latest Banurbano transactions. For the first time, everything seems more or less in order, as if someone were trying to clean things up. New deposits appear cancelling the withdrawals. The financial payments are smaller, and mostly directed to NGOs with rigorous financial oversight. Clearly their inquires have produced greater caution and scrutiny, but probably also great anxiety. No one likes to have the cash spigot turned off. Something will have to give.

The two men agree they should see the Pricewaterhouse audits, to make sure Ignacio's telling the truth.

"Ibrahim, is there any chance these threats have to do with your own company?"

Ibrahim coughs. "What do you mean?"

"All along we have assumed that the threats you've received have to do with your appointment to the board. But what about your textile factory? Has anyone tried to shake you down here? A disgruntled employee?"

"I treat my workers as family. There is absolutely no union activity. Ask them. They love me," Ibrahim says, somewhat offended.

"What about suppliers?"

Ibrahim closes his eyes, then puts a hand over his tightening mouth. "Well, actually," he says, before hesitating. "No, never. There are crooks everywhere, certainly in the textile business. People who want to offer me Italian cloth that they have somehow gotten into the country without paying import taxes, or that is actuality manufactured in Singapore or China. You know that I believe we are entitled to pursue wealth without government interference, but I won't break the law to become richer. I don't need to do that. That's not how my parents educated me. And if you think I would do something illegal to prosper, Guillermo, then you really don't know me."

Juancho used to say the same thing. "I was only asking. I believe you, completely, but I need to make sure I am not missing any viable source to these threats. I want to be absolutely sure these calls are the result of your work on the board."

"You can be absolutely sure of that."

"And what about Samir or anyone else in the Lebanese community?"

Ibrahim smiles. "Maryam's husband is an ass. And the others, well, they admire me."

Several minutes later, Ibrahim's secretary comes in to say that his daughter has just driven up and will wait at the first-floor gate to take them home for lunch.

Ibrahim stands up and motions to Guillermo that it's time to go.

"I am going to have to take a rain check on this lunch."

Ibrahim looks disappointed.

"I promised to go with Rosa Esther to talk to my daughter's teachers."

Ibrahim shrugs.

"Please convey my regrets to Maryam." Guillermo is a bit disappointed that he will not see her, but at the same time he thinks that a cooling of his interest in her might be for the better. He doesn't want to lose the upper hand in his courtship. Besides, he has some serious research to do. He doesn't really know how he would go about improving Ibrahim and Maryam's security systems. He has promised Ibrahim he'll look into it, but he doesn't have any strong connections with the security apparatus or the telephone company. Still, it shouldn't be too complicated.

This much is certain: he now has Maryam's phone number, a way to contact her independently of her father. And this makes him more than a little excited.

## CHAPTER NINE

# GREAT EXPECTATIONS

**G**uillermo sits on Maryam's phone number for almost a week. Each day, instead of putting all his attention into his work, he lobs the idea of calling her back and forth. He's certain she likes him, but he's still not sure if he wants to mix pleasure with business. And the fact that he is hopelessly attracted to her might lead to something more explosive in his life than the occasional sexual romp with Araceli.

One Tuesday morning, when he finds himself especially distracted at his law office working on some incorporation papers, unable to concentrate and sporting a formidable erection, he texts her.

*Maryam.*

A minute later. He receives a *Who is this?*

*Guillermo, your father's lawyer.*

*Oh hi.*

*Would you consider going out to lunch with me?*

There, he has taken the plunge.

When he doesn't receive an immediate response, he begins agonizing. Was his message too formal, or baffling in its purpose? Should he have been a bit more direct? He might have said something more urgent, like, *Maryam, I need to discuss a security issue about your father in private.* That certainly would have piqued her interest, but it might have also worried her.

Guillermo is certain that Ibrahim has not discussed the threats, the hang-ups, and the static noises on the phone lines with his daughter, since he also made Guillermo promise not to. But she has to be aware that he has been making himself a nuisance at the Banurbano meetings by asking very provocative questions—discussion of this has taken place during their Wednesday lunches. Her father, she must know, has a sturdy moral soul and is the type of person who will question discrepancies—even those committed by his own family—until the truth about them is revealed.

By noon, Guillermo is in a panic. He wishes there was a way to retrieve the text he has sent and that he had called Araceli instead for an after-work rendezvous. Why hasn't she answered him? Has he offended her? Is she on the tennis court?

He decides to text Araceli and hopefully hook up with her at the Stofella for a quick lunch fuck. He hears back from her immediately that she will be at the hotel at one.

*Perfect*, he answers her, and then he calls Rosa Esther. The maid answers the house phone. "Tell the lady of the house that I won't be coming home for lunch today."

"Yes sir."

"I have an emergency meeting. And I will be coming home late tonight. Please tell her that," he adds as an afterthought, not knowing why the maid needs to know this.

"Would you like to tell her yourself, Don?"

"That won't be necessary."

As soon as he says this Rosa Esther gets on the line. "Lucia has prepared veal Milanese and buttered potatoes," she says rather abruptly.

"I really can't make it. Sorry. Enjoy it."

"You know I'm eating vegetarian."

"Of course. You had her make that veal for me. Thank you, but I'll have to take a rain check." He is so distracted. "How are you?" he asks, as if talking to a distant relative.

"What's wrong with you, Guillermo? Do you know who you're talking to?"

"Of course. Sorry. I've been extremely busy this morning. How was the French conversation class today?"

"You know my teacher is a bore. She loves to tell us how *fatigué* she always is. Everything has to do with *quel dommage*."

"Yes," he says. "I know she only talks about herself."

"That's it. How great Paris is, blah, blah. As if we're all Indians living in the cornfields."

"So, why not tell her?" He wants to get off the phone but feels these questions will earn him points.

"What for? Madame Raccah is oblivious. I can understand exactly what she is saying, but Claudia keeps interrupting her to ask her to repeat everything because she can't follow the dialogue. After class she told me she's going to drop French. I don't know if I want to study alone. Claudia wants to start taking Pilates with me."

"What's Pilates?" Guillermo asks, wondering if it is some kind of Italian dialect.

"It's an exercise. I've been doing it the past five years at the Pomona. How can you not remember?"

"Like yoga?"

"It supposedly tones your muscles and enhances flexibility," she answers flatly.

Guillermo sees his cell phone vibrating on his desk and looks down. He unlocks his phone and reads a new text: *I thought you'd never ask.*

Without thinking, Guillermo looks up at the ceiling, smiles, and says, "Yes!"

"Did you just win the lottery or something?" Rosa Esther asks.

"I've been courting a new client for some time and he has just decided to go with our firm. This could be lucrative. I have to go, amor."

"Well, good luck, Guillermo," she says, and surprises him by blowing a kiss into the phone. He should feel guilty about all his maneuvering, but he doesn't. He has successfully managed to compartmentalize his life to the point that his own wife accepts all his cubby holes as normal.

As soon as Guillermo hangs up, he texts Maryam.

*What about today? Now.*

*Are you joking, Guillermo?*

*What about tomorrow?*

Instantly he receives a text back: *I can't.*

He is beginning to feel annoyed, the I-call-the-shots annoyance. He is about to tap out *Let's forget it!* when he receives, *I'm free Friday.*

*Your apt at noon?* he answers.

*?????????*

*Where then?*

*Better at a restaurant.*

*La Hacienda Real?*

*No! 2 many people. The Centro Vasco at 1.*

*See you there. And then.*

*;-\**


Guillermo drives to meet Araceli at the Stofella singing the Cuban bolero "Dos gardenias para ti." He feels almost childishly elated. It has not been as easy as he imagined, and her spunk makes her even more sexy. Clearly, though, Maryam is sweet on him. There's no other explanation. She has been bold, what with her *What took you so long?* or *I thought you'd never ask.* Which was it? He can't remember, but either way she has taken the bait. Still, he has the nagging feeling that he needs to change his way of thinking from *She has taken the bait* to *She wants to see me.* She is a woman with her own thoughts and resources, not a stupid fish.

So he must wait three days to finally be alone with Maryam. Almost an eternity. And he is not about to change his routine based on the supposition of what might or might not happen in three day's time.

He receives a text back from Araceli saying she is running a few minutes late. Normally he would be angry at her lack of planning, but he is so excited to see her that as he walks into the Stofella he trips on the front steps and almost falls. The clerk at reception gives him the key for his reserved room: number 314, top floor, at the end of the hall, away from the elevator, with no connecting door and only one neighbor.

He lies in bed wearing only his underwear. He knows that he and Araceli are going to have a grand time. He will fuck her hard, really hard, and will imagine he is fucking Maryam for the first time.

## CHAPTER TEN

# THE NAKED MAJA, OR *LA PETITE MORT*

The Centro Vasco is an old Basque restaurant on Reforma Boulevard that had its heyday in the sixties when everyone acknowledged that it was the best restaurant in all of Guatemala City. Now, in 2008, it is a place for viejos rucos—old codgers—who are still impressed by waiters in tight black jackets, white long-sleeve shirts with cuff links, string ties, black vests, and matching shiny pants. There are little ceramic oil and vinegar sets on the starched white tablecloths, and furniture that is meant to be Spanish but has actually been transported from a San Marcos province farmhouse. The salt and pepper shakers are Tyrolean, made of wood, and have cranks.

It is actually an ideal place for them to meet for lunch because no one Maryam or Guillermo knows would eat there now, with so many new gourmet options in Guatemala. The paella is overcooked and salty, the cod tastes like clods of white flour, and the oily red peppers that the restaurant had once been famous for taste artificial, straight from a bottle. Maybe the restaurant has never been good and had only been a kind of novelty of Spanish cuisine back when going out to eat in Guatemala City meant hamburgers, steak, or an occasional chapin meal.

Friday is a lugubrious day, with low clouds and a constant cold rain. Guillermo pulls into the parking lot of the restaurant and scans the entrance for valet service since he has forgotten to bring an umbrella. Instead he sees a handful of cars in the dirt lot. He is sure that one of them is Maryam's since he is—at least according to plan—ten minutes late, and he expects her to be like her father, who is very punctual.

He parks his BMW next to a blue Hyundai Accent whose chassis is half underwater. There's a man sitting in the car texting on his phone. When Guillermo opens his car door, their eyes meet momentarily.

As Guillermo steps out, his shoes sink into a puddle of mud, which rises over his soles. He walks to the entrance door on his heels, pulling up his pants legs, cursing the weather, the choice of restaurant, the lack of valet service . . . He hates not having everything under his control. Before pulling back the restaurant's heavy door, he wipes his shoes clean on the towels piled high on the entrance mat.

To his surprise, Maryam is not there. He takes a four-top corner table and waits. The waiter comes up, asks how many people are eating. Guillermo raises two fingers into the air. Then he asks what kind of Scotch they have, and when he learns they only have the scandalously bad Vat 69, he orders a double highball. He downs his drink quickly, sucking on the ice cubes and then munching on the stale cashews and peanuts served on a chipped little plate.

The minutes crawl by like snails. The waiter who served him the drink comes by again and puts a dish of dried sausage on the table, and two salad bowls holding the obligatory iceberg lettuce chunks with spicy tomato dressing on top. Guillermo orders a second drink and texts Maryam a curt message: *What's up?*

It is only one fifteen p.m., but Guillermo is about to fester. He texts a second message, *??!!??!!*, less than five minutes later, but again receives no reply. The Scotch arrives and he takes it down gulp by gulp. He is thinking that as soon as Maryam shows up, he will have to give her a good dressing down and explain to her the rules of the game.

Guillermo asks the waiter if anyone has called the restaurant and left a message for him. The man simply raises his eyebrows as if he has just been spoken to in Tagalog or Mandarin. He does not seem to want to understand.

Guillermo is fulminating internally. He considers his options: order a third drink and get truly soused, or simply leave.

He looks around the restaurant with its framed posters of bullfighters, the erstwhile Picasso drawing of Don Quixote and Sancho Panza on horseback, Goya's *La maja desnuda*, Velázquez's *Las Meninas*, and Dali's *The Persistence of Memory*, which after two drinks is possibly the worst painting he has ever seen in his life. He shakes his head at the half dozen winebotas with their absurd red rings and shrunken black penis spouts dangling from the walls. Dirty chandeliers with low-watt bulbs hang above each and every table—he is sure they were purchased from his father's store fifty years earlier.

What the hell is he doing here waiting like a stupid old secretary for her boss? What is he waiting for?

He decides to call Sofia Muñoz. He leaves her a message on her cell phone to meet him at the Stofella at precisely six p.m. This is the first time he has ever left her a voice message. It is a risk since she is married to an insurance agent who might know how to retrieve her messages. Guillermo doesn't care. He does not want the day to go totally to waste. And he will have to leave the Stofella at exactly seven thirty p.m. because he is meeting his children across the street at Tre Fratelli for dinner and then going to the nearby Oakland Mall to see the ten o'clock showing of *Kung Fu Panda*.

He puts a five hundred quetzales on the napkin dispenser and walks in a straight but lumbering line toward the front door. From the corner of his eyes he sees his waiter begin to approach him, then angle over to the table, probably to examine the bills.

As he starts to push on the door, someone pulls it open. It is Maryam.

"What the fuck," he says as he crashes into her.

She keeps him from falling, but he is annoyed for having lost his balance. Before he can express further displeasure, however, she kisses him on the lips and whispers in his ear, "I'm sorry. I was running late. The rain, the traffic, my car stalled, I forgot my cell phone, please don't be angry—"

"I've been waiting for you," he says huffily, pulling away from her. Her lips taste of mango chapstick. His head is spinning.

"Yes, I know." She tries to grab his hand, but he impulsively pulls back. "I'm not really that hungry," she says to him. "Can we go somewhere else?"

She is wearing gray woolen leggings and a matching gray sweater top.

A maroon skirt, more for show than comfort, hugs her hips. A knit scarf is tightly wound around her neck. She's holding an umbrella and sporting yellow Hunter rain boots.

"Sure," Guillermo says. She hooks her arm into his and they leave the restaurant. It is still raining, so he borrows her umbrella and goes to get his car—she'll leave her Mercedes in the lot—while she waits for him under the overhang.

As they drive away, he notices the car beside his put on its lights. It is the blue Hyundai.

At the Stofella Guillermo gets his key at the reception desk while Maryam waits by the elevator. As soon as they walk into room 314, she takes off her clothes and throws herself stark naked on the bed. She closes her eyes, letting out a childish little giggle. Her ample breasts flop to the sides of her chest.

"I'm waiting for you," she says.

Her undressing has happened so fast that Guillermo doesn't know if he is pleased or upset. This is not how he had planned things would play out. Instead, he struggles to take off his shoes (still stained with mud), his brown suit, his brown tie, his cuff-linked white shirt, his T-shirt—like a college sophomore.

Because Maryam is ten years younger and is married to a much older Lebanese Arab, Guillermo has imagined that Samir is the only man she has ever slept with. He assumes that though she has sensuous qualities, she will be shy in bed and terribly inexperienced. But already she has outflanked him.

He has imagined a more traditional encounter: some goofy and awkward talk, slap-dash touching, then a couple of deep kisses, a hand into her blouse or a detour under her skirt, Maryam's feigned reticence—the lady doth protest too much—tearing off her clothes, exhorting her to relax, to enjoy the explorations . . . he would be the aggressor, but in time she would surrender to his entreaties.

Instead, Maryam watches him, amused as he struggles to take off his clothes. When he is nearly naked, she sits up on the bed on one elbow and looks at him mockingly. "Are you going to make love to me wearing your black socks?" And then she laughs.

Guillermo glances down at himself, black socks up to the ridges of his knees and his penis ascending through his baggy white jockeys toward his belly button. He feels ridiculous. If he could watch himself from a distance, he too would laugh, but he finds it impossible to see humor in his own absurd maneuverings. He is even ashamed of his penis flagpoling through his shorts.

"Off with them, off with them," she commands, swinging a forefinger in the air as if signaling decapitation.

Guillermo sits on the edge of the bed and pulls off his socks. His head continues spinning because of the Scotch, and he wonders if Maryam's friskiness is also the result of drinking.

He turns to her and starts kissing her deeply, as deeply as he can go. He is grateful that he can still taste the mango flavor of Maryam's lips. She does not resist, begins exploring his mouth with her tongue. They are both enjoying the rise in passion. He pulls his underwear down to his ankles and perches over her. Sitting on her thighs he begins rubbing her nipples softly. She arches her back and purrs with pleasure. He flattens his body against hers and tries to place his penis into her, two or three times, but each time she closes her legs.

"Is anything wrong?" he asks, feeling totally lost, adolescent, and out of his element. Maybe it's because he hasn't put on a rubber. He is nagged by the memory of catching herpes from Chichi and so he typically protects himself when screwing women for the first time. Once his trysts evolve he insists that his girls be checked for AIDS almost monthly and take the morning-after pill as soon as they are done making love. He does not let them go until they have taken a pill, or otherwise proved to him that they will not become pregnant. He doesn't need any illegitimate children.

She points down to her sex and says, "Eat me first. I want you to imagine that you are eating the sweetest baklava you've ever tasted."

He obeys, slides down to the foot of the bed, and places his mouth squarely above her pubis. She once more arches her back, this time in anticipation, so that her vulva rises up to meet his mouth. While he begins to lick her, she starts running her hands feverishly through her hair and pulling down on her earlobes. She is moving her hips from side to side and raising her legs, forming a small Arc de Triomphe.

Without warning, she grabs his head and pushes it deeper into her crotch, so that he feels the cartilage of his nose flattening against the top of her pubis, her clitoris. He can barely breathe.

She doesn't let him stop licking, even though his tongue has lost feeling. She continues to press his mouth into her. She squeals a few times, she must be coming—that's how he interprets her trembling—and when he feels that his tongue is about to fall off, she pulls him up, reaches down for his penis, and shoves it inside her.

Guillermo and Maryam make love all afternoon. In truth, she appears to be using him for her own needs as if he were a practical handmade tool, maybe a canvas dildo. He is more than grateful to oblige, but continues to feel a loss of control. She wants him to rub against her clitoris, to drive into her, to fill her up completely, to come into her from behind. Whenever he feels he's about to come, she relaxes and induces him to push through layer after layer of curtains to reach the spot where she can finally let loose. And when she does, she trembles in his arms the way a willow shuffles in the crosswinds of a storm, with all its vines fluttering.

But even then, after the storm has passed, she will not let him stop.

"I need this," she keeps repeating, and she won't let him rest. He's unsure if it is the drink or her passion that makes him stay hard.

She is directing him, telling him what to do and where to go; it's as if she has been crossing a desert for years, and finally finds an oasis that might run out of water if she stops drinking from it. Whenever his strength seems to flag, she urges him forward, or goes back down on him and slurps his penis in her mouth, trying to get him ready for the next penetration.

At one point he climbs off her, exhausted, and wraps himself up in the sheets. She lays next to him, faceup and covered in sweat. He can smell her body odor, which is strong now, no longer mango, a bit fetid like a rotting guava. He likes the smell.

It is four thirty in the afternoon. Through the green curtains of the Stofella he can see a strip of sky and a range of thick clouds, like a rumpled gray sash, signaling the coming of more rain and darkness. Where has the afternoon gone?

"Maryam?" he asks, tightening the sheet around him like a papoose, afraid that she might want to begin again.

"Yes, Guillermo?"

"Shouldn't we be going?"

"Where to, my love?" The words *my love* echo in his head. They say too much about their commitment and it makes him extremely nervous.

"Home. Your house. Your father's." He can't bring himself to say her husband's name.

"They can all wait. You don't know how much I needed this. It's been years. I've felt things I didn't know existed. You have such a manly body." Maryam grabs his hips and gives them a tug. "Thank you," she says, staring at him without blinking her eyes.

He offers a fake smile and closes his eyes. Making love to Maryam is something special, not anything like what he expected. But still, he has a difficult time enjoying the moment. He is worried about what's going on in the office while he has been philandering. This is the way his mind always works. And then he starts speculating if Maryam uses birth control, or if she has any communicable disease like herpes or chlamydia.

She seems to be in no rush to leave, covering herself with one of the big pillows.

"What about your husband? Surely he must be worried," he says stupidly.

Maryam lets out a sprawling laugh. "Samir? Well, he is like an old, smelly goat. The kind that climbs up a dry mountain—all skin and bones, no muscles—looking for bits of grass to eat." She rolls over and grabs Guillermo's behind. Her eyes are almost on fire. "I like this," she says, squeezing his cheeks. "Fleshy and hard." A second of silence flits by and then she laughs heartily for a second time.

"What's so funny?"

"I shouldn't be telling you this."

Guillermo braces. "Yes?" he asks, shifting in the bed. He is sure she's going to tell him that she's in love with him. Then he will have to tell her he's not interested in breaking up his marriage—or hers, for that matter; that time has to pass before he can get together with her again.

"From the start, Samir refused to eat me. He thought it was unmanly." She is moving her hand around under the sheets and he is certain that she's touching herself.

"Many men feel that way. Especially in the Middle East, I would imagine," he says, just to say something. He isn't prepared to discuss these issues with a woman he barely knows. And he doesn't want the image of Maryam's husband going down on her to be central in his mind.

"I would imagine, Guillermo, that you don't know what you are talking about," she says smiling, almost laughing at him. "I assume you know nothing about the Middle East. Have you ever been there? I mean to Lebanon?"

"You are right, I haven't been," he replies, relieved. His eyes are closed and he would like nothing better now than to fall asleep. He hears Maryam shifting.

"Beirut is an international city, like Paris or London, but by the sea." He opens his eyes to see her straddling a pillow. "Would you like me to tell you what's wrong with Samir's lovemaking?"

Guillermo doesn't want to know anything. He wishes she would just be quiet, but without thinking, he says to her: "This is between the two of you."

He sees her green eyes sparkling. She touches her chin and says, "I thought it might have something to do with the thickness of my pubic hair, which is normally dense as a hedge. I shaved it just for you."

She pauses, waiting for Guillermo to say something. All he can think is that five hours ago he had no idea they would be sleeping together.

"So once I gave it a really good trim and I showed him my vagina. He looked at it as if it were the ugliest thing he had ever seen. He insisted that I cover myself up, that I lacked modesty. He swore that he was too old to try something new and that he had never seen anything so repulsive. He made me swear never to shave it again. But there, I've done it."

"I guess you disobeyed him," he says awkwardly.

She shakes her head, laughs, and says, "I knew you would like it. You have the face of a man who will do anything to satisfy a woman. You've been raised on *Playboy* magazine and *Esquire*."

He laughs a fake complicit laugh and then says nervously, "And I thought you read the *Economist*."

"I do! But I also like *Playgirl*. I have a stash of them in my closet!"

Guillermo is not amused. "Well, I should be going," he says. He remembers that he had earlier called Sofia to meet him at this very same hotel, in this very same room, at six. He needs to find a way to call her.

Maryam sticks her hand under the sheets, grabs his dormant pecker, and begins to softly squeeze his testicles. "Can't you stay a bit longer?"

"My kids will be waiting for me," he says, moving away from her, very much aware that his penis, sore as it is, is growing hard again in her hand.

"I don't know, my love, but it seems to me that you wouldn't mind it if they waited a bit longer." She is stroking him gently.

"We're supposed to go for pizza at Tre Fratelli and see a movie at the Oakland Mall. They will be awfully disappointed if I'm late."

"I don't know anything about children. Are yours house-trained?" she asks, licking the tip of his penis.

"Very funny. Ilán is nineteen and Andrea is seventeen. They are both at the Colegio Americano."

"Sweet," she says. He is not sure if she is referring to the taste of his penis or his children's education.

He tries to pull away from her, not out of displeasure, but fear. She refuses to let him go. "Maryam, this isn't the time to tell you about them. I must go. Really."

She continues looking up at him and licking as if hasn't said anything. "I bet you're afraid of your wife. That must be it." As she says this, she pushes his penis away and recedes from him.

Maryam cannot possibly be jealous of his wife. "This is her bridge night, with *les girls*—her girlfriends—I swear. I am meeting my children." He leans over and kisses her on her right ear—he notices again that it is flat—before getting out of bed.

It has begun raining again and the droplets are smacking the window in the room, slipping into the ledge from a crack in the glass. The hotel clerks can't understand why he always selects the same ugly room without a view. "We do need to go, Maryam."

She smiles at him like a vixen. "Well, if we are going, I need to shower, my handsome man. It'll take me a minute."

While Maryam is in the bathroom, Guillermo grabs his BlackBerry. He quickly texts Sofia to tell her that an emergency has come up and he cannot meet her tonight. *Don't come to the hotel.* He wants her to text him back to confirm. Then he lies back down.

What is wrong with him? He realizes he's still a bit drunk, spent. He feels that he and Maryam actually fit together, sexually and otherwise. There is a sense of compatibility which he never experienced—not with Chichi or Araceli. And it scares him because it reminds him of what he felt in New York with Meme.

He hears the water from the shower spraying full force. Maryam is singing loudly in what is probably Arabic. Guillermo feels untethered. His wife is becoming more impatient over his excuses for getting home late, for acting bored with her and disinterested in their kids. Maybe they should make a clean break of it. The only ones who might suffer would be the children, but Guillermo is convinced that since they have their own lives, their own group of friends and activities, they would hardly care. It's not as if they are still six or eight years old. And he is sure they will do whatever their mother asks of them—

His phone chimes; Sofia has texted back.

*Fine!!!! You are a prick!!! You've ruined my Friday night.*

He will have to deal with her anger some other time, maybe give her an extra five hundred quetzales.

Before they leave the room, Maryam asks: "Guillermo, what are we getting ourselves into?"

He answers frankly, "I don't know."

She hugs him as if they have just seen each other following a ten-year absence. She does not want to let go. "I needed this, to feel this animal plea-sure. I've been lonely for so long. But I also know that tonight I'm going to feel ashamed. I fear that what we've just done will ruin lives, our lives as well as others." It comes out like a sudden uncontrollable confession. "But I don't regret it, no matter what happens next."

"Neither do I," he responds, surprised to hear himself speaking hon-estly. He realizes he cannot undo what has just happened. It can't be taken back.

Maryam pushes away from him and touches his nose. "And look at you. Who would've thought you could give me such pleasure?"

He smiles.

"Do you love me?"

"Maryam, we just—"

"I know that my legs could be longer, my tummy flatter."

"You're delicious," he says, meaning it, remembering the taste of mango.

"You make me feel like a beautiful woman, you know, and all of a sudden I don't really care about my defects. Toes that are too long, the big mole just above the small of my back. Making love with you this afternoon has made me forget any doubts I might have about myself . . ."

He is feeling grateful, but cornered at the same time. It has been an in-credibly intense afternoon. And suddenly he is hungry. "We must go, Maryam," he says tenderly.

"Samir never made me feel that I was more than a vessel."

Guillermo feels the stirrings of another erection. Almost to shut her up, he begins kissing her again. They kiss for a few minutes before she pulls down her leggings. She is not wearing her underwear, and so pulls down his zipper and puts him inside of her. She is already so wet, there against the wall. She pulls his shoulders into her, and then grabs his butt. She is breathing heavily, panting, and then she moans and begins talking: "You know that my father is very fond of you, but if he knew—oh God—this were happening—no, no, no, no, no—he would be extremely, extremely—there, there, there, just like that, oh God, please put your finger in there—oh my God. No, no, Guillermo, there, there, there!!"

She throws her head back and Guillermo has to hold her body up, otherwise the two of them will collapse onto the floor.

Still inside her, he carries her back to the bed.

"You have to pull out or we'll never get out of here."

They both lay on the bed, on their backs, gasping, trying to relax their breath. Guillermo closes his eyes and feels that he is about to drift off to sleep.

In almost a whisper, Maryam says: "He's a very stern and moral man."

"Samir?" Guillermo asks in a trance.

"No, my father, silly!"

This surprises Guillermo. "Maryam, from the beginning your father has been scheming to bring us to together. He was the one who invited me to your house that first time, remember? And he is the one who always insists that we end our Wednesday meetings with lunch."

Maryam touches the thinning black hair on Guillermo's head. "Love, you can't confuse his desire to have people like each other with actually setting up a scenario like this. He would be horrified to know I had *la petite mort* with you."

"Is that what you just had?"

"Yes, my sweet man. I had about half a dozen in a row. This has been something more, like touching the sky with my hands."

## CHAPTER ELEVEN

# REDUCED LIBIDO

**A**nd that's how the relationship between Guillermo Rosensweig and Maryam Khalil Mounier begins. From the outside, it looks like a series of carnal encounters behind curtained windows, in hotels where they can't be seen—never in the public eye. It is a clandestine affair, recognized only by its two participants, mostly negotiated through salacious text messages that are almost immediately erased. They park in different garages near the Stofella and are constantly looking over their shoulders. They are suspicious of everyone. Guillermo doubles his tip to the concierge, a short balding man in his sixties who always hands him the keys of room 314 in a plain white envelope.

Initially, their texts are extremely short, almost telegraphic. They are meant to reconfirm times and dates. But soon Maryam's messages to him become quite pornographic. Guillermo is extremely shy in responding at first, though eventually he answers in kind. It's as if a floodgate has been opened and he begins telling her about his constant erections, his wet dreams, his desire to go to the bathroom at work and masturbate. He realizes they have embarked on an uncharted course, but he is happy, deliriously so.

*Are you hard? I am lying in bed naked.*

*Where are you? I want to eat you.*

*I just painted my nails green. Next time I see you with my father I will wear sandals so you can see my sexy feet and imagine how wet I am for you.*

*I almost came last night just thinking of slipping between your legs.*

*I shaved tonight.*

And then their messages become more elaborate, like the one he receives one Saturday morning when he's taking Andrea to her swimming lessons at the Pomona.

> *Guillermo, last night I couldn't sleep thinking of you. I feel like such a fool. Here I am married to Samir and you are quickly becoming the most important person in my life. My phone has become an extension of my body, awaiting your next text message. And what if I were to become aroused when I am having dinner with Samir or my father? It would be a disaster. Yesterday, re-membering some of our get-togethers, I cursed you for how much you mean to me. I don't know what we've started, but it feels not only a bit crazy, but also quite dangerous. And who knows where this romance is going, or how it will end. I want to see you all the time, but am beginning to see the danger that this will put us both in. We must be more careful.*

He realizes he can't simply give a brief answer to a text of this complexity. So while Andrea is taking her backstroke and butterfly lessons, he drinks a coffee in the café at the Pomona.

> *Maryam, your e-mail made me very sad. Everything you say is true. Maybe it has all happened too quickly and it would have been better if we had not taken our feelings for each other to the next level. I know you think you are at a huge disadvantage but it isn't so, since both of us are married. It seems senseless to even expect that one day the two of us might end up together. And I know I couldn't ask that of you. Making love to you is like finding heaven on earth and I don't really believe in those things. I don't want your father to find out about us because, though I know he is my friend, he would hate me for tampering with your marriage.*

* * *

When Andrea's swimming lesson is over, she scours the Pomona looking for her father, who she finds hunched over his phone in the café.

"You were here all this time," she says.

"Something came up at work," he responds, smiling awkwardly.

"Dad!"

He smiles tensely and says, "Yes, my dear?"

"Don't you remember telling me you'd watch my lesson?"

He looks at her wet hair and red eyes, barely recognizing who he's talking to.

"Forget it!" she snaps, stomping out.

He gets up slowly. "Wait, young woman! Don't run out on me like your mother."

The café's glass door has shut, as if to define how Guillermo relates to his children: as if through a filter.

Sometimes their text messages are short, almost salutations.

*Good night, my love.*

*Good night, my king.*

Or they erupt, like the Pacaya volcano, into a stream of words.

*I feel better this morning, though I still miss you terribly. Maybe we shouldn't text each other so much because it just increases my level of anxiety, especially on weekends when I imagine you having lunch or dinner with your wife and family. Sometimes I think I have fallen in love with your words more than with you. I don't enjoy feeling enslaved to your words, which enslave me to this fantasy, which I can't even talk about. And then when reality sets in, I realize we've embarked on a dangerous path that can only end in pain. But then I start thinking that there is something very unique and strong between us and that it is foolish to cut it off just as we are getting started. What are we going to do? Tell me, you who have more experience in these kinds of things . . .*

Their text messages are full of contradictory feelings, as one would expect between people in the throes of an illicit love—to commit or not to commit; to risk all or to risk nothing and go back to their humdrum lives.

They meet only at the Stofella in the beginning, which is both exciting and dangerous, and at some points terrifying. At any moment someone in the hotel restaurant or meeting rooms might recognize them walking in or out, or dropping off their cars in the nearby garages. After all, the hotel is in the heart of the Zona Viva, where all strata of Guatemala's upper society circulate, where they are safe from assault but not from curious eyes. All in all, Guatemala City is a small town.

Guillermo thinks of blowing several hundred bucks to meet Maryam at the Grand Tikal Futura Hotel on the Calzada Roosevelt. But the Futura is just minutes away from Ibrahim's textile factory, and is managed by a Lebanese man she knows. It's also risky because there are always huge traffic jams getting in and out of the hotel and neither Maryam nor Guillermo can afford to be late. They could go to the Quinta Real just outside of town, but his law firm represents the owners.

Guillermo makes other inquiries. The Mercure Casa Veranda rents suites and rooms by the month on 12th Street in Zone 10, and so does the Barceló, but the cost would be a small fortune, and the possibility of being seen at either would be greater than at the Stofella. In the end, he decides to rent a furnished one-bedroom in an innocuous building overlooking the Plazuela España, which is less than a mile from his offices in the Próceres building. It is also only two blocks from Rosa Esther's sacred Union Church, but since she only goes there on Wednesdays—the day he eats over at Maryam's house with her father—and Sundays, a day the lovers will never meet, the apartment is ideal. They are no more than a ten- or fifteen-minute ride from each of their homes and from Guillermo and Ibrahim's offices, and there is a garage in the basement allowing them to come and go largely unseen.

Before either one of them realizes it, they are seeing each other three days a week. They make love two or three times each afternoon. There's never enough time for simple conversation. Neither is the least bit interested in the daily particulars of each other's lives, but they would both likely discuss music, books, movies, food, the increased violence on the public buses, and the poor neighborhoods of Guatemala City if they had the time.

But the only place that really matters to them is the bed. Before they know it, two hours have elapsed and the last few minutes together are filled with showering and dressing, and sometimes with slight recriminations for not being able to find a better way to be together more.

One day Guillermo promises to devise a plan for them to get away for a long weekend to Ambergris Cay in Belize.

Maryam looks at him with doubt. "You must be dreaming."

"I can make it work," he tells her. "Just watch me."

In the end, they are afraid to even take an afternoon in La Antigua, only thirty-five kilometers away.

Thursday when they meet, Maryam insists they talk.

They sit in the ersatz living room, he on a chaise longue and she in an overstuffed green chair that overlooks the fountain in the Plazuela España. They are sitting as far from each other as they ever have in this apartment.

"I can't go on like this, Guillermo."

When she says this, his heart panics. He suspects the end is near. Both of them are fully invested in the relationship, but he feels he has no right to insist they continue to see one another secretly. He is afraid to divorce Rosa Esther for what it might do to her and their children: he is convinced his family is helpless without him.

Guillermo and Maryam's relationship is not ideal—what in life is? He doesn't want to change anything. At least they are able to be with one another on a regular basis. And a divorce, even a separation, could affect his business.

"What do you mean, my love?" he says, trying to be tender.

"I hate all this skulking around. It's as if we're committing a crime." He can see that she is very upset.

"Some would say we are."

"I know that . . . Maybe it's something else," she says, scratching the palm of her hand. "I hate it when we part. I want to be with you all the time."

He thinks about this and finds himself saying something he has never said to Araceli or any of his other lovers: "I do too."

She slaps her knees. "I can't just leave Samir. We got married eight months after his wife died of cancer."

"I didn't know that." This is the first time she mentions anything about how they met. Or about her thoughts of leaving him.

"He's a leader of Guatemala's small Lebanese community, and highly respected. Even my father admires him because, though we are Maronites, Samir has forged contacts with our Islamic and Jewish brothers. Do you even know what he does for a living?" she challenges him.

Embarrassed, Guillermo can't recall.

"He owns a hardware store on Eleventh Avenue, downtown. He barely makes ends meet. He works hard and is respected by everyone. He has grown children, a boy and a girl, who have gone back to live in Lebanon. Did you know that I am the stepmother of children almost my own age? As much as he repels me, I can't abandon him. Not only for where that would leave him, but also for what he might try to do in revenge."

"No one is asking you to leave him," Guillermo counters somewhat testily.

"Please don't raise your voice at me, Guillermo. I am not Rosa Esther. Whenever we plan to see each other, I have to come up with a pretext: *I'm going shopping, I've gone to Sophos*."

"I know."

"You don't know. This wears me out, all this sneaking about. I can't just walk out on him, not at this stage. Any day someone will see us, and I need to know where we stand. To be honest, I have no idea where our affair is going."

This comment echoes some of their earlier text messages, before they started seeing each other more regularly and Guillermo rented the apartment. Every few weeks Maryam seems to have a panic attack: she reaches a point where she wants things to change, to adjust to the new reality of their relationship, to demand more commitment. She believes that they can't just keep fucking each other three times a week for forty years. He's not so sure.

"Why do we need to decide this now? I promise to come up with a better solution," he says, as if he is trying to calm a client. "But can't we just enjoy ourselves in the meantime?"

Rather than answer this question, Maryam simply ignores him. She refuses to be deflected from her own train of thought. "Samir asks so little of me. I am nearly twenty-five years younger than him. You might not want to hear this, but he isn't interested in coming inside of me. He is happy if I masturbate him once a month. Thank God he's happy with my hand and not my mouth—"

"I don't need to hear this, Maryam," Guillermo says, standing up.

"It's his age or his reduced libido," Maryam continues. "He has no desire for me. He's more interested in having me manage the home while he goes to work. He spends most of his time staying in touch with old friends in Sidon, which is also where his children live with his younger sister Dahlia. He is a man of simple pleasures who would prefer to wear slippers and a robe on Sunday mornings instead of playing golf."

"Uh huh."

"Do you understand what I'm saying, Guillermo?"

"What can we do?" he finally says, fighting the urge to touch her.

Her eyes are swollen red, holding back tears, and she is gripping her chair. "Samir suspects that something has changed. Maybe he has spies, for all I know. Or maybe he can tell I'm distracted. What frustrates me is knowing you won't do a thing."

He walks over to her and strokes her hair. "Give me a chance to think of something . . . Maryam, are you about to have your period?"

She glares at him. "You think this is about *hormones*?" she says, getting up to leave.

"Maryam, where are you going?"

She slams the door without saying a word.

One night, almost two months after Guillermo and Maryam first met up at the Stofella, Rosa Esther takes Guillermo's cell phone out of its belt case while he's having one of his evening showers. She's always been too afraid to do this and assumes he would be cautious enough to use a password anyway.

When she awakens his BlackBerry, she notices he has eleven saved-as-new text messages. She closes her eyes briefly, anticipating that the next step will lead to a place where she shouldn't go. In fact, she doesn't want to go there. Not this night. So she puts the phone back in its leather case.

The next time he takes an evening shower, she's determined. She wants to know what's happening on the flip side of Guillermo's life. Her face darkens as she begins reading the texts he has stupidly saved.

Words like *divino, amor, querido, corazón* dot the messages, some of which are sexually quite graphic: *Divino, I just got off the tennis court and my underwear is wet—for you*; or, *Habibi, I'm shopping, and when I touch the cucumbers and the badinjan I begin to perspire*; or, *Corazón, the dream I had of you, with your erect penis, made me touch myself till I came twice in bed.* Then she checked his sent messages: *at a meeting with some corporate lawyers, and I only think of licking you*; or, *I see you naked, with your lush breasts swinging above me*; or *Amor, I can't get up from the table because of the huge erection I have, thinking of you. I thirst for you and want to taste your peppery cunt.*

This is enough for her. She thinks of having it out with him when he comes out of the shower, but decides she should be calm if she wants her words to be effective. She decides she will plan her escape strategically so as not to be foiled. She needs to do what's best for her and the children.

The moment will come.

She waits weeks, documenting the number of times he offers lame excuses for not coming home for lunch or coming late for dinner. She wants to have an accurate tabulation before confronting him. In the meantime she has contacted her uncle in Mexico and told him about her husband's affair. He cautions her to keep silent, at least for now. He wants her to settle all the details about her move to Mexico with Andrea and Ilán, so that once she has decided to leave, there's no way he can stop her. The last thing she needs is to get involved with a lawyer who might accuse her of kidnapping her own children.

Though she will have to leave her sister in Guatemala, Rosa Esther likes the idea of going to Mexico, escaping all the tawdry gossip and looks, and beginning a new life where no one will know or care how many times Guillermo has betrayed her.

She sets up a Wednesday appointment with Pastor Huggins at the Union Church. Right off the bat she tells him that her husband has always had affairs, but is now falling in love with a Muslim slut. The pastor, originally from Louisville, Kentucky and quite conservative, is taken aback by Rosa Esther's choice of words. He suggests they seek counseling and can recommend a therapist. He no longer advises married congregants at cross purposes. He has found the few sessions he's held with accusing couples distasteful—he's embarrassed to hear salacious allegations, sordid details. Moreover, his counseling sessions never work out, and he ends up losing both parishioners.

Rosa Esther is disappointed with his reaction. She wants action or concrete advice, and all she receives is a pat on the hand, the voicing of platitudes, and a call for greater patience and devotion to the sanctity of their marriage. The Union Church is perfect for drawing congregants closer to God, but fails at resolving the problems of modern marriages.

She thanks the pastor and leaves, knowing she must act on her own, without blessing or benediction.

Rosa Esther hatches a workable plot with her uncle. For Easter, she will be taking the kids to Mexico to visit him and her older cousins. They will stay a few days in her uncle's home in the San Ángel area and then go swimming for another couple of days at a luxurious hotel in Cuernavaca. She knows that Guillermo will not want to accompany them, since he isn't able to get away from work for ten days. Besides, he would not pass up the opportunity to visit freely with his new whore.

The kids are only told that they will be visiting their great uncle and Rosa Esther's cousins. And everything seems normal. Ten days in Mexico with her only other living relatives.

Guillermo goes to Aurora Airport to meet Rosa Esther and the children when they fly back from Mexico.

"Where are the kids?" he asks, when he sees Rosa Esther coming out of the baggage pickup area on the lower level with a man pushing her two bags on a four-wheel cart. Guillermo has no idea what is going on, but is not to any extent suspicious. He knows nothing about his children's school calendar. Maybe the cousins are hitting it off and want to spend another week together.

"I thought they might stay in Mexico a little longer," Rosa Esther says, kissing him on the cheek.

The only problem is that Guillermo's ego is a bit bruised for not having been consulted. "And you made this decision without me?" he asks as they make their way to the car in the parking lot.

"Guillermo, if you cared for Ilán and Andrea as much as you think you do, you would never have taken up with that whore."

"That *what?*"

"Your Muslim whore. I know all about it. I read your disgusting text messages to her. Is she your princess? *Does* that make you her prince or have you been elevated to king or ayatollah?" Rosa Esther's face shows no emotion. No hurt, no resentment; an almost cold-blooded dispassionate expression is stamped upon it.

There's no point in denying the affair at this point. The proverbial beans have been spilled. He will have to deal with the fallout. "What do you want from me?" he asks.

"A separation to start, followed by a divorce. And your agreement not to contest the custody of our children. I want half the money in our bank accounts and I want you to sell the apartment. We can share the profits. I don't want you living there with that whore."

"We bought that apartment with the money we made from selling the Vista Hermosa house that I paid for with my parents' inheritance. In truth that apartment should be all mine."

"Well, it isn't. And no judge in Guatemala will let you keep what is now common property, especially when I present proof of your affairs. I deserve the full value of the apartment, so I believe I'm being very generous with you. Plus, I want you to send me sixteen thousand quetzales each month in child support until both of the kids are out of college."

"And where are you planning to live?"

"In Mexico City."

"And what do you expect me to live on, after I wire you that money?" he asks contemptuously. "Water? Air?"

"To be honest, Guillermo, I don't care what you live on. Hummus, for all I care. And I don't deserve your scornful tone. *You* are the transgressor. You might have considered being a bit more forthright with me about your whore, and maybe the terms of our separation would have been more favorable."

"Maryam is not a whore."

"The whore has a name," she says sarcastically.

"She does. And I think her name's beautiful."

Rosa Esther is about to slap him, but holds back. "You disgust me."

"It sounds as if you were planning to leave me all along."

"Oh, Guillermo, talking to you is pointless. You're always the lawyer. You have piles of arguments and briefs and you know how to use them. What I wonder is, when did you lose the thoughtfulness, the humanity you had when I first met you at Pecos Bill? You've become so crass, and a coward on top of that! I've given you two beautiful children and you've given me nothing but heartache and a venereal disease that makes my face break out in a rash every few months. Thanks for ruining my life."

"Nice," is all he can say. She's still bringing up the herpes stuff that occurred nearly twenty years ago.

And before he can say anything else she adds, "Tell me, when did I become your enemy?"

"You're not my enemy." He feels unjustly accused. And unjustly forced to respond.

She laughs heartily. "Oh, but I am. I know you have other enemies that you *consider* much more important, like the president and his wife, liberal journalists, tax reformers: anyone who can stand in the way of achieving your state of total freedom. Well, you are now free to fulfill your dreams. And the price that I am extracting from you is cheap. Very cheap. You won't lose your children forever: you will be free to visit them in Mexico. And they can visit you in Guatemala as long as you are not living with that whore. There won't be any talk of kidnapping, or of you trying to block my leaving. You can have this poor excuse of a country all for yourself. Is that clear?"

Guillermo fumes. From a legal point of view, he knows that Rosa Esther is being uncommonly accommodating. He's well aware of Guatemalan statutes regarding divorce and culpability. He knows when he's been beaten and also when he has been given a pass, a good settlement. What upsets him is that there is nothing left to negotiate with her, not even her refusal to accept the fact that anything good, other than the children, has come from their marriage.

He cannot say anything in his own defense.

Rosa Esther is through talking. "Could you start the car? I want to go home."

So they drive home together like a civilized, uncoupled couple. Rosa Esther moves into Andrea's bedroom, full of posters and pictures and pink stuffed animals. She stays in Guatemala for two weeks, packing up the kids' things and saying goodbye to her sister—who promises to visit her within the month—and all her friends before flying off to Mexico.

There are no big blow-ups; there's no more terrain to contest. In fact, there is no need for lawyers. Rosa Esther has brought her own divorce contract from Mexico and only needs Guillermo to copy the terms on the Guatemalan writ for divorce so that their separation can become official.

Pastor Huggins is more than willing to prepare a legal Unitarian divorce in which both parties are rendered guiltless as subjects who have come to realize that they have irreconcilable differences. Rosa Esther does not want to create a scandal by accusing him formally of infidelity. Since divorce is illegal in Guatemala, she is willing to have their marriage annulled under the proviso that they were never in love, and that their marriage was only contractual in the eyes of man, not sacred in the eyes of God.

Guillermo, naturally, agrees.

Every night, while Rosa Esther is finalizing her affairs, he calls the children on Skype. The phone conversations end up with Andrea in tears, but Ilán is more stoic, as if there has merely been a soccer trade or the aging star of the team has been axed. Guillermo promises frequent visits to Mexico City. He does not want to lose them, or so he says.

## CHAPTER TWELVE

# AN ARABIC BALLAD: *HABIBA, SHARMOOTA*

**W**hen Guillermo tells Maryam what has happened, she is very much surprised. All along she has assumed that she would have to be the one to take the first step if there was ever a chance for her and Guillermo to be together. Now Rosa Esther has acted and Maryam gives her lover the necessary space to figure things out. It is a difficult period because so much has to be done quickly, and there is no time to get together.

Within a week of Rosa Esther's return, Guillermo puts their apartment up for sale. Property in Zone 14 is selling like hotcakes because there are armed guards patrolling the residential areas and rich Guatemalans want security above all else.

He lists the apartment at four hundred thousand dollars. Guatemala is flush with drug money, and within two days he finds a buyer who will pay in cash.

Guillermo gives Rosa Esther her half and then signs a lease for a compact two-bedroom apartment in a new nine-floor rental building in Las Cañadas. As the first occupant of the building, Guillermo gets a large discount on his rent for the first year. He likes that it is a rental: it reflects the impermanence that characterizes his new life.

Rosa Esther hires a moving company, which will transport the kids' belongings and some pieces of furniture to Mexico City by land. On the day of the move, she insists that Guillermo be at work: she doesn't want him around to interrupt any emotions she might want to express.

When he comes home, he discovers he has been left a bed, a bureau, and a couple of end tables and lamps. The living room has one chair, the dining room is completely empty except for the pole lamp in the back corner and a modern crystal chandelier in the center, both leftovers from his father's store. The walls have shadows where hangings and paintings once were displayed.

With no family to fill up his nights, Guillermo is lonely. But he is stuck here for another week before he can move into his new, smaller quarters. He is surprised by his feelings of loss, something he hadn't anticipated.

One late afternoon, days after Rosa Esther has left for Mexico, Guillermo and Maryam are lying in bed in the apartment in the Plazuela España drinking Chivas on ice and munching almonds after having made love. Their sex is always an unpredictable adventure, with a newness that Guillermo no longer questions, but clearly loves. Maryam swears she has been faithful to Samir all these years, but as she has aged, she has become aware of her increased sexual drive and her desire to have it quenched. Her years of reading *Playgirl* have helped her realize what she wants in bed.

"What's next?" he asks, caressing her hair.

Maryam looks at him quizzically. "What do you mean?"

"What are we going to do?"

"That's a big question. Have you even told my father that Rosa Esther left you?"

Guillermo stops stroking her hair. "I told him that my marriage was ending. I didn't have the nerve to tell him that Rosa Esther had moved to Mexico."

"Well, I can't tell him!"

"Next time we meet I'll tell him. Though I'm sure it won't make him happy. Your father likes order."

"And what am I supposed to do with Samir? Am I to continue happily married?"

"I hope not," Guillermo says, tipping his drink at her. Maryam is lying with her head on his lap, looking up at him, holding her own glass in one hand. She sits up whenever she wants to have a sip, which is what happens now.

"You don't love him."

"I don't, it's true. But I am afraid of him," she says, taking a sip of her drink and stirring the ice with her tongue. "He may seem calm to strangers, but he has a violent temper. I've seen how he screams at the workers in his store. At times he isn't even aware of it. And he sometimes screams at me."

"Do you think he would ever hit you? If that's the case, then we should tell him together."

"That, Guillermo, is a horrible idea. It's one thing for me to tell him privately, another to have his replacement bearing witness as I tell him. I mean, how would you feel if you were told by Rosa Esther and her new lover that she would be leaving you?"

"I would want to kill them both—on the spot."

"Exactly. It would be better if I told him. I just need to find the right moment."

"When?"

"Not now." She is thinking. "Maybe in a couple of weeks."

"Maryam!"

"You have to give me a few weeks."


Ten days after Rosa Esther has left, Guillermo gives up the furnished flat in the Plazuela España building. Why pay the extra rent when he is now living alone and Maryam can visit him in his apartment at any time? He never thought he would escape his marriage; furthermore, he never thought he would be interested in living together with another woman. If he did ever leave Rosa Ester, he'd always imagined living alone.

But the weeks pass. When he tells Ibrahim that his wife has left him with Ilán and Andrea and is now living in Mexico, Guillermo is surprised at his client's response: Ibrahim is taken aback, but asks no questions, says nothing other than to offer his condolences. He must suspect that there is more than a friendship between his daughter and his lawyer and is wondering what might happen next.

Maryam says nothing to Samir. Guillermo is incensed by the lack of progress. He trusts Maryam, but wonders why she's so hesitant to simply tell

Samir that she no longer wants to live with him—it's not as if they have kids together.

Guillermo fills his nights working on cases, especially Ibrahim's. After months of nearly perfect reports with no suspicious withdrawals, he notices new discrepancies in the Banurbano monthly accounts, but now in increasing quantities. Something tells him that while other money-laundering channels are being shut, there's added pressure to use the bank as a way to move funds and to support programs that have not received legislative approval. Guillermo feels a bit out of his element since he is not an accountant and doesn't fully understand certain transactions, but he knows that something illegal is going on.

Guillermo does not confess his confusion regarding some of the bank transfers to Ibrahim, since the older man relies on his judgment and has staked his reputation on making the bank's transactions completely transparent. When Guillermo reports the irregularities, Ibrahim tells the other members of his advisory board. When their response is muted, he tells them he is considering discussing his findings with the press, since he doesn't trust the president and the judiciary doesn't seem to care about his allegations.

An appeal to the people might lead the Banurbano managers or even the president to make a public clarification of what's going on.

Guillermo, aware of how the government can manipulate the truth, advises otherwise; he feels that proof—not accusations—is what they need. He advises that they should collect more evidence, but Ibrahim is incredibly stubborn and impatient—he feels the moment has come.

What follows is ominous. After delivering his threat to the board, Ibrahim receives an increasing number of hang-up calls and anonymous threats. Someone wants him off the board, pronto.

Obviously the president or his wife won't ask him directly to resign. Oddly, Ignacio Balicar has stopped defending presidential pet projects at the meetings; he seems to be waiting for something. Nothing is done directly in Guatemala. It is all subterfuge, behind smoke screens, curtains, clouds, blankets. It is clear that something cataclysmic is about to happen—this is the calm before the storm—but Ibrahim wants to go public

* * *

Meanwhile, Guillermo is feeling greater and greater loneliness. He is deeply in love with Maryam, but old ways die hard. One night after work he gets together with Araceli at the Stofella, but it is pretty much a disaster. In fact, he has a hard time keeping his erection even when she is touching him. She suggests the little blue pill, which pisses him off.

He doesn't need the little blue pill. He needs Maryam.

That night he texts her.

*Can you talk?*

*I can't.*

*Why?*

*I am writing to you from the bathroom. No matter where I go, Samir shows up. He is tailing me in our own apartment!*

*You have to tell him about us.*

*Maybe he already knows. I can smell the change in him.*

*Maryam, I can't take this any longer.*

She does not text back any words of assurance.


And so one night after Samir and Maryam have had a light dinner of Lebanese mezzas and their maid Hiba has left, she decides the moment has come. Later, she blames her precipitated actions on Assala Nasri's voice, as if her songs were responsible for the confession.

They are sitting in the living room, with walls decorated in framed campy photographs depicting images from the Lebanese homeland: olive fields, jagged mountains, the American University campus; all touristic scenes from their trips, separately and together, to Beirut.

Maryam is wearing a dark blue dress. She looks like a nineteenth-century milkmaid, and is on the sofa reading an article in *Poder* discussing Barack Obama's election and how it will affect Israeli and Arab relations. Samir is stretched out on the Barcalounger, with his bare yellow feet up in the air. His eyes are closed. He wears a smoker's robe over his clothes and he might be dozing.

They are listening to Assala Nasri's latest recording of plaintive Arabic ballads on the CD player. Something about the way Nasri sings about love, adoration, and her terribly broken heart in an Arabic that Maryam does not fully understand unhinges her. She feels her heart is like the River Jordan about to overflow its banks.

She walks over to the CD player and lowers the volume. There are tears in her eyes.

"What's this?" Samir says, startled, sitting up.

"I need to talk to you about something."

Her husband shakes his head. "Why is it always when I am enjoying something and in a state of blissful happiness that you feel obliged to interrupt my pleasure? Is the music bothering you? Do you want me to use my headphones?"

Maryam's heart is pounding. They are both listening to the same music, but their reactions are so dramatically different. She is thinking of Guillermo's long and powerful legs, how the hair grows in mild grassy ridges along his chest, how his hands are so sure when he is stroking her. How he knows how to move his penis inside of her so that she is constantly being surprised by where it takes her and what she feels. And the way she comes.

And she cannot imagine what Samir is thinking. Perhaps he is recalling the love he once felt for his wife, long dead after twenty-two years of marriage, or his childhood in Sidon. Maybe he is thinking about the shortage of pliers and extension cords in Guatemala. The price of brackets or tortillas.

But this is the moment. How can she bring it up? Should she cast her love for Guillermo by explaining her unhappiness in sharing a life with an old, unattractive husband? Can she actually blame Samir who she knows might resort to calling her a woman with a fickle morality or, plain and simple, a harlot? Or should she begin apologetically, instead: admit her guilt as something beyond reason and control, plea for release, and accept the fact that she has acted duplicitously and has betrayed her nuptial vows? Should she say that there is something wrong with her, that she has always felt she was born defective and that in actuality she is self-centered, numbed, impulsive?

In the end, she opts for the raw truth, couched in what she feels are the kindest of words, even though she knows as she begins speaking that he will not reward her for this kindness.

"Samir, I am no longer happy sharing a life with you."

He closes his eyes and gets a pained and sour look on his face, now creviced with moles and deep gullies. There is nothing attractive about him. He pushes down on the footrest of the Barca so that he can sit up properly, a bit hunched over.

"We have been sharing more than a life together, my habibati." He puts his feet into the leather slippers at the foot of the recliner, even though he will not stand up. He lets out an amused laugh through his thin, discolored lips. "Am I interpreting your words correctly: you want to break your vows, to divorce *me*?"

Maryam is disgusted by his mocking tone, but tries not to wrangle with him. "I want to leave you. I don't make you happy." She wants to put all the blame, with dignity, on her own shoulders, but then backtracks. "We can't give one another what we need anymore. You don't please me. And I can't give you what you need."

"And what is it that you think I need, young lady?"

Maryam can feel that she is on the verge of losing control, but tries to stay on course. Under no circumstances can she refer to any of his shortcomings, which he is sure not to acknowledge, or digress to his level of sarcasm. "What you have always needed: a woman to admire you, to comfort you, to mirror your being."

Samir lets out a little laugh that is beyond scorn. "You have never mirrored my being, habibati. When we first married, you were a sweet pretty thing, simpleminded, to be sure—like a strip of plain, shiny copper. I assumed that your heart had never opened itself to any man, but I thought because of the respect I held for your father, and the respect you had for me, that you would be faithful. This is all I wanted."

"I did open up my heart to you," she confesses, dropping her head in penance, avoiding the issue of faithfulness. "I have been a good wife."

He scrunches one eye as if this will allow him to see better. His voice rises: "These last few months you have slipped away from me like a doe jumping over a fence at night who returns in the morning with its fur soiled. You may claim innocence, but the facts speak for themselves, my habibati."

"My intent was never to betray you."

"Of course it was, let's not be insincere. Betrayal is the perfect word. If anything, you have attempted to destroy me with your insolence and your unwillingness to fulfill the simplest of your marital obligations to me while hiding behind a false smile. Am I so abhorrent to you?"

She peers at Samir, a shrunken, nasty-looking man now, who often goes days without shaving the white hairs that sprout like icy weeds on the hollows of his cheeks. There's a bit of spittle at both corners of his downturned mouth, and his teeth have yellowed at their flattened tips. He reminds her of Yassir Arafat, who she always found utterly unattractive. She thinks of Guillermo, with his elegant face, the dark wavy hair, the intensity of his eyes. His eyes have fire, for her at least, wildfire, while Samir's eyes are nestled in sleepiness.

"I can't go on like this. I feel that I am dying, little by little." She sees his wrinkled penis in its thicket of gray hairs, dozing, moldy. In contrast to Guillermo's rising tusk.

Samir nods his head. "I see, I see. It's not that I am simply so abhorrent that you cannot lie with me as a woman should lie with a man. I make such few claims upon you and have even stopped asking you to open your legs to me. But that I am sending you to the grave now . . . how horrid a man I must be to put someone as innocent and pure as yourself into a landscape of so much suffering . . . But let me ask you a practical question: how do you plan to live without me?"

"I have my father's money."

Immediately Samir smiles. "You have forgotten that when we were married, your father gave me your dowry. The money you had is now mostly ours. I have him and you to thank for that generosity."

"I have considered that. I am sure my father will take care of me, habibi."

"Please! Do not say that word. It is blasphemy in your mouth."

"Yes, Samir." There are tears again in Maryam's eyes. It is an existential moment: she never thought it would be this hard to ask for her freedom.

"From the moment you leave me, because you are the one who must leave this house, I will not give you a single cent of support. What do you say to that?"

"I understand these conditions." She knows she will initially have to rely on her father or even Guillermo for support, but she also knows she has the talent, the skill, the perseverance to live on her own, without props. She can admit her sins, her inability to love him, but she will not crawl to him. How stupid it was to put all the money in their name, sanctified by a marriage contract. "But I must tell you again that I am not happy. Isn't my happiness worth anything?"

Samir now stands up. He wants to lord it over her, to express his triumph. "Do you have a rich lover? Is that what it is? It's the most common thing, and it's what I have suspected all these months. Some younger, stupid-looking man, I would imagine, with sentimental eyes, who is as common as you are."

"You know nothing about it," Maryam flares back, and immediately realizes she has said too much.

"Ah, so it is as I expected. I have exposed a raw nerve in my little hamama," he says in a surly voice. "It must be someone I know. Yes, that's it. Someone from our church. A Lebanese man half my age. Or perhaps an associate of your father's?"

"There's no one," Maryam says, trembling, certain that her voice betrays her words. She has allowed Samir to unhinge her.

"Oh, but there must be. You would not have the courage to confess your lovelessness unless you had someone else. I've suspected something all along, knowing how untrustworthy you are. Why, you are just like your father."

"Please, don't bring him into this. My father has nothing to do with it."

He grabs her wrist. The magazine with Obama on the cover falls from her lap to the floor. He is twisting her arm with his own spindly limb. "Do you think Hiba is beholden to you, simply because you are both women? She has served my family through two wives for thirty years. Do you think I've not known all along what has gone on here while I have been hard at work? That lawyer must have had an easy time fooling your father with his charm and his arguments. Or has your papá enjoyed taking on the role of a pimp so that the two of you could create a situation in which your legs, must I say it, are spread wide open to a stranger even as your heart is now closed to me?"

She sees the venom in his eyes. Maryam's wrist is hurting and she is afraid. It is not going well at all. But she's physically strong enough to push Samir away, back down into his seat, where he falls and starts laughing.

"You are a sharmoota. Like Gomer in the Bible."

"You wretched man! Calling me names won't accomplish anything."

His eyes are shining. "You are as evil as Tamar, although as far as I know you have not committed incest with your own father. You are not that depraved, I suppose."

Maryam is in tears, she is trembling. She runs into the hall bathroom, locks the door, and texts Guillermo: *Something awful has happened with Samir. I must see you tonight. I will text you when I can get out of here. Please don't turn me away.*

She puts the phone down on the sink counter and washes her face. She scrubs the back of her ears as if to clean away the poisonous words Samir has spoken. She knows she is not innocent, but she is not a whore. Her hands are still shaking as she tries to put on fresh lipstick and dab a bit of mascara on her wet eyes. Five minutes go by, but it feels like three days. What is taking Guillermo so long? Maybe he's talking to his children in Mexico via Skype or has fallen asleep after too much drinking.

She texts him a second time: *Guillermo, please answer me. Now.*

Through the bathroom door, she hears Nasri's voice again, fuller and more plaintive than before. She can't understand why Samir likes her singing, since it is so over-the-top with romance and emotion, while he seems to have wilted like a prune and paradoxically developed a heart of stone.

What had she been thinking when she married him? That she would be happy with a life of order, boredom, discipline, obedience? That marrying a respectable older man was better than living alone?

She opens the door, goes quickly to the hall closet, and grabs a sweater jacket. She has to get out of the house, go somewhere, anywhere, whether or not Guillermo calls or texts her back. Maybe she will go down to the car and drive around the hilly campus of the Universidad del Valle, where it is safe and quiet. There's a lookout at the very top where college students go to kiss. Maybe there, protected by a crowd of lovers, she will find peace.

Before she closes the apartment door, she cocks her ears. Samir is actually trying to sing along with Assala Nasri, as if their two voices could form the same anthem of lost love.

While Maryam waits for the elevator, her tongue itching, her cell phone vibrates. One new message.

*Ven, mi corazón!*

## CHAPTER THIRTEEN

# THE HARLOT

**A**s soon as Maryam is out of the house, Samir ponders his next step. It is only a little after nine, still early, so he decides to call his father-in-law. Ibrahim will not be happy to hear that his daughter has confessed her sin and is about to be cast out of the house by her affronted husband. A scandal in the small, tight-knit Guatemalan Lebanese community would be considered unseemly.

"Ibrahim, this is Samir."

"Why, Samir, so nice of you to call. I was just reading in the *Beirut Times*—"

"How long have you known that your sharmoota daughter was having an affair with your very own lawyer?"

Ibrahim is silent for a couple of seconds. "You have no right to use that kind of language when referring to my daughter. Your words also cast a dark shadow on me. You owe me an apology, Samir."

"I have proof that your daughter is a harlot."

"Please, do not refer to my daughter, to your wife, with that kind of language."

"My language is not the issue here. Let's focus on the facts. Maryam has been carrying on an affair with your lawyer behind my back for several months and you have not only known about it, but have actually encouraged it—"

"I have done no such thing!" Ibrahim interrupts, his voice rising. "The idea that she and Guillermo are doing anything together repels me."

"Your daughter is a whore."

"I must ask you again not to use that kind of language. I know you're angry, and to be honest, Samir, if what you say is true, then I will be deeply disappointed in Maryam. But I can assure you that this is the first I've heard of it. Please temper your words."

"This has been taking place right under your nose, akhi."

"Toz feek. I have played no role in encouraging it."

"You did, Ibrahim, by welcoming that Jew into your life and into your home."

Ibrahim is again repelled by Samir's incendiary language. "To begin with, Guillermo Rosensweig is not Jewish. And if he were, you, more than anyone else, should know that it would make no difference to me. I think you need to calm down before you say something else I will not be able to forgive."

"You were complicit."

"Samir, you're treading on very thin ice." Ibrahim hangs up on his son-in-law, realizing he's heard enough.

Guillermo is reading when the guardhouse buzzes to announce that he has a guest, a woman, and she's coming up to see him. He knows it's Maryam because of her text message. She'll let herself in since he's given her the passkey from the basement parking lot to his apartment on the top floor.

As soon as she opens the door, Maryam falls into his arms, sobbing against his shoulders.

"What's wrong, my love?"

"I told Samir I'm leaving him. He was awful, simply awful. He called me a whore. He knows all about us. Samir won't give me a divorce."

Guillermo strokes her thick hair, trying to calm her down. "I didn't realize you were going to tell him about us straight out. I thought you would first ask him to move out."

"There was this romantic Arabic music playing . . . It just came out of me. If you had been there, you would understand." She begins rubbing the small of his back, and his buttocks, to calm herself down. Touching his body helps anchor her to their reality. Guillermo really does exist. "Please hold me," she cries.

He wraps his arms around her, then moves back and kisses her lips, which still have the peppermint taste of the toothpaste she dabbed in her mouth before coming up. He feels a stirring in his groin, but his mind is elsewhere, plotting and calculating. He pulls away from Maryam and says: "There's nothing more I want to do than make love to you, but I think it's better if we talk."

Maryam stares at him, her eyes burning wet. "I need a drink. Something strong."

Guillermo obliges and goes into his kitchen to get a bottle of tequila. He opens a cabinet and grabs a Don Julio Reposado, and fills two shot glasses to the top. He walks over to where Maryam is sitting on the small sofa he bought a week earlier. He sits beside her, looks her in the eyes, and clinks. "To us. To the road that has brought us together. To the long road that will take us away from this mess."

As they sit closely, Maryam tells him about her exchange with Samir, the full story, all the details, all the insults. The whole time Guillermo's shaking his head. He's disgusted by Samir's comments. At the same time he's trying to figure out their next move. He's a lawyer, after all: he should come up with a plan, a strategy, as he does for his clients. But his mind draws a blank. Twenty years of legal experience have not prepared him for the affairs of the human heart.

"Oh, Guillermo," Maryam sighs, clasping him again, "what are we going to do?"

"I don't think it's wise for you to stay with him. Especially if you are trying to get a separation and a divorce. Samir sounds angry and vindictive."

"I'm afraid he is."

"Can you go live with your father until we straighten out this situation?"

Maryam takes a long sip of her drink and winces. "No, I don't want to get him involved in that way. It would put him in an awkward situation within the Lebanese community, and, well, it would strengthen Samir by supporting his argument that my father somehow brought you and me together. And frankly, I don't even know if my father would take me in. You know, in many ways he is just like Samir—tough and very moral—and I don't think he will be very happy when he finds out about us."

"I think you're probably right. It's one thing to enjoy working with your lawyer, another to have him carry on an affair with your own daughter right under your nose."

"I hate the power that men have over women."

Guillermo would like to defend his gender, but really doesn't know what to say. He is no exemplary specimen of the judiciousness of the masculine sex. His attitude, he realizes, has always been as paternalistic and sexist as those of both Ibrahim and Samir. "And what if we rent the Plazuela España apartment again?"

Maryam shakes her head. "That will be too expensive and will give Samir ammunition to use against me. No, I will simply move into the guest room in our apartment. There are two twin beds there. Samir is many ugly things, but he will respect my privacy. My unwillingness to move out will strengthen my position at home by showing everyone that I have nothing to be ashamed of."

"I don't think that makes any sense. The simplest thing would be to move out and begin living separate lives—"

"If I separate from him, Samir will make my life hell. I will be ostracized by the whole Lebanese community. Everyone will believe him because he is a man, an elder. Even if he says nothing about us, he will be seen as a victim of his scheming and lying young wife. And I will be no better than a harlot."

"I want to live with you, Maryam, you know that. But I am willing to wait. I am very disciplined. I can wait a long time."

Maryam smiles at this. The one thing she most loves about Guillermo is that he knows how to wait: he can hold back his orgasm for hours, urge her forward, let her use him for her pleasure, over and over, top, bottom, from the back. Yes, he can wait for a long time. For anything. She is sure of that. Whether it is making love or waiting for her to be free.

They start kissing on the couch and then roll down to the brown shag rug on the parquet floor. There is ferocity to their lovemaking: strong, violent, a kind of expiating rhythm to it. And when he finishes inside her, they lay together, intertwined.

"I wish I had met you twenty-five years ago," he says, "before I met Rosa Esther."

"I would have been barely fourteen! I wouldn't have been interested in an old man like you," she replies, and plants a big kiss on his cheek.

And afterward, after more cries and tears, as they both lie half covered by scattered items of clothing on the floor, Guillermo says: "We don't know what's going to happen next, my love. I want to be with you. We should be celebrating because we are closer than ever to being together. But this is Guatemala and anything can go wrong. We need to plan, consider all the possible outcomes, in case we are forced to separate. Samir's unpredictable. You may not have noticed, but I suspect there are people out there monitoring our movements. I felt it the first time we met at the Centro Vasco. There was this blue Hyundai in the lot—"

Maryam kisses his cheek again. "I know you're always looking over your shoulder."

Guillermo nods. "For good reason. We need to be even more strategic now because we're in a position of weakness. If something happens, we need to set up a place for us to meet secretly."

"I'm tired of letting my mind rule my heart, Guillermo."

He shushes her. "I'm not talking about that."

"So should we simply say goodbye and plan to meet in Paris next Christmas?"

"Very funny. We don't have to separate immediately."

"Not with what's going on with Samir?" Maryam looks at her tequila but doesn't reach for it.

"Look, your father hasn't wanted to worry you, but he's been getting more threatening phone calls because of his work exposing Banurbano, although it may have something to do with the way he is managing the textile factory. I don't know."

Maryam's eyes well up again. "Why did he ever accept that appointment? My father is so stubborn."

"He is, but I'm his lawyer and the president wouldn't dare touch him. I'm pretty sure of that. But, of course, there are spies."

"So what's our master plan?"

Guillermo gets up off the floor and goes over to the table. He pours more tequila into his glass and brings back to Maryam what is left of hers. "I suggest a less romantic place than Paris to meet. A town closer to home. Maybe in El Salvador. There's this ugly little seaside town, La Libertad, about forty-five minutes from the capital. There's really nothing there, an ugly church on the main square. If anything should happen, we can plan to meet there, in front of the church, on the first of May. No phone calls, no text or e-mail messages between us, because our movements will be monitored. Should anything come between us, let's meet there starting next year and every May 1 after that."

"If something were to happen, one of us *wouldn't* be there."

"And the other person would know that and act accordingly. And plan to be back there at the same time the following year. Can we promise this to each other?"

"Oh, Guillermo . . ."

They stare into each other's eyes, then touch glasses and drink.

"There's something else. Something we haven't even realized."

Maryam curls her body into Guillermo's on the rug as if into a huge, absorbing sponge.

"We're free, Maryam, totally free. Do you realize that?"

She nods, though her face shows worry. She knows that soon she will have to drive home and the battle royal between her and Samir will begin. "We are free, but in chains," she says.

"Yes, like Prometheus."

## CHAPTER FOURTEEN

# YOU CAN'T KIDNAP A CAR

**M**aryam is now sleeping in the guest bedroom of their apartment. It's her decision not to move out, but Samir tells Hiba that he's banished her from their bedroom because she has admitted her affair with "Rosensweig," even though she's never admitted anything. Samir taunts his wife for sleeping with a Jew, though he knows that Guillermo and his wife have been attending the Union Church for years.

Maryam prefers to be alone—she no longer has to see Samir's body. She no longer has to endure the rough texture of his skin next to her in bed, nor witness the spots that appear almost daily on his face, soon becoming moles.

Many men age gracefully, but not Samir. All of his physical deficiencies are amplified after her confession: his shoulders are unquestionably slouched, he shuffles more than he walks, and when he removes his shoes and puts on his slippers, a terrible smell permeates the living room. Maryam is certain that he wears the same socks for several days at a time just to upset her.

Though she can barely tolerate Hiba, Maryam makes sure the woman lays out clean socks and underwear on Samir's bed every day for him after he showers. Though showering has become less frequent—does he want his wife to move out to escape the stench? She closes the door to her room at night, but the odor of dirty socks is inescapable as it slides into her bedroom from under the door.

In truth, her confession came at the right time: there's no way she could have spent another night in his bed.

* * *

Guillermo and Maryam begin spending two afternoons together every week in his new apartment. With only three renters now in the whole building, it resembles a fortified castle, a private haven.

Since Samir refuses to grant her a divorce or annulment, Maryam realizes that she and Guillermo may never share a life together. In Guatemala they cannot live "in sin."

"What's wrong, my love?" asks Guillermo. They are sitting up in bed drinking green tea.

"It's nothing, really."

"I don't believe you," he says, brushing her hair from her forehead. "We shouldn't keep secrets from one another."

"Okay," she says, setting her cup on her night table. "Where are we going?"

"By which you mean . . . ?"

"What's our future?"

"I don't know. Just imagine: only three months ago we had no future together, but now we at least have this—"

"You mean our twice-a-week tryst?"

"It's more than that. I am out of my marriage—"

"And I'll never be out of mine. I feel that I am still lying about us to my father. I am certain that Samir has told him. I should just tell him the truth and see what he says. It's not right for me not to tell him."

Guillermo knows that this will depress her further, but he cannot hide the truth. "You're right, your father already knows. Samir called him the night you spoke with him. Ibrahim asked me not to talk about it, out of respect for him, and to remain discreet. I promised him I would. He does not approve of our affair in the least."

"I wish you'd told me."

"I'm telling you now. Didn't you wonder why your father stopped inviting me to have lunch with you?"

Maryam slumps in the bed. She wants to hide under the sheets and pillows.

"Sweetheart," Guillermo says to her.

"You shouldn't keep secrets from me."

"I promised your father."

"My father's not me. I need you to be honest with me. Samir and I are at a stalemate. All I can do is wish him dead . . . or maybe we should just kill him."

"What a wonderful solution, Maryam—both of us spending the rest of our lives in the penitentiary with Kaibiles, murderers, rapists, and drug addicts for having plotted to assassinate your husband. Even if we hired someone to kill Samir, what would we achieve? It's true, 90 percent of the crimes in Guatemala are never solved, but this murder would surely be traced!"

Maryam raises her right eyebrow.

"I'm not joking. It's easy to hire assassins. It's done almost every day here. Do you know that only eight out of every one hundred crimes are ever prosecuted, and only one of the eight criminals is brought to justice? This means that 1 percent of all murders in Guatemala are solved, but if the killing involves an act of love, it goes up to 50 percent."

"I couldn't live with blood on our hands."

"And neither could I," Guillermo says. He knows they are simply talking loosely. There is no crime in talking about it, but he realizes he could easily contract someone to murder Samir and be done with him.

"There's no hope. What are we waiting for?"

"What if you and I just eloped to some other country? I have friends in Honduras, Nicaragua, and Costa Rica who could help us get set up. And my sister is still living in San Francisco, last I heard."

"I couldn't simply run away with my tail between my legs—not as long as my father is alive. It would literally break his heart if I went off." She pauses. "And I don't think you would want to get any farther away from your kids than you are already. Isn't Mexico far enough away?"

"It is." Guillermo gets up and heads to the bathroom.

When he comes back, Maryam has wrapped a sheet around herself and is sitting on the bed watching television. He glances at the set and sees a boy and a girl crying on the screen. "Watching a soap opera?"

"Not a soap opera, Guillermo, real life. A woman from Vista Hermosa went shopping to Paiz in her Ford Explorer. When she returned home, she parked for a second to open the gate and a car with tinted windows drew up and two men pounced on her. This was according to the maid, who saw everything from inside the house. They shot the woman dead. The thieves killed her to kidnap her car."

"You can't kidnap a car—"

"Damn it, Guillermo, you know what I mean. They hijacked her car. She has two teenagers. There they are crying," she says, pointing to the TV. "The family is ruined. All this over stealing a stupid car!"

Guillermo sits down beside Maryam and hugs her tightly. All in all, this has not been a good day. Maryam is so upset over her life with Samir that she is feeling desperate, almost hopeless. And then the talk about their future further depresses her. And now this senseless killing.

"I can't keep doing this," Maryam says, bursting into tears. "I won't do it. I love you, but this is going to kill me. Kill us. We need to find a way to get away from this life—"

"And take your father and his factory and my law firm with us?"

"You know I don't mean that. It's gotten to the point where it's no longer safe to take a bus anywhere because you'll be assaulted, robbed, or raped. Now you can't even go shopping in your own car without being killed. The other day my maid Lucia was crying because her thirty-year-old nephew had just been killed—sprayed with thirty-two bullets because he refused to join the gang operating in his neighborhood. He was a good boy, attending the university, crossing the street to avoid the Maras until they said to him, *You are going to be one of us.* He kept walking away till they isolated him below La Plaza Berlin. They filled him with bullets and left him to die. Lucia's sister Mirta wants to kill herself. He was her only son."

Guillermo holds Maryam, though she tries to push him away. He refuses to loosen his grip until she finally stops resisting him.

"I want to propose something."

Maryam reaches over to the night table and grabs a tissue.

"Please listen to me."

She nods like an obedient puppy.

"From now on, I want you to take your passport and a thousand dollars with you wherever you go, whether to the hairdresser, the gym, the tennis court, or to go shopping. I will do the same. I want both of us to have the documents and the money to leave this piece-of-shit country at the drop of a hat."

"You think we need to do this?"

"Absolutely. We can't just sit here waiting for our future to happen. Maryam, I don't know what's going to happen with Samir. I assume you think I was kidding about killing him—"

"You better have been kidding," she says, slapping him hard, quite hard, on the chest.

"Okay, so it was only a stupid idea," he says, just to calm her down. "We have to figure out our next step. I don't want you to spend another year under the same roof with Samir. We have to figure something out," he repeats. "But one thing I know: we have to be ready to run. Do you understand?"

"I understand," Maryam says, grabbing her cup of tea and drinking it down.

"And we have our plan to meet in La Libertad."

"I hope to God we are just spinning our wheels."

"Me too. I'm an optimist, but I don't want to be taken by surprise. We need to have an alternate plan."

As he says this he sees that the television station is showing a clip of the woman in Vista Hermosa as she's gunned down. Apparently it was filmed on a phone by a teenager living across the street.

Guillermo is scared for himself, and more than a bit scared for Maryam.

Something has to change.

## CHAPTER FIFTEEN

# LET'S BRING THE MOUNTAIN TO MOHAMMED

One late Tuesday afternoon, as Maryam is playing solitaire on the dining room table and wondering how long her stalemate with her husband will last, Samir comes home early from work. He shuffles over to her and announces that his niece Verónica Handal will be coming to visit from Tegucigalpa, Honduras that very night and will be spending a few days with them.

"Don't I have a say in the matter?" she says, looking up from her cards.

"It is through my kindness that you are still living in my apartment. Someone else would have thrown you out a long time ago for your indiscretions."

"You don't need to throw me out. When I leave, it will be voluntarily."

Samir nods at her disparagingly. He is wearing a three-piece herringbone suit with an open white shirt. "I have told you I will not be made the laughing stock of the Lebanese community. You will go when I tell you to go. In the meantime, as you have observed, you are free to come and go as you wish . . . But Verónica is my only niece and is taking care of my brother and his wife in a nursing home. My home is her home. I can invite her here whenever I want without consulting you."

Maryam has always disliked Verónica. She is some ten years older than her, in her early fifties, and has never married. Since both her parents developed dementia, she has acted as the world's only true, suffering martyr for having sacrificed her happiness in order to care for them. In reality, she's never had a life of happiness to sacrifice. She is severe in her tastes, dowdy in her dress, and enjoys criticizing anyone who has an ounce of spunk or defiance. Her features are exceedingly big: her ears, her lips, and certainly her breasts, which hang like huge, shapeless eggplants that no man would want to touch. But it is not her looks that upset Maryam as much as her lack of sincerity, and her habit of probing into everything as if picking at a scab. The two women have never gotten along, not from the moment they met at her and Samir's engagement when, at the home of Jorge Serrano Elías—a former president of Guatemala of Lebanese descent—Verónica began criticizing her for her low bodice. Instead of reveling in the moment and feeling beautiful, Maryam spent the evening pulling up her dress to cover her breasts.

Oddly, both women are the same height and have the same hair and eye color. But the similarities end there. Verónica has no light of her own and is a poor reflection of the light of others. If she were to die, Maryam thinks, no one on this earth would miss her. Not her ailing parents, not even Samir.

"And how long is she staying?" Maryam is turning over three cards at a time, having lost track of her game. Four kings are already displayed and she might win.

"Just a few nights."

"Has she been sent on a mission here by your brother Saleh?"

"You mean my poor demented brother in the nursing home? Your sense of decency has escaped you."

Maryam is in an awful mood. Her period is two weeks late. She fears she is pregnant. And she is also having cramps that are particularly intense. Is she falling apart?

"You have always detested your niece."

"I don't have any idea what you're talking about, Maryam. Every day your ideas become stranger and stranger. You know that Saleh and Hamsa are in the same nursing home. They hardly know each other, much less who I am. And certainly they have forgotten who you are. My niece is a godsend."

"So if Verónica is irreplaceable, why is she coming?"

"I am her only remaining family. I have asked her to come to spend time with me. You might find this difficult to understand, but I am in mourning. I have suffered a death. My marriage has died."

Once again Maryam decides not to engage him. He is always trying to provoke her, jabbing at her as they move around the shared areas of the apartment like wary boxers in a ring. When they first married, they would often play backgammon at night, and a common tactic of Samir's was to leave one of his chips vulnerable to see if she would abandon her strategy simply to land on one of his men. After a few losses, she learned to ignore his ploys and play her own game. And she often won.

"I suppose you've told her about the trouble between us," she comments as she continues to flip cards.

Samir takes out the gold watch from his vest pocket and looks at the time. "There's no trouble between us, Maryam. You've simply betrayed the trust of our marriage. But to answer your question: I won't deny that I've told her about your affair. Why keep it a secret? She is as disgusted as I am. What else would you expect?"

"I won't tolerate her interference."

"Well then, why don't you just mind your business and let her come to spend some peaceful time with her admired uncle?"

Maryam almost chokes on the word *admired*. Samir has such an inflated image of himself, as if he were some kind of brave corsair or fighter pilot, and not the owner of a hardware store in a part of town even buzzards have abandoned. "If she feels anything for you, Samir, it must be hate. She knows that you are mean and despicable, and that you are cheap: you don't lift a finger to help her parents even though you easily could."

Samir ignores the comment. "She is coming in on the TACA flight tonight. It would be nice if you were to accompany me to the airport and at least pretend that we are capable of being civil to one another."

"Will you grant me a divorce if I come?"

"Not on your life."

"I'm sorry then, Samir, but you will have to pick her up alone." Maryam gets up from the table and starts walking to her bedroom.

Samir shuffles over to the table where the cards are and sees that Maryam has beaten the odds. As she exits he says to her: "It seems you've won at solitaire. It is a game that is appropriately titled for your situation—a woman all alone, bereft of companionship. Congratulations."

"Sometimes it happens," she replies unguardedly.

Before she closes the door, he says loud enough for her to hear, "What I wonder is if you won honestly or had to cheat."

Torrential rains begin as the sun goes down. The flight is expected in at eight p.m., but will be delayed. Maryam feels a bit tired and eats a leftover chicken leg with tabouleh for dinner. Once she is sure that Samir has left for the airport, she calls Guillermo.

She recounts her conversation with her husband. Guillermo merely listens. They talk for about twenty minutes and then Maryam cuts the call short to get ready for bed.

At around ten thirty she hears voices. If she were polite, she would get out of bed and put on her robe to greet Verónica. But why should she? She hears them speaking loudly in Arabic, perhaps even arguing. Maryam hears him say, *Ibn sharmoota*. Her niece says something back, which obviously angers him—she imagines Verónica is telling Samir that Maryam was a whore from the beginning, or that he should do more to care for her parents.

Then she hears the unmistakable sound of a slap in the face.

Verónica screams a saying in Arabic that roughly translates, *You have a penis for a nose*, a common insult she has heard before. What a family, lacking a corpuscle of decency.

Ibrahim's day has begun normal enough. His chauffeur dropped him off at the front door of the textile factory and then went back home to do some household chores. Ibrahim plans to spend the whole day meeting with his employees in groups: the machine operators, the foremen, the sales personnel, the cleaning staff. He wants to make sure they are all content, because in the coming year they will be challenged by the recession in the United States. Orders are also way down, thanks to the ferocious competition from Bengali and Haitian sweat shops. Ibrahim can hardly compete. All he can do is offer quality, timely service at a premium to his customer.

Maryam rises earlier than usual to avoid confronting both Samir's probing eyes and her niece's interrogation at breakfast. She eats a bowl of sliced papaya and melon with homemade yogurt standing at the small kitchen table, then goes to a nine a.m. exercise class at the World Gym on Los Próceres. After exercising, she decides to swim fifty lengths in the pool and take a quick sauna. Exercise is her way of dealing with the tensions at home.

The swimming and the hot sauna weaken Maryam more than usual. Maybe she should have exercised less, given her condition. She drinks several glasses of water and then takes a long cold shower, hoping the change in temperature will refresh her.

The gym isn't far from home. She needs to go home to change before picking up her father at the factory at twelve thirty for their weekly Wednesday lunch. Ever since she admitted her affair to Samir, Maryam and her father have been going to his apartment for lunch instead of hers. She doesn't want to risk Samir joining them, for fear he may begin hinting about her affair with Guillermo. Jokes about Maryam's infidelity would kill her father. It's very Lebanese to avoid awkward issues, she tells herself—better to hide and pretend to be lighthearted.

The shower has not helped, and Maryam still feels faint from the exercise. She prays that Samir has left for work and that Verónica has gone out for a walk.

No such luck. "You look very pale," Verónica greets her, and plants a kiss on each of her cheeks. "Come, give me a hug. I hear you have been running around a lot. You shouldn't put your health in jeopardy. "

Maryam doesn't know how to take this. Is Verónica making a reference to her affair or is she actually concerned about her well-being? She hugs her niece a bit stiffly and says, "I'd like to lie down, but I have to go pick up my father and bring him over to his apartment for lunch."

"Why don't you take it easy? I can drive him."

"You wouldn't know where to go. You have no idea where the factory is or where he lives. Because he has a driver, he stopped paying attention to where he was going long ago. He doesn't even know his way around the streets of Guatemala."

"Well then, just have your father's chauffeur drive him from the factory to his apartment."

"I should really go." She does not want to miss seeing her father. She insists on treating him with the same respect and deference as always, if only to prove that nothing has changed despite what Samir may have told him. She wants her father to know she will continue to dote on him, no matter what. It is a Lebanese custom to neither discuss nor feign ignorance of what both parties know. But in truth she feels too lightheaded to drive to the factory, and doesn't know what to do.

Verónica has read her mind. "Why don't we go together? You can sit in the passenger seat and give me the directions. If I can drive in Tegucigalpa, with its crazy drivers and steep hills, I can certainly drive here."

Maryam concedes. "Let me go to the bathroom first." Her stomach is hurting. She takes a Midol to ease the pain. It crosses her mind again that she might be pregnant. She and Guillermo have been so careless lately. He never wants to pull out, certainly not the last few times they have made love. He enjoys coming inside of her. And she enjoys it as well.

Maryam gives Verónica the keys and they take the elevator down to the parking lot basement. She sits in the passenger seat and directs Verónica to take the turnoff to Aguilar Batres, just before the Roosevelt Hospital entrance.

On the way there, Maryam suddenly realizes she needs to lie down. She asks Verónica to pull over and gets out of the front seat to lie down in the back. By this time, they are less than a kilometer from the factory.

Because they are arriving a bit late, Ibrahim has come down from his office and is standing talking to Fulgencio, the guard, near the factory parking lot. As soon as he sees Maryam's car, he stops the idle chatter and begins walking over to the gate to wait for the car at the lot entrance. Due to the tinted windows, he doesn't see that Samir's niece is driving until she rolls down the window on the passenger side.

"Hello, uncle," Verónica says, unlocking the car.

"Well, this is a surprise, Verónica. I had no idea you were in Guatemala. Where's Maryam?" he asks.

"I'm back here, Papá, lying down. I'm not feeling very well," she says.

Ibrahim sticks his head through the window and blows her a kiss. Then he opens the door and sits down in the front passenger seat. He adjusts the seat to give Maryam more room in back and talks softly to Verónica so Maryam can get some rest.

Verónica drives in a circle before pulling out of the gated lot. With little sense of direction, she turns right instead of left once she is on the street. She assumes she is going the right way, especially when she sees that there is a car following her—obviously another vehicle going back to the main highway. Ibrahim, lost in thought, doesn't notice. Maryam is fast asleep

Samir's niece soon realizes she is lost but is unable to remember how she got to the factory in the first place. All of a sudden she finds herself in a fairly abandoned area near the Ciudad Universitaria, a construction site that has been partially developed and then neglected because funding ran out.

She stops at a stop sign and the car stalls. She starts the car again and drives deeper into the construction area. Ibrahim begins mumbling directions to her, trying to get her back on the Calzada Roosevelt. But now he too is lost.

"Where are you going?" Ibrahim asks uneasily, leaning forward.

"You are making me very nervous, uncle," Verónica says, shifting into a higher gear, which makes the car hiccup. She takes her foot off the clutch and the car stalls once again.

"Now what have you done?" he snaps, lowering his window, looking around to get his bearings. He is beginning to panic.

Maryam, in the backseat, begins to stir. She is vaguely aware she should be giving directions, but she's still half asleep.

A gray Nissan pulls up alongside the passenger side as if to offer help. Ibrahim sees its shaded windows and becomes extremely anxious.

"Stupid woman, start the car and drive off!" he yells, slapping the dashboard.

Verónica cannot find the ignition and begins to weep.

Finally she is able to start the car and Ibrahim lets out a sigh of relief. Then she inexplicably begins to lower his window to thank the Nissan for stopping.

"Raise it, you fool. Drive! Drive!" he shouts.

What happens next happens very fast. Ibrahim catches a glimpse of a man racing out of the Nissan from the passenger side. He scrambles around the front of his car and rushes toward where Ibrahim is sitting. He is sweating and waving something wildly in his hand. Ibrahim pushes the button to raise his tinted window with one hand and tries to loosen the seat belt with the other, so he can crouch down.

The gun, a nine-millimeter pistol with a detachable cartridge, is the last thing Ibrahim sees before he hears, *PUM! PUM! PUM! PUM!* The tinted window, three-quarters raised, immediately shatters. Verónica starts to scream but is cut short by the spray of bullets.

Then the assassin, for good measure, pumps another three shots into Ibrahim's corpse. The explosion of shots, the shattering of glass, and the screaming all fold together into one spurt of cacophony. Maryam drops her face into the backseat and covers her ears.

A second later there is only a deafening desert silence. Maryam can hear her heart beating loudly in her chest and feels tears leaking out of her eyes and down her cheeks. She is terrified for herself, well aware that a massacre has just taken place.

This silence feels protective so Maryam slowly sits up. Through her own tinted window she sees the shooter walking casually back to the passenger seat of his car. She cranes her head forward, making sure she stays out of his line of vision, and sees that both her father and Verónica are slouched over the dashboard, and that the front windshield, miraculously intact, is splattered with blood.

Maryam feels the silence building in her ears.

She knows that her father is dead but she is in too much shock to cry. She looks back at the Nissan, which hasn't moved an inch. It's as if they're in the middle of a wasteland. She sees the gunman open the back door and pull out a large plastic container. He tosses the gun into the car.

Maryam lies back down and listens. She hears some odd movements and what sounds like liquid being thrown onto the hood of the car. She knows what is happening, what will happen next, but she doesn't know what to do. She is certain that if she says a word the man will shoot her as well. Her heart is beating so loudly it makes a thumping noise against the backseat, which she hopes the killer cannot hear.

Then there's a flicking noise and a huge flash of light over the hood—

flames shoot up into the air. She hears the flames crackling, followed in a few seconds by the noise of the Nissan screeching away. The flames begin to engulf the sides of the car.

In one motion Maryam jacks up the handle of the backseat door on the driver's side, grabs her purse, and rolls out of the car onto the gravelly pavement. The odor of burning gas and paint is nauseating.

She stands up and begins to run to the entrance of one of the abandoned buildings when she hears the car detonate behind her, the body of her father and Verónica still inside.

Once she is safe, she turns around to see an inferno rising ten meters into the air. If she had hesitated even two seconds, she too would have roasted inside her car. She feels a bit of urine running down her legs, her eyes are a burning tear of rage and pain. Her car is a ball of fire.

Maryam is still in too much shock to cry. Someone wanted both her and her father dead. This someone has probably been aware of every single step both of them have taken. What the killers have not planned for is Maryam's illness and Verónica's visitation, and now Verónica is dead and she is alive.

At least for the moment.

She opens her purse and sees her passport and the tiny purse with ten hundred-dollar bills, realizing how smart Guillermo's advice was. She thinks of calling him now, to let him know what has happened and that she is alive, but quickly changes her mind. Guillermo has told her many times that all their phones are tapped. The only way to communicate privately would have been to purchase disposable phones with untraceable numbers but they've never taken the time to do that. She turns off her phone, knowing she has to get rid of it.

She is so tired that she slides down the wall of concrete and sits on the ground. She needs to think clearly.

Why would anyone want her dead?

Her father has enemies, this she can understand: his advisory role in Banurbano and his constant, undisguised accusations about governmental corruption; the rumor that her father has purchased textiles from contra-bandists importing bolts of cloth illegally into Guatemala without paying duties; the handful of disgruntled employees, lazier than hell, who say they will sue Ibrahim if he makes good on his threat to fire them.

Plenty of people have issues with her father.

But her? What has she done to any of them? She hates no one and no one hates her.

Well, almost no one.

Just Samir, with his cloying smile and vituperative voice.

Would he be brazen enough to kill her and her father because she wants to leave him? In a normal world, such criminality would be beyond anyone's comprehension. But this is Guatemala, where children prey on their parents and vice versa.

There is so much unknown. So much that can't be known and perhaps never will.

Time is passing.

Maryam pushes herself up. She is covered with dust. She brushes herself off as she hurries back toward the street. It is quiet still, save for the smoldering vehicle. The stench of rubber, plastic, and cotton is disgusting.

A huge plume of smoke billows up from the remains of the car into the blue sky, drifting toward the top of Roosevelt Hospital's highest building and flitting swiftly as if from the end of a pipe into the surrounding hills and mountains.

Maryam begins walking away down a broken sidewalk. After three blocks, she hears sirens approaching and sees two fire trucks and an ambulance racing toward her.

She is tempted to flag them down and wants to tell them that they should just go back, that it's too late, for the car and for everyone in it—including her beloved father, who has been rendered into a dark, flaky ash; that she is the only survivor. But then Maryam realizes she is in a dangerous predicament. The assumption will be that she is dead. She doesn't know if she was the actual target or just collateral damage, but she understands that her next step has to be counterintuitive: that is, it must fly in the face of any sort of expectation.

As painful as it might be, she must do something completely unexpected. And what would that be?

Her mind is spinning faster than a roulette wheel, and she is trying to review her options.

Her heart is broken, but she is alive.

All of a sudden she hears the screeching of tires, the opening of doors, and the sound of people running toward her.

She rushes into the construction site. A bullet zings past her ear, then she hears shouting and screaming.

She keeps running through a maze of concrete and wooden beams.

Four or five bullets ring out. Then more sirens and burning rubber.

Maryam drops to the ground, squeezes her eyes tight, and waits for a bullet to pierce her.

## CHAPTER SIXTEEN

# A PILE OF ASHES

**One thing that can't be disputed** about Guatemala is that mistakes—very serious ones—are always happening. It is almost like a national epidemic, a defining characteristic, a part of the genetic makeup of the population whether you are Indian, Latino, or Caucasian. The wrong people are kidnapped, the wrong people are killed—there is an ineptitude that is endemic to the country. This extends to even the smallest of matters, like the purchase of fruits or vegetables.

For example, you go to a hardware store and order a fixture for your stove but get something more suited to your refrigerator. You order a Jaguar XJL—illegally, of course, to avoid import taxes—and receive an XKL instead. There is nothing you can do to rectify the mistake unless you want to return the purchase and risk being arrested.

You can have an invoice stating what you have ordered—say a table lamp with a green shade—but in the end you have to pay for what you get: a pole lamp with yellow plastic jackets. Even if it isn't exactly what you wanted, you are better off simply zippering your lips and keeping what you have, which is *almost* what you purchased. Not quite.

This is just the way it is.

Guillermo is in a meeting with Favio Altalef, a client who is hoping to establish a consulting firm to help existing factories conform to the new environmental laws regulating the release of fossil fuels into the atmosphere. Favio is an engineer with the ambition to run his own company. He knows a lot about converting waste to harmless gases, but knows nothing about setting up a legitimate business. He is hoping Guillermo can facilitate his firm's articles of incorporation, and get the necessary federal and municipal licenses so he can begin advising others. Guillermo informs him that in addition to his standard hourly fee, he will require a deposit of two hundred thousand quetzales in order to smooth the progress of what he calls "the wheels of government."

Favio knows that he isn't being hustled. Bribery is part of the price of doing business. He has gone to Guillermo because his reputation among the Guatemalan business community is impeccable. Favio knows he is in good hands and not about to be led down a financial rabbit hole.

Thirty minutes into the meeting, Guillermo's secretary Luisa rushes into his office and calls him into the hall. She says, "Don Guillermo, we just received a call that Ibrahim Khalil has been in a serious car accident about a kilometer from his factory near Roosevelt Hospital."

Guillermo tenses up; his nose starts dripping. He pulls out a handkerchief and wipes it; his right eye is beginning to spasm.

"Was anyone else in the car?" He is afraid to mention Maryam's name to Luisa, though she has put calls through to her in the past.

"That's all the man said. He sounded official. I am so sorry, Don Guillermo."

He has no time to figure out who "the man" is. There is always a secretive "man" in Guatemala who somehow becomes the messenger of bad news.

He asks Luisa to tell Favio to leave all the documents on his desk and have him reschedule the appointment for later in the week. He walks over to the receptionist's desk and calls Maryam from the office phone. The line rings six times before it goes to voice mail and he hears her sweet voice asking the caller to leave a name and number. *"I will return your call as soon as I can."*

He finds this strange. Maryam is never more than a few feet from her cell phone unless she is showering, which she wouldn't be at two o'clock in the afternoon. He pulls his BlackBerry out and calls her phone again; this time it goes straight to voice mail.

This is even stranger: first six rings, then none. Why would she turn her phone off? Something is up.

He wipes his nose on his coat sleeve and calls Maryam's apartment. Hiba says that the madam is not at home. She is gruff and uninformative, as usual.

When he persists, she says, "If you want more information, talk to her husband," and hangs up.

Guillermo calls Ibrahim's apartment and his maid Fernanda picks up, all in a huff. After he identifies himself, she says that it is now two o'clock, lunch is getting cold, and neither Ibrahim nor his daughter have arrived, or called to say they would be late. More matter-of-factly, she adds that she has just received a call from the police, asking for Ibrahim. She told them what she just told Guillermo.

"How do you know the call was really from the police?" he asks, agitated.

"Because the caller identified himself as Sergeant Enrique Palacios."

"Sergeant Enrique Palacios my ass," says Guillermo, hanging up. He is losing his cool. Rage is taking over his chest.

He leaves the office and drives his car straight to Ibrahim's factory, weaving in and out of traffic, pushing down on his horn as he goes. He zooms around the Plaza del Obelisco and heads west. In two minutes he is passing by the huge IGGS center on the south side of Calzada Roosevelt. He passes the Trébol entrance leading to Roosevelt Hospital and goes down Ninth Avenue toward the factory on 12th Street. As he approaches the guardhouse, he sees at least five police cars parked there, with lights spinning and intermittent sirens sounding. He sees more than a dozen policemen talking, laughing, kicking at the pebbles under their feet. It all seems oddly festive, as if the president of the republic has come to pay his respects to one of Guatemala's leading industrialists, or to bestow upon him an international business prize.

Guillermo leaves his car outside the gate and jogs up to them.

"What's going on here?"

One of the policemen takes a few steps toward him. "And you are?"

"Guillermo Rosensweig. I am Ibrahim Khalil's lawyer," he says, struggling to pull out a business card from his coat pocket. He notices that his nose is still running, but now he doesn't care what he looks like. "I received a phone call telling me that my client has been in an accident. I would like to talk to him right away."

The policeman's cap is too large and falls over his coppery forehead. He has to keep pushing the rim up in order to see, but since his hair is greasy it slides back down. His ears stick out like unruly cabbage leaves. He tilts his cap up again and examines the card. "I don't think you will be able to do that, Don Guillermo . . ."

"And why is that?"

"Mr. Khalil is dead."

"What?" Guillermo screams, confused.

"And I am afraid to say that so is his daughter."

Guillermo runs his right hand through his thinning hair. His scalp is sweating and begins to itch. He scratches his neck so hard he draws blood. He is totally lost, about to lose the capacity to breathe. The spinning lights and noise further disorient him.

"He's dead? Ibrahim Khalil is dead?"

"So is his daughter," the policeman answers.

"If this is your idea of a joke, I don't find it funny."

"It's no joke, Don Guillermo. Samir Mounier, the husband of the deceased woman, has just confirmed that the car that blew up belonged to his wife. She and her father—apparently—were in the car and driving home together. They burned to a crisp, like a pan francés," he adds, as if he has been waiting all his life to say something as foolish as this.

"Samir Mounier is a joke of a man. He knows nothing. And why isn't he here now?"

"He has gone off to make arrangements for the funerals."

It's all happening too fast. The phone call to the office. His inability to get through to Maryam. His call to Hiba, then to Fernanda. The zigging and zagging to the office and the factory. His mind is fizzling.

"I am telling you that there has been some kind of serious, very serious, mistake here—" Guillermo is grasping at straws, but at this moment he doesn't know that. He only feels something like the weight of a bulletproof vest pressing heavily against his chest, making him tired and clumsy.

"If you come with me I will show you the car, or what's left of it. Perhaps you will have something more to add when you see it."

Guillermo follows the policeman into his car, saying angrily "I don't know what you're talking about. I really don't."

"Be calm, Don Guillermo."

He gets into the front passenger seat of the police car, which is filthy, full of paper cups, brown towels, empty plastic bags, three sets of sunglasses, garbage bags, balled-up cellophane. He pushes the side lever back so he has more leg room in the car.

All of a sudden he starts getting nervous. Why has he just gotten into a cop car? This is a dangerous situation. They may be kidnapping him. "Where are we going?"

"To the crime scene."

"Bring me back to the factory!" Guillermo screams, afraid he is being abducted.

The policeman points to the rising smoke blocks away. "That's where it happened. We are almost there."

Within a minute they are there, in the middle of an abandoned construction site with gravelly streets. On the side of the road is a blue tow truck with its engine running, starting to lower an enormous metal plate. In the middle of the street lies the burnt carcass of a black Mercedes with a piece of twisted metal—one of the doors?—next to it. The plate is about to scoop up the remains.

The car is surrounded by five or six men in ill-fitting suits. There are more clumps of metal on a sea of sticky, multicolored oil. There's the faint but unmistakable smell of charred flesh and bones. He sees no bodily remains.

Guillermo pushes himself out of the police car and goes over to look more closely at the car, whose front half, up to the backseat, resembles a brittle charcoal briquette. As soon as he looks at the trunk door he knows it is Maryam's car because he sees the shreds of a green blanket on the asphalt; Maryam sometimes put it on her father when he felt cold. He crosses to the driver's side and sees the blown-out door and window, the dashboard turned to pulverized ash and burnt rubber, a blackened iron cross dangling from the roof: the remains of the mirror. On the wired vestiges of the front bucket seats he sees piles of charred mineral compounds, like the simple white residues of old bones.

The passengers have been cremated, largely vaporized.

And then it finally hits Guillermo that Maryam and Ibrahim have ceased to exist. If they are there, they are the small mound of charred white splinters covering the seats.

Guillermo tries to get closer to the car. He sees the passenger door held to the chassis by one little hinge. He touches the door and notices that the metal handle is still hot. One of the detectives stops him.

"This is a crime scene, sir. You cannot touch the evidence."

"Evidence? What kind of evidence do you need? I mean, don't you see what's happened? The passengers have been vaporized. They're gone. My Maryam is dead!" he hears himself saying, shocked at his own words, seeing an image of her in her tennis outfit with the little pink balls on the heels of her sneakers; and then her voluptuous body stretched out on the Stofella bed. Guillermo tries a second time to touch the handle, open the door maybe, but the hinge has soldered it in place.

"My darling is dead. She's dead. Oh my God, my love is dead."

The detective grabs Guillermo by the waist and tries pulling him away. He signals to the policeman who brought him to the scene for help. The cop tosses his oversized cap into his car and scampers over. Both of them pull the grieving lawyer away and sit him down on a curb in front of the half-constructed buildings. The policeman explains to the detective why he brought Guillermo over, that he had just driven to the factory. He adds in a sly whisper that obviously he is the lover of Ibrahim Khalil's daughter, since the husband has already been there and has left to make the funeral arrangements.

"But he knows nothing," Guillermo hears.

Filled with thick cumulonimbus clouds that funnel up, the sky has darkened but nobody really notices or cares. It starts to rain, a soft, steady, and enduring patter that douses the burnt cinders and creates new chemical reactions releasing vinegary clouds of smoke into the air. The whole area seems lifeless, like a battlefield filled with stinky corpses.

Guillermo buries his face in his crossed arms and feels the policeman's hand on his shoulder. He again sees Maryam lying naked on her stomach in the bed at the Stofella, her head resting against her folded arms, her ample breasts, the flatness of her feet, the broad curve of her ankles, her toes hanging over the bed and wiggling, the tattoo of a smiling red bat above the dimple on her left butt cheek. He can hear her slightly husky voice talking to him as he stands by her feet, ready to massage or lick her toes, with their green nail polish. In a dreamlike trance, she is telling him that he can do anything he wants to her body; hurt her even, hurt her more than a bit. She likes pain, as long as he stops when she asks him to stop. She wants to hurt but only a little, perhaps enough to know she is alive, not dreaming, not in a state of unfeeling. Hair pulled back, hard bites on the neck.

"What am I going to do now?" Guillermo says aloud. His nose is no longer dripping, he suspects. He can't be sure because the rain is splattering his face and his suit is damp. He feels he will never again be sure of anything in his life, now that Maryam is dead.

"You have nothing to do here, Mr. Rosensweig. You should go home. We may want to interview you later this afternoon or evening since you obviously knew the victims well."

"There must be something I can do," says Guillermo, wondering if he can help shovel the cinders on the seats into separate urns. He has always believed there are things to be done, that nothing in life is final, save for the death of his parents. "What am I going to do at home, alone?" He thinks of his children and Rosa Esther in Mexico City enjoying their lives. He feels nothing. The memory of them stirs no feeling in him.

"Samir Mounier was just here," the detective repeats. "He's the husband. The next of kin. He identified the car, since there are no bodies to speak of. Maybe he could use your help."

"Fucking Samir," Guillermo cries. "How do you know he isn't the one behind all this?"

The detective smiles. Nothing is more absurd. The grieving husband is so decrepit he could hardly pick up a broomstick.

The policeman starts talking: "You're a man in mourning, Don Guillermo. You will do what grieving men do. Be a man, a decent man, and go home."

Guillermo turns to look at him without his cap. He notices more clearly that he has a pointed head and, yes, cabbage ears. Then he glances at the detective, who may as well have been talking to him in Urdu or Tagalog.

"But I don't want to go home. Isn't there anything I can do?"

"You are going to let the husband handle the details. And like a good lover, you are going to cry. And then you are going to cry some more. And when you are done mourning the death of your lover, you are going to join with us and get the bastards responsible for this crime."

The words *la petite mort* come to Guillermo's mind. This is anything but *la petite mort*, something he will never again experience with Maryam. This, he realizes, is the real thing. Pure and simple murder.

And cry he does, realizing that one of Guatemala's most common mistakes has happened to him. Through a crazy turn of events, his love Maryam Khalil has been killed when the target had to be her father.

Unless, of course, Samir—

It cannot be.

He wouldn't be such a bastard. Would he?

## CHAPTER SEVENTEEN

## TYING UP LOOSE ENDS

**Samir Mounier is the only person who knows what has happened.** And because nothing of what has happened has managed to betray his strategy, he proceeds on course.

He had invited his niece to visit him so she would bear witness to his grief at his wife's infidelity, to help give him some solace, and to get under Maryam's skin, since she disliked her immensely. And if she had minded her business and not offered to accompany Maryam, she would still be alive today to help him plan his father-in-law and wife's funeral. That she has also gone up in flames doesn't really change anything.

She will not be missed. With her parents Saleh and Hamsa in a nursing home in Tegucigalpa, and Verónica a spinster living alone, her disappearance from Honduras—the country with the highest homicide rate in the world—is sure to raise no suspicion. Tegucigalpa is a city where bridges lead to nowhere. Her incineration is only a minor occurrence—dozens of people vanish in Honduras every week and nobody cares.

The most Samir will be required to do is fly to Tegucigalpa and close up his niece's apartment. If he were decent and had the time, he would also stop by and see his brother and his brother's wife in their nursing home one last time. But what would be the point? They'd have no idea who he is, and if they end up being wards of the state in a hideous urine-infested facility, then so be it.

*No one will miss Verónica.* The thought makes him smile. *The Guatemalan*

*police have no idea what actually happened. They suspect absolutely no foul play.
The only danger is if they discover any evidence pointing to a third person in the
car. In truth, no one gives a damn about my niece. Certainly not me, Uncle Samir.
And even Ibrahim and Maryam Khalil: they are today's news and tomorrow's old
papers.*

He had seen the mass of twisted metal that remained of Maryam's Mercedes at the crime scene. He is no scientist, but he suspects there will be
no forensic evidence to cull from, no DNA that could possibly prove three
people had died. Guatemala is years away from genetic testing, but DNA
cannot be recovered from cremated remains anyway. All the pieces of jewelry,
the few chips of gold from fillings, will be traced back to Maryam because the
truth of what happened is too complicated to investigate.

It was wise of him to give Hiba the morning off and ask her to come in
at twelve thirty to make lunch. For some reason, he had assumed that Hiba's
presence would have inhibited conversation between Verónica and Maryam
in the morning, thereby delaying his wife's departure to pick up her father.

The fact that Hiba came in later in the day would awaken no suspicion.

Samir has no trouble faking his grief. He has lost his wife, his beautiful
young wife, and the texture of his life will have to change in the eyes of the
world. He can fabricate real tears just thinking of his dead mother or father,
but to look at him, no one would know that he is feeling absolutely no grief
as he cries. He doesn't need to plaster gloom all over his face, it is naturally
disfigured by a lifetime of disappointment and the distortions of age. Adding
a heap more sorrow will not change things at all.

He calls home and tells Hiba matter-of-factly that the madam is dead,
and to please go home. He is surprised by the maid's display of sorrow over
the phone. "There is nothing else you can do," he snaps at her. "I will call you
when I need you again."

When he arrives back to his apartment, he unlocks Verónica's door and
gathers together her few belongings. He examines each piece for a label or
marking that might identify them as hers, and finding none, he puts her
clothes back into her suitcase. As he drives to the San Francisco Church
downtown to make funeral arrangements with Father Reboleda, he stops by

the edge of the small park bordering the Simón Bolivar Plaza on Las Américas Boulevard and places the suitcase on the sidewalk. Poor Indians are taking down their food stands for the day, and the contents of the luggage will easily find their way into a needy family's hands.

The beauty of living in a country as corrupt as Guatemala is that evidence can vanish as easily as smoke. Scarcity creates a society in which the truth of any situation can be variable or even paradoxical, and very few people will care. It happens all the time.

Samir has a mordant smile on his face as he drives downtown. Everything has gone smoothly enough. The killers seem to have been as discreet as they were paid to be. He can't imagine the explosion traced back to him. The detectives, God bless their souls, will come up with enough believable theories of who was behind the killings.

He is well aware that Ibrahim has at least three or four enemies who would want him dead. Crooked textile suppliers, fellow members of that idiotic presidential oversight committee he was on, and even Guillermo Rosensweig, if he felt the man was an obstacle to his plan to steal away his daughter.

No one will suspect Samir. As a former leader of the Lebanese community, his reputation is sterling. He is an ideal citizen. Yes, he knows he will have to get rid of his jovial smile before he meets the priest. It is, in the end, a small price to pay.

They are all such fools.

And he knows that with Khalil and Maryam gone, he may soon inherit another bundle of money, enough to keep him, his children, and his relatives in Lebanon going for many years. The money will come just in time, as he is planning to leave Guatemala and return to Sidon.

Everything is falling perfectly into place.

## CHAPTER EIGHTEEN

# THE DOG CHASES ITS OWN TAIL

Ibrahim and Maryam's ashes—or rather what is assumed are their ashes—are placed in two ceramic urns for burial. If the remains had been found in a mass grave in the Ixil Triangle, international forensic anthropologists would have been called in to lend their expertise to the prosecution of, for example, a former Guatemalan president for the genocide he undoubtedly committed. But this is just the explosion of a car on an abandoned street in a worthless neighborhood. If there had been remains beyond the small splinters of bones and a few chips of teeth, a postmortem might have been required, but the detectives on the case feel it is unnecessary to examine the ashes for organic matter; Fulgencio, the guard at Ibrahim's factory, told detectives that he saw his boss get into his daughter's Mercedes. Forensic testing would have proven that the ashes held human remains, but no proof as to who the victims were. And what would a chemical toxicology report reveal? The ashes were so con-taminated by oil, gasoline, and burning hydrocarbons that the existence of drugs or poisons would never be found.

There is no reason to extend the investigation. The dead are the dead. It is an open-and-shut case.

The police know that Ibrahim is dead because they have found vestiges of his pacemaker. Guillermo knows that Maryam is dead because he phones her every day and his call now goes directly to voice mail. Still, he wonders why the police department or federal officials are unwilling to do a thorough investigation. Since Samir is the closest living survivor, he is the only one who can authorize an inquiry into their causes of death. For his part, Samir has told the authorities that he is consumed by such overwhelming misery that he wants the matter closed as soon as possible. He insists that sending the remains for examination and analysis in the United States would not bring his wife and father-in-law back to life. The only thing he claims to want is to be at peace, and to forget these horrid killings. In fact, Samir says that as soon as he can, he will travel to Honduras to see his ailing brother and sister-in-law. He is seriously thinking of returning to Beirut or Sidon, to spend the rest of his days with his children, surrounded by the only family he has left. In sum, he wants nothing to do with any further investigation. There are over 6,400 killings in Guatemala in 2009, and the few viable forensic teams are routinely sent all over the country by the president to examine the dozens of newly discovered mass graves, dating back to the early eighties. Confirming who perished in a car explosion is of little national interest.

A bigger issue is whether the municipal police will ask the federal government to convene a grand jury to investigate why Ibrahim and his daughter were killed. Indeed, as soon as their murder is made public, there is substantial speculation as to why they were killed. When Guillermo is interviewed by the detectives, he suggests that there has to be a formal inquest to determine who killed them, and to bring the guilty parties to justice.

He knows he cannot cast a shadow on Samir.

Four days after the murders, Samir organizes a small memorial service for his wife and father-in-law at the San Francisco Church in downtown Guatemala City. Guillermo knows that his presence is not wanted, but there is no way he will not attend. He is consumed with sorrow and feels entitled to grieve as if his own wife has died.

He drives downtown alone. He sits in the back of the church and stares in disbelief at the two urns placed side by side on a table by the altar. Guillermo is stunned that Samir has chosen to collect their ashes in urns and entomb them in a wall at the Verbena Cemetery, rather than pony up for two stately coffins and a decent Christian burial.

Father Robeleda barely knew the deceased and his comments are of a generic nature, commending the good souls of Ibrahim Khalil and Maryam Khalil Mounier to the kingdom of God. There are perhaps a total of sixty people in attendance: a handful of Lebanese friends; former associates of Samir and some girlfriends of Maryam; the cook Hiba; about a dozen illustrious leaders of the Lebanese community; Maryam's tennis instructor; some high school friends who have read the obituary in *Prensa Libre* and *El Periódico*; a couple of government officials who seem nervous and impatient, including a representative from the presidency who keeps looking down at his watch. Guillermo guesses that he has another three funerals to attend that day and simply wants to get away.

There are also four men—plainclothes detectives?—sitting near Guillermo in the back, off to the side, constantly checking their cell phones.

After the priest delivers the funeral oration and says a few words about the deceased, Samir gets up and begins to speak to the guests from a lectern surrounded by glass vases with sparse flowers.

"We are gathered here today to pay homage to two wonderful people, Ibrahim Khalil and his lovely daughter Maryam, my wife, who were prematurely and unjustly murdered for reasons we may never know. For those of you who didn't know this extraordinary little family, Ibrahim came from the Levant to Guatemala in 1956 with his brother Leo to seek their fortunes in their adoptive country. They arrived with no money in their twenties, but with the desire to make their mark in the new world. Leo started a photography studio on Sixth Avenue while Ibrahim opened a fabric store in the downtown area, on Fifth. The business began modestly but continued to grow as Guatemalans realized Ibrahim was honest and reliable and worked incredibly hard. A few years later Ibrahim went to Cobán to look at a small café finca he considered purchasing and met Imelda Beltrán, the pretty daughter of a papaya grower. They married in 1965. Their first child died in childbirth, but two years later, in 1970, Imelda gave birth to a lovely daughter. Maryam, whose name means *beloved*, and was also the name of Moses's sister, came into this world when Ibrahim was already thirty-six years old, and she became his pride and joy.

"When Ibrahim decided to open a textile factory, he practically gave the old store to Leo, which Leo continued to manage in Ibrahim's style until—

well, you all know what happened to this lovely downtown area. He was forced to abandon the store and moved back to Tripoli, in Lebanon. Now the whole area on Fifth Avenue is a series of cheap Chinese stores and cantinas. It breaks my heart—" Samir gasps for breath and brings tears to the eyes of many of the attendees.

"Imelda died of cancer in 1980, when Maryam was only ten years old. Ibrahim loved his daughter—he doted on her the way any proud father would, and gave her whatever she needed to grow up a loving girl, one without a mother.

"I don't need to tell you that Maryam was completely devoted to her father and, in fact, had lunch with him every week, especially when Ibrahim began to suffer from vertigo, which made it impossible for him to drive. She would pick him up at the office in the factory by Roosevelt Hospital every Wednesday and bring him to our apartment for lunch. The devotion she showed to Ibrahim was beyond dispute.

"And it was during one of these lunchtime pickups that I lost my wife and my father-in-law in a cowardly attack. As I said earlier, we may never know the motives for their murder, but we do know we have lost two remarkable human beings—" Samir becomes overwhelmed with tears again, and the priest holds him, then escorts him down to his seat in the front row.

It is clear to Guillermo that the priest is in a rush to finish the service. He now knows why. One of the government officials is circling a finger in the air, as if to tell him to wrap it up. Glancing across the pews, Father Reboleda asks the mourners if anyone else wants to say something.

Guillermo is shocked by the silence, by the fact that no one—absolutely no one—gets up and speaks a word about Ibrahim or Maryam. Maybe it would have been different if Samir had gotten a Lebanese Maronite priest to lead the service.

Few of the mourners know of Guillermo's existence, and he suspects that Samir will be angry if his wife's lover gets up to speak—even if he were the only one to know of his role in Maryam's life. But little by little, Guillermo is realizing that, with his love gone, he has nothing to lose. He looks at the statue of Christ at the rear of the altar and shakes his head. He then stands up and walks down the central aisle of the church and up the steps to the lectern. He wants the audience to know that Ibrahim was an honest man and that Maryam was an exceptional human being, a person who was cultured and educated, who read the *Economist* while many of her girlfriends read *Vanidades*.

He glances at Maryam's urn and gasps. Tears begin to choke him and he is unable to speak. A church beadle approaches him with some tissues, and whispers a few words in his ears, trying to help him regain his composure. Guillermo glances at Samir, who is sitting hunched and silent; he knows that he can't confess his love for Maryam in front of her supposedly grieving husband and friends, but he does want to say a few words about the woman he has just lost. To some degree it will be an open confession, and he realizes he needs to focus his remarks more on the death of his friend Ibrahim.

Guillermo grabs the lectern with both hands to steady himself. Finally he begins to speak: "As some of you know, I was Ibrahim Khalil's private attorney. He had many legal counselors to handle his varied interests: a real estate lawyer, a tax lawyer, and even a corporate lawyer who handled the petty suits that were filed against him each year by aggrieved employees and customers. I had a special distinction: I was his privileged friend and his personal lawyer. I also happened to work with him on issues related to his appointment to the Banurbano advisory board—I will talk about that more, later, but I want to say that I was more than a lawyer: I considered Ibrahim a close friend.

"I can assure you that in the coming weeks I will provide you with new, uncontroverted evidence supporting the revelation—I won't call it a theory—that Ibrahim and Maryam were murdered. While I was aware of some rumors regarding Ibrahim's purchase of textiles and cloth from Germany and England, I believe these were a smoke screen perpetrated by his true assassins. When I have gathered the appropriate evidence, you will hear the truth. I will provide proof that he was on the verge of exposing dozens of questionable if not illegal transactions at Banurbano involving elected officials at the highest level of government—perhaps going as high as the president himself."

Guillermo glances down at the mourners who are staring blankly back at him, almost as if he were lecturing to them in Chinese. At the same time, he realizes he is saying too much. There are individuals in attendance who may have vested interest in his accusations, like the four men sitting in the back.

"But this is not what I meant to say at this memorial service. Some of you may know that through my friendship with Ibrahim, I had the privilege of meeting his daughter Maryam." Guillermo nods his head to Samir, who now sits straight up in the first row of the pews, immutable as a Mayan stela, without an expression on his face.

"Because of the legal advice I provided Ibrahim, I was able to lunch with him and Maryam many times. She was a beautiful woman, gracious and intelligent, with a fierce commitment to the care of her father and, if I may add, her husband. As Samir Mounier has stated, she was Ibrahim's sole support after his own wife died from cancer. She was selflessly dedicated to ensuring both his health and his happiness. She was a lovely human being with a heart of gold."

Guillermo begins wiping away tears. His heart aches so much that he is afraid he will actually confess his love for Maryam to the mourners. He has to find a way to finish.

"In closing, I only want to ask all of you to remember the goodness of Ibrahim's and Maryam's souls. Let's not forget their dedication, not only to one another, but to all the friends and acquaintances gathered here today. It was our privilege to know them. They were among those few Guatemalans dedicated to justice, law, and truthfulness. In contrast, our leaders are dedicated to amassing personal wealth at the expense of people like Ibrahim who would dare to clean up the filth of their government."

Guillermo knows he should stop now, but he can't—rage has gotten control of him. "To honor Maryam and Ibrahim, I want to ask each and every one of you to combat the lethargy that has delivered our once wonderful country into the hands of drug dealers, thieves, and murderers. I know I am risking my life by saying this, but my friends were killed like dogs because they were standing in the way of those who want to continue laundering ill-gotten money—"

With tears blinding his eyes, Guillermo cannot speak anymore—and he shouldn't. He makes his way back down the steps of the altar. Hands are clapping loudly, and there's a palpable stirring of emotion in the church for the first time. Guillermo has struck a nerve and everyone is feeling it.

The priest returns to the lectern and delivers a few closing comments about devoting one's life to Jesus Christ. Religion has never seemed so hollow to Guillermo as now. As if useless prayers can erase the loss that he and many in the audience feel.

The service has come to an end, and the public mourning of Ibrahim and Maryam is about to expire.

Guillermo sits alone in the last pew as people file out of the church. He hadn't seen her in attendance, but Hiba comes over and hugs him with real feeling.

"You were her guiding star," she whispers before hurrying out.

All this time he was sure she hated him. He wants to run after her but realizes how absurd it would look. He stays seated, with the odd dignity reserved for honest people who speak their minds despite the consequences.

He can't imagine her sticking with Samir, now that Maryam is gone. Guillermo feels a bit vindicated, though he is suddenly seized by the desperate finality of it all. He walks down the nave toward Samir, who has gotten up from his seat and is talking with the priest. There is an unidentifiable smirk on his face—could he actually be happy? Guillermo wants to grab him by the shoulders and punch him in the face. Repeatedly.

A well-dressed man steps out of the third row of pews and offers his hand. "I was impressed by what you had to say." He is a balding man in his early sixties, but in excellent shape, judging by the way he fills out the jacket of his dark blue suit. Guillermo is certain they have never met, but he looks familiar, as though he has seen his face in one of the newspapers, or on television.

"Miguel Paredes, at your service."

"Guillermo Rosensweig."

Miguel smiles. "Of course, I know exactly who you are."

Guillermo feels embarrassed. "Yes, of course."

"You know, you only hinted at it, but I agree there's something here that makes no sense. You almost get the feeling that Ibrahim and Maryam's deaths are part of a larger plot. And it's certainly discouraging that both the husband and the government representatives are more than willing to sweep the Khalils' remains under the rug, as if they were dust." Paredes is not a particularly handsome man, but his gift of gab gives him charisma.

"I only said what my heart and mind told me to say," Guillermo replies by way of explanation.

"May I be blunt with you, Mr. Rosensweig?"

"Of course. And call me Guillermo."

"Well, Guillermo, some of us believe that your client and his daughter were definitely assassinated and that the murderers are being protected by the government and the Banurbano board of directors—just as you implied."

Guillermo stares at Miguel. He wears turtle-shell glasses and has a large nose that twists to the side. He has sharp, hooded crow eyes, unsentimental and prone to blinking in a kind of nervous twitch, black and hard as obsidian, and unusually mesmerizing. His long arms hang to his sides as he speaks. He is grandfatherly, but his bulk suggests that he boxed or lifted weights when he was younger. Guillermo is immediately taken in by him, even seduced. Miguel reminds him of his old friend Juancho—or what he might have looked like had he taken up weights and lived into his sixties. He wants to trust this man.

"And you base your accusations on?"

"Some of the same information you have just alluded to. But you know, we should find another place to discuss this," Miguel says, glancing around the church. "Are you in a rush?"

"A rush to do what? Clean my apartment?"

"Why don't we go over to Café Europa on 11th Street where we can talk a bit more openly. It's my treat."

Guillermo nods. The two urns, weighing approximately two kilos each, will be placed in the wall of the church crypt at the Verbena Cemetery. He doesn't want to stay to see this, and he can't imagine going back to his office or apartment. He could call his children but he doubts they would neutralize his gloom. In reality, if it weren't for this man's invitation, he would go to some random bar, get stinking drunk, and weep.

## CHAPTER NINETEEN

# PLAY IT AGAIN, SAM!

**G**uillermo imagines that drinks with Miguel Paredes might produce some very interesting information as they walk single file down Sixth Avenue to Café Europa. It's a short walk, but there are dozens of street vendors blocking both the sidewalks and access into the stores selling the cheapest conceivable merchandise: plastic dishes, generic electronics, shoes made of synthetic materials. Guillermo remembers when Sixth Avenue was the epitome of elegance, when he used to "sextear" with his friends: ogle the legs of the young secretaries as they walked to work in the adjoining buildings. But not anymore. There is talk that Mayor Aroz is considering turning Sixth Avenue into a pedestrian mall, but that may be years away.

They take a corner table on the second floor of Café Europa overlooking the Rey Sol Restaurant. It is the kind of bar that is perfect for discreet conversation: few customers, tables set apart; the ideal atmosphere for loners who want to drown their sorrows or talk without fear of being overheard. It has no charm: it simply is.

Miguel orders a black tea and some champurradas for himself while Guillermo orders a Cuba libre—rum and Coke—which is fast becoming his preferred anesthetic.

"So what do you have to say that requires so much privacy?"

"Guillermo, you are a typical lawyer, aren't you?"

"Why do you say that?"

Miguel waits for the waiter to put down their drinks before continuing:

"You don't like to waste time on niceties or idle chatter, do you? I noticed that in your comments at the church. You cut to the chase!"

"Well, usually I am a busy man," Guillermo says.

"And suddenly you don't seem so busy."

Guillermo doesn't really want to talk about himself. "And who are you, Mr. Paredes? How do you fit in? I mean, why were you at the church? Ibrahim never mentioned you. I doubt you are a family friend." He jiggles the glass in his hand, takes a huge gulp, and winces.

Miguel leans back in his chair and breaks off a tip of a cookie and dips it in his tea. "Well, I have held many positions and have done many things in my life. For years I worked as a business consultant providing firms with the necessary information and documentation required for government approval. You could say I was a facilitator who made sure entrepreneurs had the proper business permits to avoid too much government scrutiny—not that there ever was any."

"I do a lot of that for my clients. I guess we are both facilitators."

The waiter comes back with a small wire basket of chips and peanuts and sets it in front of them.

Guillermo orders another Cuba libre, grabs his half-empty glass, and clinks it against Miguel's teacup, saying: "To the truth."

"To the truth," Miguel echoes.

Guillermo takes a final slug of his drink and uses his tongue to coax the liquid from the remaining ice cubes. "So from what you tell me, I surmise you were or are the necessary go-between for the Guatemalan way of doing business. The master of the soborno, the mordida. The bribe."

Miguel laughs. "Not a very elegant way of describing what I have been doing for so many years, Guillermo. As I said earlier, I prefer to think of myself as a facilitator who made things happen." He blinks his crow eyes several times. "I made sure things worked out smoothly, with minimum expense and delay. I still am a facilitator, only I don't need a fully staffed, separate office to do that. You could say that I have downsized, and am now working more independently."

"The grand facilitator has become an elegant independent contractor, it seems to me. And where do you work from now?"

Miguel lowers his eyes till they rest on his gabardine suit. He is wearing an Armani, a lovely blue outfit with the slightest of sheens. "Well, I do own a men's clothing store in the Fontabella Mall in the Zona Viva. Maybe you have passed by Raoul's. It's on the second floor, near the Sophos Bookstore, where I sometimes stop to purchase a book on history and have my tea—a better kind of café than this, I must say."

Guillermo laughs at the way Miguel tilts his teacup. "I can imagine. I've eaten at several of the restaurants on the first floor of Fontabella, but I don't really have time to read books . . . Your store must be lovely. Well beyond my means, I'm sure." Guillermo's second drink arrives, and he attacks it more gingerly now that his head has begun to spin.

"I don't know about that. We have suits for all budgets. And the shirts we sell are custom-made by our own tailors, and much cheaper than those you can order from fancy stores in Miami or New York. If you know where to buy your silk and Egyptian cotton, by the bolt, custom-made shirts need not be so expensive. Well, yes, you can't compare the price to the store-bought kind. But if you consider the difference between a shirt made by a Guatemalan tailor and one made in a sweatshop in Hunan Province, the price is decent. I must tell you, though, that my store is not my sole source of income. It is more or less a hobby."

Guillermo is warming up to Miguel. He appreciates his unpretentiousness, which also reminds him of Juancho. He is less impressed, however, by Miguel's volubility, which renders the simplest declarations circuitous. Without intending to, Guillermo has raised his eyebrows as if the conversation were boring him.

Paredes gets the hint and says, "I am sure you are wondering why I asked you here."

Guillermo smiles.

"As I said before, I am still a kind of facilitator. I can make things happen. I enjoy playing that role, but not if it involves filling out forms, waiting weeks to have meetings, and getting permissions for others. I prefer to be an independent contractor. It gives me the opportunity to ensure that the right kinds of transactions take place quickly. Speed has become a kind of obsession for me." He pauses.

"How interesting. You sound like a track star educated at the University of Heidelberg."

Miguel is smiling. "Thank you, but I was educated at the University of Life."

Guillermo laughs, but presses on: "So you clearly have a set of favored transactions."

"Yes, and the best transactions also help me accumulate knowledge."

"What can knowledge bring you? More money?"

"I knew you would ask me that. Each bit of information is like a piece in a puzzle. When you first look at it, it's unique but indistinct. Sure, it is colored and shaped, but initially you have no idea how it will fit together with another piece of information. But if you turn it around, looking at it close up and then from a distance, you will know exactly where to put it. In time, all the pieces will fit together, and you will have a very clear picture of things. And that can become extremely profitable."

"It's that easy?" Guillermo wants to be cordial, but he isn't buying Miguel's metaphor.

"My friend," Miguel says, taking a sip from his tea, "in my line of business, as in yours, knowledge is a valuable commodity. When that knowledge or information becomes actionable, it gives you lots of power. Let me give you an example. Did you know that there are several video cameras at the front of Ibrahim Khalil's office and factory?"

"I've seen the one at the entrance to the building," Guillermo says indifferently.

"I am not talking about that one. I mean the ones attached to the guardhouse, which captured the events outside the textile factory on the day of the murders."

Guillermo is now swirling the ice of his second drink in his mouth. "What could they possibly show? Maryam's car arriving and waiting? Ibrahim walking through the gate and getting into the car? The Mercedes driving away? The murder took place six blocks away."

"So many questions, but I venture to say that the tape shows a lot more." Miguel pauses. "But you have to want it."

Guillermo runs a hand through his sparse hair. "In that case, I believe the police might be interested in seeing it. Personally, yes, I would like to get hold of it. Maybe I can see Maryam alive for one last time."

"I already have the tape in my possession."

"How did you—"

"Guillermo, in my line of business the question is never how or why something is done, but what it shows and how you can use it."

"So what are you getting at?"

"It is a very interesting tape. Extremely interesting. It is what I would call a piece of *actionable information*. Would you like to see it?"

"Of course."

"Then let's go," Paredes says, taking a huge bite of the champurrada and standing up.

"Right now?"

"You have your car?"

"Parked at the lot on 13th Street. Near the post office."

Miguel waves at the waiter to bring him the bill.

"Meet me at my store in twenty minutes. The Fontabella garage entrance is on 12th Street between Third and Fourth avenues."

"Can't I give you a ride?" Guillermo is drunk enough that a little company in the car might help steady his driving.

Miguel shakes his head. "My chauffeur is downstairs waiting for me."

"How did he know where we were going?"

"I never go anywhere without my driver. See you there," says Miguel, changing his mind about waiting for the bill. Instead, he simply puts three hundred quetzales on the table.

Guillermo wobbles over to his car at the 13th Street lot and drives down to Tenth Avenue, where he turns toward the Zona Viva. The traffic is dense, all first- and second-gear driving, until he reaches Villa Olimpica and Mateos Flores National Stadium where he's finally able to get into third gear. He guns the accelerator and races down the ravine next to the stadium, not letting up until he reaches the blue polytechnic school, the Justo Rufino Barrios statue, and the old Casa Crema on Reforma Boulevard. He loves all these landmarks, still standing, on some level belying the fact that Guatemala City has devolved over the years into chaos.

He turns left on 12th Street in Zone 10 and drives past the Mercure Casa Veranda Hotel, where he once spent a weekend cavorting with Araceli. The parking lot entrance to the Fontabella Mall is a few blocks north. He turns in, drives slowly down the ramp, and finds a parking spot next to a post, which he grazes, lightly scraping the fender of his car. Given his state of inebriation, the dent is small potatoes.

On the way to the elevator, he passes a blue Hyundai and jumps. He remembers seeing one the first time he met Maryam at the Centro Vasco. There must be hundreds of them in Guatemala. But still, why here?

He looks inside the Hyundai, but it's empty.

Guillermo stumbles into the elevator that will bring him to the mall lobby. From the lobby he takes the escalator to the second floor. Raoul's is down the corridor from the Sophos Bookstore, as Miguel indicated, in a hidden corner. The display windows show only the finest of clothes, tastefully arranged on lifelike mannequins. The store could be on Coral Gables' Miracle Mile or even on Michigan Avenue in Chicago. But now it's totally empty except for the one salesman sitting on a stool facing out from the display counter. He absentmindedly files his nails.

As soon as Guillermo walks in, a bell sounds. The salesman looks up, but doesn't move. Miguel comes out of a door in back, by the dressing rooms, and signals for Guillermo to join him in his office.

To his surprise, Paredes's office is all computer screens and file cabinets—no trace of the ledgers or cloth swatches that befit a haberdashery. Instead, it resembles the headquarters, the huge central brain, of an extensive informational spy network. Clearly Raoul's is a front for some other kind of business.

"Take a seat here," Miguel gestures to a gray swivel chair facing a huge Mac computer screen.

As soon as Guillermo sits down, Miguel moves the cursor over to a still open video window and clicks *play*. "Watch now," he says.

The black-and-white film is very grainy, but despite his drunkenness, Guillermo recognizes the driveway leading up to the guardhouse and the parking lot of Ibrahim's textile factory. There's a light-colored car near the top of the screen, which is not moving. There's no way to read the license plate from this distance. For four or five seconds everything seems frozen, then a man steps out of the parked car and looks down toward the guard-house through binoculars, though the distance is less than twenty feet. He gets back into the car, and about two minutes later does the same thing, only this time he appears startled and quickly gets back into his car.

Miguel is leaning over Guillermo. "That man's a lookout. Watch the next part very carefully."

Guillermo glances up at him, not understanding.

"No, no, don't take your eyes off the screen!"

Guillermo lowers his eyes back down just in time to see a black Mercedes come into view. He feels a pain in his chest as he recognizes Maryam's car, and his eyes well up. The car's moving very slowly, much more slowly than Maryam would normally drive, even in a blurry video. Whenever she picks up her father, she turns the car around by the chain-link fence so she can drive away as soon as he comes down. This time, the car stops about ten feet from the factory and office door, which will force her father to walk over gravel to her. Five seconds later, a man steps into the camera's view and moves slowly toward the car.

"That's Ibrahim!" Guillermo shouts incredulously, as if the man was still alive.

"What's surprising about that?"

"Nothing, really. It's just strange to see him alive like this, walking toward the car, toward my Maryam." Guillermo realizes what he has confessed, but he's beyond censoring his words.

"Look, *look*, Guillermo. Tell me if you see anything strange."

Guillermo does not enjoy Miguel's warm, stale breath on his neck, but he's totally mesmerized by what's happening on the computer screen. It's almost like he is there, witnessing the event in real life, or on reality TV.

Guillermo sees the car inch up a few more feet and stop dead. Instead of getting into the car as Ibrahim normally does, he places his forearms on the door and looks in as the passenger window rolls down. From this angle there is no way to see the driver.

A conversation ensues. How strange. Why doesn't he just get into the car? Guillermo can only see Ibrahim's right shoulder. Suddenly he notices what looks like a dark blob moving in the backseat, blocking the light from the back window for a fraction of a second. Either the passenger headrest has been raised or there is someone in the backseat.

"What's that shadow?"

"Look, Guillermo. Look."

Ibrahim raises his shoulders, opens the door, and sits down in his usual place. A few seconds go by as he puts on his seat belt, and then the car makes a right-angle turn and drives off slowly, back the way it came. At one point it is no more than ten feet from the car parked on the side of the road. About five seconds after Maryam's car disappears from the camera's view, the light-colored car whips around, throwing up a cloud of dust, and follows. For another ten seconds nothing can be seen but the driveway, the same edge of the guardhouse, and the cloud of dust rising from the pebbly ground and disappearing into the air. Then the view is frozen, there is no movement, and the screen turns black.

"You can play it again if you'd like. Move the cursor over the *replay* button and click." Miguel shuffles away.

"There was someone tailing Maryam," says Guillermo. It's obvious to him that something made Ibrahim hesitate before stepping into the vehicle— perhaps there were three people inside—but for now he says nothing.

Miguel comes up to him with two goblets in his hand. "I think we both need this. Zacapa Añejo rum, twenty-three years old. It's like drinking a Hennessey XO."

Guillermo takes his goblet in his trembling hand and swallows it in one gulp. Another man who has been in the office the whole time—Miguel's driver?—comes over with a bottle in his hand and refills Guillermo's goblet.

"Just click on the button and the video will play."

Guillermo watches the video again and discovers nothing new or strange.

He keeps wondering if there's someone else in the backseat, and believes Maryam may not be the driver.

After his third run-through (by this time, Miguel has sat down in another swivel chair beside him), Guillermo pushes back from the table. Miguel asks him if he has seen anything at all that might shed some light on who was in the light-colored car.

"The image isn't very clear. And the camera's too far away to read the license plate. In fact, I can't even tell what kind of car it is."

"The guard thought it might have been a Nissan; a Japanese or Korean car for sure."

"That's what Fulgencio said? I don't know. Too grainy for me to see."

"Anything else?" Miguel persists. "Anything that surprised you?"

Guillermo sits back in his chair. By now he has had three glasses of Zacapa in addition to the two rums he had at Café Europa, and his head is whirling out of control. Even as he talks, he replays the tape in his head. He has seen a couple of things that don't make sense. He's wavering, but finally decides to reveal his doubts to Miguel, whom he is beginning to embrace as a kind of guardian angel or a kindred soul.

"You know that I came down with Ibrahim several times from his office and joined him with Maryam before returning to work at his office in the afternoon. Never in all those occasions did I see Maryam stop the car short and wait for her father to come to her. And certainly Maryam would never roll down the window and speak to her father from the driver's seat while he stood outside in the sun. He would simply get into the car, and she would drive away."

"So what does that tell you?"

"I don't know. It's a bit crazy, but maybe Maryam wasn't the person driving."

Guillermo signals for Miguel to watch the tape with him for a fourth time. When he gets to the part where Ibrahim is about to step into the car, he stops the tape. "Take a look into the car. For an instant you'll see a dark blob block the sunlight from the back. It's as if someone in the backseat suddenly sits up for a split second and then lies back down."

Miguel takes the tape off pause and it begins rolling again. It all happens very quickly. There is little to see, nothing more than a strobe blocking a spot of light. It doesn't seem significant to him, not enough of a clue to matter. "You are seeing things, Guillermo. Sometimes your mind wants your eyes to see something that's not really there."

"It's there, all right." Guillermo rubs his face with both hands. "I know what I know."

"What would a third person in the car mean? And who would that person be?"

"I said I don't know."

"Think, man!"

"Her husband Samir," Guillermo lies. "Maybe he came along to watch them die!"

Miguel pauses, then touches Guillermo's neck. "My dear man, you're consumed by grief. I only showed you this tape so you could see the unmarked car. The killing was set up, but not by Samir. I know you were in love with Maryam, and that she wanted to leave her husband to marry you, but you can't let this passion of yours confuse you."

Without opening his eyes, Guillermo shakes his head. "How do you know these things about me? We kept our affair an absolute secret."

"My friend, there was no other way to interpret your comments at the memorial service. Anyone would have guessed you were sad over the death of your client, but grief-stricken over the death of his daughter. If Samir Mounier wanted Ibrahim and Maryam killed, he wouldn't be lying down in the backseat. He would simply hire someone to murder them and be miles from the scene. Actionable information develops from credible evidence. I'm afraid you are not providing credible evidence. No, I suspect there's someone else who wanted to have Ibrahim killed, and had the means and the connections to plan it. That's where we must look to find the murderers. Maryam, as much as you loved her, was collateral damage. She was never the target. Once the assassins planned to kill Ibrahim, the death of his daughter became just one more unfortunate piece of news."

"But what if Samir wanted them both killed?"

Miguel scratches his chin. "It's fair to assume Samir may have wanted

Maryam killed to prevent her from getting together with you. I know you separated from your own wife and children months ago, and that they're living in Mexico City with her uncle. Only *you* know if Maryam would have ever left her husband. It's also true that with Ibrahim dead, Samir will now inherit the factory and the business, which will make him a very rich man, but I don't find any of this likely."

Guillermo drops his head onto the desk. He's tired. And drunk. Moreover, he's angry, full of hate, and quite confused. He glances up at Miguel, who has a knowing look on his face.

"You've set me up for this. You went to the funeral service hoping I would be there so you could talk to me afterward."

"Guillermo, I did no such thing."

"You had this tape ready for me, ready to roll as soon as I walked in."

"It's true. I was hoping someone would say something that would make me want to show him this tape, but I didn't know it would be you. Not today. I was planning to call you at your office in a couple of days and invite you to lunch."

"You know so much about me."

"Yes," Miguel says, putting a tender hand on Guillermo's shoulder. "But I know much about a lot of things. It's my business to do so. Here, let me help you get up. I will have my men accompany you. They can drive you and your car home."

## CHAPTER TWENTY

# JIMMY CRACKED CORN, AND I DON'T CARE

**I**n the weeks that follow there's a big brouhaha as the president appoints a special independent prosecutor to investigate the deaths of Ibrahim and Maryam Khalil. Since Miguel is the only one in possession of the tape, the query is nothing more than feathers flying in the hen house with no trace of the fox. The prosecutor assembles a team of investigators to study the circumstances of this double homicide and uncover the actual assassins. But since no one ever really wants to know what's happening or has happened in Guatemala, the investigation resembles a 1920s silent movie in which a dog chases its own tail for forty minutes.

Every week dozens of dead bodies appear in Guatemala City: corpses in alleys, in ravines, on street corners, at bus stops, and even inside of city buses, mostly at night. Of every hundred deaths, the police and detective squads are able to bring one or two culprits to justice. And even in these instances, those found guilty are often merely the hired hands of the true agents of the murder.

All this begins to gnaw on Guillermo, like some undiagnosed bacteria. This, together with the immense loss he feels, is enough to debilitate him. His only remaining purpose in life is to find those responsible for the death of his love.

He becomes obsessed with the idea of impunity, that crimes can be committed and proof presented, but nothing done because the judge is paid off to render any concrete evidence inadmissible or tainted. He begins to see impunity everywhere: in people throwing garbage on the streets and driving off; horns sounding near hospitals; screaming in churches; people blowing smoke in your face on the street; moviegoers cutting in line to get the best seats; people tossing cigarette butts in restaurant glasses . . . everything revealing the absence of consequences.

Guillermo actually longs for the days of armed conflict when the guerrillas were the clear enemy, setting fire to Guatemala, The Land of Eternal Spring. Back then Ríos Montt and his lapdog Pérez Molina vowed to establish military order by using a heartless slash-and-burn policy. What were they expected to do? Play footsies with the guerrillas? Turn the country over to bearded thugs and masses of barefoot Indians supporting them?

What is happening now, with no distinct enemy, is more unnerving.

He knows for a fact that Ibrahim and Maryam have been unjustly eliminated and that no one, not even Maryam's very own husband, cares why or how it happened.

The only one who seems to care is Miguel Paredes, and he is an expert at manipulation. He drops clues like bread crumbs to a starving man. Every time Guillermo's desire to bring the murderers to justice flags, Miguel is there, ready to share some tasty tidbit to pique his interest. It is uncanny how this happens. Miguel, the master operator, knows exactly what to do and when to do it, and Guillermo obeys like a trained seal.

Very often the two men meet in the late afternoon at the Sophos Bookstore café. They like one table in particular, the one that looks over the patio below. It is in a corner and just steps away from the bathroom. As far as they know, the store is free of cameras.

The bookstore café fills with shoppers and writers, drinking lattes and macchiatos, ordering thin slices of pecan or lemon pie. Mild classical music plays softly from speakers in the background. It is the perfect venue for their conversations, much more so than Café Europa downtown, which is probably bugged. And meeting in such a quiet, sedate place gives their discussions a hint of respectability, as if all their dialogues about sinister plots and hired hands were legitimate possibilities.

In this setting, Guillermo orders a bottle of red wine and reveals everything he knows about the shenanigans of Banurbano. Miguel is more than happy to let his new friend talk as if to a father confessor. Guillermo feels that a load is being lifted from his shoulders and his heart as he's allowed to speak openly about things he has held hidden. He repeats his theory that there was a third person in the car, but Miguel is not convinced. It doesn't really matter: Guillermo is no longer the only person who knows what he knows, and this provides relief.

Within two weeks of the church service, Miguel Paredes finally feels confident enough to discuss with Guillermo his master plan: he lets the proverbial cat, which has been mewling and scratching more vigorously than ever, out of the bag.

"We need to consider that the government is behind Ibrahim's death."

"That's what I've been trying to tell you! The question is *why*."

"To shut him up."

"The president wouldn't sink so low as to commit murder to silence an opponent."

Miguel touches his friend's hand. "Oh, but he would. Ibrahim's investigations into the Banurbano accounts were making a lot of people uncomfortable. I wouldn't be surprised if the president and his lovely wife were responsible for the murders. Guillermo, did you notice how quickly the special prosecutor disbanded his group of investigators? Ten days of investigation, no postmortem, no subpoenas of the files that you and Ibrahim have accumulated, no inquiry into the dropped calls and threatening messages. Whoever was behind this wanted the investigation to end. And you, my friend, are the only one who cares enough about the truth to change things."

"Did you ever show anyone in the administration or the police the security tape?"

"Are you joking? Why would I? They would simply confiscate it and force me to provide them with every copy of the tape at the risk of death. I am brave, but not so brave as to smile down the barrel of a gun."

A sober Guillermo Rosensweig would never have fallen for this ploy, but the absence of Maryam amplifies his sense of hopelessness. To counter his desperation, he takes a weekend trip to spend time with his children, who are now living in Mexico's fancy Chimalistac district. The first thing he notices is that the teenagers are happy to be out of the butcher shop Guatemala has become, and are even resentful they didn't move to Mexico earlier. They treat him with a certain coldness. The major issue for them is not the death of his girlfriend, but his own betrayal.

He wants nothing more than for his children to tell him about their lives, to feel close to him, to offer hugs and kisses. When he takes them for a Sunday lunch at the San Ángel Inn, he realizes that his children care more for the macaw repeating words and phrases in the main dining area than about his grief. Truth be told, they find his mourning, his propensity for tears, embarrassing if not morbid.

Guillermo takes the TACA flight back to Guatemala City in a state of utter resignation: he finally understands he is all alone now.

His only recompense is to drink himself to sleep every night. Every single night.

# CHAPTER TWENTY-ONE

# THE VAPORIZING FOLDER

After two weeks, the special prosecutor appointed by the president delivers a report claiming that Ibrahim was either killed by an ex-employee for having been fired or by a contrabandist he had double-crossed in a sketchy textile purchase. Maryam's death, in either case, is ruled accidental, collateral damage, the result of being in the wrong place at the wrong time.

"That's what the government claims," says Miguel. "It's always easier to blame the victims, who are unable to defend themselves. Don't you think?" He and Guillermo are talking in his office, where the privacy is greatest and the liquor most abundant.

"This is a major cover-up," Guillermo agrees. "The regime fed the prosecutor these findings so he wouldn't discover the documents Ibrahim and I were prepared to release. Banurbano *was* making illegal loans to the friends of the president and his wife. It's a cover-up, a cover-up, a cover-up."

"Maybe you can share some of that information with the press, Guillermo. You know I have friends at *Prensa Libre* and *El Periódico* who would be more than happy to publish any information you have to discredit the president."

"I don't want to talk to anyone. Tell them yourself and say I'm a reliable source."

Miguel shakes his head. "Everyone knows I've opposed the president since before his election. For years I have been considered either a malcontent or an unreliable source of information. You, on the other hand, are completely credible and trustworthy. You are a forthright citizen. You might just give them copies of some of the documents . . ."

Though Guillermo and Ibrahim had sworn to one another not to discuss their findings with anyone until they were certain their accusations could be corroborated, the older man's death changes the equation. Guillermo can use Miguel's connections to reveal what they had uncovered; there's no point in keeping it hidden. He needs help, lots of it, and Miguel's press contacts could supply it.

"Well, I know for a fact that Ibrahim warned certain Cobán coffee barons that they needed to return the interest-free loans Banurbano had given them or he would report them to the newspapers. Remember, these funds are supposed to help thousands of entrepeneurs, not a handful of moguls. Ibrahim was enraged. And it didn't stop there. He discovered some unusual bank transfers to a Canadian nickel-mining company operating out of Alta Verapaz."

"Where's the proof?"

Guillermo squirms in his seat. "I don't have any. Ibrahim would never let me make copies. The documents exist, but they are probably locked in his private office."

"You mean that even though you were working together and you were his personal lawyer, the old buzzard didn't trust you enough to give you duplicates?"

"I wouldn't characterize it as mistrust. Ibrahim was paranoid. He didn't fully trust anyone, not even Maryam. Let me backtrack—he trusted Maryam with his life, but he did not want to share any information with her. I imagine it was to protect her, in case he revealed things that put his life, and therefore hers, in jeopardy."

"That's too bad—I mean the part about not giving you copies."

"Had he told her, she never would have said a peep, not even to Samir. That much I know!"

"Well, he loved his daughter and despised his son-in-law. Who wouldn't? He's a freeloader."

Guillermo is surprised once again that Miguel knows so many personal details about Ibrahim, Maryam, and Samir, though he has said many times that his work as a facilitator gives him access to information. Guillermo Googled Miguel once but found no useful information about him, as though he never existed. All this makes him feel more lonely and despondent. He needs someone trustworthy in his life to help alleviate his depression. He can't turn to Araceli or Isabel, both of whom he cut off rather abruptly. This leaves Miguel.

"I'm sure Maryam would never have betrayed Ibrahim to Samir, whom she had begun to detest. But you know all this! Samir was twenty-five years older than Maryam. She married him when she was twenty-four because she was desperate; he claimed to be rich. Besides, the Khalils and the Mouniers were both from the same clan in Sidon, Lebanon. But her allegiance was always to her father, not her husband. Ibrahim didn't fully trust me and I was his fucking lawyer!"

Guillermo isn't making much sense and Miguel wants to stay on point. "So you don't have *any* of these documents?"

"No, none. None at all."

"And do you think he would have brought any home?"

"I don't think so. He lived alone with a maid who came in at nine and left at six. I think he kept everything important in a locked file in his office."

"Do you know where?" Miguel asks offhandedly.

"In a drawer on the right-hand side of his desk."

"Not in a safe? Are you sure?"

"Absolutely. As soon as I'd come into his office, he would unlock the drawer and bring out two bulging manila folders. And before we would leave, he would place these same folders in that same drawer and lock it."

"Well, those folders have vaporized."

"How do you know?" Guillermo may be despondent and alcoholic, but not asleep.

"You won't be upset with me?"

He stares at Miguel. When Guillermo reaches this man's age, he wants to be retired, playing tennis or golf every day, not operating a men's clothing store as a front for clandestine activities. The facilitator wants to come across as sheepishly innocent. Still, there's something about him that makes

Guillermo suspect he might be a wolf in sheep's clothing. In Guatemala so many people fit this bill that you simply have to navigate through the layers of deception and trust somebody, even if that somebody might one day betray you.

"Of course not," says Guillermo, realizing he and Miguel are becoming increasingly frank, almost wedded to one another.

"The night after Ibrahim and Maryam were killed, I sent some men to break into his office to see if we could find the folders. We searched everywhere—in his desk, the closets, behind paintings, even under the rugs—but found nothing."

Guillermo is full of questions. "But how did you even know those folders existed? Supposedly, we were the only two who had perused them. Did you know each other?"

"In a manner of speaking."

"I can't believe this! I thought I was the only one who knew."

Miguel backs off. "We crossed paths a few times at various meetings, but we were not intimate. Let me put it this way: we were professional colleagues. I was given the information that someone had copied some of the Banurbano files. I suspected it was Ibrahim, but honestly, this was pure intuition on my part."

"So you had to break into his office to see if he was the one duplicating files?" Guillermo is alternately startled and furious at this revelation. He is slowly realizing that Ibrahim had duped him as well, claiming he had no other dancing partner.

"Oh, my dear Guillermo, I've built up my network over the last twenty-five years precisely *not* to be surprised—like you were by the existence of the video. I don't like surprises. I have planted dozens of sources in Guatemala to keep me informed of things: they are cheap to hire, and when I need information, I get it. As you know, Ibrahim's factory has continued operating since his death under the supervision of a court-appointed manager. But did you know Samir is already moving ahead to take over ownership of it? You know very little about me. In time you will know more. Suffice it to say that I have been gathering and supplying information to generals and presidents going back twenty-three years—even to Vinicio Cerezo's administration. You could say that in my role as facilitator I double as a kind of senior ambassador without an office."

Guillermo is beginning to understand. "So you were a colleague of Ibrahim's. This is why you were at the memorial service at the San Francisco Church."

"Anyone can walk into a church. I wanted to pay my respects. But then you gave your speech: I loved it! I knew I had to meet you. Your eulogy revealed to me not only your passion, but your loyalty. Yes, I have known about you for many years, long before you began working with Ibrahim. I have approximately ten thousand dossiers on the most important people in Guatemala. You might say I have admired you from afar, from a distance that has varied with the passing of time."

"And what about my personal life?"

"My dear Guillermo, you're forgetting what I told you. In my line of work, nothing is strictly personal. Can I get you another rum and Coke?" He signals to his chauffeur who is monitoring screens from across the room. He looks vaguely familiar. Was he the man who was sitting in the Hyundai at the Centro Vasco that rainy afternoon?

"So you must have known that Maryam and I were having an affair."

Miguel grows silent. He adjusts his blue silk tie that has swordfish knitted into it. "I don't know the particulars about your romance, but I do know the exact date when your affair began—"

"Your driver was tailing me." Guillermo is embarrassed.

Miguel puts his hand on Guillermo's. He has beautiful hands: long fingers, scant black hair on his knuckles. They are the facilitator's loveliest features.

"How much do you know about me?"

Miguel keeps his hand still. "I know that many men would admire you for your dalliances. I know when, with whom, in which room, and exactly how many times you had sex with your different lovers at the Best Western Stofella. And I know about the apartment you rented in the Plazuela España."

Guillermo pulls his hand away, as if he has been burned by hot metal. He feels crushed, discovered, found out, revealed, standing naked with his pants down at his feet. To think that someone knew about the Stofella, the apartment in the Plazuela España.

"What about my texts?"

"We intercepted some."

"Some? Just some? And were there hidden cameras and microphones when Maryam and I made love?"

"Guillermo, you were the one who insisted on having the same room at the Stofella."

"Oh my God! I could kill you."

"Instead of looking so upset, Guillermo, you should be pleased that I respected you enough all these years to consider you both worthy of my pursuit *and* deserving of my silence."

"Araceli?"

"Araceli, Sofia, Isabel, and even Micaela, though you only slept with her twice." Miguel says this matter-of-factly.

Guillermo doesn't know how to respond. "Why were you investigating me?"

"I already told you: you were a person of interest. I have thousands of dossiers."

"Do my political views matter to you?"

"Not at all. I don't believe in politics. I dislike the president, not necessarily because of his policies, but because of his inefficiencies. He contaminates the air we breathe with his coal plant while I prefer nuclear energy. I believe we have an obligation to release less waste into the atmosphere."

Guillermo cannot believe what he's hearing. He can't get a word out.

"You know that the 1996 Peace Accords were a sham. This brought no peace, only opened the gate for Guatemala's homegrown maras to prosper, and for bloodthirsty Mexican drug dealers to buy out our police department. Now the generals and the former guerrillas can congratulate themselves for having negotiated peace, when all they agreed on was to split the foreign aid that came pouring in to help us achieve democracy."

"Miguel, I wish you would just shut up. I told you I don't care what you believe in."

"But you should."

"Okay, so where did you stand during the armed conflict?"

"Where I have always stood: on the side of order."

"And what's your attitude toward money?"

"Well, it is a very attractive and useful commodity. I would even go so far to claim that it, more than religion, motivates human action."

"And do you work for the president?"

"I dislike his inefficiencies. I already told you that. Are you even listening to me?"

"Of course I am." Unprompted, Miguel's driver delivers Guillermo another drink. He takes two huge gulps as if it was only Coca-Cola.

Miguel taps the arms of his chair. "The president and I are presently feuding, but that could change any second, depending on the decisions he makes."

"What do you mean?"

"He presents himself as incorruptible and above temptation. He conveys a smug and superior attitude when we all know that he, his wife, and her cohorts are robbing this country blind. If he were to acknowledge his humanity, all would be forgiven."

"Humanity? What a strange choice of words. Don't you mean that if he were willing to share the wealth with you and your associates, you would reconsider your attacks against him?"

"As I said before, he is like the rest of us: not above temptation."

Guillermo is shocked. He feels he is suddenly in deep water without a lifesaver. "And who else are your enemies?"

Miguel looks at him suspiciously.

"I ask you this only to understand your point of view better."

Miguel leans back in his chair. "Well, I am not a big fan of Ignacio Balicar. Or Mayor Aroz, who is making himself a billionaire by buying up all the real estate downtown so he can convert the whole area into a commercial Disneyland—that only he will own. I believe in sharing the wealth."

"So what do you want from me, Miguel?" Guillermo asks, exhausted.

"For the moment I only need your trust and devotion. Everything else will fall into place. In time you will see what I mean."

## CHAPTER TWENTY-TWO

# THE MASTERMIND, MAYBE

This last conversation convinces Guillermo that the facilitator not only has great power but even greater fluidity. Because of his dozens, perhaps hundreds of connections, Miguel has access to information that Guillermo can only dream of. The only territory Miguel cannot penetrate is his mind. Guillermo decides to be more cautious with this man. He realizes he is likely in mortal danger and if he is to survive, he has to learn restraint. The problem is that, though he knows he can survive, he isn't sure he wants to.

Each day that passes makes him realize more and more that Maryam is gone and not coming back, that without her he is nothing, not even a shadow. He is barely alive. He tries to keep in touch with his children, more for his sake than theirs, but it's obvious they really don't need him. Their great uncle has filled the vacuum of the absent father. Rosa Esther's uncle has the wealth as well as the emotional commitment to welcome them with open arms into his family.

If Ilán and Andrea were living in Guatemala, perhaps proximity would allow him the chance to rekindle their affection for him. As it is, hundreds of miles apart, his love for them is superfluous, totally expendable. He talks to them as if insulated by glass, and they are disinterested in having normal conversations with him about swimming or dance or soccer because they recognize he is not there for them.

He is alone and lonely and staring down a deep, bottomless hole. At some point he makes an appointment with his doctor to get a prescription for antidepressants. Dr. Madrid does a full examination and tells him he is in good physical shape for a man nearing fifty years of age, despite having high blood pressure. Guillermo confesses that he is drinking a lot and sleeping very little. He has panic attacks that increase his level of anxiety—that's what he wants the doctor to address.

Dr. Madrid prescribes a thirty-pill bottle of Ambien to help him sleep. He also prescribes Cymbalta, a new-generation drug similar to Prozac that will prevent suicidal impulses. He warns Guillermo not to mix these drugs with alcohol because he could provoke a stroke that could lead to temporary or permanent paralysis, or worse.

Guillermo nods, though he is not sure he can stop drinking. He is sliding down a greased hill without brakes. The jury is still out regarding his desire to live.

Nonetheless, Guillermo Rosensweig is not as simple-minded as Miguel Paredes might think. He has lied to the great facilitator: he does have a folder with copies of the documents that Ibrahim had shown him—they are locked in his apartment desk. One night, with all the lights off, he opens the drawer, takes out the folder, and places it at the bottom of his gym bag, which he covers with dirty socks. He is afraid to look at the documents either in his office or in his own apartment because he suspects that Miguel has both under surveillance. Microscopic cameras, sensors, and microphones have been planted everywhere, on the corners of walls, in the crevices, in keyholes. He is sure of it. His degree of mistrust grows when he receives phone calls in which he can't hear the caller, or the caller hangs up—he is sure that Miguel's henchmen are monitoring his whereabouts, trying to unnerve or panic him so he will do something desperate.

When he drives to his law office or visits Miguel at the Sophos Bookstore or Café Europa, he is sure he is being tailed by Korean cars of varying colors. And he imagines that complete strangers with whom he makes random eye contact are following his every move. He sees suspicious faces popping up everywhere, like bats hovering at the entrance of caves. He imagines eyes scrutinizing him at coffee shops and grocery stores. He is under surveillance even when he picks his nose.

Guillermo changes his cell phone number and for two days he does not receive any mystery calls. But then suddenly the hang-ups return.

He takes an Ambien to sleep every night and thirty milligrams of Cymbalta each morning when he wakes up. Sometimes he takes two of the latter, with a shot of rum, even though it makes him groggy and a bit nauseous in the morning. When the medicine is working he feels invincible: he wants to live and bring the guilty to justice. But it is a momentary high. He is unable to conquer the inertia that keeps him from shaking off Maryam's death and remaking his life. He is stunned by this, never having depended upon anyone to survive, not even when he was aimlessly walking the streets of Europe. Certainly he never had to rely on tiny colored pills.

And he has lost all sexual desire. He hasn't had an erection in weeks.

The medicine makes him less anxious, even jacks up his mind so that he sometimes has a clear will to live, but his heart is like a mechanical toy from which all the coils and gears have fallen.

One night he almost calls Rosa Esther to ask her if she will take him back. He is ready to move to Mexico. He is willing to chuck his lucrative law practice, all his clients and connections, to go back to his wife and children and get a decent night's sleep.

But is a good night's sleep enough reason to try to remake your life with a woman you no longer love? He nixes the idea of calling her and doubles down on another shot of rum.


Guillermo goes to see his accountant one day to see if he can get a better idea of his net worth, to see if he could possibly sell his law practice.

The accountant is not encouraging: he tells him that his firm is worth next to nothing, especially since it has continued to lose clients. Guillermo is incapable of returning phone calls whenever he finds himself in a fit of panic. He confesses to his accountant that he is sure there are people planning his demise, and perhaps even plotting to kill him. He has drafted a new will, which he asks the accountant and his secretary to witness and notarize. It is a simple will that bequeaths his total estate to his children. He wants to have everything squared away, just in case something happens to him.

Guillermo leaves his accountant feeling there's nothing that can bring him back from the brink. He has become the mastermind of nothing.

## CHAPTER TWENTY-THREE

# IT'S NOT OVER TILL IT'S OVER, OR THE FAT LADY . . .

**Guillermo learns from Rosa Esther** that his children, though happy to be living in Mexico, are having problems. Ilán worries he is not masculine enough and is teased by his classmates for not being aggressive or daring. He might be gay. Once when he was around eight and saw a particular boy's muscular chest, he told his mother that he felt excited, and that he wanted to caress the hair on the boy's arms. The feelings have continued with other boys. Andrea is treated like a social outcast; she worries that she has an untreatable case of halitosis and that her underarms reek. She wonders why none of the boys seem to like her. Both are having difficulty fitting in with kids who have known each other since nursery school.

But one thing is certain: they do not want to return to Guatemala City.

Guillermo listens to Rosa Esther's complaints and blames her for their children's indifference to him. Why did she have to tell them he had fallen in love with another woman, a married woman, a younger, more beautiful woman? A slut, in her words, who worships a god who encourages men to take on multiple wives. As teenagers, Ilán and Andrea think their mother is the most perfect woman on earth, even if she constantly spars with them over their laziness and slovenly habits. They don't care that Rosa Esther's once-thin figure, so gorgeous and svelte at Jones Beach in New York, has sagged, nor that the once-cute freckles on her white face have widened so much that they've become splotches.

Guillermo is bottled up in mourning and feels a whistling pain flitting constantly through his porous body. He can't believe Maryam will never come back to him, that she is gone, killed by a slew of bullets before blowing up with her car. It makes no sense, none of it does. Half the time he is drunk, reeking of booze and slurring words that he often only whispers to himself. His eyes are puffy: they look, but do not focus. They are bottomless murky wells. His tongue is a soap pad in his mouth. He has swollen cheeks and constantly itching ears.

One night he takes a flashlight and his gym bag to the roof of his building, climbing up the circular staircase to the upstairs terrace, where the maids hang laundry on poles between the huge gray containers of bottled gas. Guillermo brings a yellow legal pad, parks himself against one of these containers, and starts going through Ibrahim's papers. Lines referring to *interest-free loans* and *worthless collateral* spring up at him. Advances for projects that will never be built assault him, but he is unable to concentrate. Maybe it is the quivering of the light, the shuffling of the wind, the batting of his eyelashes, but Guillermo is not able to form a single cogent thought. And of course he has forgotten to bring a pen or pencil.

He puts everything down and stares up at the sky. There is a high crescent moon and the lightest smattering of stars. He sees a compact trail of smoke off in the distance and wonders if the Pacaya volcano is active once again. He should read the newspapers and find out what's going on in the world. He seems to remember something about a build-up of troops in Afghanistan, more chaos in Iraq, Daniel Ortega hunkering closer to Hugo Chavez and talking about building a transoceanic canal through Lake Managua with Chinese funding, Putin flexing his muscles in a challenge to Russia's oil barons.

Why the fuck should he care?

He is looking at a beautiful night sky which could make him cry, but all he can think about is that he has to find someone to pay for Maryam's death. Miguel keeps insisting that the government was behind the murders, and it is easy for Guillermo to agree. He hates the skinny president, with his horn-rimmed glasses, his mole-infested skin making his face resemble a large conical chocolate chip cookie. He looks like a ghoulish funeral parlor director with his gray suits and white shirts and blue ties, constantly rubbing his hands to express sympathy even as he convinces relatives of the deceased to purchase more expensive coffins. He is a self-proclaimed patriot who is constantly paying tribute to the Guatemalan flag in public while using it as toilet paper at home. Whenever he is filmed sitting at his desk, stroking his hands, he speaks with so much conviction—despite his speech impediment—that Guillermo thinks he might actually believe what he says. With his thin lips and his high, unmanly voice, he is a dead ringer for a chompipe, a turkey, clucking his way through an argument, a man whose discourses are so absurd that only fools would believe them.

Guillermo cannot accept that Guatemalans elected him their president—a hideous wild turkey killing off his enemies each time he gobbles or bats his flightless wings. Miguel has now completely convinced him that the president killed Ibrahim and Maryam. Guillermo is also sure that the president has signed agreements with the leaders of the main drug cartels not to pursue them, as long as they don't interfere with his looting of the treasury. He can easily imagine the president and his wife hobnobbing with the leading drug dealers in Guatemala, serving them delicious canapés and French champagne. The president is a talented manipulator who hides his backroom dealings perfectly.

Guillermo hates the First Lady even more. He is certain that she models herself in the tradition of Corazon Aquino and Lady Thatcher, a powerful woman who wants the poor to consider her another Mother Teresa. To him she is just a duplicitous chimpanzee: when she smiles and reveals her crooked teeth there is no way the people can believe what she says. Just because she has a social work degree from the Landívar she professes to know how to solve the ills of the country, and thinks that people more skilled than she should follow her lead. She definitely sees herself as another Cristina Fernández de Kirchner; as soon as her husband's term is over, Guillermo suspects, she too will announce her candidacy for the presidency of Guatepeor o Guatebalas, even though the constitution does not allow the spouses of sitting presidents to run for office. What will she do to accomplish her goals? Divorce her husband, just so that she can become a candidate all on her own? Is she that cold-blooded?

Guillermo's hatred of her has nothing to do with her being a woman. He admires Michelle Bachalet and Angela Merkel for reaching the presidency of their respective countries on their own, not using their husbands as stepladders to the podium. It is her hypocrisy that rankles him. *Guatemala has become Guatemess.*

Guillermo prays every day that no one assassinates the president; if that happened, his wife would make a convincing case for being allowed to finish his term. After all, she is one of his most trusted advisors. If someone tries to kill him, his wife would be sure to escape; she might even be behind it. Somehow she would be sitting two rows in back of him at the National Theater, or, at the moment of the assault, in a bathroom stall, rehearsing her inaugural speech. Under no circumstances would she allow herself to die with him.

It is unclear to Guillermo how corruption this deep developed so quickly in Guatemala. When he looks at his country's history, he is convinced it all began with the overthrow of Ubico, the end of the rule of law—yes, no matter how harsh it was. Most Guatemalan sociologists and historians blame the overthrow of the constitutionally elected Arbenz in 1954 for turning the tide.

He wishes he could wake up one day and feel good about being a Guatemalan, without thinking about soldiers, narcos, maras, cartels, whatever. Maybe no single event was the cause of it, but instead decades of horrible luck and corruption. He thinks back to how Guatemala changed during the two years that he and Rosa Esther were in New York: he left a country at relative peace and returned to mass murders and killings.

In his drunken stupor he has crazy dreams. One night he dreams he's attending a beauty pageant in which the wrong girl gets crowned Miss Guatemala simply because one of the judges didn't know how to add up his own points. When he gets up to decry the mistake, he is arrested and thrown into a prison without any clothes.

He knows that all Central Americans complain about their own countries. He remembers the time a pilot on a flight from Guatemala to Nicaragua landed at Comalapa Airport in San Salvador. The passengers had to disembark and wait two hours for another flight to Managua, their original destination. No apology, no explanation, no reimbursement. Just another screw-up.

And in the hospitals? Patients are given each other's medicine and both die. There is no foul play, just incompetence, plain and simple.

There must be something in the Popol Vuh that set the whole thing off like this.

All of Guillermo's dark thoughts are accompanied by rivers of liquor. He can't control himself anymore. He has stopped exercising, stopped eating correctly. His diet consists of fast food, potato chips, and soft drinks. He doesn't recall when he gave up riding his bicycle; his ankles and feet are swollen, red as beets.

Guillermo buys a new cell phone every couple of days and shares the number only with his secretary, his ex-wife, and Miguel. Within hours of each purchase he begins receiving more garbled messages and dropped calls. His anxiety is out of control. Someone wants him dead.

A month after Ibrahim and Maryam's funeral, he asks Miguel if he knows anyone he can hire to be his bodyguard and chauffeur now that he is afraid to drive. Someone who can take him to work and back, who can fill the car with gas. Someone who can make sure he doesn't become another statistic. Miguel instantly suggests that he hire Braulio Perdomo. Braulio was the driver of the blue Hyundai at the Centro Vasco, but Guillermo is too far gone to notice or care.

In addition to the hang-ups, Guillermo sometimes receives typed letters at the office saying things like, *We are watching you, stop drinking cheap rum.* Or, *You were reading quite late last night* (when in fact he had passed out with the night light on).

On rare occasions something nice and unexpected happens.

Ilán and Andrea call him for his forty-ninth birthday and sing "Las Mañanitas"—they are already so Mexican! For the first time in a while, Guillermo feels connected to them. He cries on the phone. The kids cry with him. Andrea blurts out that she misses him. Guillermo blows them each a kiss and tells them he wishes he could make things right for them. For the first time ever, they say that he has been a great father. He knows it's not true, but still he feels embraced, even if their warmth is only related to his birthday.

* * *

During Braulio's first morning on the job, he brings his new boss to his office. Before going down to meet him, Guillermo rinses his mouth with mouthwash. He has shaved his face for the first time in days. He is wearing a pressed suit, a clean shirt.

No one is in his office since he furloughed his secretary. He opens his mailbox and finds lots of bills and thick envelopes. He has stopped paying his office rent and is merely weeks away from being evicted. Does he care?

Less each day.

Among all the annoying mail he finds a plain white envelope with no return address. It is postmarked May 20.

Guillermo goes to the cabinet across from his desk where he stashes bottles of liquor and pours himself a big whiskey. He is sure this is another threat. He has half a mind not to open the envelope, but curiosity gets the better of him. Inside is a gorgeous color postcard of a beautiful beach with white sand, palm trees, a palapa, mostly blue skies, a couple of white cirrus clouds. Gold lettering on the bottom reads, *Playa del Carmen, A Golden Beach on Mexico's Riviera Maya*. When Guillermo turns the card over, he sees that it is blank.

He looks back at the envelope. It has a cancelled Guatemalan stamp from the town of Chiquimula overlaid with the date. Why a card displaying a beach in Mexico?

He thinks maybe it's a coded message from Maryam, announcing that she's still alive, staying somewhere between Mexico and Guatemala. But he knows he's just grasping at straws.

## CHAPTER TWENTY-FOUR

# CHRONICLE OF A DEATH FORETOLD

**T**he night after his last big bender and Braulio's arrogant phone call about the Monday morning pickup, Miguel calls Guillermo and says he needs to talk to him immediately.

"In private."

"Here I am."

"No phones. I'll pick you up at six at your apartment and we'll go to the usual watering hole downtown."

They chitchat on the drive along Las Américas Boulevard and Reforma to Zone 1. The streets are empty of people and cars, not surprising for a Sunday night.

"What's on your mind?" Guillermo asks as soon as they are seated at Café Europa.

"I want to know how you are."

"To be honest, I wish I were dead." He confesses to Miguel that he has thought long and hard about it and wants to take his life: he simply doesn't want to live anymore. He knows that the cocktail of antidepressants, mood stabilizers, and sleeping pills, plus all the booze, are not helping him to think clearly, but he has nothing to keep him alive. Not even his children—the birthday call was, after all, an exception.

"My life is over," Guillermo says, without much emotion. He has just downed three straight shots of Flor de Caña rum. When his eyes meet the waiter's, he orders two more shots.

Miguel is sipping Ron Zacapa, to give his friend company. It is his first and only drink of the night. "But you must consider your children—"

"They would be better off without me."

"How can you say that?"

"I know. They are doing well in Mexico City. Rosa Esther is a marvelous mother. When I call to talk to them, I get the feeling that I am pulling them away from something they would rather be doing."

"But this is natural. They are angry at you." Miguel is not only a self-proclaimed facilitator and the head of his own private spying network, but also a bit of a psychologist. "They would never recover if you were to simply kill yourself."

Guillermo nods. He remembers their voices on his birthday. Sweet. They were concerned. He looks back at Miguel and nearly forgets why they are there. "I don't know anything about you. Are you married? Do you have children?"

"None of that matters. You know you can trust me."

Guillermo answers this comment with a blink.

Miguel pats him on the shoulders. "My private life is so boring. I've been married to Inés Argueta for thirty-eight years. We have four children, all in their thirties. Two of them, the girls, are living in the States, married. The boys are in Europe. One is studying theater and working part-time in a restaurant in Seville. The other works for a Scottish bank in London."

The waiter arrives with more drinks and a basket of potato chips. He looks at Miguel before putting them down. Miguel nods, making Guillermo laugh.

"And to think that I have someone I don't really know, a father of four children, watching over me," he says, gulping down more rum.

"You're drinking a lot these days. I wonder if the depression you feel is related to it. You should cut down on your alcohol intake, if you don't mind me saying."

Guillermo runs his hand through his hair. Drinking is the least of his problems. He needs to sleep peacefully, but his mind has become a feeding trough for nightmares and sudden fears. "And what would you have me do? Drink milk? Become a choir boy? Study for the priesthood?"

"You can't let your life deteriorate like this. You need to sober up a bit. You have to get control of yourself. The liquor is poisoning your system."

Guillermo has read such poppycock in popular magazines. As befuddled as he is, he is not brain-dead just yet. You can't control your life as if it were a steering wheel. He knows why he doesn't want to sober up. "So what do you advise, Mr. Freud?"

"Well, if you want to die, make sure your death has meaning."

"Make sure my death . . ." he says absentmindedly. He takes his glass, swirls the golden liquid, and drinks it down. The rawness makes him wince, as if he were drinking grain alcohol. He can't stop thinking about himself with a morose self-pity. This is the source of his inertia: his inability to rouse his soul.

Through the fog, he hears Miguel declare: "Well, if you want to kill yourself, then at least make it worthwhile. Meaningful. You can help bring the government down like a house of cards, for example."

"Say what?"

"Let your death count for something. Make it meaningful. To your family, to the country you love so much. Look," Miguel says, grabbing Guillermo's hand and moving it away from the rum, "I am very fond of you. The last thing I would want is for you to kill yourself. At the same time, I cannot judge the depth of your depression. Your wife has abandoned you, your kids are living in another country. Your law practice is in disarray. A friend and client has been killed and so has the love of your life. If I had suffered all those blows, perhaps I too would be as lost as you are. But you can't continue to indulge yourself like this. What I do know is that no matter what you decide to do, it should have some sort of meaning beyond yourself. And that meaning can create a positive outcome that will be useful to others, maybe even to society. You should consider that."

Guillermo picks up a new glass. He has no idea where Miguel is going, but the train of thought has sobered him up: he wants to hear more. He sounds like a priest with a direct line to God, and the message he is delivering is not garbled, though it is in a code Guillermo has not yet deciphered. "All this sounds like some kind of variation of your theory of actionable information," he finally slurs.

"Not at all," says Miguel. He is clearly bothered by how Guillermo is muddling things up. "My actionable information theory is related to producing something tangible: making money based on truths that you and no one else has, or creating a positive situation based on the destruction of something rotten. Right now I am talking about something incredibly powerful: sacrificing your own personal desire for the greater good. *True* love of country."

"You sound like a Marxist."

Miguel shakes his head. "It is quite the opposite. I'm not arguing for you to usher in the dictatorship of the proletariat, but for you to execute a patriotic act," he says triumphantly. "Guillermo, I know that you love Guatemala."

"I do. The quaint Indians, the majestic volcanoes, Lake Atitlán," Guillermo responds, citing some banal tourist-brochure claptrap. What he wants to say is that he has dedicated his whole life to making Guatemala a better place to live for his children and grandchildren—who will now spend the rest of their days in Mexico.

"Did you ever read Camus's *The Stranger?*"

"I read it in French in high school. *L'étranger*—in Madame Raccah's class. She was our French teacher from Tunisia. She later tutored Rosa Esther. All my classmates thought the novel was a superb piece of fiction."

"Well, I think it is totally stupid."

"I only remember that it takes place in Algeria or somewhere in Northern Africa. And that it is terribly hot."

"Exactly," Miguel says. "The protagonist is a guy who kills an Arab simply because the sun is driving him crazy and he discovers that someone has placed a gun in his hands. I personally can't imagine a motivation so stupid. The French protagonist kills an Arab—a bad Arab for sure, a troublemaker—but for no real reason. It's a murder that has no effect on anything other than his own death by hanging. Can you imagine anything so foolish? To kill someone because you can't stand the heat? His death has no repercussions in society beyond the act itself! How insipid is that?"

"Well, if I could kill Samir I would be extremely happy."

"But what would killing him actually accomplish? It would be an act of malice with no benefit to the greater society. Maybe if things were switched:

if killing him would bring Maryam back to life: that would make you happy, and therefore return you to a position to benefit society. But to kill that old man—what would be gained? You would be arrested for murder and eventually sentenced to death. Even if Maryam were alive, the two of you would never be together. It would be something else if you killed Samir and you and Maryam were able to escape to live together somewhere, happily ever after—"

"In Paris! In Paris! That's where we would go. But Maryam is dead."

Miguel pauses to wet his lips on his drink. "Do you really want to die?"

"As things now stand, I do. My life tastes like shit. I wish I could find someone to kill me because I am too much of a coward to kill myself. I would pay him to do it."

The bar is quiet; there are only a few clerk types drinking beer at the bar and watching the TV screen—Comunicaciones is playing soccer against its crosstown rival Municipal. Guillermo had no idea that local soccer games were now being transmitted on cable.

Miguel inches closer toward him. "I can help you kill yourself painlessly—but only if you take someone else down with you."

Guillermo's head is spinning. "I have a dear friend who read a shitty French novel and wants to help me commit suicide," he says softly to himself. "What a wonderful friend."

"Only if you want to."

Guillermo doesn't know what to say. His own departure from this planet has already become a given—according to Miguel Paredes. "Who do you want me to take down? Samir wouldn't be enough. He may have wanted Ibrahim and Maryam dead, but I don't believe he would actually have done it. I doubt that a suicide letter accusing him would change anything. It would be seen as the rantings of a madman consumed by grief."

"You're right. Accusing someone as unimportant as Samir wouldn't make a difference. But there are others who make living a decent life in this country impossible. And both you and I have the evidence to prove it."

Guillermo is confused. "Oh yes, I know who you mean. Mayor Aroz, for example. He is buying up this whole neighborhood so he can turn it into Disneyland."

"I was thinking of someone higher up."

"Óscar Berger? Who gives a shit about that useless ex-president? You are simply wasting my death."

"What about going after the president himself? You yourself have said that Khalil had documents proving his financial shenanigans. I think we could create a scenario where we might force him to resign—in shame!"

Guillermo stares into his now-empty glass. "You're crazy! No one would take my word over the president's. Ibrahim Khalil believed he could bring him down—see where that got him? Killed, and he and his wife are still roaming around free. No thank you. I'd be dying in vain."

"If we plan this thing correctly, we could bring down the government—the whole house of cards."

"You're dreaming, Miguel."

There is a pause. For some weird reason Guillermo thinks of Carlos, who worked with his father at La Candelaria. He hasn't thought of him in twenty years. But at this very moment Guillermo wonders if he is still alive. He was such a loyal employee—maybe he thought that one day he would inherit the lamp store and that's why he was so devoted. Guillermo should try and contact him. When he awakes from his reverie, he sees Miguel looking dead at him.

"What?"

"*What* what?"

"Why are you staring at me in that way?"

"I want you to know something: what I am thinking is not a dream."

"What would you have me do?"

"I'll explain, but it requires bravery."

Guillermo peers at Miguel through glassy eyes.

## CHAPTER TWENTY-FIVE

# LIGHTS, CAMERA, ACTION!

**"I think we should make a video."**

Guillermo picks up his nearly empty glass and runs his tongue along the rim, fishing for the remaining drops of rum. Suddenly he feels Miguel's hand on his wrist.

"Listen to me!"

Guillermo ignores his spinning head and puts his hands down on the table, fingers entwined, as he did in grade school when his teacher demanded attention.

"We set a camera on you and have you tell the audience, the good citizens of Guatemala, your story. You say that if they are listening to this particular recording, it's because the president of the republic has had you killed. You will have died to make your country better—"

"*Our* country," Guillermo corrects, snickering.

"Yes, our country."

"I don't like pain. An overdose of pills is not painless."

Miguel looks at him impassively through his sharp, hooded crow eyes. "I could guarantee that your death will be painless—"

"I can't imagine a painless death."

"Imagine if you were playing tennis and had a heart attack that killed you instantly. One minute you are running across the court with your racket, smashing backhands, the next minute you are down on the asphalt, dreaming of making love to 70,000 virgins."

As Miguel explains the scheme, Guillermo realizes that he has given the matter much thought. He is to look straight into a camera and say, "If you are watching this recording, it is because I am dead." He'd then go on to accuse the president, his wife, and their inner circle of plotting to not only kill Ibrahim Khalil, but him as well, as the only other person who knew about the secret transfers and loans at Banurbano.

Miguel insists that to make the video convincing, Guillermo has to sober up. There can be no hint that his accusations are being made because he is a mourning alcoholic or that depression got the best of him. For this plot to work, the video needs to show that Guillermo is alert, very much alive, and with much to live for, even though he is grieving the loss of his lover. A bungling drunk would not be able to convince anyone. On camera he would have to be passionate, courageous, and clear as a glass bell—an individual who has become so fed up with corruption and money laundering that he is willing to sacrifice his own life to get the truth out.

"I don't think I can do it."

"Yes you can. You are a strong man."

"Look at me. I'm a shadow of who I was, if I ever was a strong man."

"We can do this together, Guillermo. We need to get you into shape."

"What do you suggest?"

"Braulio Perdomo can help you get off the bottle."

"Your spy?"

"Come on. He's not spying on you. Think of him as an ally: he can bring you to the gym, oversee your training. Of course you can do it. With his help, you can get into shape within a week."

Guillermo nods. He understands how far-reaching Miguel's web is. He sits back in his chair and sighs, realizing that his death could indeed have its benefits. He can imagine that Ilán and Andrea, even Rosa Esther, would see him as a hero, willing to give up his life to once and for all rid their birth country of the plague and stench of corruption. His death could begin the healing, the process of clearing out all the filthy leeches that are sucking Guatemala dry. His sacrifice could be the first act initiating a movement of national cleansing.

"What's your favorite form of exercise?"

"Cycling."

"Let me buy you an Italian aluminum alloy bike tomorrow."

"That's not necessary. I can repair my old Pinnarello."

"That's the spirit," Miguel says.

"Two weeks is all I need to get into shape and sober up."

"I think you can do it in one."

Miguel is clearly calling the shots, but Guillermo truly no longer cares. He is sure that nothing he does will redeem his pointless life, though his death might help.

The suicide has to be perfectly planned and executed. Miguel will help make the arrangements. The first step is to hire people to begin calling Guillermo's phone number with all sorts of threats. Guillermo needs to react appropriately to these calls, with the right degree of anger and fear in his texts and call-backs. The incoming and outgoing calls will be registered on his phone's SIM card as proof of the threats. Guillermo neglects to mention the hang-ups and other strange calls he's been receiving.

Then both he and Guillermo need to buy another set of disposable mobile devices so they can communicate privately and discuss the details of the filming and Guillermo's death—an assassination. Miguel will provide him with the contacts. He knows hit men who would kill their own mothers for five thousand quetzales. But he insists that Guillermo make the arrangements. Miguel doesn't want to be directly involved should something go wrong. The strategy is to keep as many layers between Guillermo, Miguel, and the hired killers as possible, so that nothing can be traced back to them. The whole scheme would collapse if Miguel's name were to be implicated in the preparations.

The single assassin will think his orders came from the president.

Carried out in secret, with great finesse, Guillermo's video and apparent murder will be seen by his countrymen as the final, desperate act of a courageous patriot obliged to hold the president and his band of thieves accountable for destroying the country.

\* \* \*

The first day—a Monday—that Guillermo is on the wagon his body rebels, giving him stomach cramps and wreaking havoc on his bowel movements. He drinks gallons of Gatorade to build up his electrolytes, and eats spoonfuls of peanut butter straight from the jar to increase his iron. He stops consuming all kinds of junk food—no more chips or pitchers of coffee—and feasts on plates of papaya and scrambled eggs in the morning, a can of tuna fish for lunch, and, continuing his high-protein diet, a steak every night, with boiled potatoes and broccoli.

He slowly finds himself climbing out of his dark hole; his thoughts, too, are beginning to develop some level of coherency.

He has Braulio bring him to the gym, where he jogs, swims, and lifts weights to get his head clear enough to make the recording. He also has the chauffeur bring his bike to the Raleigh repair shop near the Oakland Mall. It is fixed immediately and on the first afternoon of his rehab he begins to ride it again on the roads near his condominium. At first his legs are stiff and cramp up often, but little by little they start to hurt less and achieve a bit of fluidity.

He stays on the Cymbalta but starts weaning himself off the other medications, reducing the dosage a little each day. For the first two nights, Guillermo's sleep is interrupted—he has horrible, violent nightmares—but then he sees an improvement. He is beginning to heal.

Despite the physical recovery, Guillermo's desire to live does not return. He wishes he were dead, though the thought of actually going through with the planned suicide still gives him the chills.

Meanwhile, Miguel works full throttle to arrange the filming for Friday night. No one will ever suspect his apparent murder was a suicide. It will be another sleight-of-hand trick, something common in Guatemala, where the audience, fed up with violence, becomes a willing and necessary participant in the success of a totally fabricated production.

Throughout all the planning, Guillermo realizes that for the first time in his life he has given up total control. He has always seen himself as the driver of his own destiny, a mastermind who controls all the buttons and levers. Now he has ceded control to Miguel Paredes, and this makes him nervous.

Since their last meeting at Café Europa, Guillermo feels like a machine programmed to respond to the other man's slightest provocation.

What troubles Guillermo most is that Miguel is not as transparent as he acts—there's something of the manipulator about him. But Guillermo is so alone now, he is grateful that *someone* has taken any interest in his life, his ideas, and what he has lost. He could not plan this act alone, and has come to need Miguel.

Guillermo also doesn't like that he has to involve others in the arrangement of his own death. He fears it will not be executed exactly as planned. He wonders why he can't just put a bullet in his brain or overdose—he has the pills—and leave a suicide note. Why bother to engage others? What will that do? According to Miguel it will transform his death into a salutary movement, ridding Guatemala of disease.

And by dying he will also refocus scrutiny on the circumstances surrounding Ibrahim and Maryam Khalil's deaths, and perhaps flush out the real killer. Though he still wonders if Samir was somehow behind it all, Miguel has all but convinced him the president was involved. He welcomes the idea of surprising and exposing him.

He is not afraid of dying. In truth, he is afraid of living, of continuing to live a life that holds no meaning. A life without Maryam.

Guillermo continues to have disjointed dreams of her, especially as his body works to eliminate the alcohol from his system. He breaks into night sweats, and his breathing is hard and sporadic.

Once he finds himself standing in the middle of his living room, sleepwalking. In a deep sweat. With a fork in his hand.

He has a recurring dream in which he sees Maryam walking across a foggy landscape. He tries to grab hold of her arm, but she slips away—she always manages to escape his grasp. He sees her walking to a cliff, seconds away from jumping over the edge, or he sees her ejected without a parachute from a small plane.

He is troubled by her lack of corporeality. And the fact that she is always beyond his reach.

* * *

The filming of the video is planned and will be carried out downtown. Miguel has decided it is best done in a two-room storage facility above a barbershop in Zone 1, on 9th Street, between Sixth and Seventh avenues, very close to Café Europa and Guillermo's father's old lamp store.

At first, the idea is to film Guillermo sitting on one of the barber chairs in storage, but Miguel worries that the comical staging will undermine the seriousness of the video. He wants to set up the filming as innocuously as possible, without too many details, so that the recording has a sense of authenticity, and so that no one can locate the actual filming site.

Only three people will be at the filming: the cameraman, Guillermo, and Miguel.

The cameraman constructs the set in one room: camera on a tripod, spot-lights pointing to an empty black folding chair before a card table, and a dark blue sheet in the background. The only contrasting color is the red microphone on the table.

Once the room is set up, the cameraman calls Miguel, parked on 9th Street, and tells him it is safe to bring Guillermo upstairs. Both of them wear wolf masks over their heads so the cameraman won't recognize or remember them. He sits Guillermo behind a six-foot table, and does a test run while Guillermo still wears his mask. The sound and light are tested; there's no problem. The cameraman suggests that Guillermo relax, which he does by trying to sit as comfortably as he can on the folding chair.

The test run complete, the cameraman resets the video recorder and goes to sit in the anteroom so that he cannot hear or see what is going on. He is sworn to secrecy, and amply paid for it, but Miguel doesn't want any mis-takes. Once the recording is completed, Miguel and Guillermo will replace their masks before the cameraman comes back in to shut off the camera. They will make multiple recordings until they get it right.

With the video running, Miguel sits on a chair by the door and signals for Guillermo to start. Guillermo hesitates for a second. He has spent many waking hours thinking about what he wants to say on the tape, since it will be his final will and testament. Not only will it be his opportunity to set the record straight, but he will be able to tell his countrymen what he believes is ailing Guatemala. With any luck at all, he might actually be the spark for real institutional change.

Guillermo takes off his mask. He is dressed in a natty dark blue suit and a light blue silk tie; he is very nervous at first. He feels awkward looking straight ahead into a video camera, with the lights on and only Miguel present. He is sweating in the windowless room and aware of moisture dripping from his armpits into his shirt.

He begins by identifying himself and saying that if the public were unfortunately watching this tape it is because he has been killed by the president. His opening statement is delivered in a stiff monotone, as if he is reading from a poorly edited transcript. His eyes seem unfocused, his tongue tied. Sweat patches form on his temples. After about a minute, he slows down and his comments become deliberate and clear.

He reveals that the only reason he's dead is because he was the personal lawyer of Ibrahim Khalil, who was cowardly killed along with his lovely daughter Maryam in a hideous drive-by shooting and that their murder was planned by the president and his wife.

Deaths like theirs have been occurring in Guatemala for decades, year after year. It's the same old story. Guatemalans do nothing because there's nothing to be done. Whoever kills does so with impunity and with the protection of gangs that control the government, or military cells intent on camouflaging their true identities. Guatemala no longer belongs to the people, but to corrupt government officials, narco gangs, and the individual murderers and thieves who have jointly conspired to destroy the country. He contrasts the intentions of these malevolent forces with the goodness of individuals like Ibrahim Khalil, a man who showed up to work at six forty-five a.m. every day because he felt a personal responsibility to all his employees. Industrialists and factory owners were defying the endemic corruption in Guatemala by showing they could be transparent and honest, work for the betterment of society, and still turn a healthy profit—something they were entitled to.

He eulogizes Maryam Khalil as an obedient daughter and a beacon of goodness in an increasingly corrupt country. Once a week she would come pick up her father at twelve thirty and bring him home for lunch. She doted on her father and served her husband in the same proper way.

Ibrahim Khalil did nothing to deserve to die like a dog, but even worse was for the assassins to have taken Maryam along with him. The special prosecution concluded that their deaths were either gang related or had something to do with a factory-based vendetta. As Khalil's lawyer, Guillermo knew much more. For two months they had been meeting twice weekly to determine if there were any illegal shenanigans going on at Banurbano, where Khalil served on the board as the president's appointed representative. Khalil was tolerated until he began focusing on certain inconsistencies and discrepancies which indicated illegal loans to vested parties.

Guillermo goes on to stress that he has direct knowledge of why Ibrahim and Maryam were killed. As an advisory board member of Banurbano, Ibrahim had discovered fraud and had physical proof to present to the press. But before he could do this—and disrupt the theft of hundreds of millions more quetzales—the puppet president and his henchmen liquidated him.

After saying this, Guillermo pauses. He is suddenly aware that when this tape is viewed he will be addressing millions of Guatemalans. He feels the full thrust of his power and relaxes: his shoulders drop, his voice assumes a more natural tone, and he is able to spin the narrative in a more cogent form. He remains focused, though there's loud music coming up from the floor—a strange medley of rancheras. The more he talks, the greater his animation and the more distorted his face becomes. His anger is rising and it is important that the audience see this, as if they are reliving with him the cruel events of the last months. He wants them to know that merely stating these facts is making his blood boil. He feels his heart is being compressed, but this they cannot see. Two or three times Guillermo brings a hand from under the table and places it inside his shirt, as if trying to touch a cross or massage his heart. He tries to control his facial gestures now, but every ten or fifteen seconds his mouth tightens, on the verge of spitting out words from his polished teeth.

Soon the music dies down, and Guillermo starts flashing his hands left and right as he refers to the Banurbano managers as ruling over a den of thieves. The bank is where money is laundered, elite businessmen are "loaned" government money for personal use: in sum, it is a wholly corrupt institution. Every single honest banker in the country knows that this bank, set up to serve the poor, is a sham.

Guillermo, pausing in his speech, begins to think of himself as Robin Hood.

The camera runs on. He is speaking again, but has lost his rhythm. He restates the same accusations, confusing things, saucing up his language like an actor improvising on the stage.

He wonders aloud if some viewers might think this is all a plot to besmirch or overthrow the government by a cabal of malcontents, but he has the proof, pointing to a closed brown folder on the desk, that the president is at the head of a rotten administration.

And for simply raising questions about the financial policies of Banurbano, Ibrahim Khalil and his daughter were killed. Like dogs, he repeats.

Guillermo is tired. He wants to stop talking but can't. He thinks of his family in Mexico and says that there are those who might say that he, like Ibrahim, has a death wish, and should just shut up. He tells the camera that he has two wonderful children who he loves with all his heart and who are living safely in Mexico. He has no desire to die, but he needs to tell the truth, to expose the cancer eating up the body politic of Guatemala. His children won't be better off with his death, but hopefully the country will, as long as the people rise to the challenge and confront the president and the cycle of corruption he has perpetuated.

And if in fact Guillermo has been killed, then he implores the vice president to take over the reins of power and rid the government of the liars who swept Ibrahim and Maryam's deaths under the rug.

At this point, Guillermo can't control himself any longer. He needs something to drink, preferably alcoholic, to steady his nerves. He starts calling the president, his wife, and all his cabinet ministers clowns, drug dealers, malcontents. He goes on to say that he wasn't born to be a hero, just a decent Guatemalan. And this is why he is making this accusation, to reestablish a sense of decency in a wayward country.

"We need to rescue Guatemala from all these thieves, drug dealers, and murderers. Let no one deny that the murdering president, his thieving wife, and all his henchmen are responsible for the destruction of Guatemala. Don't let them hide. Ladies and gentlemen, let my death have a first name and a last name . . . There's still time for you to do something to liberate us. This is the time for action."

When Guillermo finishes talking, he puts his hands on the table and waits. His fingers stop moving. The camera rolls on for another minute, during which he sits perfectly still. He is about to collapse, to vomit really, but he knows he cannot lose his composure. He has to stay still. He knows nothing about the editing of film or video. He hopes that the editor will be able to delete all his repetitions and make him less a fool.

Guillermo grabs the mask from the floor, stands up, and starts walking toward the door where Miguel is sitting. The latter puts a finger to his lips and indicates that Guillermo needs to put the mask back on. But first he gives Guillermo a hug and places a kiss on his cheek. "Your courage overwhelms me," he whispers. "There's no point in refilming this. The recording is absolutely perfect."

Miguel releases the lawyer, puts on his own mask, and taps on the door to let the cameraman in. Then he tells the cameraman, "You have fifteen minutes to finish up here."

"Yes sir."

"Remember, put the tape in the trash bin at 13th Street and Ninth Avenue at exactly nine p.m. and simply walk away."

The cameraman nods.

Miguel and Guillermo leave quickly. When they are halfway down the stairs they take off their masks. Guillermo breaks into tears, convinced there's no way to stop what's been put into motion.

"You were amazing. That is all I can say. Simply amazing."

"You think so?" Guillermo sniffles. He feels he has just hammered the final nail into his own coffin.

"You're a true patriot, Guillermo. What a brave speech. You'll be remembered for generations to come, you know that? You will appear in the history books—"

"I just need a drink."

"Well, let's get out of here and go to our usual spot."

"What happens next?"

"A film editor will create a straight recording from the time you sat down at the table to the time you stopped talking. It won't be edited in the least, should someone later claim that the video has been tampered with. The editor has been instructed to make fifteen copies of the DVD, which will be given to me. I'll keep them under wraps until the second part of the plot—your death—can be put into motion."

"My death?"

"Of course. But it will all be painless, as promised. The country will be plunged into mourning by your death. And at your burial, we will hand the press the copies of the DVD and see how long the president stays in power."

"It sounds foolproof." Even as Guillermo says this, he is wondering if there is any way to get out of this. Yet only Miguel can throw him a lifesaver.

"It is, my friend. It is foolproof."

"And when am I supposed to die?"

"This Sunday morning."

"What if I change my mind?"

Before they get into Miguel's car, he hugs Guillermo tight and whispers, "You won't."

It's obviously too late to retreat.

The fuel is there. It just needs a match.

## CHAPTER TWENTY-SIX

# A BICYCLE BUILT FOR TWO, MAYBE THREE

**I**t is seven a.m. Sunday morning and Guillermo gets his Pinnarello mountain bike out of the back bedroom and parks it in the living room. He truly loves his bicycle now that Braulio has had it restored. It has twenty speeds and is made of the lightest of carbons, so that it can be lifted with one hand. It's a model of engineering genius. Actually, it can be balanced on two fingers once it's been hoisted up.

Guillermo goes out to the terrace of his apartment. The sun is shining. The flamboyant tree below is about to burst into bloom. Soon there will be orange flowers falling on the grass and into the central fountain, something he will not live to see. He stares off in the distance and sees the tranquil surface of polluted Lake Amatitlán. Beyond the water he sees a plume of smoke rising up from the Pacaya volcano against a blue sky. He is horrified by the thought of never again seeing the people and places that have accompanied him for nearly fifty years.

Guillermo opens the refrigerator and takes out a plate of frijoles volteados and tortillas wrapped in cloth. He puts them in the microwave for twenty seconds and then pours himself a glass of orange juice for the dead man's last meal. Within the hour, the world will be spinning without him, though he imagines his face will be plastered across the front page of every website reporting Guatemalan news. He wonders if anyone at this very moment is even thinking of him. Perhaps Ilán or Andrea.

Who is going to call them to tell them their father has been killed?

Miguel has helped Guillermo devise a perfect plan, so that there will be no way to trace the killing back to him. Miguel called a cousin who had been affiliated with the Mano Blanco back in the eighties, when the guerrillas were threatening to destroy civic catholic society. The cousin has anonymous connections to three assassins: a cashiered sergeant whose brutality is known throughout the country and is now working with the Zetas of Mexico to bring Colombian cocaine to the US via landing fields in the Petén; an oreja who serves in the presidential guard and is a member of Opus Dei; and a glue-sniffing criminal who has been in and out of prison for years and is reputed to have murdered half a dozen people for a handful of quetzales.

Any of these criminals would be happy to execute a stranger, no questions asked, for the paltry sum of 2,400 quetzales. The killer will do the shooting and disappear.

Guillermo looks at the food on the table one last time and is unable to eat a thing. He had been drinking all night, still gathering the courage to go through with his suicide. He is beyond depression and yet keeps thinking about his kids and his desire to see them again. He is upset by the thought that they will be ushered through college by Rosa Esther's uncle, or by a new rich Mexican boyfriend. Still, he has set something in motion—the video has been made, the murderer hired. Guillermo can already hear the outraged speeches that his cohorts will be making at his burial at the accusation that the president was the architect of his murder.

The mole-faced president is about to wake up to the biggest surprise of his shitty life, thinks Guillermo. He has no idea what is awaiting him. A downside to the suicide is that he will not get the chance to see the president's face blanch, tick nervously, and tighten up like a ball of tissue when he is served the news that even the dead want him out of office. And the president will glance around to see the face of his wife, that sow who believes the world is fooled by her constant photo opportunities in which she hands over a thirty-dollar monthly payment to an Indian family to demonstrate the government's generosity.

Maybe the president will be placed in the same prison as Byron Lima who oversaw the murder of Bishop Gerardi in 1998. Let's see which of the two makes it out of jail first.

Guillermo is sure the manila folder he is leaving in his gym bag with Ibrahim Khalil's documents will be a trove of incriminating evidence for independent investigators. He hopes Ibrahim's discovery that Monsieur and Madame President were siphoning funds from Banurbano to place in secret accounts is sufficient evidence to have them both arrested.

Miguel Paredes's brilliant plan is to have Guillermo at the designated assassination spot at eight a.m. A ten-minute ride from his building.

Guillermo is ready at seven thirty. He has a splitting headache—his body is rebelling against him. Dying, putting an end to it all, is obviously the only solution.

He goes down the hall to the bathroom overcome by excruciating pain, brought about by the nonstop ingestion of almost pure alcohol. Nothing comes out—it must be gas. He goes back to bed to lie down, just for a minute. He is tired, extremely tired. He doesn't intend to sleep, but he does. When he wakes up it is ten to eight. He needs to hurry.

He races across the apartment, gets his bike, and takes the elevator down to the basement. As usual no one is in the elevator. The doors open and he walks his bike across the nearly empty garage and up the back ramp to the door, which leads to the garbage dumpster on the side of the building. From there he can take the alley, used only by the garbage trucks that come every Thursday, to the main road.

His route through the alley is the only way to avoid being seen. Actually, it doesn't matter if Guillermo is seen or not, by either the lobby or parking attendant. Once the news of his death is announced, who cares who has seen what?

He doesn't need anyone's permission to go for a bicycle ride on an early Sunday morning. Still, he prefers to be cautious and not to be seen. Or rather he doesn't want to get into a conversation with a tenant or the guard in the guardhouse. None of the usual banter: *It's a beautiful day, sir. Any news from the family? I have a package for you.* All the innocuous *blah blah blah.*

Guillermo goes out the parking lot door, which for some reason does not shut behind him. Should he go back and close it to protect his few neighbors from any potential burglars? He frankly doesn't care, since he won't be coming back. The door can remain ajar.

It is a spectacular morning. The wind blows softly and it's cooler than it has been in recent days. He walks his bicycle along the alleyway that smells of stale beer and, oddly enough, almonds, though there are no almond trees around. When he reaches the avenue he notices the long shadows from the eucalyptus trees growing on the lawns of the houses across the street from his building. His neck feels a bit sore, but the tightness eases as he stretches, moving his head in gentle circles. He leans the bike against his hip and extends his arms to the side.

Enough stretching: he's ready to go.

He mounts his bicycle and begins peddling. What a pleasure to ride a machine so carefully designed as to nearly ride itself. The gears shift effortlessly with hardly a trace of sound or friction, only the soft click of the derailleur. His legs are pedaling at a good clip. Maryam loved his lean and powerful legs, like those of a stallion. She liked grabbing his ass in her hands, trying and failing to shake it loose from his trunk.

Guillermo glances around. He has never been as conscious of nature as he is this morning. It's as if he has awakened to a newly created world, one that dazzles him with its beauty and serenity. He hears birds chirping, yes, *birds chirping*, and feels the sun warm his face. Where has he been these past weeks? Has he lived with his head deep in the ground? Even when he had gone riding to get into shape and shake off his drunkenness, it was on a mission to expiate pain, fatigue, booze, and frustration, rather than to enjoy the beauty of a sunset ride. Nature had once been important to him.

Maryam's death crippled him. He lost the desire to engage with anyone. With himself. He knows that he has become a worse father than his own was to him. He demonstrated more sympathy for the elephant La Mocosita than he has for his own flesh and blood.

It isn't the solitude that destroyed him. What he can't survive is this taste of ashes, the refuse of something that had at one time nourished him but had now decayed. Music, art, meals, all taste burnt, flaking, putrid.

*Rotting*, now that's a better word for what he tastes. Everything has putrefied to the point of rotting. Rot and mold.

Guillermo is crying so hard now that he can barely see the road on which he pedals. He squeezes the brakes with his hands, puts his legs down, and stands still momentarily before wiping away his tears on his sleeves.

He stays there on the side of the road, his thoughts racing. When Maryam told Samir she wanted to leave him, he laughed at her. In fact, he told her he would never accept her wish to dissolve their marriage. The only hope for Guillermo and Maryam would have been for Ibrahim to intervene on their behalf. But given his stern morality, they would have had to emphasize the allegedly platonic nature of their romance, built up over the weeks of dining and conversing together with each other, and with him. They could not have admitted the carnality of their relationship, the unquenchable thirst. In this way Ibrahim might have allowed a relationship to develop between them, for he was dedicated to the happiness of his daughter.

Guillermo wipes his eyes on his shirt again. Why had Maryam been killed? What did she have to do with the filth of this world, the drugs, the corruption, the venality? The thought of her burning up, that sweet aromatic flesh, repels him. She did not deserve to die like that.

Guillermo glances down at his watch. It is after eight and he is still not at the appointed spot. He's no longer sure he wants to die, but he needs to put an end to his despondency.

He remounts his bike and pedals slowly. It hurts him to consider that no one will mourn his death. There will be something unfortunate about his death, but nothing tragic.

Facing a steep incline, Guillermo forces his legs to churn harder. His muscles, nearly atrophied by so much booze and apathy, strain at the task. His legs begin shaking, threatening to cramp, but he simply puts a steadier foot to the pedal.

The agreed upon spot is one hundred meters away, on a grassy ridge at the edge of a pine forest. Across from it sits one of those oversized houses, wedding cake–shaped, with a V etched just below the intercom. It is a hideous house owned by Boris Santiago, the millionaire narco chief.

Guillermo is supposed to dismount his bike at the crest and wait for the assassin to approach by car. It is to be a simple undertaking—a man rides his bike on a Sunday morning, quite innocently, possibly before going to church services. He gets winded from the climb and dismounts his bike to rest for a minute or two before going on.

Guillermo switches to a higher gear and continues up the hill, wondering what he will do when he sees the car approaching. Maybe he will crap his pants—how indecent a way to leave this world—or try to run away into the woods and get shot in the back.

Or will he simply meet his fate by awaiting the bullet, with his mouth open as if to accept the Host of Hosts? Will one bullet be enough, or will he lay there squirming, with his brain oozing out of his skull like blood sausage from the pork skin, waiting, begging for the second bullet, or the third, the shot that will deliver him from the suffering his life has become?

What if the second shot never comes? What if he is condemned to spend the rest of his life in a wheelchair, dumb and blind, blowing on tubes to make the wheelchair move, attached to a tank of oxygen?

Oh please, Lord, not that!

Halfway up the hill, a jackrabbit appears below the hedges of a house on the right. When it reaches the curb, it pauses ever so briefly, twirls a floppy ear, then bounds across the road as if its legs were on pogo sticks, and disappears into the forest.

Guillermo glances toward the sky—there's an oddly rectangular, dark cloud resembling a chalk eraser. He wishes it weren't there. He wants to die under a spotless blue sky, as under a coffin's dark blue velvet casing. Is that too much to ask for?

His legs feel sore as he nears the top. Boris Santiago's McMansion now comes into full view, taking up the whole crest of the hill. Looking up, Guillermo sees a glass-encased hexagonal cupola at the top—it must be the playroom for the children, or where the ex-lieutenant and his buddies drink bottles of Zacapa 23 and snort samples of the cocaine they fly from Colombia to the Péten fields to the United States.

Immediately Guillermo realizes his mind is exaggerating things—on several occasions he has seen children staring down from the cupola to the road as he cycled by. It is a four-story house, and he can well imagine that from the third-floor windows someone could see the Izalco volcano in San Salvador miles to the southeast, or Lake Amatitlán a stone's throw to the south. He expects one can see the volcanoes of Fuego and Pacaya belching their endless plumes of gray-black smoke from any of the windows in the house.

As he reaches the plateau he notices that there is no one in the cupola now; the whole family of the mutilator-turned-cartel-chief must still be sleeping, or vacationing in Disneyland.

Guillermo takes a deep breath, filling his lungs with cold, clean air, and slows. To be alive is glorious, he thinks, with tears welling up in his eyes again. If there were a guard in the guardhouse protecting the McMansion, he might have gone up to him to confess his desire not to die, but strangely no one is there.

Just past the house there is another incline, so steep that no houses have been built there yet. Guillermo is supposed to wait at the notch on top, at the edge of the curb, in front of a young eucalyptus tree that was planted four or five weeks earlier on a grassy spot. There is no way to miss it.

He reaches the top of the knoll, stops, and dismounts his bicycle. His heart skips a beat when he sees another bike and what might be a backpack lying on the grass immediately in front of the spindly eucalyptus. What could this be? A large rodent? A sack of oranges? A small dead mountain lion?

Guillermo is confused. He rubs his face to make sure this is not a mirage. He pinches his nose to test if he is still alive. His mouth gasps for air.

As he approaches the backpack, he sees the soles of a pair of sneakers and realizes that a man is lying there. A Diamondback Sorrento mountain bike lies behind him. Why would a cyclist be sleeping at the side of this road?

Guillermo inches closer. He sees a muscular back in a white, hooded pullover riding above what look like shiny blue boxing shorts. The man has a shapely ass, that's what Guillermo notices, and hairless legs. The back of the man's head is bald. Though the sleeper appears to be short, he has a thick neck. A bull's neck.

Guillermo puts his bike down and goes over to shake the man awake, to ask him to move along and find his own spot to recline. How dare he take a snooze at the spot of Guillermo's presumed encounter with death?

He nudges the man gently from the rear, rocking him back and forth a few times, but there is no reaction. He shoots a quick kick to the small of the back. Nothing.

Guillermo sits down next to the man, as if to have a chat with him. It is a cool morning, but up on the hill the sun is shining powerfully and Guillermo begins to sweat. The truth is beginning to dawn on him. He gets on his knees, careful not to dirty his beige pants, and begins to turn the man over with his gloved hands. The body rolls over lightly, and Guillermo lets out a loud gasp and feels a chill in his back.

This is definitely a dead man, not a sleeper. He can't recognize the face because the nose has been completely blown off, and there are bloody craters for eyes. The whole visage is a disheveled mess of blood and cartilage, rubberized, like a ghoulish Halloween mask.

Guillermo vomits on the grass before he can close his mouth.

*Oh my God,* he thinks, as he wipes his maw with his left arm. Is this man me? He is confused from the previous night's hangover, from the weeks of binge drinking and indulging. Everything is muddled.

He holds his breath, frozen, as if blue smoke were issuing from a gun he's unable to shake loose from his hand. He hears no sounds except the pecking of a woodpecker—*rat-a-tat, rat-a-tat*—somewhere behind him, and a mourning dove in the distance cooing stupidly.

Guillermo sits next to a corpse that could be him but isn't. Miguel Paredes's cousin's assassin—whoever it was—has killed the wrong man!

How strange.

Who is this guy? Part of him wants to figure that out, but then he snaps out of his stupor. He has to get out of there quickly, before the army or the police show up and accuse him of murder. He isn't sure if he's more afraid of being arrested as the accused murderer and dumped into the penitentiary with drug addicts, pimps, and gang members, or being sought out by Miguel Paredes's henchmen for failing to orchestrate his own murder successfully.

Something has been botched. Has another cyclist passed by the appointed spot at just the right time and been killed by mistake by the hired assassin? This seems like the most obvious answer. Guillermo looks down at his watch. It is eight fifteen. He has arrived fifteen minutes late. So what? Assassins aren't taught to distinguish between cyclists: all Guillermo knows is that the bullet meant for him has blown off half the face of someone completely innocent.

Then it clicks. He thinks he knows the dead man. From the shape of the body, he believes it's the narco capo Boris Santiago.

Guillermo starts to cry into his hands, saying aloud, "Oh dear Maryam, how much I love you—and miss you." He realizes that he has been minutes away from joining her in heaven.

Through a fortuitous, incomprehensible case of mistaken identity, Guillermo is still alive!

He takes a deep breath. What's he to do?

Birds are chattering loudly, as if relaying the news of the murder to their avian brethren. Guillermo cocks his ear to listen for sirens, but he only hears more sounds of nature. Apparently, no one has heard the gunshots. Otherwise, this area would be overrun with medics and chontes.

Guillermo pats down the body to find some ID to confirm his suspicion. But the poor schlep is only wearing shorts, a white pullover, and a pair of sneakers worth several hundred dollars.

Guillermo places his Pinarello next to the corpse, then takes the other bike without thinking. The seat needs to be raised, but he has no time to look for pliers and tinker with it. He hates abandoning the Pinarello, but he has no choice. The Diamondback is actually a nicer bike anyway.

He backtracks across the plateau and coasts downhill, passing several blocks of houses on the way to his apartment building. He hears a few dogs bark, but no one comes out. He takes the dirt path back to the trash door and finds the door still propped open, thank God. He crosses the garage and takes the elevator straight up to his apartment. No one sees him.

Adrenaline is directing his movements.

He goes into the bathroom and takes a short, hot shower. Afterward, he puts on a pair of jeans, a short-sleeve shirt, and a light jacket.

His mind is racing but focused. He has to move quickly if there's any hope that he can extricate himself from this mess of a situation.

He has to get out of there. Now.

## CHAPTER TWENTY-SEVEN

# A BUS TRIP TO EL SALVADOR ("THE SAVIOR")

L ife is full of opportunities. The difference between the follower and the maker of his own destiny is that the former is willing to accept his fate while the latter forges it. Guillermo feels he has reached a summit and sees his future clearly. He has the opportunity to escape the tawdry conspiracy he has helped to weave and to be free.

He has to leave town at once. Get the fuck out of Guatemala City.

As he prepares to flee his apartment, both his cell phones start ringing: the personal one that recorded all the threatening phone calls and the disposable cell he had only shared with Miguel, Rosa Esther, and his secretary.

Guillermo realizes he has to discard both phones and disappear. When they stop ringing, he shuts them both, takes out the SIM cards, and dumps them in the garbage disposal under running water. He flips on the switch. The grinding metal makes a horrible noise at first but within seconds there is a quiet whirring, as if he were grinding walnuts in a blender.

He hurries to his closet and retrieves a shoe box from the top shelf. It contains a forged passport he bought years ago for four hundred quetzales, just in case, and five thousand quetzales in twenties and fifties, just in case. The only way to survive in Guatemala is to plan for *just in case*.

And there are many just-in-case situations, as he and Maryam once discussed.

He checks the top drawer of his desk to make sure his legitimate passport is there and, leaving it visible, takes the fake one and the cash with him. He fills the backpack with other essentials—several shirts, a spare pair of pants, socks, underwear, a toothbrush, deodorant, a comb. He does all this in a flash. The last thing he puts in the bag is Ibrahim Khalil's folder—one day it will be of use. He grabs Boris's Sorrento and quietly leaves his apartment. His heart is beating hard in his chest, thumping to get out.

In the basement, he adjusts his backpack so that it is firm against his shoulders and flat against his back. He takes a deep breath. It's time to go.

Guillermo pedals slowly in low gear up the garage ramp toward the gatehouse. When he gets close to the garita one hundred meters away, he sees that the guard, thankfully, has his head inside a car window and is checking the driver's identification papers. It is barely nine thirty a.m.

Guillermo knows it is too risky to cycle by. Someone will notice him. He needs to remain invisible. What to do?

To his right, Guillermo sees a footpath running into the woods, one of the many used by squatters before the shanty town on the hill had been cleared for development. It is still used by servants who work in the private houses, a quicker beeline to the main road, with access to the public buses on Los Próceres.

The path, tamped down and smooth, is a shortcut to 18th Street and Seventeenth Avenue. When he rides out of it, he sees several buses, a truck, and a smattering of cars going the other way, toward Vista Hermosa. He decides to avoid Los Próceres, where someone might see him, and takes a series of small streets through Zone 10 toward the Zona Viva.

Guatemala City is sleeping in, slumbering through the pleasant eucalyptus aroma around him. On a typical Sunday, when Rosa Esther and the children were still around, he would go riding toward the Obelisco and turn down Reforma Boulevard, which was closed to car traffic from six a.m. to six p.m.

But this is not a typical Sunday. He turns down Fourth Avenue and rides north toward the Radisson Hotel, where the first-class buses leave for San Salvador every other hour. When he reaches 12th Street, he gets off his bicycle and walks alongside the Fontabella Mall, where Miguel Paredes has his faux men's shop. He notices a wooded lot next to the Hotel Otelito, facing the plaza. Using his Swiss Army knife, he pries off the little license plate and leaves the bicycle leaning against a tree. It will be stolen in a heartbeat.

He walks down Twelfth Avenue by the Geminis 10 Mall and the Mercure Casa Veranda hotel. There are Chiclets and cigarette vendors on the street, an old half-blind Indian woman selling sweet rolls on the avenue, but none of them pay him any notice. It is as if he were gliding invisibly through the Zona Viva.

There is a long line of cars snaking along First Avenue toward the Radisson valet. Breakfasters get out of their cars, receive ticket stubs from the valets, and watch their cars disappear into the basement garage.

Beyond the driveway, the ten a.m. Pullmantur bus to El Salvador drives up. Guillermo hurries toward it. As soon as the driver opens the door, he edges up the steps.

"You have to buy your ticket inside the hotel," the driver says.

Guillermo gives the driver two hundred quetzales and tells him to keep the change. Before the driver can say a word, he hastens to the back of the bus and nestles himself in, curled into a ball, about to pass out.

When did he last sleep? Two nights ago? He hardly knows.

His eyes simply close on their own.

But his mind is alive and he cannot sleep. He recalls that the Stofella is less than two blocks away. His thoughts turn to Maryam and the various afternoons they cavorted there with total abandonment. He remembers the touch of her body, her full breasts begging to be embraced by his mouth. He starts crying, half asleep, as he recalls her mango-flavored mouth, the perfect fit of their bodies, the hunger with which she would ride him thrust after thrust until she would let out a low, widening scream.

Guillermo remembers reading what García Márquez wrote in *The Autumn of the Patriarch*, that "el corazón es el tercer cojón." *The heart is the third ball.* He was so right. And at this very moment Guillermo's heart is throbbing. He remembers that someone in *Love in the Time of Cholera* had said that "el corazón tiene más cuartos que un hotel de putas." *The heart has more chambers than a whorehouse.* And he knows this is also true.

He opens his eyes to see the bus driving down Los Próceres, en route to the highway that will take him to El Salvador. Guillermo needs alcohol—his body aches for it. His throat has clenched and he feels a tug that turns his insides out. But there is nothing on the bus to indulge his craving.

Eventually, fatigue takes over, he settles into his seat, and finally sleeps.

He wakes when the bus stops at the Guatemala/El Salvador border an hour later. All fifteen passengers have to disembark and go through immigration in a small, concrete, windowless building surrounded by empty wooden pallets and half a dozen uniformed soldiers lounging on broken chairs under blooming jacarandas. This is a first-class bus, but the procedure is the same: everyone has to bear the insufferable heat which within minutes speckles Guillermo's cotton shirt with sweat.

The passengers are directed to some high tables and instructed to fill out tourist cards. They are told to line up single file in the center of the room once they have finished filling out the cards.

Guillermo is the fifth person in line, behind a middle-aged woman whose jewelry jingles whenever she moves her rather impressive behind. She is wearing so much perfume that his nose suddenly twitches and he sneezes. She turns to look back at him.

"Salud."

"Thank you," he says, sniffling a bit.

"Why do they insist on demeaning their own citizens?" she whispers to him.

"I beg your pardon?"

"This doesn't offend you? If we were on an airplane they would simply usher us through. Is it because we want to save a little bit of money by taking the bus? I don't know about the others here, but I'm scared of airplanes." She winks at him knowingly. "And though I *could* drive my Lexus, I'm afraid of the kidnappers. Communists and kidnappers rule this country."

Guillermo nods at her. She must belong to the Salvadoran elite, the fourteen families who have ruled that little crumb of a country for over a hundred years.

"I know you are a chapin from your passport."

Guillermo's Central American passport indicates his Guatemalan nationality with embossed gold lettering on a blue background.

She smiles. "You don't know how lucky you are, Mr. . . . ."

Before he has a chance to answer, a man calls out to her: "Come over here, lady."

Guillermo can see the three customs officials sitting at the same table. The first examines the woman's passport for its validity. The second evaluates the tourist card, matching it to the passport, and asks some mundane questions that have already been answered on the card. The third official sits with an open ink pad and stamps the Salvadoran seal with the date of arrival and waits for the visitor to ink his or her finger onto the card. When he asks the woman for her fingerprint, she goes into a tirade. She yells something about the misfortune of living in a shitty country—not exactly an effective way to charm customs officials.

When it is Guillermo's turn, the first officer beckons him with one finger. Guillermo hands him his fake Central American passport. As the agent opens it to the photo and information page, Guillermo realizes that from now on he will be Rafael Ignacio Gallardo, a resident of Los Aposentos, Guatemala—a new man with a new identification number and a totally new identity. The questions are all normal enough: name, address, passport number, place of residency while in El Salvador, length of stay. The agent looks up at him and smiles, handing his passport to the second man, who validates the information on the card against that on the passport. When he reads the address Guillermo has given for where he is staying—the Hotel Princess—he says, "I hope you enjoy the *princesses* of San Salvador." He smiles lasciviously and passes the card to the man with the pad, who looks at Guillermo and adds, "We don't need your fingerprint. You don't look stupid enough to want to stay in our country illegally," and waves him through.

Guillermo feels relieved that he hasn't had to provide prints, even pleased to be visiting a "shitty country" where his passport, looks, and birthplace give him greater status than the woman before him in line.

Before getting back on the bus, he takes a leak in a stinky bathroom, then buys a squash blossom, a red bean pupusa, and a large Coke. He wolfs them down as if he hasn't eaten for years, and then reclines his seat to watch the thick vegetation catapult past him. He hopes that the Coke will ease the migraine behind his eyes, but no such luck.

He should sleep, but is kept awake by a machine gun of questions running through his mind. He has no idea what he will do in El Salvador, or how he will survive. He only knows that he has died, and he hopes to rise like Lazarus and live again in another land.

When the Pullmantur stops at the Radisson in San Salvador's San Benito neighborhood, a wealthy enclave of huge walled-in homes, boutiques, and expensive restaurants, Guillermo decides it would be a big mistake to stay in the nearby Hotel Princess. If the police believe he has somehow eluded death and crossed the border into El Salvador, they will most likely look for him in hotels like these. He needs to find simple, safe lodgings in a working-class neighborhood where no one will think of searching for him—where he can grow a mustache or a beard, shave his head, disguise himself. He's better off finding a room in a cheap pensión or boardinghouse amid the junk dealers, the modest, cavernous stores selling suitcases, shoes, or toasters right on the street.

He has not brought a single suit. He gets off the Pullmantur with only his bulging knapsack and walks down 89th Avenida Norte to the Paseo General Escalón. Here he takes a mostly empty public bus toward the cathedral on Plaza Barrios, where Archbishop Romero was gunned down, and to the north end of Calle Rubén Darío.

The cathedral looks out onto its own crowded square. It is Sunday and there are hourly church services until five.

It's tough for him to navigate the 2a Calle Poniente with so many people, though he is happy to be where he is. It's scorchingly hot, but what the hell. He's alive.

He stops at a corner kiosk. "I'm looking for a decent place to stay," he says nervously to the street vendor.

The man behind the counter has a grizzly face, eyes that have seen enough horror—the butchery of a civil war—that nothing surprises him. He sizes up Guillermo in a flash.

"Don't look south near the Mercado—the maras have taken over most of the buildings, whole blocks. You wouldn't survive more than a minute there, with all the stick-ups and robberies. There are a few good places a couple of blocks from here, near the Plaza Morazán and Calle Arce. Look for the rental signs in store windows. There's the Pensión Cuscatlán on Calle Delgado. I've been told it's safe."

Guillermo thanks the vendor and walks up Avenida Cuscatlán, plowing through the crowds on the narrow sidewalks. Before looking for any rental signs, he decides to first check out the pensión on Delgado.

The building, which also houses a number of jewelry stores, has two armed guards on twenty-four-hour duty. He takes the elevator, with room for just two passengers, to the top floor. It reminds Guillermo of the place he stayed in decades ago on the Paseo del Prado in Madrid.

Pensión Cuscatlán is a modest place on the top floor. It has six rooms with private bathrooms, says the proprietor, a woman who is wider than she is tall. She barely looks at him as she escorts him down a dark hallway.

"This is the only vacancy."

He's shown a dark room with bulky antique furniture facing an inner courtyard. He presses down on the bed; the mattress seems new.

"You get fresh sheets once a week. Friday. That's when we clean." He sees a large white towel on the bed. It is actually fluffy.

The room is simple, clean. The bathroom is big, but not particularly modern, and has a broken window that lets in the hot, sour air from an airshaft. While he is looking around, the landlady goes to the window and turns on a small air conditioner that runs surprisingly quietly.

"What's the rent?" he asks.

"Twelve dollars a day or sixty a week. This includes breakfast between eight and nine and electricity."

"I'll take it. By the week." He's surprised to realize how accommodating he has become, how quickly he's adapting to a new reality. A day earlier he wouldn't have even stepped foot in a room like this, but now it's about to become his home.

"Is that all your luggage?" she asks, lifting a paw toward his backpack.

"For now," he answers. "Next week I'll have the rest of my clothes shipped to me."

She nods as if she's heard this story before and gives him the key. "You can pay me for the first week. I don't allow visitors in your room."

"I understand," he says, handing her sixty dollars. He asks where he can get something to eat. She suggests going to any of the sidewalk comedores lining the streets of Plaza Hula Hula.

"The food is good, the dishes clean. You won't get sick. Try the sopa de res or panes de pollo."

The restaurants run down the south side of Plaza Hula Hula and have tables on the sidewalk. They are so crowded on a Sunday after Mass that there's hardly a place to sit. San Salvador is broiling. He finds a comedor that has somewhat cool air blowing out from the inside and orders the sopa de res with bolillos.

It is a hearty soup and Guillermo is satisfied. He goes to a used bookstore on Delgado and buys a Spanish translation of Steinbeck's *The Grapes of Wrath*, a book he has meant to read for years. He also buys a bottle of rum at a convenience store next door.

He goes back to his room, starts reading, and falls asleep by eight o'clock. He sleeps twelve hours without waking up, but he has many disturbing dreams. In one he is visiting a zoo and all the animals are running free, trying to claw him.

He has eggs, red beans, and a cheese pupusa for breakfast. The coffee is watery, almost tasteless. Guillermo goes downstairs to look for newspapers and see how his botched suicide has played out. He heads back to the same corner kiosk where he was directed to the pensión and finds a teenage boy, perhaps the owner's son, manning it. He buys a copy of *La Prensa Gráfica*. Plastered on the front page is a photograph of the dead bicyclist with a good part of his face blown off. He rolls up the paper, in a sweat, and looks for an empty bench to sit down.

Guillermo's left leg thumps as he begins to peruse the front-page article. He reads about an as-yet-unidentified cyclist being shot in the exclusive Zone 14. It is assumed by his dress that he lives in the neighborhood. There are interviews with some neighbors who worry that the increase of violence in the city has reached them in their oasis. The article alludes to some controversy between the police and the armed forces regarding who has the jurisdiction to do the forensic analysis and determine the cause of death and the identity of the victim. Does the municipality or the federal government have jurisdiction? Once this has been settled, the identity of the victim can be investigated. The standoff could take days.

Guillermo smiles. The really good news is that his name does not appear anywhere in the newspaper. He assumes that Miguel Paredes's plan to release the DVD recording has been aborted and he wonders what the facilitator might be thinking. Surely he knows that Guillermo is not the dead man on the crest of the hill, and must be wondering if the assassin botched the killing or if their plan coincided with an entirely different murder. It is a wrench in the machinery, but knowing Miguel he will figure out how to turn this to his advantage.

This fortuitous development has given Guillermo more time to decide what he wants to do. The greater the time between the murder and the start of the investigation, the better for him to develop his new identity. He may be the only person to know that the dead man is Boris Santiago, the ringleader of the Zeta gang in Guatemala and owner of the pink McMansion at the top of the hill. Guillermo wonders why Boris's family has not stepped forward to claim the body, but then deduces that he probably shipped them to Miami Beach long ago, or they're hiding out in a hacienda in Zacatecas, Mexico. Whatever the reason, the longer it takes to identify the body, the better.

Guillermo puts the paper down on his lap and lets his mind wander. Clearly there's no rush within the cartel to file a missing-person's report given that knowledge of Boris's death will probably start a civil war among his lieutenants. The narco capo has to have a full staff working in his house, a chauffeur or two, half a dozen bodyguards, but maybe they have been instructed by Capo Number Two to remain silent if he were to ever go missing. Or perhaps Number Two himself is responsible for the assassination.

In any case, criminals like to clean up their own messes with their own brand of justice. Or maybe a fake Boris was killed and the real Boris Santiago is on a secret helicopter mission, care of the Guatemalan military, to the Petén, where he can oversee another shipment of cocaine through Guatemala to the United States. It's plausible that someone masquerading as Boris has had his face shot off while going for a bike ride. These bullet heads are always conniving and scheming, and they don't want weak-kneed staff filing a missing-person's report every time the head honcho disappears to Miami to arrange another shipment or to cavort privately with his dozen whores.

So the reporter can only conclude that a poor fucker going out for a Sunday bike ride has been killed: a typically vicious crime in Guatebalas that will produce no guilty party for now and forever more.

On Tuesday morning Guillermo buys *La Prensa Gráfica* again and sits down on another park bench, this time across from the cathedral. The front-page headline shows the same picture from Monday, but it's half the size as the day before. The caption reads, "Sospechado narco-traficante mexicano asesinado en frente de su casa" ("Suspected Mexican Drug Dealer Murdered in Front of His House"). Below the headline, the boldfaced type declares that the dead cyclist is, in fact, Boris Santiago, the alleged leader of the Guatemalan Zetas cartel. He was shot from less than twenty feet with five or six bullets from a Beretta 92, blowing the features off his face. The article speculates that Santiago has been killed by a rival gang rather than by unhappy members of his own mob. The reporter goes on to posit that Santiago may have been killed by a secret paramilitary force within the Guatemalan army fed up with the Mexican domination of the drug trade.

There's a second, shorter article on the bottom of the front page. It states that the Guatemalan military has been tasked by the president with carrying out the investigation and reporting its findings to him and the Congress. An anonymous congressman claims that an elite squad within the army might be behind the assassination—Israeli Mossad style—but wouldn't claim credit for the killing in a hundred years. "Everyone is free to speculate," says the congressman, who refuses to give his name, knowing that Boris's killer will never face justice and he himself could be killed for his speculation. "We may never know what happened. After all, 97 percent of the murders in Guatemala go unsolved."

Guillermo sits back against the park bench. He's surprised that his planned suicide has brought about such unexpected results. There's no mention of him anywhere in the newspaper, certainly nothing about the release of the DVD. He realizes that Miguel will not release the recording now that Boris has been murdered and Guillermo has gone missing. For all he knows, Miguel might be thinking he has been kidnapped by the same assassin who killed the drug dealer, or that he had a bout of nerves and simply decided not to go through with it. Unless he resurfaces or is discovered, Miguel will most likely say nothing publicly, and will put all his resources into finding him.

Guillermo has to lay low to escape detection. For the first time in weeks, he feels true relief—the sensation that he is not required to do anything for anyone. He's not despondent, he is not angry, he's no longer consumed by the deaths of Ibrahim and Maryam. The rage has turned into a loss that is quiet, private, and constant—one that is part of him and colors his changing view of the world. He feels fortunate to have been given the opportunity to vanish into thin air. The only regret he feels is over his children and what they might think when they fail to hear from him, and eventually get the news that he cannot be found, or is presumed dead.

For the next three mornings Guillermo follows the same ritual of eating breakfast in the pensión at eight thirty and then going down to a park bench to read *La Prensa Gráfica*. He turns the pages each day expecting some new revelation about Boris Santiago's murder. Each succeeding edition of the newspaper has an article about the murder, shorter than the last, full of conjectures about who might have wanted the drug kingpin dead. And then on Friday there appears a larger "weekend" article claiming that an autopsy has shown the dealer was killed by the second shot to the face, and that fingerprints and dental records have certified the victim's identity beyond a doubt. As he is about to close the paper, he finds on the next-to-last page, in a section of Central American news briefs, a headline that mentions his name. His hands start shaking as he reads, "Guillermo Rosensweig, Guatemalan Lawyer, Missing."

Guillermo reads on. Braulio Perdomo, his bodyguard and chauffeur, has reported him "disappeared" going on the third day, when in fact he has been gone now for five. This report is confirmed by his secretary Luisa Ortega, though Guillermo had furloughed her two weeks ago. The article says that his ex-wife Rosa Esther has no comment about his disappearance, but is concerned for his safety. The unnamed reporter claims there's no evidence of foul play because no ransom note has appeared. Perdomo testified that his boss was not depressed, so the police won't presume that he disappeared on his own. Miguel Paredes, a friend, contradicts the chauffeur—Miguel's own employee—by claiming that Rosensweig was still despondent over the brutal deaths of his client Ibrahim Khalil and his daughter Maryam Mounier outside Khalil's factory near Calzada Roosevelt the month before. The reporter mentions that the lawyer's valid passport was in his top drawer, implying he hasn't run away. The article ends with a police request that if anyone has any information regarding Guillermo Rosensweig's whereabouts, to please contact them immediately.

Guillermo stares out across the square to the cathedral. The morning sun is hot, making his face sweat. He is surprised by these developments, the fact that no one wants to *presume* anything. It's odd that no one has noticed that the missing lawyer and dead drug dealer live in the same community, blocks apart. The fact that both disappearances happened at about the same time has not been mentioned. He wonders if he should call Rosa Esther and tell her that he's alive to calm the children, but he immediately nixes the idea: the less she knows, the better for him. Her telephone might be tapped. He also cannot rely on her silence, and he needs time to plan his next move, whatever it might be.

He's surprised, however, by the lack of curiosity of both the police and the press. It seems to him that they accept everything as it is, at face value. Why not investigate further? There might be a connection between the murder and the disappearance, he conjectures, as if he were a detective assigned to the case. Why did it take Perdomo and Paredes so many days to report his disappearance, and why did they contradict one another?

But then Guillermo thinks he understands: there's nothing to be gained by connecting the two events. In truth, keeping the investigations separate will in effect contribute to a confusion ideal in preventing both crimes from being solved. Better to move on to investigate or report the next gruesome crime, since every day five to ten Guatemalans are reported missing. Vaporized. Disappeared. Departed. And every week a dozen new bodies appear, with slit throats or chests decorated with bullet holes in the shape of a clover.

Guillermo had assumed that, because he is a lawyer—a respected member of Guatemala's upper crust—his vanishing would awaken further scrutiny and outrage. He's not just a pordiosero.

And there are facts worth noting that the reporter skipped. Guillermo was recently separated, his law practice was going south, and the murders of two of his closest friends, father and daughter, remain unsolved. Wouldn't any of those pieces of information be enough to draw interest in his absence? Maybe it all hinges on the words *apparent disappearance*. In Guatemala, a country of speculators and myopics, the word *apparent* has great significance: nothing conjectured is ever really worthy of investigation, until corpses are unearthed.

Indeed, why would the police start a manhunt for a wealthy lawyer, a womanizer, a divorcé? For all anyone knows, Guillermo Rosensweig decided it was time for a change in his life, bought a fake passport, and is living happily in Palermo or Malta, drinking wine and sunning himself, going fishing for sea bass every couple of days, or practicing yoga in Ambergris Caye.

Guillermo keeps a low profile in the days that follow. He eats out in inconspicuous greasy places near his pensión, like a simple bookkeeper or unemployed accountant, with no apparent—there's that word again—expectations that his life will ever change. He takes long walks in the mornings through the many parks in downtown San Salvador, peruses newspapers, and dips deeper into *The Grapes of Wrath*. Once he even walks down the crowded Salvadoran streets to the rather large Parque Cuscatlán a good kilometer away from his pensión. It is almost a forest in the city, the vegetation so thick that, though it starts raining, Guillermo stays dry under a canopy of trees. He realizes that San Salvador is really a tropical city.

He has many observations that contradict his expectations of what living in El Salvador would be like. Despite all the reports in Guatemala about the dangers of gangs and a left-wing government incapable of maintaining law and order, Guillermo is never assaulted or even bothered. Of course, he makes sure to be back in his room every evening by eight o'clock. He finds the Salvadoran people to be open and helpful, not the beguiling traitors Guatemalans think them to be.

Guillermo's life starts changing in so many ways. Where before he owned dozens of expensive slacks, shirts, and sweaters, for work and pleasure, he now buys simple, functional clothes appropriate for the heat and humidity. Dacron instead of gabardine and wool, cotton in place of silk. It is tactical not to stand out in the largely working-class neighborhood where he lives, but his purchases also suggest his new preferences. He is glad to be downsizing.

He buys light colorful guayaberas and multiple packages of Fruit of the Loom underwear and socks from vendors on Plaza Barrios. He is starting to drink less, and is losing weight—the two pairs of pants he traveled with are already too big on him. He buys three meters of light poplin and takes the material to a tailor on the second floor of a building on Avenida España to make him four pairs of pants. He purchases new brown and black shoes from the store across from his pensión. They cost twelve dollars each and are imported from Brazil.

He wants to be totally inconspicuous: a thin middle-aged man working quietly, staying below the radar, seeking a job as an accountant or bookkeeper in a small business in downtown San Salvador. A man with no family and little ambition, pleased to be alive and enjoy his next meal. He wants to blend in and be ordinary—as common as his father Günter was.

He knows he can change, he can learn to take pleasure from simple delights. And if he wants sex—after all, he's a healthy man—there are plenty of whorehouses on 8 Calle Poniente where the microbuses to Comalapa Airport line up.

Guillermo is becoming a new man, shedding old layers of being, like a lobster discards its carapace once a year. What he cannot change is his desire to understand what has happened. This much he knows: his elaborate and meticulous murder-suicide plot has been foiled by a series of coincidences.

Had his assassin killed Boris Santiago by mistake? More unbelievably, had Miguel hired an assassin to kill both Guillermo *and* Santiago to at once bring down the president and take control of the Guatemalan Zetas? The murder of Santiago has led to many new killings among drug dealers according to the newspapers. Obviously there's a struggle to see who takes control of his business.

In the meantime, Guillermo would like to think that his old associates, clients, friends, neighbors, his ex-wife (for the sake of their children)—all the people who'd had no role in the plot but who were extensions of his own life—would want to know what happened to him. If nothing else, simply to close the chapter on his worthless life. But nothing of this appears in the press. Despite his assumptions about his own importance, Guillermo is of no more interest than the salesman who gets killed for not giving part of his salary to the local gang.

Guillermo realizes he cannot spend the rest of his days reading books and newspapers on park benches or watching television in his air-conditioned room. He will, in time, run out of money. He needs a plan.

He cannot return to Guatemala, now or perhaps ever. It would not be safe. His coconspirators have invested too much time and money trying to overthrow the president and his wife to simply fold their cards and say, *Oh well, let the chap go.*

This is why he must assume that Miguel has assigned some of his foot soldiers to find him and have him silenced. Guillermo alive is undoubtedly a risk, especially if Miguel wants to hatch another, more successful plot against the president. Guillermo even wonders if Ibrahim Khalil's appointment to the Banurbano board was part of the plot that Miguel Paredes had hatched to pressure the president to resign. There is no way to know now, but this possibility underscores the danger that Guillermo would be in should he decide to casually reappear.

He knows too much. Miguel would be smart to want him dead; he has become a huge liability.

One evening Guillermo lies in bed assessing his options. One idea would be to go to Mexico City and try to be a good father to his children, far away from the dangers of Guatemala. He would have to be willing to truly devote his life to building some kind of relationship with them. His Columbia University degree would help him get permission to be employed in Mexico; he could even volunteer to do legal work for the Guatemalan exile community.

But he knows this happy reunion would last for no more than a few days, and then Guillermo would begin screwing up again, out of despondency or heartache. He misses Maryam too much to assume he could turn around his life with Rosa Esther. It would be a lost cause from the start. And besides, Mexico City would be one of the first places Miguel would be looking for him.

Thinking of Maryam, he once again thinks back to the night many months earlier when they had vowed to meet—or try to meet—on May 1 in La Libertad should they ever become separated. It is mid-June and he would have to wait nearly ten months before seeking an imagined reunion in a town named Freedom, in a country called The Savior. How ironic. Perhaps he should go there simply as a way of remembering her.

How long, Guillermo asks himself, can he live under the radar? He could wait a couple of years and simply emerge in El Salvador, convincing the world that he has been living here all along, that he's happy with his new life. He could willingly come out of the fog like Assata Shakur did in Cuba forty years ago. But even that might be too dangerous. It had been dangerous nearly sixty years earlier when members of Árbenz's cabinet, having been granted asylum by the Mexican government, had gone happily into exile only to be beaten up by Guatemalan goons collaborating with the Mexican police. Memories are very long, especially for those who feel double-crossed.

Payback would be Guillermo's fate no matter how many years have passed. Miguel would make sure of that.

So for the moment, Guillermo needs to get a job and stop languishing. After all, he's a corporate lawyer who speaks two languages, and has a law degree from Columbia University! Even without his actual diploma with him, perhaps he could use his skills to advise others on how to legally establish new businesses. But it would be too risky to open an actual law practice in downtown San Salvador. Miguel would first sniff and then snuff him out.

## CHAPTER TWENTY-EIGHT

# PUPUSAS AND YUCCA FRITA

**A**fter two months of staying at the pensión, Guillermo decides it's time to find his own digs. He rents a small furnished apartment on Calle Rúben Darío across from the Parque Bolívar. The furnishings are not to his liking, but it doesn't matter. He is far beyond caring whether his mattress is firm or not, if the sofa is covered in soft leather or naugahyde, if he has real art or framed posters on the wall.

Another change: before he sought solace in drink; now he is committed to sobriety. He is down to the occasional beer.

Rather than risk working for someone else, he decides to start a consulting service for individuals or small groups of investors interested in opening firms. His legal background is useful—he's an expert on business applications, articles of incorporation, legal filings—so it should be a breeze to do lawyerly stuff but charge consultant rates.

He rents a small 200-square-meter, air-conditioned office for three hundred dollars a month in the same building that houses the tailor shop where he had his pants made. He buys secondhand office furniture and an old desktop computer, an ink-jet printer, a scanner, and a small desk copier from the nineties.

At a carpentry shop by the market he has a business sign made: *Continental Consulting Services, Rafael Ignacio Gallardo, Proprietor*. He also has five hundred business cards printed. And as another act of self-determination, he buys a cell phone under his assumed name.

Guillermo Rosensweig is slowly ceasing to exist.

* * *

There are various decisions Guillermo can help entrepreneurs consider: what kind of business to open given the existing competition; deciding whether to manufacture goods, provide information services, or simply sell retail or wholesale products. Though much of his advice could be considered obvious, potential customers might not know that to establish a business, you should know the profile—age and sex—and the estimated disposable income—individual or corporate—of your potential customers. You also should extrapolate future competitive trends and whether or not you are entering a growing, shrinking, or a mature market. For example, if you are selling smart phones, the market would be growing, but anyone interested in selling sewing machines would be entering a mature market where only product innovation would lead to increased sales, and then only to a few customers.

The financial considerations are huge: Does the entrepreneur have a financial analysis identifying the costs related to starting the business? Additional sources of financing should the new business require it? Personal or family money, bank loans (at what interest rate?), outside investors—and a projection of weekly, monthly, and yearly wages and expenses? A budget spreadsheet with the cost of raw materials, labor, rent, transportation, utilities, administration expenses (payment to the consultant!), cleaning, and unexpected maintenance expenses? Guillermo can help the potential business owner identify the price point for the successful sale of products as well as estimate profits.

The only problematic part of the consulting business is that Guillermo cannot legally execute incorporation in El Salvador, or secure valid licenses, file proper municipal papers, etc. At some point he has to work with a local lawyer to complete the process to avoid awakening any suspicion with his fake passport. Luckily, downtown San Salvador is full of these kinds of lawyers.

Although he is unfamiliar with the laws of El Salvador, he knows from his legal work that documents and licenses are all fairly routine in the Central American Common Market. With a computer and the Internet, he can download any required documents from the government offices.

To publicize his consulting firm, Guillermo prints fifty flyers on colored paper and asks proprietors if he can tape them on the inside of their store windows; he also posts them on bulletin boards along Delgado Street. He drops off flyers with his former landlady and with his tailor as well. He displays them in the restaurants he frequents, on any open wall space.

Soon enough, he begins signing up clients, most of whom decide to pay the hundred-dollar application/consulting fee since they have not done sufficient research to mount a new business on their own. These clients, rather than being resentful or frustrated by Guillermo's probing questions, are, in fact, grateful to him for his thoroughness and his ability to see the larger picture. In the end he will be saving them hundreds, perhaps thousands of dollars in setting up businesses that otherwise would have been bound to fail.

What Guillermo has to offer is experience and an agile mind.

He throws himself into his work like never before. It's as if he has been given a second chance in San Salvador, and like a carpenter working with his hands, he finds his job immensely satisfying. He enjoys problem-solving and motivating his clients by the promise of success. He discovers he has the skill to empower them. And most of all, he is surprised by how little he misses his old life, with the exception of Maryam.

He attempts to make up for his loneliness by going to whorehouses. One in particular, La Providencia, he finds under escort service listings in *La Prensa Gráfica*. It's more high-end than those near the marketplace and the cathedral, but in the end he only feels temporarily relieved.

There are days when, while listening to Liszt or Debussy or Delibes on a cheap CD player in his apartment, he feels a lump in his throat. The music saps him at the same time that it humanizes him. He listens to Bill Evans's "Peace Piece" and Cole Porter's "So in Love." He feels that Maryam is with him: *I'm yours till I die.* He allows himself to imagine that she got away, like him. Maybe she escaped from the carnage realizing that to survive she had to disappear. These thoughts are not the ravings of the Guillermo in Guatemala City. His thinking is clear; this could be possible.

There was no forensic evidence of her death—just a mound of white powder that found its way to an urn in the wall of the church at the Verbena Cemetery. Of course, there was no proof of Ibrahim's death either, yet he knows that the textile factory owner is dead. It is more of a sixth sense about Maryam—there's a small chance she is still alive. He remembers the anonymous card he received several months back—could it have been from her?

Maryam was so beautiful that he could imagine a kidnapper or would-be assassin deciding like Clegg, the protagonist in *The Collector*, to capture her and keep her enslaved instead of killing her.

In darker moments he imagines the explosion has disfigured her, and she has vanished knowing that Guillermo would be sickened by her appearance. Would he still love her with her face grafted over in layers of pink, curling skin? Does one love the body, the heart, or the soul, or a combination of all three?

Why can't she actually be alive, running some Middle Eastern restaurant in La Libertad? There wouldn't have been any way for her to contact him during the weeks after the explosion, just to set his mind at ease. But since he too has vanished, without a trace as it were, there'd be no way for her to reach him now. He has done too good a job of erasing his tracks for her to find him. He has entered the ranks of the disappeared.

Every weekend he goes to the Biblioteca Nacional across from the Catedral Metropolitana on Plaza Barrios and reads through all of the previous week's daily Guatemalan newspapers—the *Diario de Centro América*, *Siglo 21*, *El Periódico*, *Prensa Libre*. He looks for any mention of either of their names. He examines each and every page, scans the ads, gossip columns, and wedding announcements as well—he believes he is now an expert in decoding hidden messages.

Of course he finds nothing. Maryam Khalil and Guillermo Rosensweig have both been relegated to the realm of the forgotten. He never imagined his notoriety could allow him to disappear like this, so quickly, without any serious inquiry, like the thousands of massacred Guatemalan Indians dumped in unmarked graves. It sobers him.

Unlike him, the Indians have relatives to mourn them, to seek their bones or their corpses, a vestige to bury, proof that they had lived.

Reading the Guatemalan papers proves futile, but it does give him the opportunity to follow the political developments in his country. The president and his wife have managed to dodge all the accusations of money laundering by the dozens of Guatemalans who want to force them out. It appears the president will finish his term to keep the US from gaining leverage by manipulating a premature regime change so it can restrict the sale of weapons. In another year there will be new elections, and it looks as if the right wing will win. The president's wife is going to divorce her husband. She is willing to sacrifice her marriage to run for the presidency.

Oddly, Guillermo feels no animus toward the president and his wife, as if recording the tape and the bizarre events that followed have cured him of his hatred for them. He is rankled when the Catholic Church expresses its willingness to annul their marriage so she can run for the presidency. There is no more cynical act imaginable, to eliminate a sacred covenant for political expediency. (Guillermo still pays lip service to the sanctity of marriage even though he has betrayed the precepts dozens of times.) More than anger, he pities the president, who clearly does not want the divorce but is incapable of curbing his wife's single-minded quest for power.

On one Sunday, Guillermo smiles and shakes his head when he reads that the president has named his old buddy Miguel Paredes a special advisor on economic affairs. He has also been tapped to replace Ibrahim Khalil as the president's envoy on the Banurbano board. This turn of events makes Guillermo laugh aloud—what a skillful chameleon Miguel is.

He wonders if he had been Paredes's pawn all along. Now the facilitator can freely funnel money to pet projects where his participation is hidden by governmental sanction and layers of deceit. Was his intention to force the resignation of the president only a ruse?

*Prensa Libre* shows Miguel Paredes and the president holding hands in the air like best friends, astronauts launched together into space, survivors of a rocket explosion after having parachuted successfully back to earth. Has Miguel replaced the First Lady as the presidential confidante now that she is divorcing him?

All this teaches Guillermo that he has made many serious mistakes. His love life has been an utter disaster. There were mistakes of judgment he has to own up to: he was dismissive of his father and his father's hope to have him take over La Candelaria; he was jealous of those classmates who had the means to go to colleges abroad; he was duplicitous with both his wife and his children; he was obsessed with finding a cursed, manipulative hand behind everything he did not fully comprehend. His understanding of evil has been simpleminded, and he has never seen the whole picture of anything, choosing to totter from crisis to crisis or success to success without ever considering his actions, not even his own sexual desires.

Guatemala is a hopeless disaster, a country sinking deeper and deeper into its own lies and denials. The newspapers are reporting it day after day. With thousands of citizens involved in the drug trade, Guatemala has become a bazaar of graft and payoffs, piled as high as a basket of dates. His expressions of outrage and his tendency to mistrust all governmental agencies failed to change anything. He had come to believe that even loyal friends, excepting Ibrahim, were involved in plots to destroy the country he loved.

Now he knows that his own bile, his unwillingness to believe or trust in colleagues, has also contributed to his country's malaise. Like Candide, Guill-ermo believes he should "cultivate his own garden" in this life. This would be the best of all possible worlds, since so many powers-that-be work day and night to control how things develop. He is no match for them. No honest people are a match for them.

Living in San Salvador, he is learning that he can simply apply his skills to advise and counsel others without investing his own ego in anything. He can apply his own capabilities and draw pleasure in his own accomplishments, like helping an entrepreneur open a legitimate business. There is no need to act courageously, to see himself as purer than others, to feel outrage when things don't go his way. He wants to live and to let live instead of trying to create a world in his own image.

And the odd thing is that years earlier the mere thought of being in El Salvador would have made him feel imprisoned, since his freedom of move-ment would have been restricted. Instead he feels freer in exile than he ever did in his life of relative freedom in Guatemala. This gives Guillermo a kind of peace of mind that he hasn't experienced since he lived across the street from the Symposium restaurant in New York. He is now controlled by the simple desire to do what he knows he has to do: work, listen, and advise. And endure his present condition with something like gratitude.

The fact that he has given up drinking, except for the occasional Suprema, has helped clear his mind for the first time in twenty years. The clouds have dissipated and he can finally see the occasional ray of sunlight.

And there is something else: he actually likes San Salvador, even more than Guatemala City. It hurts him to say it but it's true. While Guatemala prides itself on being the beautiful queen of Central America, its smugness is a bit dated, like that of an English dowager. While many Guatemalans will admit that civil society has temporarily gone awry in their homeland, they will also say it's a gorgeous place and that it's only a matter of time before their country assumes its rightful place as a Latin American leader.

El Salvador, on the other hand, is a crazy, chaotic country, much too violent and polluted to have any such pretensions. Santana wrote a song called "Blues for Salvador" in 1987. It is a tragic, five-minute electric-guitar riff with absolutely no lyrics. The country lacks Guatemala City's broad boulevards and faux French look, and its glorious, eternal-spring climate. But its citizens are humble, and real. Everyone is trying to survive the best they can with no airs of entitlement. Salvadorans are open, humorous, self-deprecating. The civil war they have endured has affected them each personally, with bombardments, killings in their own backyards, the horrific raining down of bombs and explosives, the extensive loss of life. No one has survived unscathed.

In Guatemala City, the armed conflict was abstract because it mostly took place in a countryside only the Indians thought to inhabit. Here in San Salvador, the craterous wounds of the conflict are visible and palpable, and this makes the citizens more honest, unwilling to hide behind any sort of delusion or distortion.

And then there is the weather, the torrid heat, which makes everyone respond fairly directly, not like in Guatemala, where reality is hidden under sweaters, jackets, or layers of cloth. The lava-like heat in San Salvador strikes everything: Guillermo swears that the walls sweat as much as the plants.

There is a plain, if brutal honesty in El Salvador which Guillermo never encountered in his homeland.

And so his life is not the life he imagined, but for the first time in a while, he can call this life his own. It is a prescribed picture—office, furnished apartment, mercado, whorehouse, library, greasy comedores, café de olla, and pupusas.

How long it will last is anybody's guess.

## CHAPTER TWENTY-NINE

# SWITCHING HORSES MIDSTREAM

**M**iguel Paredes had been eating a croissant and sipping a cappuccino at the Café Barista just below his Fontabella shop when he got a call around nine in the morning announcing, "Goal." It was as simple as that, and it told Miguel that the mission was accomplished and Guillermo was dead. For the moment there was nothing to do but wait and let the wheels of the press do their work. There would be plenty of time to plan his response to the murder and figure out the right moment to release the tape incriminating the president. He could hardly wait to see the owl-faced leader's reaction.

To Miguel, life in Guatemala had become a comedy erroneously portrayed as tragedy. He knew there was no such thing as a perfect crime, but he had been riding on a string of successes that implied that if he applied total vigilance, much could be accomplished. Befriending Guillermo at the funeral had been a brilliant move, allowing him to exploit the man's vulnerability. Miguel knew that injustice alone would not have been enough to convince Guillermo to join him on his quest. The shock brought on by the deaths of Maryam and Ibrahim, the specter of Samir's potential role in the murder, and Guillermo's implacable weakness created the ideal situation to pull off his plan. All the pieces seemed to fit together, and he was right where he needed to be. The only thing required of him was the demonstration of sufficient amounts of sympathy, guile, and money to ensure victory.

The revelation that something had gone awry in his master plan came while he was in his office at Raoul's trying to plot the exact moment to release

Guillermo's recording. One of his orejas at the national police texted that things at the murder scene didn't quite add up: the dead man was shorter and stockier than Rosensweig, and he had a buzz cut, not patches of wavy black hair.

Miguel immediately called Braulio Perdomo to see where things had been left with his charge. Everything seemed copasetic to Braulio, with no inkling that Guillermo was going to pull out of the scheme at the last minute.

"Do you want me to go check out Guillermo's apartment? I have the keys and no one would be suspicious. I could just go there quickly and sniff around."

Miguel liked the idea. Maybe he would find Guillermo there, sprawled out on the living room floor in another of his alcoholic extravaganzas.

By noon Braulio had reported back. Nothing seemed suspicious or out of place: the apartment reeked of alcohol; there was half-eaten food on a plate on the kitchen counter; Guillermo's bicycle was gone. Braulio found the man's passport in the officer drawer and noted that his car was still in the garage, the engine cold.

But something was not right. By one o'clock Miguel heard from a contact at the morgue that the dead man had a huge tattoo of an apocalyptical horse galloping on his hairless back. With no forensic evidence, the coroner wouldn't say who the dead man was—he needed to take DNA samples and send them to Miami. He would only say that the victim had been shot by a high-caliber pistol at a short range and had died immediately.

Miguel had never seen Guillermo without a shirt, but he doubted he would have a tattoo like that. Miguel grew troubled: he had been too complacent, too confident. He contacted his plants at Aurora Airport and asked them to make inquiries into the departure of Guillermo Rosensweig or someone fitting his physical description. He had underestimated Guillermo's guile, and now suspected he had purchased a fake passport and would try to escape.

Miguel contacted his orejas at the central bus station, but no one reported seeing a man fitting Guillermo's description. He had some of his men make discreet enquiries in the downtown hotels and those in Zone 9 and 10, in case Guillermo had decided to hole up for a few days. By sundown Sunday, no one had seen hide or hair of Guillermo.

He had vanished into thin air.

On Monday morning, he had Braulio contact Guillermo's secretary and discovered that he had furloughed her several weeks back. She mentioned that she still had keys to his office and as far as she knew, Guillermo hadn't moved his files out yet. Did he want her to check it out?

Braulio thought on his feet and said. "No, no. I must have misunderstood when he asked me to pick him up early this morning. I'm sure he's okay. Wait for further instructions."

When it was revealed that the drug lord Boris Santiago was the murder victim, and when it also become known that Guillermo was missing, Miguel was surprised that no one suspected any connection between them. Oddly, Boris's family made no effort to claim his body, and though Guillermo had vanished, neither his wife nor his children seemed very concerned.

Miguel realized he had to move fast on two fronts if his master plan were to succeed: first he had to patch things up with the president, and second, scour the earth for traces of Guillermo. The former he would deal with personally, with all the finesse and force he could muster, and the latter would be handled by his henchmen.

Through intermediaries, Miguel let the president know that he was tired of opposing his government and would be willing to join his economic team and take Ibrahim Khalil's place on the Banurbano board. He would do so with the utmost respect for the presidency and with the sole interest of serving with honesty, discretion, and loyalty. Miguel, the inventor of actionable intelligence, had had a long career in government serving as advisor to many of the military officers who found themselves promoted to the presidency.

The president agreed instantly, happy to have one less adversary throwing darts at him and his wife.

With his appointment to the president's administration behind him, Miguel can turn his focus to finding and killing Guillermo. But no one knows where he's gone. He sends Braulio to San Salvador and Edgar Rocio to Tegucigalpa and San Pedro Sula in Honduras, but after a week of investigating, they both return with no leads, no sightings. He fans immigration agents across all the land crossings in and out of Guatemala with pictures of Guillermo and a 10,000-quetzales bounty for information leading to his whereabouts.

A month passes with not even one piece of credible evidence or actionable information to go on. Miguel is frustrated that this time he cannot find the needle in the haystack, which has never been a problem for him before. He realizes that Guillermo could be anywhere—on an island in the Caribbean, in Mexico City, in Miami, or even in New York or San Francisco. A family man, a lawyer of Guillermo's standing and stature, doesn't just disappear, especially after living in Guatemala for the better part of his nearly fifty years, but that's exactly what has happened.

Miguel Paredes decides he needs to rely on his patience and sit tight: at some point Guillermo Rosensweig will attempt to come back into the country, out of nostalgia or necessity, and that's when he will be nabbed.

And eliminated.

## CHAPTER THIRTY

# FREEDOM'S JUST ANOTHER WORD

**M**aryam and Ibrahim had been killed on May 5 and Guillermo had plotted his own death several weeks later, in early June. In December, before the arrival of Christmas, Guillermo begins feeling despondent again, and lonely. He remembers the jovial Noche Buena dinners; the kids getting up early on Christmas Day to open their gifts as if the Rosensweig family were living in the United States; the numerous vacations they would take—always from the twenty-eighth of December to the seventh of January—somewhere in the Guatemalan Highlands. There were trips to Antigua and Panajachel, but also journeys up the Río Dulce to the Castillo de San Felipe and Lago de Izabal, and beach trips to Likín, in which Guillermo actually recovered his role as the head of a lovely family. It didn't matter that their bonds would dissipate after two days back in Guatemala City, the laughter of the kids and the distraction of booze made lovers of Guillermo and Rosa Esther, albeit in a somewhat forced and dyspeptic manner.

One day, nostalgia for his homeland consumes him. He recognizes the immense risk crossing borders implies, but he can't help himself. He needs to feel the Guatemalan earth beneath his feet.

He wants to go to Valle Nuevo because it would allow him to test out his fake passport for a second time. But there is another reason: Valle Nuevo has a bank and a post office, which will allow him to send Rosa Esther a bank check for four thousand quetzales along with a letter revealing he is still alive. He owes his wife and children that at least, even though he is taking a big risk, given Miguel's long reach.

The following day he takes a bus from the Radisson along with twenty other passengers. At the border crossing, the Guatemalan immigration officer barely looks at his passport because he is clearly a member of the upper class and scrutiny is saved for Salvadorans trying to make their way north to the US. On a first-class bus no one would fit that bill. The agents must be so accustomed to having dozens of illegals crossing through the brush that Guillermo does not look the least bit suspicious.

He spends the night at Las Palmeras, a hideous two-story motel on the Guatemalan side of the border that is no better than a truck stop. The noise in the lobby is overwhelming: tinny ranchera music, loud talking, and the sputtering of drunks from the bar. He asks for a quiet place in back, and as soon as he enters his room of fluorescent lights and chipped furniture he realizes he is ravenous. He is sick of eating pupusas and goes to the motel restaurant where he orders corn and potato tamales with chipilín. He hasn't eaten real Guatemalan food for months.

After dinner he goes back to his room to compose a letter in which he tells his wife and children that he is, in fact, alive. For reasons of security, he cannot reveal where he is living and begs them not to share the contents of this letter with anyone should it by chance awaken the interest of his enemies and jeopardize his survival and their security. He tells them how much he loves them and how sorry he is for all the damage he's caused them. He acknowledges that he has been a poor father, someone who has abdicated all his parental and conjugal responsibilities to pursue his own wayward agenda. And he apologizes for having vanished as he did, in such an abrupt fashion, but explains that he's not at liberty to tell them what transpired and why he felt it necessary to disappear.

He wipes away tears as he writes.

He has no idea whether his children harbor any strong feelings for him anymore, but he promises that one day he will try to earn back their love, if not their respect. In time, he writes, he will make things right, though he knows he has made this promise before. He has no idea how they are surviving financially, but he begs Rosa Esther not to attempt to claim his money and properties because it might awaken suspicion. He hopes the four thousand will be of some help. He honestly doesn't know if, with the passage of time, he'll be able to reclaim his property. He reiterates how much he loves the children and how sorry he is for the mess he's made.

As steeped as he is in loneliness, he cannot see that his words of reconciliation are just another illusion. Even so, he avoids claiming he is an altogether different man, and writes that he has learned something from his mistakes, *blah blah blah*.

It is sizzling in his room. He puts on the poor excuse for an air conditioner. It rattles like a car about to explode.

Guillermo collapses onto his bed and falls immediately to sleep on the shitty straw mattress. He wakes up a half hour later and spends the next hour tossing and turning, trying to ignore the rumble of trucks and sound of mariachi music. At one a.m. the border crossing finally closes and the noise, the loud talk, and the flashing of lights finally die down.

At eight in the morning he eats two fried eggs, black beans with cream, plantains, and delicious blue corn tortillas at the motel restaurant. Then he walks down a noisy, dusty street to the tiny Banco de Guatemala and exchanges four thousand in cash for an official bank check. He takes the check and places it inside the envelope with the letter. At the post office next door he sends the letter special-delivery to Mexico. He knows he is taking a big chance: the letter could be lost or confiscated, the check could be stolen. Even if it weren't cashed, it would be lost forever. But this is all he can do.

He returns to the motel, gathers his things, and catches a bus back to San Salvador.

Easter comes early in April of 2010 but already the heat in San Salvador is oppressive. The spring rains have failed to arrive, a pattern dating back to the deforestation during the years of civil war. Not that forests would do much to cool things down, especially in a city that is increasingly crowded and polluted. There is a density to the air that makes breathing difficult.

It has been an unexpectedly kind spring for Rafael Ignacio Gallardo né Guillermo Rosensweig and his depression is once again lifting. His consulting business is doing well and making good money: he's no longer dipping into the cash he brought from Guatemala. His clients recommend friends because, unlike many other advisors, Guillermo is dedicated to exploring possibilities and finding solutions, not whining about problems. He concentrates on getting them to focus on achieving their goals, however small. And he is honest to the core, something unusual in downtown San Salvador, where it seems like every other person is a huckster.

Guillermo acknowledges something else about the structure of his life: after all the turbulence in Guatemala, he is happy to simply go to his office, keep a low profile, and help his clients without major distractions or drama. He is no longer driven by the messianic desire to right the hundreds of wrongs in his homeland.

He lives in relative peace except for the times that the memory of his love for Maryam clutches his heart and won't let him go. Over time these memories come less often but are no less gripping. There are evenings when he falls asleep in a deep rapture, remembering their times together, the happiness they shared, the dreams they discussed. He often ends up masturbating, imagining he is entering her as she begs him not to come yet.

In quieter moments, he remembers their pledge to meet in the main square of La Libertad on May 1—in a month's time. He feels unsure about whether he should go. His fear of disappointment disquiets him. He feels that if anything could send him back into the depths of despair again, it is the realization that a dream, no matter how extravagant or far-fetched, might never come true.

The odds overwhelmingly favor it: Maryam is almost certainly dead.

But what if by some miracle she's not?

What if she somehow survived the explosion, is alive, and has built a new life for herself, as he has done?

## CHAPTER THIRTY-ONE

# LA LIBERTAD

**M**ay 1 falls on a Friday, which complicates things for Guillermo because La Libertad is on the coast and thousands of city dwellers will be going there for the three-day weekend. There will be highway blockages and lots of chaos, demonstrations, and parades to celebrate International Workers' Day.

Luckily, the day dawns cloudy and rainy. This will deter many families from getting up early and heading to the beach. By eight a.m. it is still as dark as night, and the rain is falling in steady sheets, pattering roughly on windows and roofs. No one will head for the seashore or the parades in this weather.

An hour later the rain is still coming down hard. Guillermo realizes he needs to hurry now if he's to make it there on time. He takes bus 34 from in front of his building to the Terminal Occidente to catch one of the buses that leave every ten minutes or so for La Libertad. He figures that if he catches the ten a.m. bus he will arrive on the coast by eleven, in plenty of time to explore the town and get to the appointed spot—in front of the central church on the main square—by noon.

The downpour delays the bus's departure. The streets are crowded, mostly by people trying to dodge the buckets of rain. The bus moves slowly through the San Salvador streets, on its way up to Santa Tecla, a town appended to the capital by the thousands of Salvadorans who left the countryside during the civil war of the 1980s. The bus stops for ten minutes or so on the corner of the central park for passengers to embark and disembark, and then barrels toward the coast.

On the outskirts of Santa Tecla, in an area of dense trees and crowded village outcroppings, the bus comes to a halt. The rain has caused a land-slide and large clumps of brown earth and stone are blocking access to the highway. There's utter chaos as two-way traffic tries to navigate through the single passable lane between the mounds of mud on the road. What's worse, there are no policemen to help sort out the mess. For the next half hour the bus inches forward, maybe a block at most.

Suddenly the ticket taker jumps off the bus wielding a pistol and gestur-ing wildly. He reaches the blockage and points his gun at the driver of a sta-tion wagon moving in the opposite direction, stopping him. This allows the cars in front of the bus to drive through the obstruction. Once the bus gets by, the ticket taker swings back on, cheered by the passengers.

The bus begins to wind slowly up the mountains. Guillermo is surprised by the route and asks the driver what's taking so long. The driver tells him that if he wanted the fast route, he should've taken the express bus to Coma-lapa International Airport, not the mountain route via Santa Tecla. Instead of smelling the sea air along the coastal route, Guillermo is treated to the odor of dank, fetid vegetation and innumerable stops.

The bus strains up the incline and races down the slopes. The engine is grinding, the sides of the bus shaking, and the passengers are talking loudly as they take hairpin turns at high, unsafe speeds. Several times Guillermo sees the bus heaving halfway over the ravine before managing to right itself back onto the road. But maybe in this way, they will make it through the mountains and arrive in La Libertad on time.

Once out of the mountains, the driver floors the pedal. Gas stations, small villages, and roadside businesses swirl by. Guillermo is nauseous by the time the bus slows down on the crowded outskirts of La Libertad: tire shops, hardware stores, dirt-floor restaurants. The sun has come out and steam floats like low-hanging clouds over the quickly drying asphalt.

The bus stops in the main square facing the central church a bit before twelve. Guillermo doesn't know what he imagined, but this church is no cathedral: it looks more like a large airplane hangar, with corrugated tin walls surrounded by a barbed-wire fence built, he imagines, to keep possible suicide bombers away, a relic of the civil war.

He doesn't understand why the fence hasn't been brought down. Does it still face a daily onslaughts of terrorists attempting to get in? To do what? To pray?

Guillermo is struck by the sinking feeling he has made a huge mistake by coming: better to dream desperately of her survival than face disappointment at a place as disheartening as this. It's absurd to be waiting for his deceased lover in front of a veritable airplane hangar in La Libertad, El Salvador.

He waits and waits, seeing two other buses arrive and an equal number leave, and soon it is twelve thirty. The sun is beating down now that the rain has temporarily subsided; there's no relief. Guillermo realizes Maryam will not be meeting him, that she perished in the car with her father, that his hope she survived the explosion has been a childish fantasy.

## CHAPTER THIRTY-TWO

# PAYING THE PIPER

**M**aryam's bus from San Lorenzo stops at the town of La Amatillo around eight a.m. for the passengers to go through customs and immigration control. But even before the bus reaches the border crossing, it's surrounded by nearly one hundred teachers and their families holding signs and placards protesting salary cuts and the poor working conditions in western Honduras. Maryam is sympathetic to the strikers, but furious at the delay: she had left her home at six in the morning, planning to arrive in La Libertad by eleven. She could kick herself for not having left the day before.

The driver says they will get through the protesters in a half hour. Maryam is unconvinced. She looks out the window and sees the build-up of thick clouds—the rain could be a blessing in disguise since it might force the teachers to scatter. Nervously, she begins playing with her ring. It has bands of silver filigree and there's a deep amber stone, almost ruby in color, in the center. She bought the ring in a Tegucigalpa store that sold jewelry from Mexico. The shopgirl called the stone a lagrima de la selva. A jungle tear.

Maryam bought the ring to symbolize her engagement to Guillermo. She has no idea if they will ever see each other again, but she wants to wear something on her right hand that will remind her of him every day.

In San Lorenzo, she wears her wedding band on her left hand so that the men in town will not bother her. She passes herself off as a grieving widow whose husband died in Guatemala. Here on the bus she puts the ring in her purse.

With the bus at a standstill, the driver allows two peddlers on. They walk down the aisle selling food and beer to the half-asleep passengers.

Maryam is starved. She buys two bean pupusas and gobbles them down while looking out the window. The strikers are jovial but show no signs of letting the bus and the stream of cars behind it go by. She's not sure what's going to happen next.

Loud claps of thunder shake the bus. A minute later, bolts of lightning illuminate the marchers and the rain starts bucketing down. Within a minute the strikers have dispersed and the bus driver inches down another five hundred yards to the border crossing. Years ago, crossing frontiers could take days, but since Central Americans now share the same blue passport, crossing is easy. The passengers don't even need to disembark as border agents come aboard the buses to stamp their passports.

Soon they're on their way to San Miguel where Maryam will transfer to the La Libertad bus. She drifts in and out of sleep, once again reliving the moments after the explosion.

She has no idea why the bullets suddenly stopped. She sees herself crouching in the construction site, waiting for the onslaught of more bullets. Instead, she heard a car drive away. Who was it and who did they think they were chasing? Her? Some unknown witness? Did they think whoever it was got the message and knew better than to try to come forward?

The bus hits a bump and Maryam is startled awake. A part of her is still expecting that bullet. Her carriage is no longer carefree—there's something skittish about it.

She presses her body against the window. She reminds herself that she escaped. As she dozes again, she sees herself leaning against the bus window as though crouching in the construction site. The same dream of that day takes over once more.

*The bullets stop and she knows she must be decisive. She's alone, but she tells herself the worst is over. She decides it's best to wait until dusk. She tries to quiet her mind. Breathe calmly.*

*At six p.m. she gets up and walks the back roads until she reaches Calzada*

Roosevelt where she takes a public bus to the Marriott Hotel in Zone 9. She spends the night there, not too far from Guillermo's rendezvous apartment in the Plazuela España. She knows there are first-class buses that leave from the Radisson not too far from the Marriott. She takes the first available bus in the morning. It's going to Tegucigalpa. She knows she can't stay in the Honduran capital, but it's the first step toward safety. She's sure people are trying to find her.

She decides to settle in a small town called San Lorenzo, on the Pacific coast, about two hours from Tegucigalpa. It's an inferno and has none of the conveniences she has grown accustomed to. She lives simply, renting a nondescript apartment and waitressing in a small but busy fish restaurant in the Las Cabañas area, overlooking the harbor. A few months later, she starts to teach the cook how to make some Middle Eastern dishes—tabbouleh, kibbes, falafel sandwiches, saffron rice—as a way to keep part of who she is in a place where she has absolutely nothing. These recipes are her connection to her father and to Guillermo. She knows it isn't much, but it's something.

The factory workers who eat at the restaurant love the new dishes, the way her rice explodes with taste and the lamb patties are infused with the three C's—cumin, coriander, and cardamom. She even finds sheets of filo and makes her own baklava.

Months go by and she realizes she's adjusting well to life in this small town. She feels a sense of accomplishment. For the first time in a while she's responsible for her own well-being—she's independent, beholden to no one.

One day she sees an old push-pedal Singer for sale. She buys it and starts sewing place mats and napkins to add character to the restaurant. Customers start asking her to make some custom-made mats for their homes, which she sells to earn a few extra lempiras. She becomes friendly with a woman who sells fabric at the market and Maryam learns how to use patterns to make simple dresses, blouses, and slacks. She tries not to think too much of Guillermo when she's around other people. His absence hits her as a lump in her throat and she knows she needs to keep functioning. She can't let her guard down and seem too vulnerable.

She learns how to be friendly but reserved. None of the coquettishness she carried as a second skin in Guatemala is visible here. There's nothing provocative about her manner or dress. She is absolutely clear about what she needs to do to survive—creating any kind of interest in her or her past would not be smart.

She reads voraciously. It is her escape. On rare occasions she allows herself to fantasize about Guillermo, to pretend they might have a life together one day. She keeps imagining the trip to La Libertad, that she will get off the bus and see him. She can't go too much further than that—it feels like she is tempting fate to even imagine that day. But sometimes she can't help herself, and she plays out different scenarios in her head, always hoping he will show up.

She is happy to be alone, away from the demands and strictures of her former life. This allows her to do her work without distraction and to mourn the loss of her father and lover.

On the bus to San Miguel she remembers how many times she imagined this trip. How May 1 seemed so far away.

And she didn't account for the teacher's strike and the bad weather.

What will they do if they somehow manage to meet up? She has changed so much in these months and is not the woman he knew, not the woman who waited for his calls. She can't go back to that. If they do meet, she imagines he will have changed as well. If it had been the reverse, and she had heard news of Guillermo's death, she's not sure she could have convinced herself to come to La Libertad.

Music is playing as Maryam wakes up on the outskirts of San Miguel. She gets off the bus and goes to the ticket booth to inquire about the bus to La Libertad. It is ten a.m. and her bus has arrived a half hour behind schedule. When she asks for the next one to La Libertad, she's told it's leaving at ten thirty but will be making a stop in San Salvador.

"What about an express?"

"It left fifteen minutes ago. There's another one at eleven."

She's furious at herself for her poor planning. She won't get to La Libertad until well after one. Her father used to say that women are like lint brushes, picking up thoughts and ideas as they sweep across the surface of things, never initiating anything on their own, always distracted.

Maryam has never felt like a lint brush until now. She knows her bus will not reach La Libertad on time. She could not have predicted the teachers' protests, yet she feels she's at fault for being late.

Maryam falls asleep again on the eleven o'clock bus and dreams she's in a hotel with Guillermo. They are lying on the room's industrial gray carpet after having made love.

"So what are we going to do?" she says.

He replies cautiously: "We can't go back to Guatemala. Let's assume that Samir wasn't behind the murder of your father and Verónica. Wouldn't the real assassins try and kill you? Wouldn't they be afraid you could identify them or their car? They wouldn't be happy to have us appear a year or two after the explosion holding hands."

"I could cut my hair, hide my face under a keffiyeh," Maryam says, lying across his body, covering his mouth with her scarf.

"What about your green eyes? Wouldn't they give you away?"

Maryam grows reflective, then snaps her fingers. "Come back with me to San Lorenzo! I can't imagine anyone there caring who we are."

"What would I do there?"

"Maybe you could become a fisherman!"

"Start fishing at my age?"

"Sure," she says.

"Like Santiago in *The Old Man and the Sea*? Going eighty-four days without catching a fish?"

"You could cut lumber in the forests outside San Lorenzo," she says, poking his sides.

"Uh uh, I'm not Paul Bunyan. No manual labor for me."

"What about moving to New York City? You always brag about your Columbia University law degree. It should be worth something, don't you think?"

He has turned his back to her and she realizes he has a tattoo of a horse on his back. She had never noticed that detail about him.

"And I'll grow out my hair," she says. "No one will recognize me. I'll become a famous dress designer, you'll see."

\* \* \*

She wakes up when the bus arrives in La Libertad. It is one thirty. She bounds down the steps and is surrounded by a sea of humanity.

CHAPTER THIRTY-THREE

# DREAM A LITTLE DREAM

**G**uillermo thinks that a half hour should be long enough to wait. Still, he decides to linger by the church for another half hour: doesn't love require patience?

At one in the afternoon he realizes he has wasted his time. He considers taking the next bus back to San Salvador to avoid the crowds who will be arriving soon, now that the rain has stopped and a fiery sun is beating down.

Instead, he decides to walk the few blocks to the ocean. The streets are dirty in La Libertad, paved with discarded paper, plastic, and aluminum. It's a hideous town with its dry mud, uneven streets, and pockmarked walls half-eaten by sea salt and the merciless sun. Swirls of dust prowl around the unpainted buildings, leaving a brown film on everything.

He reaches the shore. From the broken-concrete parking lot he sees a rickety pier on ten-foot wooden pilings: it's almost collapsed into a sea pounding the shore with a steady, thudding rhythm. The pier has remained standing for years in an act of pure defiance. Six-foot waves roll in and adventurous surfers to the left of a stone jetty lie flat on their surfboards awaiting the right wave to carry them to the black, volcanic shore. The sun is trying to peek out of the gray sky. All Guillermo can think about is the pain in his chest: yes, he will return to La Libertad in a year, and the year after that, but he already knows he will come back with increasingly lowered expectations.

On the way to the point at which the pier drops into the ocean, he passes food shacks with thatched-palm roofs; he glimpses oyster shells on ice, turtle eggs on sea grass, plates of fish and grilled potatoes, but he has no appetite. He senses he could willingly starve himself to death. This would be his penance.

When he reaches the end of the pier, he stares out at the brown water in a kind of hypnotic trance. The waves come ashore in perfect order, their symmetry astounding. There's a distance of fifteen feet or so between each crest and the waves break in precise curlicues, in perfect formation, like the flight of seagulls in the lowering sky.

He turns around and walks back to the square. His eyes are open but he sees nothing, as if a curtain of gauze were blocking his vision. In the square, in front of the church, he spots plenty more buses and hundreds of scantily dressed Salvadorans carrying their clothes in small suitcases or plastic bags, straw mats and thin towels rolled under their arms. The noise is deafening. He goes up to the front of the church; its metallic doors are now shut. He knocks insistently. He has no expectation that anyone will let him in.

Of course no one does.

He turns around and starts walking to the plaza. He passes vans with signs saying *Sonsonate* and *Zacatecoluca* before he sees the bus that will bring him back to San Salvador. Overcome by disappointment, tears edge out of his eyes.

When he reaches the bus, the door is open but the driver is still not there. Why should he go in and wait in the heat and smell the accumulated body odor that probably hasn't been washed off for days?

Guillermo feels a tap on his shoulder and ignores it. Why would anyone want him? Maybe it's Archangel Michael ready to accompany him to his grave.

He feels a second tap and turns around, annoyed. He sees a woman wearing a black-and-white cotton keffiyeh on her head. The scarf hides her nose and mouth. He glimpses green eyes and thick black eyebrows—a familiar sight, but aged with sparrow's feet. He can't speak—what could he say from his choked throat?

"Señor," the woman whispers.

Guillermo's not sure what he's seeing.

She begins unwinding the scarf from the base of her shoulders. He recognizes clumps of black hair that is cut short, almost like a pageboy. *Oh my God*, he says to himself, convinced he's not hallucinating. God is not unjust, a trickster intent on fooling him—it's Maryam, somewhat aged, with much shorter hair! "I can't believe it's you," he says to her, leaning in to kiss her forehead.

"Por favor, señor," the woman says, backing away from him. "If you aren't getting on the bus, could you at least get out of the way? This bag is very heavy."

Guillermo closes his eyes, overwhelmed by his mistake. His whole life has been a mistake. He has always opted for the easy solution. He has always felt deserving. He *is* deserving.

It can not have been an accident he wasn't shot. People can escape their fate.

"Por favor," he hears the woman repeat.

He can't even look back at her. Somehow his legs have climbed up to the first step of the bus. He grasps the edges of the doors and with great effort pulls himself up.

What a mistake to have come.

His legs wobble, about to give under him. He has always had strong legs, but he stopped exercising in San Salvador, and muscles atrophy quickly. He barely makes it into a seat before he collapses.

He is sweating profusely. His blue shirt has mackerel and catfish emblazoned on it. At this moment it's thoroughly wet, as if he has just stepped out of the ocean.

He realizes he's on the bus to San Salvador, on his way back to his apartment and his solitary life. He has much to expiate: his foolishness, his years of blundering and wastefulness, the pettiness of so many of his actions, and the devastating comprehension that he does not deserve Maryam, whether she is alive or dead.

Guillermo curls into his seat, placing his head against the bus window. He closes his eyes and tries to calm his breathing. He is trying to even his breaths, as he did during the weeks he practiced pranayama yoga: dispel all thoughts and concentrate on the soft point of light issuing from a blue cloud of emptiness. He feels the bus throttling along and hears ranchera music and laughter. He falls asleep.

He dreams he had met Maryam in La Libertad. In the dream she drags him by the hand to a restaurant with lime-green walls and red-tiled floors with four empty tables. It is off the beach and empty.

They take a corner table near two large windows overlooking empty lots across a muddy street. An overhead fan sputters. As soon as they sit, a boy wearing a torn T-shirt brings them a menu.

Maryam tells the boy to bring them a basket of chips with guacamol and two Supremas. Before the boy is out of earshot, Guillermo screams, "Frías como los muertos!" *As cold as corpses!*

Guillermo takes hold of Maryam's hand. It is darker than before, but just as smooth and lithe. For a few minutes they sit in silence staring at each other, memorizing each other's faces.

But something spooks him and he pulls his hand away as if they are in Guatemala and someone might catch them in a moment of intimacy.

The boy brings the beers and the chips.

As Maryam grabs her bottle, Guillermo notices that she's still wearing Samir's wedding ring.

"I wear it out of habit," she says. "It doesn't mean a thing."

When Guillermo wakes up, the bus is approaching the San Salvador terminal.

As he pulls himself out of his seat, he hears a soothing female voice say, "Inshallah."

Guillermo couldn't agree more.